A GLASS DARKLY

K E BARDEN

Cover Design by Etheric Tales

Chapter Artwork by EthericTales

Map designed by AdrianoBezerra

Typography and Formatting by Turtle Publishing

Paperback ISBN 978-1-7635308-6-7

Hardcover ISBN 978-1-7635308-8-1

eBook ISBN 978-1-7635308-7-4

Distributed by K E Barden and Lightningsource Global

OTHER BOOKS BY K E BARDEN

Finding Ever After Series
The Gilded Mirror
These Grimm Fates

To Trent,

Whose magic still lingers in every word I type.
RIP 01.02.2021

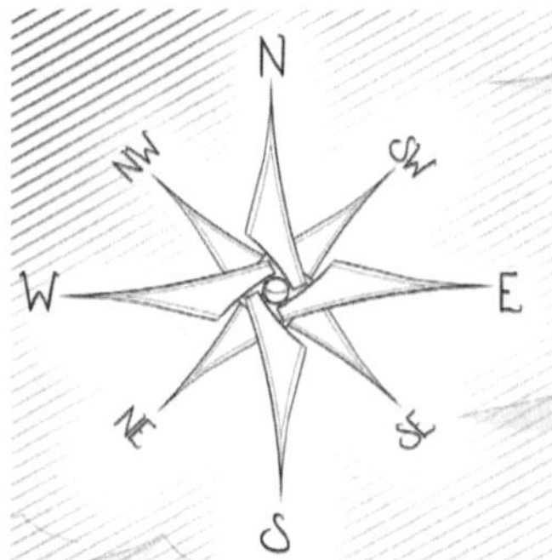

N
NW
NE
W
E
SW
SE
S
Beast Cove
CRULLFELD
ASHENFELL
Lake Moss
The Luna Lighthouse
The Tower and the Maze
Cawdor
Gri
XERSAILLES
ARDENBEAX
The Lantern Lighthouse
Annice
MOUNTAIN LE BLEU
Lake La Belle
Waters Keep
The Channel
WHITE BRIDGE
The Bla Cove
THE ISLAND OF MYORCAI
THE EVER AFT
THE REALM

g Isles
The Northern Lighthouse
AURELIA
THE CORAL COAST
THE REALM OF DRAGONS AND GIANTS
KING'S KEEP
Butterpond
Blarney Forest
The Briar Rose
The Marshes
MINES OF PARADOR
Hasleholme
MAELSTROM
Ellendale
CARNELL
PEAKS OF CARFELL
Eastborne
THE MOUNTAINS OF EYRIE
SHADOW FOREST
Arrow's Den
Ivywood
The Crystal Lake
THE SILVER CITY
Bell's Peak
THE DARK FOREST
PERRIDORM
Roserock
Dove Port
Witche's Hut
The Skinny Piglet
BELLATORRE
The Elysian Fields
Forest
Wolf's Den
The Queens Mines
ALDRYN
TEAL COVE
Nysa
ATLAS
THE ISLE OF NYSA
Lighthouse Luvon

There once lived a little lord with buttons of brass and tassels of gold.

His small estate lay by the cliffs of the sea, where the waves crashed against the rock like a violent lullaby.

Others in his realm lived the same way, though not all were as little as he. And not all held the same gentleness of heart.

Prologue

The sky shattered, illuminating Felldryn's famous towers of glass. They stood tall, reflecting bolts of grey and silver rain from the raging storm. Blinding and beautiful.

Adanna blinked as light rippled across the towers' smooth surface. The wind howled, whipping across her skin as rain drenched the twins, exposed under the lightning-swept sky. They huddled at each other's side, shivering, near the highest balcony of the castle's northern tower. The cold seeped into Adanna's bones. She reached for Odion's open palm. Her brother's hand was warm despite the cold, but it still didn't hold back the terror seizing her insides.

The storm was a warning. A promise of death from the woman dressed in black.

The woman had come to Felldryn with clever words and pretty promises. Her gifts ones of luxury and bribery. She'd been painstakingly beautiful, reminding Adanna of an old tale about another woman who had wielded her beauty like poison.

The woman in black had charmed the court, leaving them breathless and shaken. Yet, the only thing Adanna had noticed were her eyes.

Eyes like amethyst.

Adanna shook in her ruined silk, her palm slick against her brother's. Odion squinted into the dark, his onyx hair falling into his eyes. Adanna could barely see before her, their once familiar home more a stranger than a friend.

To call this evening a disaster was an understatement.

It had been a massacre. A slaughterhouse. The people of the court were the pigs, and the amethyst-eyed woman, the butcher.

There was so much blood.

Adanna's mouth went dry as the sky flashed, turning the world bright before smothering them in darkness again. She'd known for weeks something dreadful was coming. A shadow that had followed her through the dark crevices of the world. It had infected her dreams, a nightmare poisoning her waking world like a disease that rotted in her blood. But she'd always been that way: prone to the shadows, prone to feeling death, prone to reaching for the monsters that crept through the night.

Some had called it a gift. Most considered it a curse.

The people in the kingdom of Perridorm were a pious bunch, after all, praying and lighting lanterns for the magic that lay within the land.

But her people drew a fine line when it came to what was a gift and what was a curse. There was the natural magic: the kind that ran through the very soil and roots of this land. It brought forth crops, lush grass, and plants that could cure or kill.

And then there was the unnatural: the kind where magic was wielded with blood. Magic that stole from something. To manipulate. To create. To ruin.

It belonged to what they called witches, or *the cursed*.

Adanna was their curse.

She remembered the look of pity and fear in her mother's eyes when she'd told her parents of her nightmares. Of the dark claws that gripped her sleep whenever she lay down her head. She still remembered her mother's smell of gooseberries, her rosy cheeks as they'd warmed before dinner that night.

She could still feel the gentle press of her mother's lips on her forehead. The final kiss sealed into her skin like a goodbye.

That had only been hours ago.

Shame brimmed underneath her skin for not pushing it more, for not seeing things clearly when the beautiful woman had come. Instead, Adanna had cowered, leaning into her brother's arms as if he could halt all the terrors of this world.

Odion didn't feel the darkness like she did but even he'd seen the fear behind her eyes. And he'd believed her when nobody else had.

She blinked away the rain as it coated her eyelashes, running down her face in rivulets. It was only her and Odion now, lost under the thundering screams of the sky.

Her brother's eyes burned into her as he pulled sharply on her arm. 'Don't look, Adanna. We must move. You cannot look back. You can never look back.'

The words stung like a thorn lodged in her heart. She still felt the dead court behind her. Adanna couldn't help herself and spared a glance over her shoulder, her gaze falling on the broken ballroom doors, the shattered glass like broken dreams across the marble floor. The chandelier was in ruins, embedding into the mosaic floor that ran slick with blood.

Her gaze flickered over the bodies, each one twisted and gnarled in ways the body was never made for. The minstrel with his head bent above his spine. The general with his insides splayed across the tiled floor. The duke's daughter – whom she'd only just played a game of tag with that afternoon – lying with her back snapped like a contortionist bending into a glass box.

But it was the twisted bodies of her mother and father, blood still leaking from their torn chests, that would haunt her. They still looked alive somehow, tangled in each other's arms even in death. The cold, empty eyes of her mother stared back at her, the scream still on her lips from the moment the woman in black had smirked.

Adanna choked back a sob. Her brother wiped the hair out of his face, urging her forward along the balcony towards the west stairwell. She could see his lips moving, shouting a warning of some kind, but she couldn't hear it over the harsh wind. She didn't know the towers like her brother did. She'd never had the same urge to explore. Before tonight, she was content enough to draw in her rooms and wait for him to return, enjoying his vibrant tales when he'd discovered something new.

She now regretted her complacency.

Adanna was in unfamiliar territory and almost felt like she was floating, as if the dreadful things she'd tried so hard to push away had suddenly taken hold, gripping her and stealing her away into the night like so many other tales.

She bit her lip to focus and tasted the copper ache of blood in her mouth.

'One step at a time,' she said to herself. 'One breath at a time.'

This wasn't the moment for her to fly away. To lose control as she was known to do. She had to remain anchored. Focused. To keep following her brother.

Odion's mismatched eyes watched Adanna carefully as he helped her take the steep stairwell. His hands were steady as she gave him a nod that it was okay. That she was stable.

For now.

She hated it when he gave her that worried look. As if she were a fragile doll coming apart at the seams with no tailor to stitch her back together. Her mind was different, but it wasn't brittle. Not when she could control it. And right now, she *had* to control it. This was not the time to break. She could hold on. She *would* hold on. She would protect Odion, as he protected her.

The stairs shook and Adanna stumbled, her brother catching her as lightning shot from the sky. White light met the tallest point of the south tower and ran down its surface in a feral dance. From this height, she could see the ocean below and the forest along the coast. The trees bent almost to breaking, thrashing against the wind's call.

Her dark hair whipped across her face, the rain peppering her skin like sharp needles. The stairs were slick as they descended, water running down in a stream. She gripped the smooth stone wall, using its solid texture as both an anchor and a reminder as she navigated the spiralling stairwell.

Odion had called the alarm. He'd seen to that after the court had been slaughtered. He'd moved with swift surety, his focused gaze taking control when she could only stare in horror.

Frozen.

And useless.

The army had been called, their swords ripping free of their sheaths as they met the oncoming enemy invading the eastern lands. The woman with amethyst eyes had come prepared. She'd brought not only magic, but vicious men and foul beasts. And the kingdom of Perridorm had been unprepared.

The woman in black was a queen. One that ruled with an iron fist in Bellatorre. Whispers had even reached them here about her cruelty to her own people. Her strange mines in the middle of her kingdom and her powerful magic. But Perridorm had welcomed her anyway.

Adanna caught a view of the courtyard below through a slitted window and vowed they would never be so unawares ever again. That she and Odion would never allow another kingdom to swallow them whole as the Queen attempted to do now.

Odion was sure footed, helping her along. Though he appeared strong, she knew he was scared, just as she was. They might be each other's other half, but they'd never been similar in the slightest. She froze at fear, felt things on a deeper level, and could never quite understand the difference between reality and imagination. She was the feather, floating and delicate.

Odion was iron and stone. Silent and watchful. And when she would again begin to fly away, he would hold her steady and keep her feet on the ground.

They reached a doorway revealing one of the smaller staircases. 'Come on,' Odion urged, the walls blending into each other as they hurried down the dry steps.

He took charge, checking each corner was clear before moving. She didn't argue. She trusted him. Odion wouldn't run despite the sorceress invading their kingdom. Even in desperation he wouldn't falter. And though she longed to escape this place, to run far into the forest below, he would take them deeper into the heart of the palace. To where her curse became a living thing.

It was a place she feared to tread. A place where her parents sealed away her secret in the shadows of a locked room. A place she only saw in her nightmares.

Adanna stumbled as they turned another corner and Odion squeezed her hand. Her dress was heavy, the wet layers of silk and cotton suffocating as they delved further into the depths of the castle. The darkness embraced her. The whisper of the hidden treasure called like a master to their pet.

She tried to swallow her fear, but it tasted like metal and decaying fruit.

Odion only released her hand as he reached a wooden door. With a groan, it opened into an underground cavern. Rushing water spliced through its middle, cutting the room into two. Adanna eyed the massive gateway on the left wall, filtering the seawater through.

Odion stopped at the edge of the river, his forehead creased. But she knew where to go. Where *they* had to go.

Every part of her screamed this was a bad idea.

Her eyes darted from Odion to a doorway etched into stone across the water. It was unimpressive. Plain. It looked like a servant's quarter, just a timber door, weathered and aged with time. Sections of wood bulged around the iron set into its locks.

Her parents had made sure it looked that way.

Unassuming.

Forgettable.

Odion pulled at the small boat tethered to a nearby dock.

'No!' Adanna cried, yanking his hand from the rope. 'It's too risky.'

Odion swatted her away. 'Risk is a royal's duty, Adanna. You know this.'

'It's too rough! You'll die.'

Her eyes stung, but Odion's face remained calm, despite his shaking hands. He pulled away from Adanna. 'Let me do this,' he said. 'For you and for Perridorm.'

'Is Perridorm worth your blood?'

'Every drop,' he said with a sad smile. Her body shook as he began to pull the eroded rope.

A sharp pain pierced Adanna's chest. She glimpsed his death.

Her eyes bore into the water as it fought through the gates. She couldn't let him die. She *wouldn't*.

He could be stubborn, a frog that wanted to fly when it had no wings. Gulping back her fear, she eyed the lever near the cavern's entrance. She ran for it and Odion shouted her name. Her feet slipped, the slick surface of the stone hindering her steps.

The water lashed towards her, blinding and angry, but she ignored the sting on her skin. She met the mouth of the cave, and her delicate fingers grasped the lever to the gate. Adanna pulled downwards, ignoring the biting pain in her fingers and the way her body lifted to counter its weight. She grunted, using both hands to shut the gate against the onslaught. But when the gate hit the water, it struggled. Slowly, the water settled, blocking off the torrent from outside. Adanna couldn't hold the lever long, but if she could block the flow of water, even a little, perhaps it would give her brother enough time to cross.

In this moment, she would not be a feather. She would be her brother's stone.

Odion climbed inside the boat and pushed with all his might against the current. The oars were about as useful as trying to paddle with spoons against a roaring tide. Adanna winced as her arms burned, her willpower her only companion against the raging torrent.

When Odion was almost halfway, the gate groaned. Panic sluiced through her as a loud crack echoed through the cavern and the gate shuddered. The wood bulged, fractures rippling across the surface as water filtered through every crevice. Adanna screamed as the metal bolts began to bend, each twisting more with every crash.

'I am the stone,' Adanna said through gritted teeth. She closed her eyes, focusing on what little strength she had.

Odion was almost across.

Adanna felt the next wave before it hit, and she roared. The gate squealed, as if it too could no longer stand the pain.

And then the lever slipped.

The gate shattered.

Seawater crashed through and battered against the stone, taking shards of wood with it. Adanna cried out as a wave smashed into her like an avalanche. She was flung against a wall, a crack ringing from somewhere inside her body. Her skull vibrated, stars peppering her vision.

But only one thought consumed her—

Odion.

She choked on the next wave, the battering water trying to drown her on land. Her throat tasted like ash. She was a hollowed-out tree in a wasteland, waiting for something to grow but finding herself withered and without hope.

Once the water had withdrawn, Adanna craned her neck, finding Odion safely on the other side. He broke through the aged wood of the door with ease, disappearing into shadow. Adanna clutched her chest, waiting.

One heartbeat. Two.

It was moments before he came back out, his eyes meeting hers in stern determination. He held a wooden sword and lifted it above him, calling out to her.

Like the door, the sword was plain, forgettable. Only those who knew the tale of the little lord knew its true power. She attempted to stand. Whilst Odion should be the preferred choice, the sword could only be used by her. Would only cut her.

It was her curse.

Odion's strange eyes met hers. One brown. One gold. Eyes she shared.

Fear turned to resolve as she gathered herself. This was Adanna's price. Her duty.

Perridorm was not for the taking.

Reaching her arms out, Adanna shouted, 'Throw it!'

Odion's face was grim as he took a breath, and with his ebbing strength flung the sword across the waterway. Her hand grasped around the wooden handle, her wrist smashing into the edge of stone as she dived for it. Her brother cried out as she barely missed the edge, the water roaring beneath her.

But any pain Adanna had was quickly forgotten as power thrummed through her, alive and volatile.

She clutched the sword, ignoring her panting breath. Pulling all her emotions together, she staggered away from the water and braced herself against the furthest wall. She'd only ever done this once and it had been so terrifying that her parents had hidden the sword away for years. But as she stared at the weapon, she didn't feel fear. Only sorrow.

Her gaze locked with Odion as she brought forth the blade and sliced it across her forearm. Once again, he was the stone tethering the feather.

The cut burned and she held back her scream, each death a living, breathing thing inside her. She felt every soul. Every demise. The water raged. Pain flooded her senses as blood flowed down her dark skin.

With that one cut, Adanna felt her soldiers of death crawl their way out of the soil in the valley. Felt each rotted limb. Each broken soul.

The Elysian Fields welcomed war and death. And each body she had brought back to life, rose to drown the enemy in blood.

I

The Troll, The Elf, and The Royal

Days after Hansel and Eve's disappearance.

The tip of the sharp knife bit into Snow's throat. It glinted in the afternoon light as the large shadow pinned her down. Stones dug into her back. She scowled. Malak huffed a laugh before releasing her, and gave her a quick wink as she hitched herself onto her elbows.

'Not fair!' she yelled, attempting a kick that missed him by a pixie.

'Since when has battle ever been fair?' Malak mused.

'Since I've been smacked on my arse five times,' she grumbled.

He sheathed his knife and wiped sweat from his brow. 'You've forgotten your training.'

She glared at him as he reached out his hand to help her up. Swiping her midnight hair out of her eyes, she took it, eased herself upwards and dusted off her skirts.

They'd been sparring during their break for lunch and Malak was still able to put her on her arse despite all her training. Though he was far larger than her, he was still considered small for a troll, and it made him faster than she'd anticipated. Leaving her sore and a little embarrassed.

'I haven't forgotten,' Snow said, 'I've just been under a curse that ensured I couldn't wake or move, remember? So, forgive me if my muscles aren't up to scratch.'

He flinched. 'I didn't mean—'

'I know,' she sighed. 'It wasn't a dig at you. It's not your fault.'

He met her gaze for a moment, then gave a single, firm nod. 'You know my only priority is you, Princess.'

She squeezed his arm. She knew Malak was doing his best, they all were, but she also knew she'd been snippy since the grotto.

They'd been on the road for days now. Each new dawn reminded her that Hansel was gone. Lost to the chasm that had opened near the grotto. All to follow the Seeker.

Snow scowled at the thought. Pip was convinced Hansel was dead, the Seeker too, but Snow couldn't accept it. Wouldn't. Not when her heart told her otherwise.

So far, they'd travelled south under the cover of the mountains and forest. Snow was still trying to adjust. The enormity of being outside was a growing fear inside her chest. Most days she managed to squash it down. But on other days she felt as if the sky would swallow her whole.

She denied it, of course, waving it off as exhaustion when her companions showed concern, but it was becoming old. She wasn't as fragile as they all assumed. She wasn't a glass slipper that could fall off and break. But even she could at least admit this was all so … *new.*

To make matters worse, her travelling companions were annoyingly astute. Malak, the overprotective brute, and Pip, the scrutinising eye, were always watching her. Florian at least had the decency to speak to her like another royal and not some common child.

Snow's whole life had been under watch. She'd always been chided like a toddler, and even now, out in the open world, she was still being treated as such. She swallowed down the growl that itched at her throat. Snapping at Malak didn't help, nor did the guilt that sat in her belly when she did so.

The journey had been hard for all of them, and she reminded herself to not forget it.

The roads less travelled weren't made for comfort and Snow was learning fast that the luxuries such as a carriage or a full belly were not as common as she'd believed. Already she'd seen the blackened roots of the forest. The lingering effects of decay spreading through the soil like poison. She'd seen the dying crops, the traitors pinned on spikes along the main roads, courtesy of *Her Royal Majesty.*

Snow had known, of course, what Myrenna had done. But to see it from the crest of a mountain, when the sun had set in the colour of blood, had been another experience entirely. Even now, she could clearly see the flies that hung around the bodies.

She gave herself a mental slap and kicked at a small rock. She watched as it tumbled across the ground.

If only everything was that easy to control.

Pip clicked his tongue, his look one of curiosity but also malice.

Snow rolled her eyes. 'What now?'

'Deflecting won't win you a crown,' the elf said. 'Curse or not, a queen that can't defend herself is as useless as tits on a boar.'

It had been like this for days, the elf offering advice she neither asked for nor needed. And despite her and Malak's long history, the troll even seemed to err on the side of caution, both of them ganging up on her when they saw fit.

She hated it.

'That's why we're training,' replied Malak. 'She just needs time.'

Time. Another familiar conversation.

Too much time between places. Not enough time for the right reinforcements. Time was always the problem. Sand pouring through an hourglass as Myrenna and her murders of crows flew about the realm, reporting everything they had seen.

'Well, I've had enough *time* today,' Snow replied, 'and enough of the both of you trying to control me. Myrenna already took that motherly role.'

Shrugging, Pip turned to Florian, who was fidgeting with some string, bending the twine over a small twig. His nose shone bright red under the sun, and his sniffles in the night were beginning to infect Snow's dreams.

'Regardless,' Pip said, 'you've grown weak, and the only way to get strong again is to train.'

'I don't see you picking up a knife, little elf,' she sneered.

'That's because I don't need a knife to stab someone, Princess. I have words for that.'

Snow held back her groan. She took a seat on the large rock nearby and began to remove her slippers. She was too tired for Pip's quips today. Her feet hurt. Blisters had begun to grow on her slight feet, rubbing her toes raw. The flimsy shoes weren't built for hikes or long journeys. She'd only ever experienced the smooth floors of the castle, and she hadn't contemplated appropriate footwear, considering the day she'd been cast under a spell she hadn't planned on leaving the castle.

Now, the pinch on her heel took up most of her time. The slippers were unsalvageable by this point, blood permanently stained into the silk. She stared at Malak's boots in envy and pouted.

They'd chosen to rest at the top of a hill. From here she could see fields of green and the wooden fences outlining borders of farms where livestock grazed. Sunlight spilled over the trees. The wind poured through the leaves like wine into a glass.

'At least the cows are fat and happy,' she muttered before unravelling the bandages on her feet. She almost groaned at the relief.

Pip snorted from his own rock.

'What?' she snapped. Her hands rubbed along her feet, a hiss escaping at the sharp ache.

'I suppose I merely forgot how delicate royalty is.'

Malak chuckled. 'I assure you, she is not delicate.'

'Then why do you treat me like I'm made of glass?' Snow mumbled.

Malak stood beside her, his green skin shining under the high sun. He cast a broad shadow over her, and she shoved him playfully. He feigned pain and shot her a sharp grin. His eyes landed on her bloody feet. 'You know why, Princess. You're invaluable to not only the realm, but us. I know you're not made of glass. That doesn't mean we don't want to keep you safe.'

Snow only huffed.

Malak asked, 'Want help?'

She softened towards him, but shook her head. She could do it herself.

'We just want you safe,' Malak said.

'Safe is a figment of your imagination,' Pip snapped. 'It's as make-believe as goblins and unicorns.'

Snow rolled her eyes.

Malak frowned at the elf. 'Have you lost all ability to believe? Or does that sour demeanour come naturally?'

'If you mean my charm, that's definitely all natural.' The elf winked.

'What about hopes or dreams?' Malak asked. 'You never thought about what could be instead of what is?'

'I'd rather be realistic than naïve.'

Malak only shook his head and assessed Snow's blood-covered feet. 'More blisters?'

'Slippers aren't made to walk through forests and rough roads,' Snow admitted.

'We need to get you some proper shoes. I can't see the rebellion being overwhelmed by us if we bring a princess who can't walk.'

'Cauldron forbid we bring her in alive and intact and they'll be happy?' Pip said. He puffed at the nozzle of his pipe. His shirt was torn from when the earthquake had hit the grotto, and he hadn't bothered changing it. The others at least had recently stopped into a small water reserve to bathe. Pip just seemed to be above it all.

Malak crossed his arms, frowning at Pip. It was the closest Snow had seen him irritated with the elf. 'You know we'll need to make a good impression when we first meet the rebellion. Appearances matter, even in dark times.'

Snow bristled. She'd heard the same refrain from Malak for days and she was tired of being referred to as weak or lacking. Insinuating she wouldn't be good enough was completely inappropriate when speaking to the future queen. And yet, when he'd explained it, she couldn't entirely fault his logic.

'We can't bring her in bloody and battered,' Malak continued. 'She must look the part. Regal. Ready to rule. She's the symbol of hope, and if she greets the rebellion looking defeated before the battle has begun, how do you expect them to be inspired to follow her?'

A sneeze splattered on Malak's arm and he stepped back, a glare on his face.

'Sorry,' Florian said, wiping his nose.

Malak wiped the snot off his arm, his nostrils flaring in familiar agitation. His voice was a growl as he asked Florian, 'What's your opinion on the matter?'

The prince was silent a moment before he said, 'I think you have a good point. My brother used to always say appearance is everything. What people see, they believe. It's a good way to manipulate them.'

Snow rolled her eyes.

Pip laughed. 'I wouldn't be overly quick in accepting advice from your brother, Prince, but he's not entirely wrong in this instance.'

'I don't want to manipulate anyone!' Snow huffed. 'That's what Myrenna does.'

'We're not asking you to manipulate anyone, Princess,' Malak said in his gruff voice. 'We just want to make a good first impression and let gossip do the rest. You haven't been seen in over a decade. This first impression *matters.*'

He was right, though Snow was highly against her reign being dictated by how she looked and not by her choices. It was something her mother had been strongly against.

She remembered one afternoon, sneaking with her mother into her personal garden. They'd played in the hedges, ducking and swerving around each other before falling into a laughing mess by the rose-carved fountain. Her mother's dark hair had been like Snow's: the silky strands fell through Snow's fingers like water.

Leaning in close, her mother had said, *'Sometimes the best lessons learnt are outside of the classroom.'*

'*What lesson did we learn today, Mama?*' Snow had asked.

'*How to have fun.*' She had smiled, tracing her fingers along Snow's palm. '*And how to enjoy the sun. All the best things can be found outside.*'

'*Papa says it's only safe inside these walls,*' Snow had replied.

The Queen had lifted her chin. '*Your father is right and wrong. But don't ever tell him I said so.*' Her mother had laughed as she pulled Snow into her lap and held her close. '*It's a very big world out there, Snow, with a lot of people and a lot of creatures. Some waiting to bait you and gobble you up – exactly as Papa says!*'

Snow had giggled as her mother tickled her. She had lost her breath, gasping air as her mother pulled her close again. She'd smelt of roses and lilies and *home*.

'*But he's wrong that all exist to harm you,*' her mother had continued. '*Magic is neither good nor evil – just like the creatures who live in the realm. Some are kind: they will share what little they have to ensure all receive equal measure. Some are small, just like you, and choose to stay in groups to help each other. Some will seem fierce, but underneath they are the most vulnerable of all.*'

'*What about the dark monsters Papa talks about?*' Snow had asked, her blue eyes wide.

'*Sometimes a monster can be the most beautiful thing you've ever seen,*' the Queen had said with a flick on the little princess's nose. '*When you are queen, never forget that. Never forget that we all come from many paths with many destinations. But our dreams are just as important. Truth is a powerful weapon. But so is deception.*'

The memory faded and Snow wiped at a lone tear falling onto her cheek. Looking up, she found Pip watching her.

She quickly turned away, hiding whatever moisture was left in her eyes.

Malak was still rambling.

All Snow wanted at this point was to obtain new shoes, find Hansel, and to take back her kingdom. All in that order.

'How far is the next village?' Snow asked, trying to bite down on a whine.

'It doesn't matter,' Malak said. 'You're not going near any village. There are too many eyes.'

Her nostrils flared as she whirled on him. 'I'm not a caged animal, Malak. First Myrenna, and now you. Really?'

'I didn't mean …' Malak stumbled.

'It's for your protection, Princess,' Pip calmly interjected.

'Perhaps all she meant, Malak,' Florian said, not looking up, 'was that she wants something to walk in that won't tear her feet apart. Which only requires one of us to tend to. I don't think the intent was her buying new shoes herself or entering the village.'

Snow sighed and lifted her hands. 'Finally! Someone who understands. I don't want a party, I just want something that won't make me bleed as we travel halfway across the realm. Though, when we do manage to find the rebellion, a party would be nice.'

Malak frowned. 'You want a party?'

'Who doesn't?' Snow replied. 'Some music and joy wouldn't go astray after all this misery.'

Pip chuckled. 'I think she's onto something.'

'I used to love parties,' mumbled Florian. 'Even though my brothers more often than not threw me into the pond near the ballroom.'

They all stared at him in silence.

Snow never quite knew whether to pity the Prince or envy him for a normal childhood.

His skin flushed as he met their eyes, the blotched patches creeping across his neck. 'What?' he asked. Since leaving the grotto, his skin had reacted to the pollen in the air as they moved into a warmer climate, causing an almost permanent rash that crept from his neck to his forehead.

Snow shrugged. Today she would pity him. 'Your brothers really are pieces of Scarat shit.'

He smiled back at her. 'Indeed, they are.'

'Maybe we need to work on your language,' said Malak.

'Cauldron help me,' Snow muttered.

Pip stood and straightened his shirt. 'We're close to Roserock, which isn't far from the Skinny Piglet. Perhaps Florian can grab the footwear the Princess so desperately requires whilst we wait. There's also a river nearby where can freshen up to satisfy what I'm sure is an adoring group of fans waiting for their *Dear Monarch*.'

'We're all fresh except you,' Snow sniped.

Pip glared at her before Malak stepped forward. 'Marcellus is the owner there. We should be able to talk to him. He was our contact when Hansel and I went after the spindle.'

Snow huffed. 'You mean when you went after Eveline.'

Florian gasped as pollen hit his nose, and Pip narrowed his eyes at Malak. 'You went after Rumpelstiltskin's spindle?'

Malak nodded with a grimace. 'We almost had it, too, until the Seeker intervened. She kicked both mine and Hansel's arses.'

Pip smirked. 'That's not surprising. That girl is ice and fire.'

'More like pain and ruin,' Snow grumbled.

Malak watched her with caution. As Florian sneezed, Malak jumped back. Snow would have too if she'd been closer.

'Sorry,' Florian mumbled as he searched his pockets for a handkerchief. Coming up short, he made do with wiping his snot on his sleeve.

Snow held back a grimace.

'The Queen sent Hansel on a quest to find Snow,' Malak explained, keeping a wide berth from Florian. 'But when we had no luck finding her, we followed some tavern gossip about a missing spindle. Turns out it was up for sale. Being so valuable, we knew Rumple wouldn't hesitate in hiring the one person who could find it. After a few weeks, we finally got in contact with Marcellus.

'We tried to get information on Marcellus before our meeting but there wasn't much. Just that he's a smuggler and seems to have a tonne of information on a lot of important people. Eve showed up, and Hansel – the lovesick fool – struck a bargain with her to help us find Snow. But if anyone knows where the rebellion is, Marcellus would be it.'

Snow rubbed her feet again, holding back bile as dried blood flaked off her toes. The thought of the Seeker sent hot pulses across her skin. It made her miss her days in the castle. Made her miss the little secret pockets of time she'd spent with Hansel, in the small windows between shifts and his designated time with her stepmother. She understood the Seeker had technically been the one to find her, but the dwarves had also protected her, and it was Malak's love for her that had awoken her. It's not like the Seeker broke the curse. She was a human compass at best.

She wondered if breaking the enchantment had triggered some kind of tracking spell, but it had been days since Myrenna had crashed through the grotto with her fog dragon and Malak had protected her.

She looked up at the troll as he conversed with Pip on the best way to approach the owner of the Skinny Piglet. Standing beside the elf, he looked positively enormous. He'd tanned over the last few days, his skin turning a darker green than normal. He'd always been fit as a warrior, smart for his kind, and she knew she loved him. Not in the way she loved Hansel, but in the way she'd imagined a brother and sister would share. He was her shield, and when the daunting task of what lay ahead came over her, she knew he'd be by her side through every minute of it, as Hansel should have been.

Sometimes Snow had met Hansel and Malak after dark in the gardens and they would imagine what they would do if they were free. What would they see? Who would they meet?

She remembered lying on the grass, holding each of their hands as they stared at the stars. The three of them. A small army dreaming about infinite endings.

Pain shot through her heart. She focused on putting her shoes back on, ensuring not to damage her already wounded feet. Would the people of the rebellion accept her as she hoped? Or would they merely see her as a girl pretending to play queen? Having an idea of a person and meeting the real deal were two completely different things. She feared she couldn't live up to expectations.

The group moved wearily at Pip's command and made their way towards the valley. Snow took a moment to look back at the disappearing tree line that followed the forest to the mountains, wondering if there would ever be a place where she would be enough. Where her friends could be happy. Where they could all be safe. Where Myrenna wouldn't exist. But no matter how many steps they took, how many choices they made, danger followed. She shook off the memory of Hansel and followed the others. Because while her feet may be blistered, bleeding, and broken, it was her heart that hurt the most.

Hansel was hers. Had always been hers. And what the Seeker found she also apparently took. Snow set her mouth into a fine line.

'Are you coming?' Malak called.

That little witch of a Seeker may have fooled Hansel, but she hadn't fooled Snow. The Seeker was only important whilst there was a battle to win. If Snow were queen, she could bring Hansel home. Back to the Silver City.

She refused to believe he was dead. He was too stubborn. Too hopeful.

Hansel didn't know he'd made a mistake, and it was Snow's responsibility to help him. To save him.

His loyalty lay with her. His fealty and his hope.

To accomplish that, she needed more support. More power. Magic.

The rebellion would be Snow's first step to luring him back.

Malak watched the Princess as she stared at the path behind them. Her eyes watered against the light, but she put on a brave face. Malak had seen her heart shatter when they'd found the blood in the forest, Hansel's axe left behind after he'd dived for Eveline. She wore the weapon now, strapped across her back, like a lone warrior ready to slay any who stood in her path. The red, leather hilt was worn but the blade was sharp, shining under the sun. Snow polished it each night, caring for it like a sick animal. She smiled at it sometimes, as if she carried a piece of Hansel with her.

Maybe she did.

Malak cracked his knuckles, releasing the tension that hummed under his skin. The forest around them was peaceful, a stark difference to the hurt in their hearts from recent events. The grotto's destruction. His best friend gone. Even now the thought broke something in him, but he couldn't linger on it, not when Snow had convinced him otherwise. She believed Hansel was alive, not just because her heart told her so but because the whole event had involved magic. Magic that was targeted. Ancient. Even Pip had confirmed that magic was involved. And magic meant miracles.

Though, it had taken him a while to believe it too. After he'd come to terms with the whole thing, he and Snow had fought. Snow had stormed off in her grief, disappearing into the shadows of the trees. It was the first time she'd walked away instead of tearing into him. He'd eventually chased her down, finding her amongst a makeshift shelter in the forest. She'd cried so much that her cheeks were swollen, her blue eyes rimmed in red.

It had taken everything in Malak not to fold her into his arms and hold her. The soothing words had been on his lips, but he'd hesitated, letting her mourn in her own way.

He couldn't help but think of Hansel. How the Huntsman had been his first and only friend, the first kind person to acknowledge him as anything other than a *thing*, a beast. How Hansel had snuck in training time with him when they were off duty. Trolls weren't let into the Queen's guard, and Malak was lucky enough he'd been placed into maintenance and care. Even then, he'd only got the position because of Hansel. Malak had a one-way ticket in chains to the mines before a young Hansel had helped change his fate. And then, when Malak had finally met the Princess – someone so beautiful and yet just as lonely as he was – he couldn't believe his luck.

He missed the time they'd had in the castle. Missed the ease of watching Snow's raven hair blend in with the dark of night. Or how her pale skin shadowed against the snow that covered the grounds in winter. But while Snow and Hansel had planned for escape, to run away, to find another home, Malak had dreamt a different dream. Unlike his friends, Malak knew the realm. He had travelled this world from top to bottom in the hopes of having the same dream.

And it had been cruel.

Hansel had barely felt starvation, and despite the death of his sister, he'd been loved. As had Snow, before the death of her parents. Malak understood each had their tragedies but what he couldn't fathom was the humans' need to focus on what had been lost and not what they already had.

Love was not something Malak was accustomed to. It was not the troll way. His family had been harsh, unafraid of brutality in a world where strength was everything. He'd never felt kindness, never seen love, or stopped to see the beauty of it all.

He'd left Troll's Keep when he was old enough. Still too small to matter much but different enough that the world outside shunned him. No village would take his offer to work. Travellers would attack him or run. He was spat at, beaten, and given cursed names.

As a half-caste, he was too human for Troll's Keep and not human enough for the outside world. His parents never spoke about it, but his father never looked at his mother the same. Whatever had happened to conceive Malak had been hidden. Which meant Malak had never held a home, had never understood the concept of a person being 'home' until his time in the castle. It had been the first time in his life he'd held a purpose. A family.

Only to be ruthlessly separated by a warring realm.

Malak frowned at the dirt covered path. He blamed Eve, to a certain extent. She'd been trouble from the moment he'd met her, but he'd never envisioned Hansel's magnetism to her – or hers with him. He looked at Snow now, whose eyes went dark against whatever thoughts she let run wild through her mind, and he understood that, whilst he loved her, she loved Hansel. And Hansel loved the Seeker.

But that was love.

Malak's dream relied on Snow's happiness, and her ability to create something new with her crown. Something whole. If they could get her to safety and find her an army to take back the throne, then maybe others like him would no longer suffer.

He refused to believe Hansel had died – the Huntsman was far too stubborn for that. As a family they were whole; apart, they were broken pieces.

The rebellion was hope. If Hansel did survive, that's exactly where he would go. Just as they'd planned before everything began.

And then, after this mess was over, after the loss and the bloodshed and the heartbreak, perhaps Malak could also find happiness. A place where he, too, could belong.

II

The Weaver's Chance

Rumpelstiltskin didn't just get captured, Pip thought. He wasn't known to be soft, nor the type to let his spindle be stolen. Pip had been locked away for fifty years, but he knew Rumple like nobody else, and something was amiss. The spindle was powerful – exceptionally potent when it came to magic. To 'lose' it was not in Rumple's vocabulary, and it wasn't possible given the magic Rumple wielded or the connections he had. So, how had one of the most formidable beings in the realm fallen?

Pip's finger traced his pipe, noting the small engraving of $R + P$ on its side. Over a century he'd spent with Rumple, taking his commands with a desire so strong he'd have broken every rule in the realm to achieve them. Rumple may not have been overly kind, but it was in those moments of success that Pip had felt true happiness. A sense of being whole. Worthy.

Powerful.

Pip strolled ahead of the group, his walking stick in hand to help his short legs on the journey. With his free hand, he lifted the flute, tied securely around his throat. His power, his curse, and his freedom.

They were a broken group relying on a spoiled girl to save a ravaged kingdom. He'd simply stuck around out of mere curiosity, but now, with Rumple and the spindle missing, it had become so much more. Perhaps his old companion needed help. And not only that; Pip felt it was his personal responsibility to ensure the spindle's safety.

If the Queen held that kind of power, they would never win this war. All hope would be lost, despite Snow's presence.

Pip's first step was to get the Princess to the rebellion, then assess what kind of army they had. From there, he'd go his own way.

Otherwise, none of them stood a chance.

Rumpelstiltskin hissed as his knees scraped the floor of his cell. The cold stone cut into his torn and bruised skin like razors.

The guards laughed and slammed the door shut behind him, covering him in festering darkness. His threadbare clothes were torn, no more than a makeshift white cloth splattered with dirt and the stink of his own blood. He blinked into the dark and bit his yellowed fingernails; they were already down to the quick.

Without his spindle, he was wild.

Lost.

Powerless.

Never had he known such isolation. Before his imprisonment, he'd always been surrounded, always had a companion of some kind. Whether it had been his network, or those on his payroll, or … he didn't finish the thought.

Either way, he'd had plenty of visitors in his time. Many had come to him asking for favours or for help with their dreams. Trading favours and making bargains were his drug and his survival. Unless you were human, respect was a hard commodity to come by. He'd spent years building his empire, experimenting with magic, and achieving great triumphs for those indebted to him.

His spindle was a part of him. A piece of his soul split. Without her, he was hollow. He missed the blinding colours. The voices of wisdom and the clarity she brought. Without the spindle, the manic voices in his head echoed with a chorus of disturbing thoughts. They consumed him, whispering to him in awful nightmares and terrible dreams. And in the darkest, deepest parts of himself, he could still hear the spindle as she screamed.

He always heard her, even when she was apart from him. He felt it when the Tinker played with her, the pain like a brand being burnt into his skin.

He hissed at the thought, his broken nails scraping the stone wall. She was his as he was hers. She was the power and spirit of dreams. She was the tether of it all. And somehow the Queen had her in her lethal grasp.

He smacked his forehead at his stupidity. The pain throbbed through his scalp as he leaned back, resting against the wall. He hadn't seen Myrenna coming. Hadn't believed it possible. But hindsight was a bitter thing.

How could he have been so naïve?

He was old, very old, and wasn't age wisdom? Or had he become so complacent that he believed himself invincible? The only beings more powerful than him were the keepers of this realm: the Sisters Grimm. Had they been blindsided, too? Or was he the only fool here?

The Queen was a child in the eyes of the Sisters Grimm and himself. Nobody in the kingdom could outwit them. Or so he'd believed.

It had happened so fast, Myrenna's fog dragon snuffing out his dream magic. Rumple stood frozen in shock as the Queen had obliterated his network, her meddlesome murders infiltrating and destroying it from within.

His advisors had warned him of undelivered messages, told him of instances where his crew were disappearing, and yet Rumple had merely waved them away, told them to handle it. He'd thought the warnings a minor inconvenience. Nobody had come to challenge him, and he knew their dreams, their fears, and their lies.

The taste of metal coated his tongue as he chewed his nails, and he licked his lips.

Whilst the spindle remained in the hands of the filthy little Tinker, he would fight for her. She was his as he was hers.

So, in the darkness of his small cell under the castle of the Silver City, Rumple scraped his hands against the ground and smiled.

Though nobody could hear him, his was the only voice that cut through the symphony that replayed in his thoughts. 'I am hers as she is mine.'

III

The Bows of Vagabonds

Bronson's teeth chattered against the cold wind as their wagon slowly made its way along the narrow path lining the side of the northern peaks. Though King's Keep was close, this part of the journey had been the worst. Sure, they'd battled scarats, adopted a lost pixie, and won a rigged battle in an arena of trolls, but it still didn't stifle the boredom or the regret.

Bronson wasn't built for sleeping in the open, or the makeshift blankets that barely kept out the cold. He wasn't used to stale food, or the way his skin itched from the constant dirt. It had been too long since he'd had a proper bath. Too long since he'd done his nails or styled his hair or made a new outfit.

He stared at Brufell beside him. The always stoic dwarf guided the reins as the horse trotted at a steady pace. His vest was unlaced, the greyed hair on his chest visible through the opening of his shirt.

'I miss the grotto,' Bronson grumbled.

Brufell blew out a breath through his nose. 'So you've said. Repeatedly.'

Bronson pouted at the response. Talking to the surly older dwarf was always difficult, but more so since the whole debacle with Bo in Troll's Keep. Bronson had tried to respect Brufell's privacy at first and give the old dwarf space, but it wasn't in his nature, especially when the journey was so long and he had no other company besides an overly hungry pixie.

But Bronson wasn't completely heartless. He could see the heaviness of Bo's betrayal sitting on Brufell's shoulders. The way he lost himself in thoughts of the past and took the safer routes. It was why Bronson tried to talk about nicer things, prettier things – instead of the ugly truth of it all.

The Queen controlled the fog dragon.

She wanted Princess Snow.

And something *big* was coming.

The old dwarf sniffed the air, before slowing the cart.

'What is it?' Bronson asked.

Brufell frowned. 'Something's burning.'

Bronson sniffed the air, finding only the scent of rock and his own sweat soaked skin.

Brufell watched the younger dwarf from the corner of his eye. Whether he was waiting for a response or some recognition, Bronson didn't know. He didn't care, to be honest. Brufell's knack for quoting the obvious was a trait that Bronson found to be nonsensical at the best of times.

Unless the fire was a warm inn with a blazing fireplace and a hot bath, what did he care if something was burning. Bronson's attention drifted back to the crinkled letter in his hand. They'd received it from the others, urging them to travel to their cousin's home in the Peaks of Carfell once their journey was done. He'd lost count of how many times he'd unfolded the delicate paper, eyes tracing the familiar words just to feel a little closer to home.

The parchment was soft now, worn thin by his touch. It held a warmth, a comfort he couldn't quite explain, soothing the ache that had settled deep in his chest.

Bronson and Brufell had found the information they'd needed about the fog dragon, but it didn't get them any closer to stopping the Evil Queen. They couldn't go through Carnell as originally planned as it was now declared to Bellatorre, the royalty having aligned themselves to Myrenna. It was why they were headed north to secure a boat in King's Keep instead of going home. If they could stay low, they could follow the river through the mountains and hopefully arrive at the Crystal Lake in time to meet the rest of the Seven at the colony.

Bronson had never been fond of boats, nor the idea of sailing through the mountains themselves. When Brufell had suggested it, Bronson's heart had practically plummeted out of his chest, fear souring his mouth. There were hidden pockets scattered deep inside the mountains, natural traps for awful, fell things. Monsters of the deep. And he certainly didn't want to be the one of the idiots who woke them up.

Especially not after their experience with the scarats, or the dark beast that had lingered in that underground pool near the pixies' colony. He shuddered at the memory.

Brufell had only grunted at Bronson's fear, assuring him that, if they remained swift and silent, they should float through unseen. But if Bronson's bitten fingernails didn't give him away, his twitching should have.

The fog dragon was the darkness of the Shadow Forest, a magic creature old and powerful. Created from something even the dwarves had no understanding of. How Myrenna had gathered the information or the power to control it was still a mystery. Surely, with the beast by her side, they stood little to no chance of survival. He knew she ate hearts. But how many hearts was she consuming to be able to fulfil this terrible dream of hers?

Since that fateful day on the mountain pass when they'd stumbled upon the poisoned Princess, he'd been set upon a path he wasn't yet ready to face. But was anyone ever truly ready to face war?

The letter's ink was faded. It was in beautiful cursive, the swirls arching around each other like an unsung sonnet.

Brufell clicked his tongue. 'You know the words won't change no matter how many times you read them?'

'I know,' Bronson grumbled. 'It's just—'

'Comforting?'

'Yeah,' Bronson said wistfully, folding the letter carefully before tucking it into his pocket.

Brufell focused on the reins. His long beard flowed with the wind. Scars lined his weathered skin.

Bronson faced the road again. The path was narrow, barely wide enough to fit the cart, winding in a way where the sharp turns caused Bronson's stomach to roil.

The further they travelled, the smaller the cart felt. They had one sheer cliff to their left, leading towards a towering forest and valley. Steep rock shadowed their right, reaching high into the floating clouds. Bronson eyed the wall of sheer rock cautiously. For once he'd just like a smooth journey. Less of an adventure and more of a holiday, with beautiful dwarves to rub his feet. Female or male; he didn't mind. If he tried hard enough, he could hear them singing to him. He grinned, closing his eyes to daydream, when Brufell grunted, halting the horse.

Brufell swore.

'What now?' Bronson asked.

'Take a look.'

Rocks upon rocks were stacked atop each other, reaching for the grey sky and barricading their path.

Bronson turned to look for an alternative route but found none. They couldn't rotate the cart even if they wanted to, and neither of them had enough strength or magic to fit through the rockfall. Bronson rubbed his temples and met Brufell's knowing eyes. 'What?'

'What were you thinking about before?' Brufell asked.

'When?'

'When you were smirking like a fool.'

A flush crept up Bronson's neck as he avoided Brufell's rare chortle. 'It was nothing,' he mumbled.

The old dwarf let out a husky laugh, and Bronson held back his retort. He could admit it was nice to hear him laugh, even if it was at his own expense. Brufell shushed the horse and hopped onto the rocky ground.

The mountain remained eerily silent, the only sound coming from a cold wind echoing above the cliffs. Bronson searched the trees, the hairs on the back of his neck standing on end. When the pixie crawled on his lap, he jumped back. The pixie snickered and Bronson rolled his eyes.

'Ha. Ha.' Bronson said, 'Let's all laugh at Bronson today.'

Bronson leaned back into his seat and wiped his eyes. Black kohl marked his index finger, and he pouted. It would be smudged now, and not in the good way.

Ahead, Brufell ran a calloused hand down his grey beard as he made his way to the debris of rock.

Bronson stretched out his legs, trying to ease the tension building inside him. The pixie climbed up his arm and stood on his shoulder, his stitched eye red.

Bronson supposed he should help the older dwarf, but he was also perfectly happy remaining where he was. Out in the open, without things wanting to *eat* him. Yes, not being eaten was preferable.

Brufell entered a small opening in the rocks ahead, most likely looking for a pinpoint where the structure would crumble. Being a dwarf and building underground cities at least had that advantage: the ability to see the best way to move dirt and rocks.

'Anything?' Bronson called.

A slight grumbling echoed across the path.

'Very succinct, Brufell. Great work.'

Bronson picked at the beds of his fingernails. 'Anything now?' he called. He was keen to get off this narrow excuse of a path. He didn't trust that the wall of rocks to his right wouldn't start caving any moment, knowing his luck.

Silence.

'I suppose I should help him,' Bronson groaned to the pixie. 'I'll never hear the end of it if I don't.' The pixie smiled as Bronson stepped out of the cart with a flourish.

He'd taken barely three steps when the wind broke, stillness settling over the pass. Bronson lifted his head, a shiver running over his skin when there was a *whoosh* in the air. Pain shot through his arm, knocking him to the side. To his left an arrow protruded from the ground. Another *whoosh* and Bronson scuttled behind the cart, his breath ragged. He braced himself against the front wheel, trying to breathe through the pain. With a quick glance, he noticed his tunic was torn, blood staining its edges. It was just a scratch, but by the cauldron it burned.

'What just happened?!'

The pixie stared at him with a wide eye, shaking his head.

Shouts rang out across the mountain, echoing along the dirt. Goosebumps peppered Bronson's skin as he panted. Would there ever be a time when they weren't in peril, for cauldron's sake? Bronson hugged his arm to his chest, really wishing he could escape to his fantasy from earlier.

He twisted towards the cliff. While it provided coverage on this side, they were vulnerable from the valley below, which is exactly where the shot had been fired from. Before he could formulate a plan, three more arrows came flying in quick succession, imbedding themselves deep into the cliff. Tiny rocks scattered across the surface and fell like dusty rain.

The pixie shook, whimpering on the gravel. Bronson repositioned himself on his belly. His eyes skimmed under the cart, but the wheels obstructed any view of the valley. 'Brufell!' Bronson cried again. But there was no response.

The older dwarf had lodged himself into the debris. What if he'd been hit? What if he was bleeding out? Bronson's heart thrummed as more arrows zinged overhead.

'BRUFELL!' he screamed.

Sweat beaded on his brow as a shadow fell onto the road. Old grey hair peered through a small gap.

Bronson sighed with relief. 'Thank the Godmother.'

Brufell gave him that annoying warrior's nod before moving his finger to his lips to stay silent.

'Like I have a choice,' Bronson muttered.

The pixie scrambled around the wheel of the cart as another arrow hit its side, the wood groaning. Bronson closed his eyes. 'Whatever happened to just being nice to everyone?'

Why shoot when you could sing? Why fight when you could dance?

Neither of those things needed blood.

Or pain.

Bronson had barely opened his eyes when the pixie pointed upwards, buzzing with panic. Bronson followed his finger towards the top of the cart where the shining metal of their weapons glistened. They were laid on top of their things, an easy target for whatever trap they'd fallen into.

Dredging up whatever bravery he had left, he shuffled backwards, closer to the weapons. He braced himself, and lifted his head to peek into the distance. Trees lay scattered below, the body of the forest climbing up the mountains from the valley like a second skin. Despite the cooler climate, the milky sunlight washed over him, his tunic and leathers getting hot as dust and sweat soaked his skin.

Not even a bird could be seen. But there, in the distance … was a glint. A whizzing sound cut through the air, and he cried out as an arrow grazed his ear. Blood pooled on his collar, and he winced.

If this continued, he'd have no blood to give, for cauldrons sake.

The arrow shone in the murky sunlight, lodged into the dusty ground. It was lined in silver, the main shaft made of dark wood. While Bronson had seen arrows before, this was the largest he had ever encountered. It stood the height of a whole dwarf. A tall one.

The dwarves had bows in their arsenal, of course, but nothing like these monstrous weapons.

Bronson trembled, fighting back the panic that threatened to drown him. He blinked back tears as Brufell's calm voice echoed in his mind. *'In war, there is only that moment. Let fear focus you, not control you.'*

They were blind, trapped, and separated – not the greatest circumstances to find oneself in. But also, not the first time, either.

Bronson eased into a crouch, focusing on his first goal: protect the wagon and their supplies. He knew Brufell could handle himself and trusted his brethren to do so.

Bronson swallowed and eyed the cart. Before he could move, the pixie flew towards the canvas covering their belongings and smirked. Swiftly, the clever little creature unlatched the strap covering the back of the cart, so Bronson had a better reach. Before Bronson could thank him, the creature delved deeper into their belongings.

'One day,' Bronson promised himself, 'I'll be able to just play my music and get fat. When this mess is over, I refuse to be kidnapped, or shot at, or told what to do.'

Awkwardly, the pixie lifted an arrow, sliding it out from under the covering. One arrow after another fell to the ground. Bronson shuffled over to collect them.

A howl called out over the mountains, and Bronson froze. One sound turned to many as they responded in echoes, each one a different call, a different voice, haunting and ethereal.

They were surrounded.

This wasn't the Queen's doing – he knew that much. She attacked in shadows and spite; this wasn't her style. Bronson suspected raiders or robbers, and he swore at himself for being so naïve. They'd avoided the main roads, taking into consideration raiding parties may appear, but with Brufell's battle skills, they'd assumed the two of them would be okay. Brufell didn't die easily – the turmoil from the last few weeks had proven that. Had proven they had more to give in this life.

Then the mountain rumbled.

Bronson bit down on a cry as the largest stone from the blockade tumbled free, crashing over the debris. Smaller rocks followed in a thunderous cascade, the rumble shaking the cliffside and drowning out their enemy's calls.

Brufell was nowhere to be seen.

Arrows shot from the trees, clattering against the rocks.

Bronson's gaze swept the debris, searching desperately for any sign of the old brute. He couldn't lose him now. Not after everything Brufell had endured, after all the times he'd watched over him, tried to teach him to fight. He was family. He was one of the Seven. Their protector.

Brufell's hand peeked through a gap and gave a thumbs up. Despite the dread Bronson felt, he gave the old dwarf a shaky smile. Brufell was causing a distraction.

The pixie dropped another few arrows and a bow from the cart. Bronson picked them up with shaking hands, his eyes locked on the cliffs. There was no movement – until Brufell's voice rang out in a sharp cry of warning.

Bronson spun around, nocking an arrow and drawing the string back. He aimed at the shadow racing along the cliff, its figure broad and slow-moving. With trembling arms, he released the arrow. It flew like a shooting star.

Bronson's eyes widened as it barely missed the stone wall and pierced their enemy's arm. A roar rumbled over the hills and Bronson ducked back behind the cart. Arrows careened across the sky in response, splattering across the ground before him. With a *thunk*, an arrow lodged in the wood beside his head.

'Nope!' he yelped as he dived under the cart, narrowly missing the sharp edges from the next volley of arrows.

Two sets of heavy feet approached, bare and covered in mud. The pants were torn, shaped in haphazard lines around a hairy calf.

The pixie shuddered, crawling closer to the wheel to get a better view as Bronson braced himself.

Cauldron help me, he thought.

'Come out, come out, little dwarfy,' sang the husky tone of the stranger.

Bronson's breath hitched and the pixie stared at him. Did they have Brufell already? Or was it just Bronson's luck to always be the one to get captured? He nocked another arrow. If he died, he may as well do it with style.

'We have nothing of value,' Bronson called out. 'We're just trying to get home.'

The stranger chuckled as several sets of feet halted near the cart. The head of a very large, very smelly troll leaned down. His arms rippled with muscle, the veins lining his skin like a road map. Bronson gulped. Before he could do anything, his bow was snatched by a green hand. He could only blink as it snapped in the troll's fingers like fragile bone.

Bronson couldn't move. He felt like he'd been thrown back into that arena again. Fear coated his skin, fresh and wild. He should run, or fight, or do something remotely noble, but he didn't have it in him. Not when more trolls appeared, blocking any hope of escape.

The troll who had spoken dropped the broken pieces of the bow, leaving them in splinters on the dirt.

Bronson was dragged by the hair from the cart, the huge green fist tight against his skin. Bronson squirmed in the grip, failing pitifully.

'Nothing of value, aye?' the troll said, raising Bronson to meet his gaze. 'A dwarf is worth more than nothing these days, especially with the mines paying good coin for your kind.'

Bronson winced as the troll's breath suffocated him. It was hot and sticky. Decaying meat sat festering in his teeth, the mildew becoming its own living thing. Bronson gagged.

'Tie him up. Let's find the other one,' another troll gruffed. His thick arms held the largest bow Bronson had ever seen. It was made of a flexible metal, the sheen stark against the troll's dirt-encrusted skin. Noticing Bronson's stare; the troll grinned. 'Nothin' shoots better than this beauty right 'ere.' The whole side of the cliff was studded with large silver arrows from the trolls' ambush.

Bronson's knees hit the dirt with a crack, the vibration shooting straight to his hips. A scream echoed in the air. He twisted, eyes locking onto the troll, and froze as the pixie attacked. Its wings fluttered wildly as it lashed out, claws raking across the troll's face. The creature bit down hard on the troll's ear, ripping the top clean off. Blood dribbled down the troll's neck. He smacked the creature into the cliff. The pixie's small form went limp for a second before the troll walked over and caught him.

'No!' Bronson cried.

Sucking his teeth, the troll sneered down at Bronson. The dark warning in his expression was clear.

Another troll brought forth a makeshift cage and the pixie was shoved inside. The act was violent, but at least the creature was alive. The pixie screeched at them, his bared teeth covered in blood, and his wings fluttered as he rammed into the edges to no avail.

'A dwarf *and* a pixie,' the troll mused. 'Who's your other companion? An elf?'

The group of trolls chuckled as Bronson skittered back.

'Where is he then, aye? Still amongst the rocks? Why don't ya tell him to come out and say hello?'

Bronson swallowed. He felt like a youngling being targeted by bullies. Except here, he had nobody to report them to, and no parents to cry to when it was all over. Here, it was life and death.

The group of trolls moved towards him. They were a dirty lot, the smell coming off them like a decaying corpse.

Bronson skittered away, halting only when his back hit the rising cliff wall. His gaze raked over the troll's haphazard clothes. The one with the bow wore a large fur cape, a gold chain hung from his throat matched with hooped earrings, and he had braids in his long, dark hair.

As Bronson began to shift up the wall, the troll with the bow leaned down. 'Believe it or not, we don't wanna hurt ya.'

Bronson's voice came out braver than expected. 'Says the troll who laid out a trap and shot me in the ear?'

The troll laughed. 'See? We do have something in common. Considering what your little friend did.'

'We have nothing in common.'

The vision of another troll in an arena coated Bronson's vision. Where sand crusted his boots and blood coated his hands. The crunch of his spear as it pierced the troll's neck.

Before the troll could respond, Brufell called from the rocks. An invisible voice amongst the stone. 'I've been around a long time, and when a group of trolls carry weapons, it always means somebody is going to get hurt.'

The troll in front of Bronson smiled and stood tall. 'Looks like your friend finally made an appearance.'

The pixie squealed in the cage as Brufell's voice rang out. 'If you mean no harm, then let them go.'

The main troll nodded to another. Each one spread themselves out and slowly lifted their weapons. The troll with the bow widened his grin. 'I'll let them go,' he said. 'If ya come out from yer hiding place.'

'I'll come out when you let them go. Or, I'll slaughter you all.'

The trolls all howled with laughter and the one with the bow turned to Bronson. 'If he's as small as you, then his courage is as big as a troll. Maybe he ain't an elf? Perhaps he's a magic wielder? He's confident if he thinks he can beat us.'

Bronson just stared back at him, his mouth a tight line. He refused to give this animal anything.

The troll ignored him, focusing back on the rocks. 'Come out, brave one. We only want goods to survive.'

'Then take the goods and let my friends go.'

'Yer friend is stubborn,' the troll said to Bronson. 'Under different circumstances, we might have gotten along.'

Bronson winced as another troll lifted him up by the shirt and he twisted in his grip. Warm blood dripped down his side, and he wondered how much he'd lost.

'Check the cart, see if they have anythin' of use,' the troll with the bow said.

'Let us go,' Bronson said. 'Take whatever you want, just don't hurt us.'

The troll looked back at Bronson as the others started searching the cart, hauling out the dwarves' weapons and food.

'Yer lucky it's just us and not murderers,' he said. 'There are worse things out 'ere than us. There's even a dragon up in these hills.'

Bronson swallowed his terror. A dragon! It was impossible. They were secluded with the giants, locked away in the realm above the clouds.

The troll smiled, as if he could smell Bronson's fear. He turned back towards the boulders. 'Don't come out, then. But I'll keep yer friend close until we get what we need.'

Bronson's feet dragged across the ground as the troll pulled him towards the cart. The trolls took out the dwarves' packs, dropping their belongs across the dirt road. Bronson's heart ached as they yanked out his instruments, stealing the measly rations of food. Brufell and Bronson didn't have many medallions, just gems, but those had been hidden in a small compartment underneath.

'Why let us live when we'll starve anyway?' Bronson said. 'You've taken anything we can use to eat or to protect ourselves.'

'If yer a survivor, you'll find a way.'

'There's medicine 'ere,' one troll called.

'Good,' the troll with Bronson said. 'Take what ya can.'

The dirt shifted as another rock fell. This time half the roadblock opened up. Stone tumbled after stone, the ground beneath them shaking.

The hairs on Bronson's arms raised as he thought of Bonyx's tales back in the grotto. If they'd awoken a rock giant, then the trolls would be the least of their problems. At least they were larger targets. Bronson found himself wondering which alternative would be worse.

With a shudder, the mountain responded, the creaking grind of the cliff shifting under them. Shouts rang out as Bronson was shoved forward. With a defeating crack, the wall trembled, breaking open. Everyone turned towards the cliff.

And then it went to the cauldron.

The top of the cliff shifted. A torrent of rocks and dirt fell ready to wipe them away.

Bronson grabbed the cage with the pixie and dived under the cart, his heart beating like a thousand drums. The trolls ran, separating in the chaos as Bronson saw the same hairy calf from before.

He didn't know why he did it. He blamed his panic. He gripped the trolls calf and pulled, screaming at him to take cover. It was an odd sight to see, the fear in the troll's eyes – the last moments of his life flashing before him as he, too, dived for the cart.

The wall crashed around them like dark fire. One moment, they had been in sunlight, and the next they were choking in darkness. The dirt entered Bronson's lungs, and he heaved a throaty cough. His eyes stung from dust. The cart creaked, the weight of debris pressing on the smooth wood.

The pixie shivered underneath him, wincing as the dwarf protected its small, blue form.

For a moment he waited in silence. The avalanche ended and he coughed again. He had barely any room to move. The back of the cart had broken, dipping into the road with the weight of whatever stones had fallen. But the wheels at the front were hanging on and he made out the green legs of the troll.

He pulled back rock, and saw the troll had survived. Unconscious but breathing. His hulking form was barely protected by the strained wheels, and even then, one wheel held a large crack.

'Can you move?' he asked the pixie. The creature nodded, seeming unharmed. Bronson yanked at the cage doors, but it had bent in the crash, the door jarring into the bars. 'We'll have to get you out later.' The pixie whimpered but obliged.

Bronson assessed the damage. He couldn't even fathom where to begin digging, but if he didn't start now, the wheels would crumble, and his bones along with them.

On his left, the wheel groaned, ready to snap.

I don't like this adventuring business.

Bronson adjusted his position, careful to avoid the creaking cart above him. He began working, his dwarven hands releasing the dirt bit by bit. Every movement stung as dirt fell into his open wounds. Sunlight poured through the gap, widening with each shift, until Bronson finally glimpsed the thick fingers of another dwarf's hands.

He sighed with relief as Brufell's weathered face appeared through the gap.

'Sorry, small one,' Brufell said. 'I didn't have a choice.'

Bronson gave him a grim smile as they both worked to widen the hole. With one final pull, Brufell yanked Bronson free from the debris. The path was almost indistinguishable. The dwarves heard coughs and twisted. The trolls were collecting themselves. Smoke and dust particles floated in the air as Brufell ushered Bronson forward.

With the collapse, the road blockage was nearly cleared. They ran through the dust, clambering over the rocks, but Bronson's feet slipped beneath him. Panting, he'd almost breached the top when a massive green hand yanked him back. His head cracked against the ground and a ringing filling his ears.

Brufell bellowed. 'BRONSON!'

Bronson was pinned beneath the weight of the troll, the cold edge of a sharp sword pressed to his neck.

'Save our leader or yer die,' a troll growled, his voice low and threatening.

IV

The Dread of Failure

The crows of the Queen had been the eyes of the realm for over a decade now. They flew in murders, their harsh black wings a reminder of the power Myrenna held. She was their master, their saviour, their Queen. Dread had been a proud general of that small army for many years, just as his brothers had been. He now stalked through the castle, his broad shoulders grazing the stone wall in the narrow staircase. He shoved past court officials and servants, even causing one girl to squeak as he passed. He barely glanced at her, but her scent lingered. And it reeked of fear.

He smirked, tasting it on his tongue. The tart sweetness of it could have a man hooked if they weren't careful. But Dread didn't have time to linger today. Not when his queen waited.

His steel boots beat against the stairs towards the Queen's tower, where a set of golden doors waited at the top. Dread rapped his knuckles on the door three times before he pulled them open. Myrenna stood in the middle of the room, her silky, dark hair loose around her shoulders. Dread could have sworn her amethyst eyes shone brighter, the thrum of magic in the air a living heartbeat.

Bodies lay strewn about the room, girls of all shapes and sizes sprawled limply. Dread noted their wide, terrified eyes, and the blood pooling on the floor. But it was the sight of the torn-open chests of the victims that made him smirk.

Myrenna licked the last of the blood off her fingers, a wicked gleam in her eyes.

The room reeked of terror. Dread's eyes almost watered at the thickness of it. He shivered as he carefully stepped over each body, then fell on his knees in front of his Queen. Despite the death, he loved it when he saw her in these moments. Moments when she let the cool facade fade and released the animal inside. Myrenna never let others see the times when she devoured maidens for regeneration, and some part of him had always yearned to see it. To one day witness the sanctity of her *feeding*.

His mouth salivated at the thought, and he swallowed thickly.

Myrenna was silent as she sauntered closer. He held back his gasp at the feel of her sharp nail on his skin, her finger raising his chin towards her pale face. Blood coated her lips, dripping slowly from her mouth. How beautiful it looked against the harshness of her amethyst eyes. Crimson and purple truly were her colours.

An electric heat spread through his veins. 'Your Majesty.'

'It's been a difficult morning, Dread,' Myrenna said, stepping away. Her touch left a brand on his skin he couldn't ignore.

Myrenna's feet were careful as she stepped over a young maiden. Only a teen, if Dread hazarded a guess.

As she poured a glass of wine, he took in the remainder of the room and stood. Scrolls were scattered everywhere, some with tears ripped through them as if in a frenzy. He noted the spilled ink by the window, the way the chaos aligned with the bodies on the floor.

Dread was aware of the potency the magic held within those scrolls. He'd even helped the Queen locate them in Bellatorre before her reign began. Staring at them, broken and torn, left him a little hollow. So much work to find, and so little effort to destroy.

Dread headed for the carved, black chair by the desk and waited. Myrenna tapped her fingers on the wooden table in front of her. Her eyes swept towards the window over the Silver City, and she took a deep breath.

Dread watched her curves as she turned, her skin smooth against the lines of her dress. The back of this particular gown swooped low down her backside, revealing milky skin and her shoulder blades. Dread imagined putting his tongue there and tasting her skin.

Would she taste like she smells? Blood and lavender. Wine and shadow. Or would she—

'Well?' she asked, her voice snapping him back to attention.

He'd missed the start of her question, but he could guess why he was here. She wanted his report.

He gave her a revered nod, lowering his eyes in apology. 'The recruits for the mines remain steady, my Queen. We've recently come across some old graves that have yielded no further information. We've expanded the east side to widen the search area. There have been reports of tunnel collapses that have killed some of the workers, but the dwarves you sent have been able to stabilise them.'

She nodded as she lifted her glass of wine, pausing to sniff it. Her nails tapped against the glass as she spun the liquid around. 'Have the dwarves been cooperative?'

He wanted to tell her the dwarves hadn't been. That, though their talents outweighed their grief, they'd required more motivation than the others. Dwarves were stubborn, filthy things, and he'd given more than one a severe beating since their arrival from the colony.

Instead, he replied, 'As much as expected.'

'I see,' she said, and sipped from her goblet. She licked her lips. She was beautiful, regal, formidable.

Dread stood straight as she lowered her glass and faced him. 'It's been months now,' Myrenna said, 'and we're no closer to finding the object than we were then. Maybe I've left the mines alone too long. If the recruits need motivation, then perhaps I need to visit to remind them.'

Dread swallowed. To have the Queen attend the mines for anything other than a regular inspection demonstrated to his soldiers that he wasn't doing his job effectively. Loyalty ran on fear among the men and sharp clawed beasts of the mines. He dreaded to think of what those evil creatures could do, each one more twisted than the last. He'd have his head bitten off by one of the rabid bloodhounds, or his intestines pulled out with the spindly claws of the reavers.

Terror and the hard twist of shame clung to his bones, making him stand straighter. 'There's no need, my Queen. I assure you, we have everything under control. We get closer every day. You can taste it in the air. The magic is heavier the deeper we dig. It almost warps those who spend too much time near it.'

'Warps them how?' she asked.

'Headaches, mostly, but some have reported sleep being hindered, scratches on their skin from their own nails, fights breaking out.'

Myrenna smiled wickedly. 'Now *that* is good news. If the eastern expansion shows no promise, you need to continue to dig further down and not out. Recruits can be replaced, and if they're too weak, perhaps my own personal guard may need to step in.'

Dread gave a sharp nod. Ever the trained soldier. He watched her fingers, noting her index fingernail was chipped. He blinked. She was never not perfect, never not wholly put together.

She fingered the papers in front of her, ignoring his watchful gaze. 'What of the Princess?'

'Still not found,' he said reluctantly. 'I have my murders out flying the realm, but she's remained unseen since Parador.'

'And let me guess, the same for the Seeker?'

Dread felt the room change, the air thick with tension. 'They are coated in magic, my Queen, hidden from us.'

The paper in Myrenna's hands crinkled as she crushed it. She closed her eyes briefly and took a deep breath.

'But we're looking every day. At all times,' he continued. 'My crows won't rest until the Princess and Seeker are found. I'll even bring you their heads myself.'

The Queen hissed. 'Did I ask for their heads?'

Dread focused on the hand of a corpse. He felt Myrenna stand beside him, and he took a deep breath, inhaling her scent of blood and lavender. So different to the stench of death permeating the room.

'I don't want their heads,' Myrenna said, her voice brushing against his ear. 'I *want* their hearts. The others you can do with whatever you wish, but the Seeker and the Princess are *mine*. Do you understand?'

Dread clenched his tattooed hands and dropped to one knee. 'They will be yours, my Queen.'

'Good,' she replied. He heard the hint of hesitation.

Dread cracked his knuckles – an old habit – and the Queen eyed him suspiciously.

'What news of your brothers?' she asked.

'Both are posted where they ought to be,' he said. 'Trik still commands the army on the borders of Perridorm. We've kept Perridorm's army under control, but it's a stalemate at this rate. Most of the forces are in lockdown in the trenches, and the land has become nothing but ruin.'

The Queen sighed. 'Perridorm is just an inconvenience at this stage. If we can find the object in the mines, then I'll have more than enough to wipe them out despite that cursed little princess. In the meantime, Carnell can provide more men. The princes will be visiting in the coming weeks, and they'll be looking for any crack in our armour.'

Dread didn't understand the alliance, couldn't fathom why Bellatorre needed those pathetic excuses for men. But he didn't question it.

'Any news on the spindle?' he asked.

'Not that it's any of your business, but yes. The Tinker proves fruitful, despite his misgivings.'

Dread loathed the Tinker. Hated his filthy little fingers and his proximity to the Queen. When she'd brought the Tinker in, Dread could only think of a maggot crawling out of a decaying corpse, and as such had called him Maggot since the day they'd met.

'Anything else, Dread? Or will you be remaining to piss me off even more?'

Dread stood slowly, taking her question as a dismissal. 'I'm always at your call.'

As he closed the door, he took one last look at his Queen. Her silhouette was silk and shadows.

As always, his heart ached with longing.

Dread's steps echoed as he left, making his way through the castle grounds in haste. As he reached the gardens, his body shifted, morphing effortlessly into the shape of a black crow. He groaned with the change. It always hurt, the pain like searing fire as it overtook him. He flung out his wings, the crack of bone enough to make him hiss. With a jump, he was in the air, the wind lifting under his wings. It was this, the freedom of flying, that reminded him the pain was necessary.

He cawed as he soared over the towering spires of the castle. He honed in on the familiar thread that connected him in this form, it wove through the air like a web, pulling him toward his brothers, a subtle tug in the world that bound them together.

He was the middle child of the three, all of them shifters and all of them connected as one when they changed. Growing up, it had been a convenience and a pain in his arse.

I convinced her the mines are under control, he called through the bond, hoping for his brothers' answers.

He waited a heartbeat before a gruff voice replied, *'Good. How many maidens this time?'*

At least seventeen.

There was a lengthy pause before his brother – Trik – replied. *'It continues to grow. How close are you to finding what she needs?'*

Not close enough. She's getting anxious, her behaviour is erratic. But she says she's getting close with the spindle. The Maggot has been playing with it.

'I see. We'll continue holding the border for now. Perridorm is weak.'

Dread speared higher into the sky, the wind cool beneath his broad black wings. *What of the Princess and the Seeker?*

'The magic hides them from sight, but we've picked up a scent. We're investigating now.'

She'll be pleased with that. Who did you send?

Silence.

Dread tried to hold back his groan. *You sent* her, *didn't you?*

'She's the best hunter we've got,' Trik sharply replied.

And she's also a pain in the—

'I'd hold your tongue if I was you,' Trik warned.

I doubt she does when she's in your bed.

Trik growled. *'Enough. You're both just as bad as children.'*

Dread wanted to bite back but thought better of it as he heard the exhaustion lingering in his brother's voice.

Trik asked, *'Are there any reports from our brother?'*

None, replied Dread, letting Trik change the subject. The huntress was a tender topic for his brother, and Dread knew when to quit. Even though every instinct in his blood screamed otherwise. Unfortunately, their younger brother was also a sore topic. *He should still be on his mission.*

'He hasn't reached out in a few days,' said Trik. *'We'll just have to wait, but it may need investigating if he's silent too long.'*

Fine.

The connection ceased as Dread soared above the Silver City. He veered west this time, letting the wind carry him like a song. He always took the long way back to the mines if he could help it. His favourite view was the sprawling Crystal Lake beside the city. How its glossy water shone like silver under the dimming sun, throwing shards of colour across the smoky mountains beyond.

He dived towards its glassy surface and cawed in glee as his wing skimmed the rippling water.

He couldn't worry about his younger brother now – not with everything else happening. Especially when Myrenna was becoming more unhinged. He'd always come through for her, had reaped her rewards for the fear and the blood and the magic. Without her approval he felt empty. Incomplete.

Focusing, he turned towards the southeast and took flight amongst the clouds. He was close to finding what had been buried in those mines, and if he had to kill a thousand prisoners to do it, he would. Time was no longer

on his side, and with the slaughtered maidens strewn about
the tower, it wasn't on his Queen's, either.

V

The Barkeep's Companion

The Skinny Piglet was a crooked pub situated on the side of the main road just outside Roserock. Its straw-covered roof stunk of mould and the stones were almost entirely shielded in moss. Usually, its lanterns felt like a welcome beacon for weary travellers. Normally you could hear music drifting along the road, the smell of smoke and merriment in the air.

This time, the cauldron had other ideas.

Under a banner of stars winking into the sky like scattered wishes, Snow, Malak, Pip, and Florian made their way towards the forlorn tavern, its shuttered windows shadowed and foreboding. It lay silent amongst the trees, their branches reaching out, taunting and wicked.

Snow shuddered, praying the cauldron would bring some desperately needed good fortune. Her thoughts were consumed by Hansel, his axe strapped firmly against her back. She swore she could feel him in the realm, alive and breathing.

Malak halted the group, his broad form a shield against the darkness. Florian shuffled behind Snow. He smelt of mint. 'This doesn't look inviting.' he whispered, far too close for her liking.

'Wonderful observation,' Pip replied, dryly, swiping a leaf off his torn jacket.

The hairs on Snow's arms rose as Malak approached the tavern. The stories she'd heard of this place had been colourful, Malak explaining the grime and music made it *homey*. She'd laughed at the comment, thinking that nowhere with that much dirt could be a place of joy. Malak had warned her about the owner, Marcellus, calling him a dangerous man. But he'd also insisted that the Skinny Piglet welcomed creatures of all kinds. Despite herself, a flicker of excitement stirred in her chest, curious to see the place come to life.

Instead, she was faced with a rickety sign that rattled against the worn exterior, chains squeaking, and the words *The Skinny Piglet* barely legible through years of grime. It was a lacklustre dwelling, reeking of desertion and secrecy.

Malak disappeared into the shadows as Pip urged them off the road. Snow squatted down in the brush and waited in anticipation. The faint smash of a window echoed in the distance, and she flinched.

'He better not get himself killed,' she mumbled.

'Our death will be on you, Princess, if you don't hush,' Pip chided.

Snow poked her tongue out, feeling inside her pocket for her mother's familiar pen. She followed the trail of its smooth edges, centring herself, and keenly watched the road. The silence was eerie, not even the sound of a cricket daring to break it. In her travels, Snow had begun to recognise that the forest should be alive at night, the creatures of the dark opening their eyes to find food, and it made her uneasy.

Florian shuffled close by, snagging her attention. He was an odd one, that prince: allergic to everything, yet adept at hunting; brought up in a brutal and bullying environment, yet kind. And, though he lacked courage, he was the kind of clever that came from observing, from reading – two things she understood. She considered his life. Despite his siblings, had he also left pieces of his soul within the pages of those stories like she did, hoping and wishing?

Snow began to speak, but hooves hit the dirt as horses approached. She whirled, her fingers tapping her leg in anticipation.

A large, hooded stranger arrived on horseback, with another flanking them. A lantern glowed softly, casting a circle of light onto the road like a small moon as they silently dismounted. Snow and the others retreated further into the forest as the two figures tied up their horses to a nearby tree. Cloaked in darkness, they blended into the mist that dulled the glow, their figures barely visible in the shifting shadows.

Moving quickly towards the tavern, the man with the lantern unlocked the door and ushered his companion inside.

Snow swore under her breath and stood. 'Malak is still inside.'

Florian grabbed her arm and yanked her back down. She turned to bark at him when he pointed to the side of the Skinny Piglet, where Malak was already making his way back to them, surprisingly nimble in the cover of night.

Snow loosed a sigh of relief.

One of the shuttered windows was opened and a light flickered on, the two figures visible. They removed their cloaks, revealing one man with a sweaty brow and bad teeth. His companion, on the other hand, was striking in a way that mothers warned you about. Despite his slicked back hair or the cool gaze, he was all sharp lines and cheekbones. There was a confidence to him that drew Snow in, and when he smiled, her stomach flipped.

A little voice inside her head said, *Beware.*

Malak ran towards the brush, branches crackling under his heavy feet. He pulled Snow's attention from the window and ushered the group further into the forest.

'It's Marcellus,' Malak confirmed when they were far enough away not to be heard or seen. 'But I don't know who his companion is.'

Snow looked back to the gleaming lights breaking through the shadows of the trees. They cast a warm yellow glow, yet she felt anything but comforted. She'd always known the safety of the light, locked inside the castle, only to now find herself becoming the shadow within the trees outside. It shook her.

'It's strange,' Malak said, breaking her thoughts, 'seeing the Skinny Piglet closed. It's almost never closed. Not even on celebration days. Marcellus wouldn't even do it when we had the spindle. He likes medallions too much.'

Florian wiped his nose on his sleeve. 'So, is it safe?'

'I don't know,' Malak replied, keeping close to Snow. 'But there's four of us and only two of them.'

'Only two of us can fight,' Pip pointed out.

'But with your flute, we have an advantage,' Snow countered.

Pip only grimaced, his fingers wrapping around the slender flute hanging around his neck. 'I avoid using it on anything but animals. It got me into a bit of a mess last time, if you recall.'

'These are people, not giants,' she retorted.

Pip frowned. His eyes bore into hers and his voice took on an icy tone. 'Freedom should not be taken so quickly, Princess. Even if you are the future queen.'

She knew she should feel guilt, but they were desperate. There was no room for guilt when Myrenna still held all the power.

Malak met her eyes with caution, appearing to assess Snow for a moment in a way she wasn't familiar with. She lowered her gaze, feeling sheepish under his disapproving glance. He said, 'Pip will remain as a last resort if needed. Marcellus may not be the purest human, but he deserves to choose freely. Like anyone in this realm. He can help, we just need to think of the right incentive.'

Snow felt like a chastised child as Pip and Malak dismissed her, speaking in hushed tones about their next steps. Snow wondered if this was how it was to be when she took the throne: always apart, always alone.

The two men moved away from the window, heading deeper into the tavern, and Snow lost sight of them.

'What now?' Florian asked.

Snow was unsure. Malak spoke of finding an incentive, but she had nothing to offer. Pip would surely have an opinion, but she didn't care for it.

Malak shifted in the dark. His voice was rough as he said, 'Now, we knock.'

Snow wrapped her arms around herself as she followed Malak towards the Skinny Piglet. The troll gave her a reassuring smile as they approached but it didn't help the fear mounting within her.

Pip and Florian remained hidden in the brush. It was best to have backup should the plan go awry – something she fully agreed on.

She knew how to defend herself; had to remember those skills Hansel had taught her when they lived in the castle. She'd been practicing with Malak, too. Which meant she'd be fine. Right?

A haunting wind blew through the trees, bringing her back to the forest and the task at hand. This Marcellus person was someone who could help her take back her crown. Yet, fear still lingered. Books couldn't prepare her for the real world. The thought of hundreds, perhaps even thousands, of people staring expectantly at her filled her with sickening dread.

The idea had been entertaining when it was a dream. The promise of war and taking back her father's throne was wildly exciting. But now, as the darkness enveloped them, the tavern their only shelter, she felt like a small mouse finding the cheese only to be snapped within the metal claws of a trap. She was powerless.

Malak gave Snow's hand a reassuring squeeze. He rapped on the door four times, waiting a heartbeat before muffled footsteps sounded from the other side. Malak pushed Snow behind him, his broad shoulders and thick armour blocking most of her view. They'd agreed that even though Marcellus could help them, they weren't going to risk him discovering she was the Princess before they could get her within the safe confines of her army.

Her army.

The words still felt rough on her tongue. Like gravel being swallowed.

Light beamed through the door as the watchful eyes of a sweaty, burly man peeked through a gap in the door. 'We're closed.'

Malak huffed before stepping into the meagre light, leaning down so Marcellus could get a good look at him. 'All the better for a private conversation.'

The barkeep's eyes widened. 'Malak, you can't be here. I have company.'

Snow noted the sticky stench of stale liquor seeping through the door and wrinkled her nose.

Malak held the door open with his palm. 'The Queen doesn't know we're here.'

'By the cauldron, I hope not!'

'Let us in, Marcellus.'

Biting his bottom lip, the barkeep slid his gaze over the two of them before he slammed the door closed.

'You're a cowar—' Malak started when the sound of several locks unlatched.

When the door finally opened, bathing them in light, Marcellus glowered at Malak. 'You want to finish that sentence?'

'You want to let us in?' Malak growled.

Marcellus rolled his eyes before, then ushered them inside and slammed the door closed. Once the locks were back in place, he turned to face them. 'You better not be here to cause more trouble. My companion is a friend of *hers,* and he won't be happy that I have other guests.'

Marcellus headed towards the bar and picked out several glasses. He filled them with brew. Snow took the opportunity to remove her cloak, soaking in the heat from the roaring fireplace nearby.

When Marcellus handed Malak a drink, the troll only raised his brow.

'It's not poisoned.' Marcellus scoffed, shoving it into his hands.

'No,' Malak mused, 'but it's free, and you do nothing without a medallion attached.'

'Just take the drink.'

Malak accepted, a smirk forming as Marcellus muttered something under his breath.

'And your friend?' Marcellus asked.

Snow shook her head. She wasn't accustomed to alcohol, and the thought of her first drink being in a seedy bar in the middle of nowhere didn't sit well with her.

Marcellus shrugged. 'Suit yourself.'

Snow scanned the tavern, noting the wooden chairs and tables. The low ceilings and dim lamplight gave it a rustic charm. Worn cushions lined the booths along the back wall, and the floor bore the scuffs of countless chairs and heavy footsteps. It was dirty, but even she had to admit there was a certain homeliness to it.

Marcellus took a sip of his drink. 'You look familiar. Have you been here before?'

Snow blanched, but Malak stepped in. 'No. She hasn't. Forget her. I need information, Marcellus, and it's important.'

Marcellus snorted. 'So was the last time you were here, and that time you left my backroom covered with flour and lost gallons of brew. Whoever that girl was who attacked us, she's banned for life – and I ain't the only one who thinks so. I found her "wanted" posters in Roserock and stole one for myself. Just so I could put her on my list.'

The barkeep pointed to wall behind him, and sure enough Snow found the wanted poster pinned nice and high. They'd drawn Eve well, even pronouncing the high arched brow the Seeker gave when she wasn't impressed.

Snow grimaced. Even when Eve disappeared into a magical chasm, she seemed to have a knack for snaking her way everywhere else, too.

'You know she's the Seeker,' Malak replied.

Marcellus grunted. 'Found out after it all. Your Huntsman and you embraced her quickly even after that destruction. Her gift is useful, but the little bitch still owes me. You and that Huntsman do, too. You owe me medallions. Lots of them.'

Snow walked around as they talked, noting the small alcoves of cushions that would have been lush once. She eyed the one by the back corner, neatly tucked in front of the window, and moved towards it. She touched the marks indenting the table. Carved from nails and knives. The positioning was ideal, with a view of the door and bar. Each booth was clearly visible, even the hallway off to the side, giving the perfect vantage point. She smiled.

She imagined what her life would have been like if she hadn't been who she was. Would she have liked Eve then? The wandering lone warrior travelling from town to town. Free. Gifted. Fierce.

If she had been the Seeker, she would not have spat on such gifts so lightly.

'Why come to a bar if you're not going to drink?' said a silky voice from behind her.

Snow whirled around, her hand automatically going for Hansel's axe at her back and pulling it free.

The stranger raised his hands in a show of peace. His piercing green eyes melted into hers, and she swallowed. His hair was as dark as a raven; slicked back so neatly that his skin paled against it. He wasn't handsome, but he was striking.

Snow took a wary step back.

He chuckled. 'I'm just trying to start a conversation. You can put away the axe. Though, I'm surprised you can lift it so easily. It's usually reserved for those with more … bulk.'

She narrowed her eyes, not releasing her grip on the handle. 'Most conversations don't usually begin with people creeping up on you.'

He chuckled again before slowly motioning to the table. 'How about we take a seat? I'd be interested to learn the right way to start a conversation. Plus, my legs are sore from riding. It's been a long journey.'

Malak and Marcellus could be heard nearby, reminding her she wasn't alone. But that also didn't mean she was safe. She shuffled on her feet. Her blisters were flaring again inside her flimsy slippers. She wanted to sit down, too, but she wasn't inclined to give in just yet. Keeping her chin high, she asked, 'And where exactly did you come from for the journey to take so long?'

He ignored her question. 'If you won't sit, then do you mind if I do?' Without waiting for permission, he took the seat on the opposite side of the window. Sinking deep into the cushions, he released a deep sigh. 'It's comfortable. You should try it.'

'I'll sit, but I'm keeping the axe.'

'Far be it for me to get in between a lady and her axe.'

Snow sat slowly, surprised at how comfortable the cushions were despite their age. She laid the axe on the table, in clear view, her hand gripping its handle. 'Who are you?' she asked. 'Marcellus insinuated you were a friend of the Queen's.'

'Did he, now?'

She gripped the axe's handle harder. 'Don't play games.'

He waited a moment before he replied, his gaze piercing her in a way she wasn't accustomed to. 'You seem like you've had more than enough of games in your lifetime.'

She gave him a wary nod.

He leaned back in his chair. His white shirt was unbuttoned slightly at the top, his skin peering through the gap, showing a subtle smattering of his chest hair.

Snow hadn't been near many young men. Only Hansel. The rest of the castle had actively avoided her, and besides Hansel, Malak, the tutor, the cook, and the creepy little

Tinker, she'd had limited exposure. She noted the indent at the bottom of his throat. His defined collarbones and lean figure were the opposite of any man she'd ever known.

This man was nothing like Hansel.

Hansel was all sunlight and strength, his smile a bright and unending light. This man was more like the shadows she shied from within the forest. His eyes were bright but cunning, and from what she could figure, his lean frame was stronger than it looked.

Hansel was all courage and truth.

This man was carved from secrets.

Snow put on her bravest face before eyeing Malak at the bar. He was still in deep conversation with Marcellus, who looked about as pleased as a broken wheel on a cart.

'Who are you?' she asked again.

'I was hoping to ask the same question,' he countered.

She pulled the axe closer, her instincts screaming at her to run but in what direction she didn't know. She was fearful, yet fascinated, his callous demeanour enthralling.

He leaned forward on the table. 'How about we make a deal?'

She tilted her head. 'I said I don't like games.'

'Not a game, I promise.' His eyes twinkled, bringing a heat to her stomach she chose to ignore. 'How about I'll give you an answer to an answer. Three questions each. No more, no less.'

Snow smirked. She'd read the art of words used in her books – had seen the Mistress of Games herself work her magic within the walls of the Silver City. If she was to be queen, then surely answering some questions wouldn't sign her death warrant. It was practice, after all, and whilst she ran from the Queen, this man was not really Myrenna's *friend* if he didn't know who Snow was.

'Fine,' she replied. 'But you go first.'

He smiled again; those green eyes boring into her with heated curiosity. It was a tight fit in the alcove, but she was smaller than him, and if it came down to it, she was positive she could move fast enough.

'I can already see from the way you speak and the way you hold yourself, it's clear you had an education – and a good one at that. Your skin is unmarked, but you hold that axe as if you know how to use it. Considering the satin slippers and the rich dye of cobalt in your dress, your clothes suggest you come from a high-society family. But your accent is Bellatorrian. I've met most of the high families and even the royalty in that region, yet you remain unfamiliar to me. So, my first question is this: how did someone of your nobility come to be in this place with a troll as a companion and Marcellus as a friend?'

She breathed a sigh of relief. This was a question they'd already planned for out in the forest. 'My mother was a governess in Bellatorre. She taught several wealthy families' children, so I was taught the same. After her death, I ran away. Malak found me and helped me.'

The man glanced at Malak. 'He's small for a troll. Nothing like the brutality they breed up north. A half-breed, perhaps?'

She remained silent, her foot beginning to tap under the table. She hated that she couldn't sit still. Not like the way Eveline held herself.

Turning back to Snow, the man smiled again. 'A governess? I thought in Bellatorre they were unable to wed. Are you a bastard child?'

'Is that your next question?' she gritted.

He chuckled. 'No, it's not. Where are my manners? It's your turn.'

'Who are you and why are you here?'

'That's two questions.'

She frowned at him.

He raised his hands again. 'Okay, we'll take that as one.'

Snow raised her chin, daring him to answer her question.

'I'm a member of the royal guard and I'm here on business to do with the provisions of the mines. Marcellus is a smuggler, as I'm sure you're aware, so he helps me with my goods.'

Her heart faltered in her chest.

The Queen's guard.

Myrenna's guard.

It was one thing to know, and another for him to admit.

'My turn,' he said. Snow watched him intertwine his fingers. He smelt of wind and vanilla, a scent far too sweet for the malice in his eyes. 'What are you doing at the Skinny Piglet?'

'Same as you,' Snow said.

He snorted. 'I highly doubt that.'

'We're here for information. That's all.'

'What kind of information?'

'It's not your turn for a question.'

His eyes glinted but he leaned back again. Waiting.

'What kind of goods are you gathering?' she asked.

He seemed to assess her, his smirk unnerving in a way she didn't care to admit. 'The kind that will save many lives.'

Snow blinked, confused. As far as she knew, the mines killed people, not saved them.

'I see you weren't expecting that,' he said, smugly.

'No, she wasn't.'

Snow's breath caught as Malak snatched the axe from the table and shoved the edge of steel against the man's throat.

While most people would choke on fear, the man remained calm, leaning back in his seat confidently. 'Hello, *friend*. Have you come to join?'

Malak shifted beside Snow, his agitation emanating off him so much that she tasted it on her tongue.

'Everything's fine, Malak,' Snow said, trying to still her racing heart. 'Mister, um …'

The man winked, despite the blade to his throat. 'Flynn is fine.'

'Okay. Yes. Flynn and I are just talking whilst you speak with Marcellus,' Snow said with feigned confidence.

Malak's eyes remained steadfast on Flynn. 'Marcellus seems to be under the impression we're all on the same side. I'm here to check if we are.'

Snow gaped at the troll. His shoulders were hunched forward, the green muscles roiling under his skin as he leaned across the table. If there was a fight, she didn't want to be anywhere near the scene if Malak crushed this man's bones.

'Back off, Malak,' Marcellus yelled from the bar. 'I only just cleaned up this place.'

Malak didn't move, his eyes dark against the vivid green in Flynn's.

'Is that so?' Flynn asked. 'If we are indeed on the same side, we may be able to help each other.'

Silence.

Snow's foot twitched again, adrenaline running through her veins like a drug. With the snap of this man's neck, they would have to run. Marcellus might be an ally now, but Snow didn't know how he would react to murdering a colleague on his property. They were already short of allies, leaving them almost nowhere to go. But she couldn't even begin to think of how she could stop it.

Snow reached for Malak's arm, gripping his forearm with a warning. 'Malak.'

He tensed, but didn't release his grip on the axe. 'And how could you help us?'

Marcellus came to the table and placed down several glasses of brew. 'I might not know where the rebellion is,' he said, and nodded towards Flynn, 'but he does.'

Flynn laughed. 'The rebellion, you say?'

Malak frowned as Flynn placed a finger on the axe's edge and pushed it back towards Malak.

'What's it to you?' Snow asked.

Flynn shot her a wink. 'This night just became interesting.'

VI

The Madness of Bones

The sky burned crimson, its embers fading like a dying fire across the horizon as the imposing black crow soared above. The familiar scent of the mines thickened the air with sulphur and ash as Dread dipped low over the steep, onyx rock. The Queen's mines were a shadowed mark across the land, a scar left unhealed. And while he hated them, it had a deadly kind of beauty to it.

In the distance, scaled wings scratched at the air as his beasts and shaiths rotated guard, screeching across the sky. Fire roared from the chasm's depths, spitting flames and shadows as he landed near the northern tower and stretched out his mind to feel his brothers. There was a tug from Trik on the other end of the tether like the thrum of a pulse, but his other brother remained frustratingly quiet.

As his talons hit stone, the crack began in his bones, his feathers shifting to skin and sinew turning to human bone. He grunted, pain shooting through him as he slammed into unyielding black rock, cursing at the sharp throb in his knees.

The shift never got easier.

He stood and took in the wall that surrounded the mines like a warning, the black granite stark against the yellow and orange sand covering the pits. There were pockets of buildings for the recruits, all wooden shacks designed to keep them contained. From the centre of the compound fire spat forth as the forge melted what they found, and he tasted magic thick on his tongue.

He gave a curt nod to his guards and made his way down the stairwell to his inner sanctum, his shoulders taut.

The mines were monstrous in size, and though it was impressive, it had failed to deliver. Years they'd been digging with nothing to show for it, and the Queen was getting impatient. With Trik monitoring the war on the borders of Perridorm, and his younger brother somewhere in the Silver City, Dread was alone in his search for the Princess and the Seeker.

He was also alone in running the mines – the Queen's most precious dream.

Not to mention, his failure had been apparent in his meeting with Myrenna. The shame alone was enough to set him off.

As he entered his study, he headed straight for the wooden desk. His fist smashed into its surface before the door could even close. With a creaking roar, splinters flew, the edge of the table screeching as a leg broke, the papers stacked on its surface sliding onto the cold floor. Dread growled in frustration, pacing back and forth, when he was interrupted by a sharp knock.

'What?' he snapped, throwing open the door.

Before him stood the black-scaled reaver of the mines, its bulked form bowed in apology, teeth bared in a snarl. The reavers never spoke the human tongue, nor did they need to. Their job was monitoring the recruits and putting them back in their place when it was required. They were the ones who did the dirty work, who stood watch, thriving in the hot and harsh working conditions.

Dread used to watch in sick joy as they would claw, bite, or whip those who disobeyed. And whilst it was cruel, it was an effective method for motivating the recruits who slaved under the Queen's command.

But as the creature bowed, Dread's fury dimmed for just a moment, replaced by an eerie curiosity. Was this a casual visit? Or was something more pressing at hand?

His pulse quickened. Could they have actually found something? Was the cauldron that fortuitous? Had the Godmother finally listened to his pleas at night as he prayed for guidance, for the one thing that would win his Queen's heart?

A wave of unwanted longing swept over him. When he'd been at the castle, he'd wished Myrenna would ask him to stay. To take him out of this cauldron of a place. To free him from the bonds of these creatures.

Though he knew she needed him here, needed him to find the missing piece for destroying those who dared harm her, he still couldn't help the *want* that took over him whenever he thought of her. Surely, if she could take that golden-haired Huntsman to her bed, then Dread would be a superior companion?

The Huntsman had been weak. Too unworthy. Too sheltered. And somehow, she still held affection for him.

Dread couldn't help his elation when the Huntsman had finally deserted. It meant he had an opening, an invitation into her affection. He had a chance. And a chance was all he needed. He was so much more than a guardian of the mines. More than a murder or a soldier. He was devoted. Loyal.

And she was everything he'd ever wanted.

Not her crown. Not her power. Just her.

His jaw clenched at the thought. He didn't want to think of failure, not now. He looked down at the reaver, the creature's sharp claws raking the stone with nervous energy. His pulse thudded louder in his ears.

Could this be the breakthrough he so desperately needed?

Dread took a slow, calming breath, pushing his anger aside. No. This wasn't just another dead end. This could be it.

He stepped toward the reaver, his presence imposing, and motioned toward the hallway. 'Show me what you found.'

The dank air burned Dread's nose as he followed the reaver further into the depths of the mines. Everything here was hastily-made wood, or carved stone and mud. Paths varied from packed dirt to wooden bridges, the hole on the centre a looming centrepiece.

The watchful, vacant eyes of the recruits passed over him as he followed the reaper down the rickety staircases attached to the mine's edge. The despair scratched against his skin. Pain was one thing – it could provoke you, motivate you; it even brought you closer to pleasure. But despair was hollow: it was the acceptance of death, of embracing the empty black ravine of life and replacing it with hopelessness. Once you stepped into that ravine, it was almost impossible to crawl out.

Dread's boots were heavy against the unsteady wooden bridges that crossed the digging sites. The recruits were everywhere. On ledges, in tunnels, some slipping against the rocky edges with their weak limbs and sagging skin.

If they need motivation, then perhaps I need to visit to remind them.

Dread closed his eyes the memory of Myrenna's voice. He'd sworn he could do it, that he didn't need Myrenna to intervene, but staring back at him now were prisoners not easily motivated. Souls that stared back with dead eyes, hollowed shells that had lost their will to care.

He shuddered as their desperation coated his skin. Some of them flinched as the reaver passed, their breaths halting in fear. Dread tried to ignore them and stepped carefully, his large feet barely fitting onto the makeshift bridges. Whilst he could fly, he chose to walk when he was this close a powerful source of magic. It would be no good if he was stuck as a crow or if it mangled his form.

Using magic against magic was always a precarious thing.

Myrenna's amethyst eyes flashed across his vision as the pits grew darker. Dread struggled to breathe as the air thickened. It was heavy here, the magic. His vision blurred slightly as they took the wooden shaft downwards, deeper underground.

The reaver licked its sharp teeth and skittered forward as they stopped, its limbs shaking as it urged Dread forward. Dread could only stare, wondering if he'd become like them if he remained here. Either a dark creature himself or a hollow shell like those they recruited.

Perhaps he already was.

The thought unnerved and motivated him at the same time.

The copper glow from the pits flowed along the walls, the shadows dancing in glee as the deepest part of the eastern expansion came into view. In this section of the mines there lay more bodies. Unmoving corpses of trolls, elves, humans, dwarves. They all blended into one another, scattered across the rock like a waiting army.

Dread thought of what Trik had to endure. An army of the dead was no small thing, and as Dread faced the mines, Trik held the frontlines on the border of Perridorm and Bellatorre. They'd both dealt with magic, but it was nothing compared to the death magic those royal twins wove.

Some of the dead had missing limbs, others with rotting eyes or scalps. Some you could see had been played with after they'd reached the end of their life. Dread scrunched his nose as the creature beside him licked its lips again.

If I die, I hope they burn me.

He'd seen battlefields, had been familiar with piles of death and bodies bleeding across the soil. Battle held fire and passion, each side craving their own victory and glory.

This mass grave was silent. Unforgiving.

Dread cracked his neck from side to side to distract himself. He'd need a drink after this. One preferably from his cabinet where he kept all the good stuff.

As they exited the tunnel, the mine opening into a large cavern, the reaver skittered forward. An echo spread its way along the walls as its fellow guardians reavers it. Dread kicked one of the bloodhounds out of the way, and a shaith screeched as he stepped towards the group of miners near the wall. They were dwarves, newly recruited from the dwarven colony the Queen had invaded in the Peaks of Carfell. Dread could smell the stench of blood from the battle, the way the fog dragon had sucked their lifeforce. Many had volunteered after that, over one hundred of them stepping into chains as they were escorted here.

They scattered as he strode forward, revealing piles of dirt of behind them. The sharp tang of magic stung his nose as he slowed, taking in a shape in the wall. It was a door made of bone.

Dread had seen many strange things in his time working with Myrenna but nothing as intricate as this. The bone protruded from the wall, pieces crushed to shape an archway with no handle. Skulls lined the edges of the doorway like a portrait with intricate symbols outlining what Dread assumed were instructions. A small pathway of bone had been melted into the dirt like some sick invitation to follow its lead.

This had been made by an artist.

A sadist.

A creator.

Dread couldn't help but smile at its vicious beauty.

VII

The Irksall and The Deal

Brufell growled at the large green hand dragging him by his shirt towards the cart. His teeth clenched at the blade held near his throat. Blunt, but still sharp enough to draw blood. If they were going to kill him and Bronson, they would have done it already. He didn't particularly like games. Not the ones that dealt with life.

War was war. Dying honourably meant something. And he'd never been one to play with his opponent, especially on a battlefield.

Though this wasn't war, it was still a battle.

The warrior in him thrashed at his insides, looking for an excuse to unleash himself and fight back. He only refrained for Bronson's sake.

Bronson's skin was swollen, the blood caked on his face already drying with the harsh mountain winds. The sun blinded Brufell momentarily as he was dragged forward.

Defeating a lone troll in the arena was one thing, but a whole band of them was another.

At least it wasn't the Queen, he thought.

Brufell was pushed into the gravel, his old knees groaning on impact. Bronson fell beside him with a gasp, his pallor grey.

'Listen to me,' Brufell muttered, seizing Bronson's tunic, holding him upright. The blow to his head must have been harder than he'd realized. 'You're about to pass out.'

Bronson gave him a weak smile. 'Probably.'

Shadow blocked the sun as a troll loomed over them. He wore less furs than the others, his skin not as scarred. His lip worried over a gold piercing as he lifted a jagged knife, pointing it straight at the two dwarves. 'Where is he?'

Brufell leaned in front of Bronson, preparing to defend when the younger dwarf pushed him off to the side and nodded towards the cart. 'Under the dirt and debris. Near the unbroken wheels.'

His speech was slurred, his eyes half lidded – both signs that his injury was worse than expected. Blood seeped down the side of Bronson's neck, but he remained conscious at least.

'You betta not be lying,' the troll grunted as the others assessed the rock and dirt that had fallen onto the cart.

With a murmur, they began to dig, loosening the stone much faster than Brufell had when he'd dug Bronson out.

Brufell gripped Bronson's shoulder and focused his energy on finding an escape route. The road was still blocked, with a cliff on one side and rock wall on the other, not to mention the landslide he'd created had only trapped them further. Trolls were scattered, most staring him down with an itch to kill. It would be impossible to run, let alone fight their way out.

He blinked past the dust in his eyes and ignored the sweat dripping down his neck. Despite the heat, Bronson shivered beside him, his eyes drooping further. He swayed before Brufell jumped forward, clasping the younger dwarf between his arms.

'He needs shade,' Brufell shouted at the trolls. 'He's hurt and sick. Let him rest and I'll help dig.'

Their captors hesitated, but as Bronson faltered again, two trolls grabbed him by the shoulders and dragged him to the cliff side.

Thankfully, Bronson was dropped near the rock wall, sheltered in a sliver of shade. The pixie remained nearby, gnashing its teeth through the cage's bars at any who came close. The creature couldn't do much if it came down to a fight, but at least Bronson wouldn't be alone.

Brufell stood as the troll with the gold piercing loomed over him, distrust in his eyes. 'You save our *Irksall* and we save your friend.'

'Irksall?' Brufell asked.

The troll crossed his arms, showing his bulging biceps that could easily tear Brufell limb from limb. Brufell might have been a fighter, but he knew when to pick his battles.

He took a step towards the cart when the troll said, 'Irksall means leader. He protects the tribe.'

Brufell considered the troll before he nodded. If digging out their leader was what it took to save Bronson, then it was all the motivation Brufell needed. He ignored the bite in his hips as he placed himself between two other trolls, his thick fingers grasping dirt. He made sure to clear the area around the wheel first. The only sounds on the mountain came from their grunts as they cleared the space.

His mind wandered back to the arena, where another troll had swung a killing blow towards Bronson. His friend, Bo, had stood within the rafters, watching without even a twitch. He might have been the one to lead Brufell to the stadium, but he'd shown no concern for his kin. No remorse as Bronson screamed on the sand.

Bo had always been bred from steel, knew his way around a gambling den and loved a good bet, but he'd never been one to betray his kin. Would he have let Bronson die if Brufell hadn't intervened? Would he have just stood by as his kin was slaughtered, letting the horde of trolls bellow in glee?

Brufell dug faster to expel some of the rage from memory. Dwarves were strongly tied together – a lineage that ran thousands of years knotted to blood and family. Yet, Bo had sacrificed his lineage so easily. And that … that had been the biggest betrayal of all. It wasn't Bo's lies about who he was in Troll's Keep that had deeply upset Brufell. It was the fact he'd kept it from his kin and allowed the power to fester inside his own soul whilst his own kind died for entertainment.

Bronson annoyed him at times, as all family did, but he was proud and protective of the dwarf. Of all the Seven.

When everything else was lost, the Seven stood strong, as unyielding as the ancient carved walls of Parador.

Brufell's thoughts were cut off as he uncovered the thick hairy ankle of the troll. 'Here!'

The troll beside him gasped, pushing Brufell away as the dirt revealed a tattered cloak and a silver bow. The Irksall's eyes were closed but he was still breathing. Which was enough for Brufell to pull back and sigh. They might let him and Bronson live after all.

In a moment of solidarity, the trolls roared, the echoes bouncing off the cliff like a dragon claiming its prize. As one, they pulled their unconscious leader free.

Brufell took the opportunity to run to Bronson's side. The dwarf's eyes were closed, his body limp. Brufell checked for a pulse, loosing a breath when he felt a faint heartbeat.

'We need a healer,' Brufell called. Bronson had only sustained a hit to the head, but with the troll's brutal strength it could have killed him just as easily.

The troll with the piercing returned and scooped Bronson up before Brufell could even blink. Brufell reached for his weapon, then remembered he had none as the troll stood. 'You save Irksall. We save dwarf.'

Before Brufell could snap back, the troll walked away, leaving Brufell to stumble. Brufell made it three steps before he pivoted back and grabbed the cage containing the pixie. The creature glared at him, but he ignored it as he tried to catch up. Running, Brufell followed the trolls down a narrow path he hadn't seen, high enough that it made him dizzy. A shove on his shoulder urged him forward and he found himself locked in the centre of the group.

Grumbling a swear word, Brufell followed.

Brufell stared at the night sky, the glow from the crackling fire dancing shadows around him. The air was filled with the song of crickets and the snores of trolls, which drowned out any chance he had of sleep. He'd feared Malak's snores had been bad but, sitting here now, he admitted to himself that Malak had been a mere child amongst these beasts.

Bronson had been asleep for hours now, his makeshift tent only a few pixies away.

Brufell sighed. The trolls had been kind enough to return his weapons and he'd managed to spend the last few hours sharpening them to such a state that even he was wary of where he moved them.

The path they'd taken to get here had travelled further into a thick pocket of forest than expected, leading them midway up the mountain, providing protection with its sprawl of trees. The grass was lusher up here, the trees a vibrant green and silver. It made a nice change from staring at endless rock.

Whilst one troll had carried Bronson the whole way, two others had to carry their Irksall. Even without the cape and bow, the troll was enormous; one of his limbs the size of Brufell's entire body.

Blood had coated both Bronson and the Irksall, but it was hard to tell the damage due to the dirt that mingled with it. The healer had come running when they'd entered the campsite – though 'healer' wasn't a word Brufell would have used. Not when the creature had been robed like the priest from a temple and covered in blood. He wore jewellery made of bone, and the mangled scar on his neck didn't bode well. Despite all that, the troll had refused Brufell when he asked what needed to be done, choosing to ignore him while he concocted a brew made up of mostly mud, water, and some strange herb.

Brufell had hesitated, questioning their intent, before he'd seen them apply the same concoction to their leader. He knew trolls used little magic, their healers foregoing modern medicine for the basics of their history. And so, he'd waited.

That's all he'd done.

Waited as the sun set behind the horizon, before night finally crawled in. Waited as the others set up the fires and beds for the injured. Waited as they brought back the carcasses of several scarats, cutting them with ease before roasting them.

He watched as the trolls had set to sleep, each one spacing themselves out like the line of an army before lying flat on their backs. He noted one in the corner cradling a large rock as it were a children's toy meant to comfort him.

A twig snapped nearby as the troll with the gold piercing sat beside him. 'You save Irksall. We save dwarf.'

Brufell sighed at the accent, its harsh throaty sound grinding against his ears like a knife to stone. 'Yes, as you've said. Many times.' Brufell brushed his hands against his newly sharpened weapons. 'I've held my side of the agreement. What's happening with my cousin? When can I see him?'

The troll beside him leaned forward, his breath a mix of rot and meat. Brufell twitched at his proximity. His large brown eyes scoped every inch of Brufell. Without warning, his nostrils flared, the troll breathing him in as if he were a rare cuisine.

'Could eat you,' the troll mused. 'But won't.'

'My meat is too tough anyway,' Brufell snapped, gripping the smaller axe at his side. He would have no issue with slicing off this troll's nose if he even thought of trying to take a bite out of him.

The troll only grinned, revealing teeth layered in yellow film.

Brufell crinkled his nose. 'What do you want? We already saved your leader.'

The troll's grin widened as he grabbed Brufell, yanking the dwarf to his feet with an abrupt grip. Brufell growled, kicking out before the troll replied, 'Irksall is awake. He asks for you.' The troll released him reluctantly. 'You must come.'

Brufell closed his fists before he gathered his weapons, but the troll blocked his path.

'No weapons.'

'If you think for a second that I'm going in unarmed—'

'No weapons,' the troll grunted again, this time with a little more fervour. 'Irksall is healing. No weapons.'

Brufell eyed him suspiciously. 'Fine, but he better not try anything.'

The troll nodded in agreement, gesturing for Brufell to walk with him.

Brufell followed a path through the sleeping trolls, minding his step as they weaved through the camp. His fingers twitched, reaching for the weapons he wasn't allowed. His hands felt empty without his weapons, as if without the weight he would fly away.

Hacking coughs echoed through the night as they approached a section of camp filled with makeshift tents.

Most were crudely stitched from rough material. One stood open like a pavilion, its wooden tables roughly carved. Others were enclosed, likely for those of higher rank or special privilege.

But it was one of the larger tents that made Brufell slow. Though the same size as the pavilion, this one was sealed, the only glimpse inside offered by rolled-back flaps. Hay was scattered across the ground, trolls lying in parallel lines along the grassy floor.

Here, the coughs were harsher, the trolls more gaunt. Sunken eyes stared blankly, black veins sprawling across their skin like a web of disease. Brufell paused, watching another healer mix the familiar brown concoction, concern creasing their brow – until the gold-pierced troll stepped into view, blocking his line of sight.

'Come.'

Brufell hesitated, stepped away from the tent and found himself in front of one much grander. This one was mostly made of wood, the pale material resembling leather. As Brufell entered, the first thing he smelt was roasting scarat meat and his stomach churned. He'd seen enough scarats to last a lifetime.

The Irksall lay on a cot, the edges built of twigs twined with moss to make a bed frame. It was oddly fairy-esque and, against the monstrous form of the troll, it didn't suit. Towards the back of the space was the healer he'd met earlier, the troll's face slightly grim, his robes the colour of bone.

The leader's fur cape lay by the cot, his bow firmly placed on the bed frame. He nodded in greeting as Brufell entered. 'Welcome.'

The gold-pierced troll took one last sniff, the wet sound of his snot sending Brufell backwards before he chuckled.

'If he sniffs me one more time,' Brufell warned, 'I'll cut his nose off.'

The Irksall laughed – a wheezy sound – as his green hairy chest protruded from the top of the blanket. 'Tuk means no harm. He's just hungry.'

Brufell narrowed his eyes. 'I am not *food*. Tell Tuk to keep his sniffing to himself.'

Tuk laughed beside him before sauntering off, leaving only Brufell, the healer and the Irksall.

'He means well. Though I don't think he heard yer warning.' The Irksall didn't speak like the others, with short, stunted sentences, as if their tongues couldn't quite wrap themselves around the common language. He spoke like Malak, the inflection of the trolls' native tongue remaining but the use of certain words still articulated.

Brufell grunted. 'I don't care. I've killed trolls for less. The war saw to that.'

The troll nodded. He knew of the Great War – the War of Thorns – just as the dwarves did. The Irksall sat up. 'I felt the warrior in ya,' he replied. 'Even among those rocks.'

Brufell eyed him carefully. 'Why didn't you kill us? You were robbing us.'

The troll chuckled, which turned into a cough, his chest rumbling. 'Yer not our enemy. We only wanna survive.'

'Why aren't you in Troll's Keep, then?' Brufell asked. 'Why are you out here in the mountains of Eyrie?'

The troll frowned, his large eyebrows leaning over his dark eyes. 'Troll's Keep don't want us, and we don't want it.'

Brufell moved closer, eyeing the weapons strewn by the leather bags, and remained standing. 'Why?'

'Not all trolls are welcome at the Keep.'

'You're outcasts.' Brufell was intrigued, though he'd never admit it out loud. He waited a heartbeat before the Irksall spoke again.

'I must thank ya. I'd be passing through the mists of the Ever After if it weren't for yer friend.'

'Luckily for you, we were under duress,' he muttered. 'What's in that muddy concoction?' Brufell asked, changing the topic.

'It's a mix of herbs, mostly.'

The healer crunched on a bone at the back of the tent, his watchful gaze meeting Brufell's in warning.

The Irksall closed his eyes, his brow twitching in pain from his injuries. 'Sit.'

'I'd prefer to stand.'

'Please,' the Irksall rasped. 'Sit. You too, Shatk.'

The healer at the back of the room sighed, begrudgingly taking a seat. 'This is a waste of time, Irksall.'

'What is?' Brufell asked.

'So many questions from someone who won't even sit,' the Irksall mused.

'Fine,' Brufell conceded. 'But it better be worth my time.'

'With yer friend healing, all we have is time.'

The healer – Shatk – snorted. 'Time is neither fast nor slow. But it can still be wasted.'

Brufell grunted. 'That's the truest thing I've heard all night.' Stepping forward carefully, he reached out for the wooden stool against the rear wall. With a jump and some awkward manoeuvring, he sat down. 'So, what is it you want from me?'

'Arrogant species, dwarves,' Shatk hissed.

Brufell shot him a glare but was distracted when the Irksall said, 'Warrior to warrior, I want yer help.'

VIII

The Creature and Its Cage

The cushion behind Myrenna was as hard as wood. She shuffled on her chaise, trying and failing to get comfortable. Even though she'd had her fair share of hearts this week, her bones still felt brittle behind the magic it took to keep up her power and youth. She twisted her head from side to side and groaned at the crack that rippled down her back.

It was past midnight, the cool breeze blowing through her open windows to soothe her sweaty skin. Her sleep had been jumbled, ghosting her with nightmares of flesh and betrayal and blood. Sometimes it was Hansel. His warm skin on hers as they embraced before he left, following the Seeker as she took his hand.

Tonight, however, it had been the vivid blue eyes and the youthful glow of the elusive Princess Snow. The Princess had stood before her in gilded armour, the crest of her family burnt into its metal surface. The Queen could smell ash and blood. Her nostrils would burn with each suffocated breath as her own heartbeat matched Snow's, like the thrum of twins within a womb.

Myrenna would always smile, in her favourite cruel way, reaching out for that precious heart as the thrum grew, until Snow would move with such ferocity that, in one moment they were battling and in the next they became still. Myrenna would always look down to find a knife embedded in her gut, a grin of triumph etched across the Princess's face.

The same dream would pull at Myrenna night after night until she jolted awake, covered in sweat. Her hand rested on her abdomen even now, against the silk of her purple nightgown.

Her hair fell in a sleek curtain of ebony around her shoulders, sliding against her skin with whispered ease. Parchments lay scattered across the floor, surrounding her like a wreckage. She rubbed her neck – it was sore from reading them for so long, and her eyes were heavy despite the nightmares.

Surely the Princess wasn't this hard to find. Tracking spells in the past had been child's play to Myrenna – an easy fix to finding the thing that barred her from what she wanted. But Snow was different.

And so was the Seeker.

No matter how many times the Queen went over the magic scrolls, no matter how many times she demanded the mirror to search for them, the magic came up empty. Like following a trail just to find an abyss.

She rubbed her temples, growling at the nagging ache she could feel brewing. The Seeker she could understand having cloaking magic, but the Princess? She was as useless as a blunt knife. She'd never ventured outside. Had never known magic, never learnt how the world worked. Yet something or *someone* was hiding her.

It was infuriating.

Myrenna craved the chase as much as the lion craved the hunt, but only so far as when she caught her prey, breaking them, devouring them. The chase only meant something if she was rewarded for her efforts. She was tired of bashing her fists against a hidden wall that even the mirror's magic couldn't breach.

She hadn't devoured this many hearts, become this powerful, to be bested by a brat of a princess and a girl as plain as the Seeker. She needed a distraction. She needed a win. Proof that this wasn't all for nothing.

Myrenna rose from the chaise and donned her slippers. On cue, the doors to her chambers opened, the cool air drifting over her skin. Her guards bowed as she glided across the marble floors. Those who were nearby shuffled from view, hiding away as death herself walked the halls. She knew she shouldn't enjoy it, but she did. She bathed in the fear.

For so long she had lived in her own fear, enduring the sweaty palm of a drunken fool as he smacked her flesh like it was his due. She had grown up with the stain of judgement that meant trying to fade from the villagers that wanted to attack or berate her because she was different.

They had trembled after her bargain. They had fallen when she had come for them. Her father had begged on his knees for forgiveness, his eyes white at the sight of her vengeance as she entered, the rage emanating from her like a freshly born star. She hadn't seen a man in those moments, merely the shell of one. In the end, the death had been too quick. It was something she should have savoured, but she'd been too hungry, too starved for power.

And the Sisters Grimm had demanded a price.

She'd paid it.

She continued to pay it even now as she consumed the bloodied hearts of maidens that littered the realm. Her hands were coated in blood. It stained them even after she washed them clean, filling the crevices of her skin like water shaping stone.

The Queen knew what the realm thought of her. That she was the monster they spoke of at night before bed. She was the terror in their dreams. The demon hiding in the shadows.

Mostly, it delighted her. What did not was this game of hide and seek, the never-ending circle of cat and mouse, of beast and beauty.

She walked the halls, her steps echoing against the cold, stone floor. The painted white walls slowly faded from plush portraits to cold dark stone as she descended a set of stairs. The air thickened, dampness clinging to the floor and ceiling. The deeper she went, the more oppressive the atmosphere became. The dungeons had always been her favourite place within the castle. She found truth in this place, its plainness refreshing amongst the lies and deceit of the court and the politics. Not that she minded the luxury she lived in, but down here was where she found her prisoners raw, the truth of them spread wide open as they lay in despair and rot. Not like the snakes of court living behind their smiles and velvet. Snakes like the king of Carnell.

He rotted down here, too. Not that his twelve sons knew of it.

Myrenna and the King's last meeting over dinner had been in secret. The promise of betrothal his lure as he slipped away under the cover of night monitored by her crows. No promises had been made, and as such, Myrenna had not been tied by magic when she stripped him of his things and locked him deep below her castle.

His bones had been repaired since then.

Only to be broken again.

She had found it a delight after his behaviour towards her staff, watching his arrogance fade. And so far, his eldest son who had stepped up in his stead to take the crown in Maelstrom had been far more pliable. Prince Alfred was a greedy man, with no concern other than his lust for the throne.

She'd used it to her full advantage. The whole family lazy and foul.

But that wasn't why she was in the dungeons. No.

She was here for someone else.

Something else.

Her slippers barely made a whisper as she walked. She didn't feel the cold despite her thin robe. She took pleasure in watching those who remained down here scatter away to the corners of their cages as she passed them by. Her guards all knew her expectations, leaving her alone as she stopped in front of one of the cells.

The creature inside laid curled up against the wall as she placed her manicured finger on the latch. With a subtle click, the door smoothly opened, and the train of her robe rubbed against its edges as she stepped inside.

The cell smelled like rotting corpses and urine. She halted in its centre. The creature didn't even look at her, focused on the stone wall in front of him. His fingers were bleeding, the nails worn down and shattered from scraping the bland stone.

Myrenna's eyes roved over the cell's walls. The carved markings told a brutal story of those that had rotted down here, deep scratches and bloody marks that showed the desperate, last thoughts of the lost. The imprisoned and the doomed. Some had been written to loved ones, names of those who either knew them or were already dead; some were poems of grief, some held deep rage, even being as bold as to carve the Queen's name itself. Blasphemy and rumours.

She walked towards one, twitching her nose at the inscription. 'A little dull, don't you think?' she asked the prisoner. Her voice bounced along the stale air. 'Surely, they could have come up with something better than "the evil Queen", at least.'

She trailed the indents of the carvings, her nails scraping along the wall like a predator as she smiled. 'Why not "wicked witch"? Or just keep with the classic, "bitch"?'

The prisoner didn't move, his frail body frigid against the ground.

Her eyes flicked to him. 'I suppose they weren't down here for being creative, were they, Rumple?'

The creature shuffled in the corner at the mention of his name. His withering form was almost naked, barely covered by the cloth he wore that smelled like the sewage under the city.

'But you were creative,' the Queen said. 'You built an empire on creativity. On dreams and bending peoples' will. Even I'll admit it was difficult to infiltrate, to work with your moving pieces, the constraints and backups you had carefully planned. It was clever, but not as clever as my Tinker and his adeptness at breaking things.'

The creature in the corner shook, averting his gaze from the Queen.

Myrenna moved closer, her robe softly touching his back. She lowered her voice. 'Tell me, Rumple, how does it feel to have your empire taken from you? To watch those you trusted either leave or lie to you?' She sneered, waiting for the moment she knew she was owed. Like finding that perfect patch of soft skin between calloused fingers. 'Do you lick your wounds down here as we play with your toy? Pulling at her seams as we unravel the dreams inside.'

The creature hissed.

'Do you pray to the Godmother as others do? Or are you too proud for that? A king without his kingdom is no king, after all.'

He rocked back and forth, his thin shoulders hunching as she dug in the final nail.

'Do you feel it when we hurt her? Your spindle? Does the pain echo into you as she cracks under our thumbs, her scream a broken song in the Tinker's dungeons?'

He thrashed and crouched before her, seething. 'She is *mine.*'

Myrenna laughed, the bell-like sound echoing off the damp stone. 'For now,' she said. 'But like all things in this realm, she can be bent, twisted into something else.'

Rumpelstiltskin wrenched himself forward, his shackles pulling taut around his neck as he gnashed his teeth.

She clicked her tongue in smug satisfaction. 'Everything can be broken, Rumple. You and her are no exception. That was evident in the throne room when you gave up one of your secrets.'

His eyes widened in grim realisation at what he had done, at the name he had spoken.

Nona.

He whimpered and Myrenna's smile only grew. 'You broke. And so will Snow.'

His body crumbled under him, the chains rattling.

Heady satisfaction ran through her veins as she grinned at the creature. Before she left, she paused in the doorway. 'The Spindle will break, and when she does, I will bring you along just to watch the destruction that pours from her.'

Rumpelstiltskin winced as if she'd stabbed him, and she turned away. The doors of the cell slammed shut as Myrenna climbed the steps and yawned. The restlessness from earlier ebbed away from her like a dissipating fog.

Now, she could sleep.

IX

The Magic of Kingdoms

Florian sat hunched in the darkness, the patch of previously lush grass lying strewn around him as he continued to pick it out of the ground.

His gaze wandered to Pip sitting by the tree, his eyes partly shut in meditation as they waited for the others inside the tavern.

An itch ran along his skin, but he ignored it. The allergies had been a constant for so long now that he merely accepted them.

What a strange twist of fate his life had become. One moment he'd been caged by giants as food, next summoned to save a princess who'd already been saved, and now he sat next to a cantankerous elf waiting for a smuggler.

He kept trying to pinch himself, to wake up from whatever dream or nightmare this was. He never meant to leave Maelstrom, was never prepared for the wild, never meant to be in the untamed world if his body had its say. He was only forced into it after that horrible dinner on his last night. Where a surprisingly defiant voice inside him had finally refused to back down. He was sick of being told he was useless. Pathetic. Weak.

He had courage.

Or at least his mother had thought so.

Eleven brothers and yet he was nothing like any of them. Not strong or lethal or commanding. He never held sway with the women, and the one time he went hunting, he had ended up with an arrow in his arse.

He would study in the library, reading over each track mark and the tricks on trapping and finding prey. He'd thought, even though he couldn't shoot, perhaps his family would appreciate his tracking skills. His ability to quietly find the best quarry.

But instead, they roared through the forest shooting at anything that moved. And when Florian had attempted to show the one skill he was sure he could do, an arrow had shot straight into his backside.

The only bright side was that he didn't have to see any of his brothers or father for a whole two weeks. They'd never visited, and he'd not expected them to.

Even now, covered in bruises, facing a brewing war and sitting within the forest at night, he was less anxious than he'd been at home. The feeling of not being chastised brought him some comfort. When you weren't being insulted at every interval, strangely enough you started to feel better about yourself.

He still had a long way to go and a lot to prove. Snow's eyes said as much whenever they roved over his rashes. He swore that whenever he sneezed, she was about to cut him with her axe.

He'd only ever met her as a child – on a quick visit to the Silver City. They'd both played in the garden, her raven hair shining against the winter snow like fresh ink on new parchment. Florian hadn't known how alone she was then, how dark her world would turn, and yet it was a time when very little had been expected of him.

A time of happiness.

Pip shuffled a few pixies away, distracting him from his thoughts.

Florian looked up to meet his eyes: eyes that held a lifetime of wisdom and regret. Pip was cunning despite his size, and Florian was very aware of his background. He may be helping them now, but he'd also been in Rumple's service. Meaning, he wasn't always so forthcoming.

'With the right kind of magic or herb, you could fix your condition, you know,' Pip commented, his dry voice breaking the silence.

Florian continued to pull at the grass in front of him. 'My mother wasn't a fan of magic,' he replied softly. 'She said it warped people, that it was too risky for a royal to trust.'

Pip snorted. 'Carnell is a sanctimonious bunch.'

'They don't trust magic. That doesn't make them zealots.'

Pip raised his eyebrow.

Florian sighed. 'Okay, maybe a little.'

'Wasn't your mother from the west?'

'She was,' Florian replied.

'So why the caution on magic? If history is any indication, her old kingdom followed the old ways. Making offerings to the forest and the stars.'

'I suspect she adapted to survive.'

Pip grunted. 'As we all do.'

They sat in silence for a while before Pip spoke again. 'During our captivity with the giants, you mentioned once that you were her favourite even though you were last in line.'

Florian paused, his hands still for a moment as he shuffled his numb feet. He'd forgotten how much he'd shared during their captivity. 'It wasn't about lineage with her. I was her only son. My brothers are ...'

'Half-siblings?'

Florian nodded.

Pip watched him carefully before giving him a casual shrug. 'And so, she banned her only son from using magic?'

'Everyone was banned from using magic.'

'Interesting how magic is only banned when it's convenient. Don't even get me started on Carnell's alliance with Myrenna. Magic is magic. Good and bad; life and death. But I suppose it isn't for everyone.'

'Did you always want to have magic?' Florian asked, his innate curiosity for stories making him bold enough to ask the question.

'Magic is in everything, Prince,' Pip replied. His pointy ears twitched in the breeze as it whisked through the leaves.

'That's not what I asked.'

Florian understood magic existed in the realm, had read about it and even seen it used in certain parts of the kingdom. However, it had been highly monitored in Carnell. They'd accepted it existed and couldn't be erased, but that didn't mean they let it fly freely. Should a magic user be caught, his father ensured the perpetrator would be dead before dawn.

His family was known to be suspicious. To mistrust magic users and magic itself. It stemmed from an ancestor of his that had a bad experience, and it seemed to have been ingrained into the family as each generation was born.

Myrenna had been the only exception. Even now it confused Florian.

Pip traced the edges of the flute around his neck, its decorated surface visible in the dark. 'Magic is rooted in me. My very core. I would be nothing without it.'

Florian wanted to say he understood. But the truth was that he didn't. He didn't understand why his family was the way it was. He didn't understand why magic was so taboo. And following that, he didn't understand why or how Myrenna lured them in because of it. She had been a heathen to them when she'd first come to power. He remembered his father raving on about it deep into the night, and the prayer rooms filling with fear as Carnell locked its borders.

It had been an overnight transition, in a way. As if the death of his mother had twisted something deep within in his father – more so than usual.

Perhaps life was supposed to be that way, Florian thought. Not quite understanding everything but trying to learn anyway.

Snow peeked at Flynn from under her eyelashes, trying for an air of absent curiosity. She was failing miserably at it if the smirk he shot her way was any indication. She sighed inwardly.

Malak still hadn't released his grip on the axe, despite the fact it was now nowhere near the man's neck. His eyes had darkened, a threat behind them as he leaned forward. 'How do you know where the rebellion is if you work for *her?*'

Flynn remained seated, seemingly at ease though she swore she could spot some tension in his shoulders. 'Just because I'm in the Queen's guard doesn't limit my ability to seek out people in hiding. In fact, it makes me more qualified.'

Snow held back her snort as Malak's face began to redden. That was a never good sign. While Malak was normally even-tempered and honourable, he was still part troll. Meaning, when you finally angered him, something broke. Whether it was the furniture or a bone depended on the scenario, but she, for one, was too curious about Flynn to let his rage simmer too long.

Snow placed her hand on Malak's arm and gave it a gentle squeeze, reminding him she was there and perfectly safe. 'Malak,' she murmured, but the troll didn't relax under her touch. She turned to the others. 'Give us one moment, please.'

Flynn winked before gliding from his seat, making her cheeks heat. She needed to get it together. If not for her own sake, then for Malak's. Giving Flynn a tight smile back, she yanked Malak into the booth beside her. The table creaked as he knocked it.

She monitored Marcellus as he leaned forward and whispered something into Flynn's ear. They seemed far enough away enough for now.

'This was a bad idea, Princess. I shouldn't have brought you here,' Malak said in hushed tones. 'It's too dangerous, having you in the open like this.'

'Why?' Snow cut in. 'Are we not looking for the rebellion? If Flynn knows where it is, then I'd say we are exactly where we need to be.'

Malak rubbed his eyes, a vein protruding in his forehead. 'I shouldn't have brought you here. If I'd known Marcellus was working with—'

'—a servant to Myrenna's crown?'

'Yes, that,' he gritted out. 'Then I wouldn't have come. We can find others to help.'

Snow crossed her arms and glared at him. 'How long would that take? A month? A year? We have someone here who *knows* where the rebellion is and can help us *today.*'

'It's too dangerous.'

Snow scoffed. Malak had a propensity to be overly protective at the best of times, but they were desperate. How long could they wander until they were found? How long until Myrenna took her heart?

No, the answer they wanted was here. She stole another glance at Flynn and considered her options. If she told them who she was it might speed this along. She could promise Flynn and Marcellus riches, land, and a few little loopholes to help them with their endeavours. In particular, Marcellus and his illegal goods.

On the other hand, the two of them could also sell her out to the Queen, stopping the rebellion in its tracks and feeding a monster for many more years to save their own skins. Myrenna *was* terrifying.

It was a flip of a medallion. One she knew Malak would never condone.

'Surely they can be manipulated,' Snow said.

Malak's eyes darkened in response. He tried to turn in the booth but failed. 'I thought you said you didn't want to manipulate anyone.'

'Some circumstances call for a little persuasion.'

Her mother had always said a single choice had ripple effects. That power of a sole decision maker was a dangerous game. A different kind of poison.

Power was a drug, a greedy thirst never quenched.

She understood Malak's fears, knew he'd travelled further in this realm than she ever had.

And yet.

If she was to be queen, it meant making the hard choices even when those closest didn't agree. She was already climbing over the back of the seat before he could protest.

'Snow …' Malak began, reaching for her only to miss.

Snow marched towards the bar, hiding her shaking fingers as she stood before the two men. They halted their conversation at her approach, Marcellus frowning down at her and Flynn raising a brow with intrigue.

This was dangerous. She was gambling with lives, after all. But she'd made her decision.

Malak stumbled beside her, only reaching her side as the declaration slipped from her lips. 'I am Snowfall Anabella Aurelia Whitmore, the princess and heir to the kingdom of Bellatorre, and I demand to know where the rebellion is hiding.'

The room froze, Marcellus and Flynn pausing mid-drink, faces agape. Malak closed the space between them, his elbow grazing her shoulder in a protective stance despite the horror on his face.

Turns out, when you make a bold statement, a second can feel like a millennium.

What have I done? she thought.

Within a breath, Malak released his sword, the sound too loud in the silence. Snow's heart stopped when his expression morphed into one of fury, the two weapons an unspoken threat. But it mattered little. The damage had been done.

Marcellus burst out laughing, snorting brew from his nose when he couldn't contain his cackle. 'You've got spine, girl. That's not a name I'd be screaming unless I wanted the Godmother to hear it.'

She gaped at him, feeling her temper swirl at his impudence. He was a *smuggler*, for cauldron's sake. What would he know?

'Either that, or she's got a death wish.' Flynn chuckled, sipping deeply from his drink, green eyes amused.

'It's true!' she shrieked, slamming her fist down on the bar.

Flynn stopped mid-laugh and scowled. He looked Snow up and down and considered her.

Marcellus spoke first. 'You look the right age. Even share the same characteristics. But everybody knows the Princess was poisoned. Rebellion or not, nobody's seen her, and you ain't it, girl.'

They don't recognise me.

Snow tried to smooth out the wrinkles in her dress, the dirt from spending days in the forest covering her palms. Was it the filth she was covered in that caused them not believe her? Or maybe it was because she had been hidden for too long within the walls of the castle.

Her heart rattled in her chest. Maybe Pip and Malak were right. If a smuggler and the Queen's soldier didn't recognise her, then what chance did she have with the rebellion? She had expected shock, anger, greed, maybe even violence or acceptance, but she had not expected this. They had *laughed* at her, as if she were some mindless twat.

'How dare you,' she seethed, using every ounce of authority she could muster.

At least this time they didn't laugh. Instead, Flynn raised his hand towards Marcellus, silencing the man. Malak shuffled closer and Flynn noted the move. 'Even if you aren't the princess, you still *believe* that you are. Why?'

Malak nudged Snow towards the door with his elbow, axe and sword in his hands. 'It's time to go, Princess. *Now.*'

Snow stepped around him and raised her chin, planting herself firmly between him and the two men at the bar. 'No. We're not leaving.'

Malak gripped her arm and pulled her close enough that she could smell his breath. 'What has gotten into you?'

'What has gotten into *you?*' she said, pulling out of his grip. 'You've become an incessant mother hen since I woke up in that grotto. Where did my friend go? When was he replaced with whatever *this* is?'

Malak stepped back, stricken. 'I saved you. Only true love could break the curse.'

'And it's honourable and all but am I really in any more danger than I was at the castle?'

'Yes,' he hissed. 'Because Myrenna thought she controlled you then. You were safe.'

She couldn't help the tremble that took over her body at his words. 'I was never *safe.* You're the naïve one if you ever think I was. So, listen closely because I won't repeat myself. I'm done with being told what to do, or what to say and how to think.' She tried to stand tall despite being half his size.

He stared her down, their eyes locking in a silent battle.

'I don't care if they believe me,' Snow said, barely more than a whisper. 'I don't care if you believe in me. I need to know where my people are and if these dirty scarats know where to find them, then I need them. So. *Back. Off.*'

'Dirty scarats?' Marcellus shouted. 'How dare you!'

Flynn chuckled. 'The girl has a mouth. I wonder what else it can do.'

'Don't you dare talk about her that way!' Malak growled, turning around.

Marcellus reached behind the bar and pointed a knife straight at Malak as he stalked forward. 'Not in my bar, Malak. You were warned.'

Despite Malak's growl, Flynn remained calm. Did nothing affect this man?

'And here I thought I was the unknown enemy,' Flynn drawled. 'I believe we're at an impasse.' His eyes focused on Snow. 'If you are who you say you are, then prove it.'

Her muscles locked. 'Prove it?'

'I don't know the Princess, but I know the Queen,' Flynn continued. 'Tell me something about Myrenna that only the Princess would know.'

Snow swallowed, the sinking feeling in her gut growing heavier as she tried to think of something. Suddenly all the confidence she'd had before dissipated. She needed evidence, invaluable proof she was who she said she was. A hand touched her elbow, and she turned her panicked eyes towards Malak.

'Princess?'

'I …' she stumbled. 'I don't know.'

Flynn raised his eyebrow. 'Such a big declaration and nothing to show for it? How underwhelming.'

Snow grasped onto the memories she had, but they each slipped through her fingers in her panic. Her voice came out softer than intended as she said, 'She has a mirror.'

'Yes, a big gilded one, but we already know that.' Flynn gave Snow that arrogant smile, and she just … stood there as useless a blunt kitchen knife when she was meant to be a sword, a leader.

Speak, a small voice inside her echoed. *Speak and show them.*

She picked her brain, scrambling through her memories like a picture book, when one finally stayed. 'She has crows,' Snow said quickly, her breathing heavy. 'Not just a murder of them, but three in particular. Brothers. Shapeshifters. They follow her everywhere. Do her bidding in the dark. She covets them. May even love them. They are her spies and biggest loyalists. I've seen one change.'

'This is fairy shit,' spat Marcellus.

Snow ignored both Malak and Marcellus, keeping her gaze on Flynn. His eyes seemed to go an even richer green, as if her answers were satisfying enough. 'What did the shift look like?'

Malak growled. 'Enough of this.'

Snow swallowed thickly, fighting the fear that strangled her voice. 'I saw one of them change once … It's painful. Excruciating, even. I could hear how his bones snapped, and then he was covered in black feathers.'

'When?' he prodded.

Snow was frantic. 'A year ago, during the last ball of the summer, I snuck out and wandered the halls past curfew before I went to the tower with the Queen's balcony. It was reckless but my feet dragged me there as if in a dream. I knew everyone was busy, that I wouldn't be seen, and I heard voices. But when I found the door, there was only one man standing there – a man I'd seen visit before – and that's when he changed. I ran and I never looked back.'

Flynn cocked his head, assessing Snow in a new light. 'Do all her murders shift?'

'Just the three brothers, as far as I know.'

She felt like her chest had frozen. Would he believe her? Or was she another liar?

'That's an interesting story.'

'It's the truth,' she whispered.

'There have been rumours in the past about these brothers, so I'm choosing to take you on trust as being Princess Snow,' he said, bowing his head slightly.

The relief was instant, and Snow took a deep breath.

Malak had the opposite reaction. 'You can't report her.' His eyes were wide, pleading.

'I won't report her,' Flynn said. 'Though, I can't say I'm pleased to see her,' He handed Marcellus his empty drink and motioned towards the bottle. 'But we do need to talk, and it needs to be quick. If you are the Princess, I can't be here while you're here. Not with Myrenna watching.'

Marcellus grumbled something as he lowered his blade. Malak echoed the movement and Snow released a breath.

Marcellus refilled Flynn's cup and his own, glowering at Malak before leaning on the bar.

Flynn took the moment to speak. 'So, you're looking for the rebellion? I can show you the rebellion, and I can assure you they want to find you as much as you want to find them. Unfortunately, so does Myrenna.'

Snow clenched her fists, stifling the shake in her hands and her clammy palms. She would have information tonight, or everything she had just done would have been nothing.

Weak. The little voice inside her hissed. She ignored it. 'What do you know?'

Flynn sighed. 'There are eyes everywhere looking for you. In fact, I can guarantee one of her crows have their eyes on you right now. But rumours say her magic is failing. For whatever reason, she can't find you or the Seeker. Something is blocking her, and she's not pleased.'

Snow ignored the mention of the Seeker. 'Magic is hiding me?'

'Yes,' Flynn replied. 'But I don't know how long for, or why. The rebellion is weak. It's hungry, fighting for medicine and food. It is not the army you think it is, and it cannot keep you safe.'

Malak was still. 'What can?'

'You need another army. One you can bring to help the rebellion. One already on the brink of war.' Flynn swirled his drink around. 'There's Perridorm.'

'Perridorm has already refused,' Malak piped in. 'They denied the rebellion.'

'They've only refused Myrenna,' Flynn said. 'They already fight on your side. They just need a push from the right person.'

All three of them turned to Snow and she felt like shrinking inside herself. How in the cauldron was she supposed to gather another army when she couldn't even find her own?

'Bring Perridorm to the rebellion, and you have a chance,' Flynn continued. 'A slim chance, but better than the suicide you're facing now.'

'You think they'll help?' Snow asked.

'I think for you they might.'

He downed the last of his drink and he stood. 'Marcellus and I were done, anyway. I can get a message to the rebellion, tell them to collect you when the time is right, but for now, Princess, you're needed elsewhere. The twins are unique, but they are young, with a power they don't understand. If you are what the rebellion hopes you are, Perridorm is where you need to start.'

'Hold on a minute,' Marcellus said. 'We weren't done. We're still negotiating a price.'

'We both know the price I would have negotiated,' Flynn snapped, that calm demeanour cracking for the first time all night. 'You'll have it in a few days through the usual messenger.'

Marcellus went red.

Snow stepped forward. 'Why should we trust you?'

Flynn paused. 'Did I not trust you when you said you were the Princess?'

'I gave evidence.'

'No,' he mused, leaning closer to her. 'You told me a story I chose to believe.'

He was halfway to the door when she asked. 'How do I get to Perridorm without being caught?' The Queen still instilled a fear in her that she couldn't let go of. For so long, Myrenna had been the keeper of the keys that locked her away. So, despite whatever magic was hiding her, terror still nudged at her core.

'You'll need to stay under the cover of the trees,' Flynn answered. 'The border between Bellatorre and Perridorm is two thirds forest. The southern portion is fields, that's where the battle lingers. I know the forest is a dangerous place, but it's your safest bet. If whatever is hiding you falters, the trees will protect you. And, hopefully, your troll friend will protect you from the rest.'

'The rest?' she asked.

'The dark things that live there. Witches and creatures of magic. They hide for now, but they get bolder as the war rages. Something as pretty as you would be stolen in a moment. Tread carefully.'

Snow stood as Flynn donned his cloak. 'I won't tell the Queen you were here,' he said, 'but I can't promise that, if she has an inkling of my betrayal, she won't pull it out of me.'

Snow gave him a curt nod. She was walking a very dangerous road, and it grew darker as each hour passed. Somewhere in the depths of her mind, the nagging voice spoke again.

Weak.

She didn't know if she was strong enough. Could she do what Flynn was asking her to do? Or would she fail again? She couldn't see another path forward.

Marcellus opened the door, the cool night air a reprieve from the stale stench of alcohol as he let Flynn go. Though, if the scowl on his face was any indication, he wasn't happy about it.

Flynn paused in the doorway, turning that sharp gaze back on her. 'One last thing. My horse is yours. I can travel easily without it, and I'll deny he was ever mine. When you're ready, Marcellus will send me a message.'

Snow nodded again, biting her bottom lip and the door closed.

The group stood in silence for a beat before Marcellus grunted. 'Strange things are happening, and as usual I'm worse off for it.'

'Somehow, we are always stuck in the middle,' Malak replied heavily.

Marcellus sighed. 'I'd rather throw you out but, somehow, I have an inkling you'll be killed. Get your friends. I know they're outside. You can stay here for the night before you travel into a war zone, though I want you gone by dawn. Understood?'

X

The Broken Dreamer

Rumpelstiltskin felt the seams of his soul coming apart.

The darkness encompassed him like a tomb, closing in as his breath and life were slowly sucked away. His only reprieve was the kind old voice of the prisoner beside him. He'd heard tales of witches and dwarves and stories about a Seer called Nona. The *four*th Grimm.

Rumple knew her secret – knew a great many secrets about the realm – but he found he couldn't quite find the strength to speak. He knew his companion was lonely, and he was Rumple's only tie to reality. They were the voice that brought him back when he fell into the dark recesses of his mind.

It was a web of truth and lies, partly him, but a whole lot of others' dreams and hopes, too. Including their nightmares.

It was an easy trap to fall into, one he'd spent years perfecting as he built his empire. And though he knew others' secrets, very few knew his.

He'd not had many companions – ones that saw his true face, anyway. Whilst his empire had stretched far and wide, not many knew his inner tastes. Very few people even knew he liked chocolate cake or the feel of silk on a newly made jacket. Even fewer knew about how close he was to falling off the cliff inside his mind.

He shut his eyes against the memories, against the forest of voices flowing through his psyche as his body flinched. His spindle was screaming. Responding to his soul like a kite tethered to its string. It had been the only way to stay sane; to ensure the power of the spindle did not overtake him. He'd used bonding magic in the extreme and had chosen to meld with her. She worked with him, accepting him as he was, and they weaved their way into each other's very beings.

It was strange magic – old and unreliable – but it had succeeded. The token name of Dream Weaver had found its way to people's lips years after the magic had taken its toll. Rumple had owned it after a while, embracing his new identity.

Dream weaver.

Mind controller.

Thief of thoughts.

Very little had escaped his notice. Very few secrets had remained, and he had revelled in it. But now, in his cold cage, he shivered.

The spindle screamed from inside the Tinker's hands, his aged fingers bending her to his will. It was pain. It was suffering. It was torture.

His cellmate spoke from beside him, the old, weathered voice smooth as it called out to Nona again. But Rumple knew Nona would not help. She did not intervene unless she had cause. She was a survivor. Just as Rumple was.

So, Rumple let his companion be, remaining silent against the moist stone as he pulled his knees further into his chest. The spindle would not break, just as he would not break. He closed his eyes, letting the fractured images of the realm cross over him again, stroking them with his cracked nails.

XI

The Unlikely Debt

Warrior to warrior, I want yer help.

There was a cracked rasp from the Irksall as he spoke the words, a hint of desperation that lingered in his plea. It was the last thing Brufell had expected to come from the troll's leader, especially considering he had little to offer in the way of troll culture.

The stool beneath him was hard, his toes losing feeling as they hung above the floor. He had an urge to swing them if only to help with blood flow but he remained still, it paid him no favours to remind them of how much smaller he was.

'I have a story for you,' the Irksall said, slowly. 'Would ya do the honour of listening?'

The only thing Brufell could do was nod. It wasn't like the Irksall was the biggest threat right now, anyway. While he had a small army outside, Shatk was thin, his shoulder bones noticeable even under the bone dress he wore, meaning Brufell could snap bones as easily as the rock under Parador. The Irksall himself, though still a huge brute, was pale. He might not be as sick as those Brufell had seen in the tent earlier, but he was slow, his breath laboured. It was enough for Brufell to consider that he might be the biggest threat in this tent and that he could pay heed to whatever it was the Irksall wanted to say.

'Go ahead,' Brufell said.

'It's ingrained in us,' the Irksall started in his cracked voice. 'The need for survival. The need to be strong. Trolls are strength and might. We fight to live. Fight to eat. The message from our ancestors is a powerful one and it's taught to each of our littles as a warning and a lesson. We must be harsh, for the realm is harsh. We do not ask for handouts. We aren't made to beg. Our worth is in our fight. To show we are the strongest in a realm trying to kill us. It is the way. The only way.'

Brufell took in the words, hearing nothing that was news to him. He'd dealt with trolls in the great war, had spoken to Malak in the grotto for a bit, the troll answering what he could remember about his people. It was best to know your enemy, but when the society was as secret as it was, this was an opportunity he strangely delighted in. The Irksall lifted himself up to lean against the headboard, the strain causing beads of sweat to line his brow. For anyone else, Brufell might have helped, but even if he'd an inkling to assist – which he didn't – he would be denied. Trolls were proud creatures. Not to mention the fact that the Irksall was at least five sizes larger than him; his feet alone had the ability to crush Brufell's skull.

'But to be strong,' the Irksall said, 'ya must be pure. Mixed blood is not accepted at the Keep, and so we came here instead.'

Malak had said as much. As a half-blood and part-human he'd been shunned. Had Malak known about the trolls in the mountains? Or had he simply stumbled through the world alone, not knowing that just beyond his reach could have been a group that were just like him?

Would everything have turned out differently then?

Would Hansel have ever ventured close enough to Roserock to hire Eveline?

Would Snow have never woken up?

Would Nona have chosen a different path?

There were too many variables, too many moving parts. Though he was old, the experience etched into his skin, he wasn't good at linking all the moving pieces. It was why he felt so lost. There were bigger plans out there, tiny pieces of a complex game being played out by those far more powerful than him. Whether it be the Godmother, or the Grimms, or Nona, he couldn't say for sure. He merely thought of the ripple effect: how one choice could change the course of history and create a chance.

'When a troll is not of pure blood, they're outcasts,' Shatk intervened, pulling Brufell from his thoughts. 'They are shunned or killed. Usually at birth, unless the parents try to save them.'

Brufell knew little about the blood laws of trolls, but he did know it had similarities to the old dwarven kingdoms. Dwarves had, in some instances throughout history, taken on the same concept: the notion that mixing blood filtered out their heritage and history. It was a foolish law, one long forgotten now, but there were some in the colony who still held to that faith.

'I'm not half-blood myself, but my brother was.' the Irksall said. 'I tried to save him, I even called upon the Skulsheer to save him. Do you know what the *Skulsheer* is?'

Brufell nodded. He understood certain terms in the troll tongue. He'd been exposed to it during the war and some words didn't need explaining. The Skulsheer was the troll's term for the Fairy Godmother and the Sisters Grimm. The gods and life-bringers to the realm. Where most species recognised the Grimms and Godmother as a fairytale or belief, the trolls revered the Godmother as still living and breathing, the Sisters Grimm recognised as the watchful eyes of the realm.

Brufell supposed they were, but he wasn't inclined to build them a shrine. He'd leave the praising to the pious ones. Whether he bent a knee to the Godmother or not wouldn't change his fate as being deader than bones when he passed into the Ever After. He didn't see how thanking the unavoidable changed that. The Grimms were death, and a bargain with them always inevitably signed your demise.

But within the trolls, it was a heavily inbuilt belief, forged on superstition and the trust the Skulsheer would return to enact vengeance on the creatures of this realm, taking back the Grimms' rightful place as the only children of the fairies.

The Irksall smiled sadly. 'I was angry at the blood laws, so I left. Troll's Keep is the troll's home. The lifeblood of our kind. But they turned on my brother. So, I turned on them.'

Shatk growled at the mention of Troll's Keep.

'To turn against the royal house is to turn against yer own kind,' the Irksall said.

Brufell's back strained from the hard wooden stool, but it was nothing compared to the pain in the Irksall's cough. Or what the kingdom would go through if Myrenna continued the way she was.

Grabbing the water jug, the healer poured a cup and handed it to the Irksall. 'The trolls here have been banished,' the Irksall said. 'Shunned from the Keep either by blood or relative. When I arrived, the Irksall at the time was one with giant's blood. He did not care for his kin. He starved them and let them die, feasting himself on all the rewards. He locked me away before I could call for *Shafka* and I befriended my guard, Tuk.'

'I didn't lie about cutting off his nose,' Brufell said.

The troll chuckled, his laugh breaking into a cough. 'I don't doubt it.'

Brufell leaned forward, trying to alleviate the numbness in his legs. 'What's Shafka?' The word was rough on his tongue, as it didn't belong in his mouth.

'It's an ancient form of combat. If Shafka is called, then the challenged must accept or be dishonoured.'

Brufell pondered that for a moment. 'So, what happened when you called for Shafka?'

The Irksall handed to cup back to Shatk. 'If I didn't know any better, I'd say yer interested in my story.'

'Better to know my enemy than not,' Brufell replied.

'Want me to eat him?' Shatk muttered, refilling the cup again.

'Not tonight.' The Irksall laughed again. 'To answer your question, dwarf, Tuk set me free and when I yelled my challenge for the tribe to hear, the Irksall could not deny me. Not without the tribe losing all faith. I swore on the Skulsheer, and so we began Shafka.

'But we did not finish the ceremony. As soon as I was about to give the killing blow, we heard the crack of the forest. From it came a great black fog, with a maw so big that even we were pixies beside it.'

Brufell sat up straighter, his eyes wary. 'The fog dragon was here?'

The troll pursed his lips, his eyes darkening with a memory Brufell couldn't see. 'It killed everything in its path, sucking the lifeblood of the land, and then we scattered. Some of us died. Some of us followed the old Irksall deeper into the mountains. But some of us stayed here, closer to the edge of the forest. Those who stayed here chose to follow me. Shafka proved my strength as it has always done. The old Irksall still hides away with his tribe. Stealing from us and killing us in the dark. We fight back. And it has been so since that night. The Skulsheer has willed it.'

'So, there's another band of trolls out this way?'

The troll nodded. 'We fight a war.'

Brufell waited a moment before speaking, letting the story sink in. While enlightening, the story still hadn't answered any of his questions. 'You speak of strength, yet you're surrounded by feeble tents with trolls injured in ways I've never seen before. Tell me about the black veins.'

Shatk hissed, the bone necklace he wore rattling with the warning. 'That is none of your concern.'

'It's okay, Shatk,' the Irksall said. 'Only some of our wounded are from battle. The ones with the black veins are from the fog dragon. They survived with little life left in them. We haven't found a cure.'

'Does the other Irksall also have injured ones from the fog dragon?' Brufell asked.

'He does,' the troll replied. 'Though, we don't know if they're healed or not. That's why we wanted yer food and medicine.'

Brufell clenched his jaw, his memory of the mountain attack vastly different to the troll's. 'You mean when you ambushed us.'

'We do what we do to survive.'

'And what will you do when your little war is won?'

The Irksall's only response to Brufell's condescending tone was a furrow to his brow. 'I will finish Shafka, and I will find a cure for my kin. We will farm here and live out our days.'

'Will you continue to raid on poor travellers?'

The Irksall growled. 'Will you continue to anger me in my own home when yer kin is healing in my camp?'

'Because of you.'

'Enough!' The Irksall shouted.

A heavy silence fell in the tent.

Brufell stood, his fists shaking at his side. He wouldn't sit here and be lectured by a beast who had stolen from them, hurt them and then thrown any sense of common decency back in his face. He was too old for this. Too impatient. 'Go to the cauldron.'

Shatk stook and wedged himself between Brufell and the door, a snarl loosing from his lips. 'We are not like those of the Keep but, when pushed to anger, we can be more brutal.'

'Remember, yer surrounded by trolls,' the Irksall warned. 'You'll not survive should we choose to eat you.'

Brufell ground his teeth so hard it rattled in his head. 'Is that a threat?'

He assessed the doorway where Shatk blocked the only exit he could see. Brufell considered using the bone necklace Shatk wore to choke the life out of him, but thought perhaps a kick to the knee was better. Once Shatk was on the ground he would be vulnerable.

The only thing that stopped him was the thought of Bronson healing in the tent. He was still asleep as far as he knew, still weak.

'Why did you ask me here?' Bronson asked.

'You saved me, and we saved yer kin,' the Irksall replied. 'We are even, but we were hoping to share knowledge.'

Shatk's eyes flicked between the two of them, a nervous shiver to his body. He looked as if he was about to object to whatever the Irksall was about to say next.

'What kind of knowledge?' Brufell asked, slowly.

The Irksall eyed Shatk before giving a small nod. 'Go on, Shatk.'

The healer didn't hide his disdain for Brufell. 'I do not like dwarves,' he began. 'I don't trust you, but we need medicine. What do you know of the fog beast? And how can we heal our kin?'

Brufell considered the question. He and Bronson had ventured to this part of the realm to discover what the fog dragon was and how it was controlled, not to cure a camp of sick and unruly trolls from its life sucking powers. As of five minutes ago he'd only ever thought the pixie had survived an attack from the dragon, and even then, the pixie hadn't had the aftereffects of the fog. No black veins lingered under the creature's skin, nor did it have the grey pallor of those sick inside the tents.

'What happens if we help you?' Brufell asked carefully.

'We will owe ya a debt,' the Irksall said, as if it was obvious.

'And what if we don't?' Brufell asked.

Shatk's eyes narrowed on Brufell as if he were the cause for all of his problems. 'Sneaky dwarves. I told you, Irksall, they're stubborn, foul creatures.'

The Irksall ignored the healer, staring at Brufell with something akin to sorrow – and respect. 'Then yer to leave to fight future battles as warriors do.'

Brufell considered the troll, assessing the risks. He knew what Bronson would say: that he was mad for even tempting such a fate. But war was coming. If he could help them, then the trolls owed him a debt. There were more than one hundred trolls in this camp, and perhaps more wherever the other tribe was. In a battle, that was at least equivalent to five hundred men. To be owed a debt on the brink of such dark times was tempting, *more* than tempting.

He had no other choice. With a resigned sigh, Brufell faced the two trolls and crossed his arms. 'For a debt owed, I will help you.'

Dread nodded to a guard as he took the steps leading to his tower, the one place in this cauldron of a mine where he didn't want to kill anything. The papers sprawled across the room welcomed him as he entered, and the open windows gave him a clear view into the fiery heart of the forges below. Metal clanged against stone, the searing heat burning through the mines like ash and dragon fire. Dread usually loathed the heat but down here, amongst the chasm of embers, the fire burned away the reek of blood and death.

Carts were hauled across rope, dirt and rock piled in each one, heading slowly to their next location. Though it looked productive from here, Dread couldn't help but frown.

He had done nothing but wait for days on the progress of the bone door in the eastern tunnels. He hadn't been brave enough to tell his Queen about the discovery yet. Not when he could be wrong in his assumptions about what the door led to. He didn't know if the object was there. He didn't know what lay beyond the door other than more death, but it was the closest thing they'd come across since they'd cut this deep into the earth. All he knew for certain was that the magic surrounding the carved bones was palpable. Even now, he could feel the heaviness of the air, the way the metallic taste lingered on his tongue.

His Queen was temperamental at the best of times, and Dread wasn't keen on provoking her temper should his instincts be wrong. Not that they'd failed him before. But caution was best in times like these.

The only solace he had was that the bones from the doorway were weak and brittle despite the magic. Some had cracked through the middle or broken into dust when touched, the magic around it thickening in warning. The dwarves made steady progress, dusting off the dirt-ridden coating layer by layer, but there was also the question of protections and traps. If the magic was as thick as it was outside the doorway, he trembled at the thought of what lay inside.

Or *who.*

He didn't hesitate to think that some of kind spell lay over it. Would they release a plague? Or a beast? Or would they simply open it up and find that whoever ventured inside went slowly mad?

He'd seen many traps over the years and, whilst he was keen for progress to continue, he didn't long for the moment when they found whatever spells awaited them. He just hoped it was worth the wait if they found what they were looking for.

The room reverberated as a knock echoed against the wooden door.

'What is it?' Dread called, leaning against the window ledge.

Nails scraped across the stone as the door opened.

Dread slowly tore his eyes from the window and met the black eyes of a dark reaper twisting its head.

'Is it the bone door?' Dread asked, unable to hide the desperation in his tone.

The reaper's head lolled to the side as its long fingers brought forth a small scroll. Sighing, Dread tore the parchment from its claws and gave it leave, waving it away like a bug.

He carefully undid the ribbon keeping the paper together and read the note inside.

Check the Grave.

The Queen needed him.

And he needed a distraction.

Dread headed for the doorway before pivoting towards the parapet he used when landing here. Waiting wasn't a strong skill of his.

Even if it was a strange request, this was a blessing. He hadn't flown in days and the connection to his brothers remained quiet. He shivered in anticipation in the ash-ridden air. Trik still remained on the border of Perridorm, the armies of Bellatorre and Carnell fighting against an army of the dead. For every soldier they recruited, more would fight back, climbing out of the ground like some plague. But that hadn't been the only problem. They stemmed from the Princess of Perridorm: a petite girl who looked just as sick as the soldiers who fought for her. And though she had power, in Myrenna's eyes, she was just another annoyance. A spider about to be blown away by the wind.

Dread knew better. Knew the Queen better. Whilst her words said one thing, the lines appearing by her eyes said another. Perridorm was bigger than an annoyance: they were another wall Myrenna had to crumble before she got what she deserved. And in the midst of it all, Dread's patience waned, too.

He gave the Queen regular reports and usually received little in return. These days, he found her distracted, focused on something other than her usual grasp for power, and the note proved it. Dread put it down to Princess Snow and the betrayal of the Huntsman. One wall was an inconvenience, but with the Seeker out there, the Grimms still in power, and the missing artefact, they weren't storming a wall, but a fortress. His crows flew wide, crossing each kingdom with a keen eye, and yet the Queen's enemies remained hidden.

It made his Queen wane. Which made him feel weak and useless.

Twisting, Dread let the familiar pain shift over him. The change was now a part of his being and way of life. There was relief as his wings burst forth, a sigh escaping his beak. The wind was warm on his feathers, lifting him up with swift ease as he left the tower.

He cawed into the air as the forge below him bellowed fire. The smoke unravelled towards the sky like a message to the Godmother, and it singed his feathers, his wings trailing sparking embers.

He shone black against the sun, an inky shadow calling to the creatures below. The beasts under him lifted their weapons in salute and roared as he glided above them. The sound renewed him.

So, despite the slow strokes of brushes that painted their way across the door of bones, Dread knew one thing for certain: if he had to wait another few weeks to get Myrenna what she wanted, then so be it.

Myrenna stood by a low-burning lantern hanging upon the stone wall in the Tinker's toy room. That's what he liked to call the place where his experiments came alive. The room was organised, though a bit cluttered for her taste. Instruments were organised in order of the most painful to least, the rows of shelves labelled in themes, from plants to body parts and cauldron knew what else. Any sane person who entered here should fear this room. Should fear the man who owned it. If that's what the Tinker was.

But she wasn't afraid.

He'd been loyal. And useful. Skills her crows could learn to use.

Her amethyst eyes scoped over the room, the scent of blood and rot thick in her nose. The Tinker wiped his instruments with a filthy cloth, the old dwarf beside him. The dwarf lay strapped to one of the Tinker's many machines, his hairy chest exposed to the cold. His once white beard was now matted and brown, his skin grey. There were bones protruding under his skin, his ribs more visible than they'd been a few weeks ago. A few nails had been torn off from his hands, and his face was mottled with bruises, but from the defiance still left in his eyes, his soul had not changed.

She peered at him curiously, a smile curving on her face when he refused to cower before her. The dwarf could play hero all he liked, but Myrenna didn't like heroes. Didn't have time for them.

'I wonder if this is the day you break, Storyteller,' she mused. The dwarf only stared back at her, his lips cracked and silent. His defiance was answer enough, and she bristled.

'Are you staying for our session, my Queen?' the Tinker asked, holding out a thin knife and inspecting it for whatever it was he was about to do.

She'd considered it – watching her Tinker at work – but whilst she didn't fear him, she didn't enjoy watching him play. 'Not this time. I'm here to test out the spindle again.'

The Tinker nodded, his beady eyes shining in excitement as the blade flashed against the lanterns. 'The invitation is always there.'

'Yes,' she replied, eyeing a particularly infected wound in the dwarf's leg. 'Try to not kill this one yet,' she warned.

'I'll not disappoint you,' his raspy voice said as he pulled a stool beside the dwarf. The knife glinted again as the Tinker trailed it along the dwarf's cheek, a hunger in his eyes that unsettled even her.

Myrenna had always been one for quick deaths. A heart ripped here, the slash of her nails there. Or the snap of a neck. She revered her gowns and silken wardrobe too much to bother with all the dirt and blood that accompanied a slow and arduous death.

That's why she had the Tinker.

He'd been pathetically grateful for the opportunity to serve her when she'd found him all those years ago. He'd been locked away for his twisted ways, the people citing their right to kill whatever foul being he was. But Myrenna had seen an opportunity. Where doors closed for others, Myrenna had always stepped through. It was how she'd acquired the mirror, after all. Even if there were some misgivings between the magical object and herself.

Moving towards the moist wall, she paused to pick up the spindle, the wood chipped and charred. She ran her thumb over the sharp point, and watched as a thick drop of blood fell to the floor. Taking the spindle, she gave the Tinker a shallow nod. An eerie smile crept across his face as he lowered his head and bowed. Her eyes lingered on the prisoner for a moment longer before she took the stairs.

'I want a report tomorrow,' she ordered.

'Of course, I'll take care of our guest,' the Tinker called back, his voice retreating with each step she took.

Myrenna fought off the shiver as she reached the top of the stairs, leaving the prisoner's burning eyes to be dulled into black by the Tinker's spindly hands.

XII

The Wood Nymphs and Their Whispers

'I don't trust him,' Malak said. He booted a rock out of his path, brushing aside a low hanging branch. They walked west, delving further into the southern part of the Dark Forest.

Snow couldn't help but agree with the troll, but what other choice did they have? Flynn was the only lead they had, and with the warning about the Queen hunting for her, she needed allies.

Snow, Malak, Pip, and Florian had started their journey from the Skinny Piglet at first light, each of them with dark circles under their eyes. Snow had a feeling none of them had slept well the night before – except Malak, who had snored loudly – and she didn't blame them, considering they were trekking towards a kingdom in the midst of war. Thankfully, this section of the forest was far enough away from the conflict on the Elysian fields.

'We don't really have a choice.' Snow said, hating how her thighs already hurt from riding. Snow brushed her hand against the horse's cream mane, soothed by its softness. Considering the animal had been Flynn's, she'd been surprised by its gentleness.

Pip sat behind her, shuffling every few minutes with a grunt, whilst Malak and Florian walked ahead. The forest pathway was covered in debris, either used rarely, or old. All the group had to go off was Marcellus's quick directions before they were surrounded by trees, the sun blocked by the ancient branches.

Snow pulled a leaf from her unbound hair and chucked it away. Pip elbowed her from behind as he jostled again. Snow pursed her lips.

'Trust is a fragile lie, anyway,' Pip chimed in, his short legs hanging at an odd angle. 'What we do know for certain is that this Flynn person wasn't wrong: we do need Perridorm, and the only person who could even come close to getting them to reconsider their position is the Princess. Whether or not she's ready for it is the real question.'

Snow scowled, tightening her grip on the reins. She was getting tired of being spoken about as if she weren't there, like she was a doll for them to manoeuvre around and not a would-be queen.

Had she not proven herself in the tavern? She had wielded Hansel's axe, for cauldron's sake.

Until the troll took it from you, a dark voice whispered.

'I think she could do it,' Florian said, smiling up at Snow.

Ever the optimist.

Pip elbowed the Princess again as he moved, and she jabbed him back, satisfied with the *oomph* that followed.

'Thinking is not enough,' Pip snapped, shooting Snow a dirty look. 'Has anyone seen my pipe?'

Florian sniffled, his nose a bright pink as usual. 'Aren't they young? The twins, I mean. Surely, we could persuade them.'

'Young or not,' Malak replied, 'the girl holds great power. She wields an army of the dead.'

'How is that even possible?' Florian asked.

'It's rare,' Pip replied, 'but it is possible with the right tools and the right blood.' He leaned over the side of the horse and reached for the saddle pack. He dug his elbow into Snow's back *again* and she slapped at him, making him wobble and nearly topple off the horse. He grunted and latched onto her clothes like flea to skin, yanking her halfway off the saddle in the process.

'Could you stop that?' Snow snapped.

'Oh, my apologies, Your Highness,' Pip chimed, refusing to let go. 'Are my too-short legs and stature not of your liking?'

Florian snorted from beside them as he helped lift Pip back into the saddle.

'I meant the moving around,' Snow said. 'Sit still, for cauldron's sake!'

'He knew what you meant,' Malak replied, giving Pip an icy glare. 'He just wants to stir, as he always does.'

Thankfully, the elf didn't elbow her again. 'Forgive me for bringing some light-hearted joy to this mess we're finding ourselves in. Godmother forbid I make a joke when we're on our way to a battlefield.'

Malak slowed his steps in line with the horse. 'You're more dramatic than a circus performer.'

Pip scoffed. 'I don't even know why I bother at all. It's not like any of you are grateful for my help.'

Malak rubbed his eyes. His weapons were strapped across his back and the spikes in his club glinted in the morning sun. The hilt from his sword was as long as her torso. 'We *are* grateful, Pip.'

'I swear,' Pip said, 'you'll all appreciate me one day. Without me, all of you would have been dead in the grotto. Yet, there isn't one lick of gratitude from any of you.'

Snow tuned out Pip's bickering with Malak, focusing on the path ahead. The dawn glowed in red and orange, outlining the shadows of the forest. It might have been called the Dark Forest, but it didn't seem so bad to her. Supposedly there was magic in this forest, with witches and nymphs and monsters. Some of her books had warned her about maidens travelling alone, about being beware of strangers and agreeing to bargains with tricky words. Whilst she should be wary, this morning's trip had at least ignited something in her. It put her one step closer to Hansel, and no monster or bargain or witch was going to stop her.

Snow supposed she should have been frightened, but after last night she'd resigned herself to the fact that nowhere was safe anymore. Not since the time before her mother's death, anyway. And even then, had she ever really been truly safe?

It was time to stop pretending. Time to stop lying to herself. She was no longer a girl, but a woman, and she needed to begin acting as such.

Imposter, the little voice inside of her said, but she shook it off.

A breeze drifted by, gently lifting Snow's dark hair from her shoulders in a tender, fleeting touch. Leaves fell like green rain, dotting the dirt path with colour. Sunlight filtered through the forest canopy, scattering trails of glistening gold.

'Does anyone hear that?' Florian asked, his steps slowing.

'Hear what?' Snow replied.

'That scratching noise.'

Snow peered over her shoulder to Pip – his senses and hearing were far better than anybody else here, but she'd never admit it out loud. She loathed the creature.

His pointed ears twitched, and he frowned. 'It's probably wood nymphs.'

'Should we be concerned?' she asked.

Pip shook his head. 'They're harmless, mostly, but they like to play pranks on travellers.'

'You'll be the best of friends, then,' Malak retorted.

'Hardly,' Pip replied.

The path branched to the right, the trees becoming denser the further they travelled, blocking out what little daylight they started with. Snow slowed the horse, taking in the shadowed path before them.

Should it be this dark?

'I've read about nymphs,' Florian said, unaware of his surroundings. 'They can absorb into the wood, using the root system as a road of sorts. It's fascinating, when you think about it. Scorcies the cryptozoologist says they're the tree's spirits, awakened to seek revenge on the cut down forests.'

'Scorcies was a babbling idiot,' Pip muttered.

Snow's curiosity piqued. Forgetting the shadowed trees ahead, she turned to the golden prince. 'Are they anything like sea nymphs?'

Florian shrugged. 'Yes and no. They're smaller, more like fairies, as opposed to humanoid like the sea nymphs. They don't have a queen, either, but a council, and they hold little magic. Still, they move unseen. Invisibility is a speciality of theirs.'

Snow wrinkled her nose. 'They sound boring. Sea nymphs can breathe underwater and on land. Plus, their queen might be a sea witch, but I hear her treasure trove is filled with magical artefacts. Could you imagine what hidden treasures would be there?'

'I disagree,' Florian replied. 'While the seas nymphs have their famed treasure trove, the wood nymphs collect things, too. They could have a collection just as big.'

'Treasure is all well and good, but I'll just be happy if the wood nymphs don't bite like the sea nymphs,' Malak chimed in. 'The teeth on some of them could slice a troll's hide.'

Florian sneezed. 'I don't know about their teeth, but I wouldn't be surprised if it ran in their genetics.'

'Enough of the nymph lesson,' Pip said. 'If we don't make any sudden movements and don't provoke them, we should have a clear path. In and out of the forest, remember?'

The group moved slower now, all four of them watching the trees with caution. The further they went, the heavier the sense of dread.

The wind pricked Snow's skin.

Florian held back another sneeze, his face turning crimson. Pip sighed and pulled out a pouch from his pocket before throwing it to him. 'Here, you snivelling prince.'

'What's this?' Florian asked.

'Minx root,' Pip replied. 'Ah! My pipe!' Turning back to Florian with a smile, the elf pointed his pipe to the pouch clutched in the Prince's hand. 'Crush it up into tea next time we stop near water. It should help with your allergies.'

Florian creased his brows. 'Why are you being nice?'

Pip raised his brow then held out his hand. 'You can give it back if you don't want it.'

Florian clutched the herbs to his chest. 'No.'

Snow tuned out once more, focusing on a sound in the distance. She could hear it now, louder this time: the scratching of bark. The wind glided across her skin in a whisper as the leaves spun in circles across the weathered path.

'What do wood nymphs eat?' Snow asked, pulling free her mother's pen and twirling it in her hand.

Pip stopped mid-sentence, disregarding Florian. 'Mostly bugs. But they have long memories and like to hoard pretty things as payment for their gods.'

'Like the Fairy Godmother?' she asked.

'No,' Pip replied. 'Like the sea nymphs, they celebrate the old gods: the stars themselves.'

Snow had read about the isle of Nysa, the descriptions of the watery caverns and the sharp black rocks that surrounded the kingdom. It was said that below the underwater castle lay a vast array of tunnels, some natural and others etched by the nymphs themselves. They held objects of history long lost, some very powerful and very deadly. Perhaps when she ruled, she might see it one day – if she was lucky enough to visit. But she doubted the sea nymphs' distaste for land dwellers had changed despite the treaties with the kingdoms. Even Bellatorre still dealt with issues surrounding the fishing villages near the southern border.

'What kind of offerings do the wood nymphs give to the stars?' Snow enquired.

Pip was quiet before he answered. 'Alive ones.'

A chill crept over Snow as the density of the trees thickened. The once-dappled light was swallowed by the shadows, and the air grew heavier, thick with the scent of damp earth and pine. The scratching that had echoed in the distance was now a constant presence, like claws dragging across bark.

Then, a thunderous crack split the air.

A massive tree, ancient and gnarled, splintered in half, its trunk bending under the weight of something unseen. The ground trembled beneath Snow as another gust of wind blew through the forest, fierce and raging, carrying with it a flurry of dirt and debris. It whipped at her, sharp and stinging, the gust forcing her to squint and close her eyes against the onslaught.

Snow's horse bucked and whinnied at the ghostly wind, fighting her grip on the reins. It reared wildly and threw Snow and Pip to the ground. Snow shoved her tangled hair from her eyes just in time to see the horse bolt into the woods.

Malak shouted as he unsheathed his blade, taking a stand in front of the Princess.

'What in the Godmother's name ...' Pip started.

The forest came alive.

Spindly branches groaned and creaked, their jagged limbs twisting and reaching toward Snow like monstrous fingers, scraping the air with an eerie, guttural sound. The ground trembled beneath them, as if the earth itself was awakening. Snow's heart hammered in her chest, her breath coming in shallow, panicked bursts. The trees ... they were moving.

The dense canopy above shifted, rustling in ways that didn't belong to any natural breeze. Before she could fully process the horror unfolding, a thick, knotted root unfurled from the soil, pushing up through the dirt with an unnatural force. It stretched forward, slow but deliberate, like a beast testing the air before striking.

Malak struck, and the root retreated, but barely. Another sprang free, turning Snow's blood cold. She barely had time to scuttle back, her body sliding against the wet, muck-covered earth, into Malak's thigh. She could feel his muscles tense, his hand hovering near her as more branches began to shift, their wooden limbs groaning as they reached out toward them with an unsettling grace.

Snow's breath caught in her throat as the dark shapes of the branches spiralled and twisted around her, their gnarled limbs tightening with relentless precision. No matter how many Malak cut, more grew. Snow slapped at the twigs and tendrils, her fingers scraping against the rough bark, but it was no use. The forest had a mind of its own, and it wasn't letting her go. Her heart pounded against her chest, each beat a reminder of the crushing pressure around her body.

Snow's scream tore free as a branch snatched her arm, yanking her shoulder and ripping pain through her right side. The scream that clawed its way up her throat was swallowed by the weight of the world pressing down on her. It caught in her mouth, choking her as she groped along the road, trying desperately to find any purchase, any escape. But the more she struggled, the tighter the grip became. Her breath came in ragged gasps, her skin raw from the frenzied thrashing.

Her eyes darted desperately, searching for something – anything – that could help her break free. She could see the faint outlines of Malak and the others nearby, their figures growing smaller as the trees swallowed her up. But they were too far away, and the road between them was closing fast, with a suffocating wall of dark wood and writhing limbs.

There was no weapon. No knife, no sword, no tool she could use to cut through the encroaching forest. Only the endless twisting of roots, tightening with each passing second.

'Malak!' she screamed, her voice breaking through the suffocating silence of the woods.

Stars danced across her vision. Malak slashed at the branches with a sword in one hand and his club in the other. Nearby, Florian screamed, his grip clumsy as he swung at a branch aiming for his head.

Her body was lifted, her feet no longer touching the ground as the roots dragged her further into the depths of the forest. She clawed at the earth, desperately reaching for the road, but it was no use. She was sinking into the darkness, her body fighting, but it felt as though the forest was swallowing her whole.

The world began to tilt as the roots dragged her up, and in the back of her mind, she knew she was out of time.

Her voice barely made a whisper as she met the wide eyes of Pip who mouthed her name.

Then hundreds of tiny wooden fingers pulled her into the brush.

XIII

The Murder's Bidding

Icy wind billowed through Dread's feathers as he sailed over the border of Carnell and Aurelia. Despite it being spring, the northern kingdoms had always been colder.

He'd been flying all night at his Queen's demand. He'd received the scroll from one of the reavers at the mines and had left without a second to waste.

Worry gnawed at him. Icy and cold to match the skies.

His Queen never spoke of the massacre at Butterpond. Never gave him more details than he needed to be able to

161

serve her. But he knew enough to protect it, to know why it was important.

The grave of her father.

This wasn't the first time she'd asked him to scope it out, nor would it be the last. But with everything else happening, it should have been a faraway memory. A distant haze. Not something she urged him to check on when their enemies were closing in. He'd never understood her fascination with it, considering the man was dead. But Dread was her servant, her murder, her commander. And he would always follow.

The terrain below changed as he covered more miles. Much of Carnell was marsh and dry land, the rest merging into farmland towards the eastern borders.

Aurelia was far lusher. The trees and fertile soil were what separated this kingdom from the others. Its trade was mostly in crops, feeding huge portions of the realm for most of the year. It was why they were renowned for their food contests. The same contest that had freed Myrenna before she became the Queen.

He'd always wondered what she'd been like then: the baker's girl, covered in flour. Would he have followed her the same way he did now? Or would he have laughed at the girl from nothing and mocked her?

No.

He would have followed her anywhere. Her presence commanded people regardless of her powers. Any who couldn't see that were fools and deserved their punishment.

'You're lucky the Queen can't hear your thoughts,' Trik said through the bond.

Coming from you, with the dirtiest thoughts of all.

There was a pause before his brother replied. '*You sound distant. Where are you?*'

Trik had always been observant. The bond couldn't entirely wither no matter how far they flew, but it did fade, as if you were yelling through a tunnel. Even with the distance, though, Trik could always feel Dread's moods.

On an urgent errand for the Queen.

'*How urgent?*' Trik pressed.

Dread heard the concern in his brother's voice and withheld his response, wary despite their brotherly bond.

Though they were brothers, trust was still a hard gift to give. Trik had been gone for so long, detached and absent in this war. He hadn't seen the Queen and the graves of hearts left in her wake. Hadn't seen her scream as the Princess went missing, or how her power was drained by the fog dragon. Hadn't seen the worry that creased her brow or the sleepless nights.

Dread weighed the risk of revealing such information, deciding it was best not to share. *Urgent enough that I'm getting tired of your questions.*

He heard a sigh through the bond and was relieved when Trik didn't ask further questions.

How's the battle? Dread asked.

'*Unfulfilling,*' Trik replied. '*I'd hoped the Perridorm princess would have lost enough blood by now to have fallen dead, but it seems she's still kicking. We continue to move forward. Barely. It's hard to kill something that's already dead.*'

For years, the battle had been waged. The army of the dead somehow never depleting. Though, despite the undead, Trik had managed a good job in keeping his men alive. The battle was slow, but it was progress. The issue was that the border of Perridorm and Bellatorre lay on the far side of the capitol, Felldryn. Even if they could defeat the army, they still had to cross most of the kingdom to get there. Trik had mentioned coming from the forest, but without the loyalty of the creatures who lived within, the whole army might be dead before they even arrived.

Both the Shadow Forest and the Dark Forest protected Perridorm from the east and the north, leaving the only other openings from Ardenbeax or the Merkingdom. The mermaids were vicious and had laughed Bellatorre out before they could even ask. So, they attacked from where they could: between the forest and the sea.

Monsters are your speciality, Brother, even the undead kind, Dread replied. *The princess in Perridorm will die soon enough. All mortals die eventually.*

His brother laughed. *'Says the man controlling beasts of all kinds in those mines of yours.'*

Myrenna's mines, Dread corrected. *I'm just the keeper.*

'You found anything yet?'

Something, Dread said quietly.

'It's progress, at least.' There was a pause. *'Nothing from our brother, then?'*

Silence, Dread said. *I'll put out word. See what I can find. It's been too long.*

His brother mumbled something back through the bond, but Dread missed it as he judged the small village ahead. A temple sat atop a crested knoll, its wooden frame twisted from years of use.

I have to go, Dread said, diving towards a graveyard.

'Be wise, Brother.'

Being wise wasn't a trait Dread had, but he did have enough common sense to not be stupid. He sliced through the air in silence and landed near the shade of a tree. The grass was unkempt, tickling his legs as he twisted into a human. He panted as the noon sun glared down, the wind warmer closer to the ground. He found the unmarked grave immediately near the outer edges but was distracted when the temple doors swung open. Dread stood frozen as a group of villagers left, cheering, and singing as they threw petals. A woman in pink held hands with a man in black, their faces beaming in joy. Typically, weddings in Aurelia used a lot of flowers, pink being the customary colour. Of course, red worked too. Most of it was in tribute to the Princess Briar Rose, from the War of Thorns.

Even now, hundreds of years later, they honoured her name. But nobody ever recalled her general's name.

Would Myrenna be remembered the same way?

Dread took his eyes off the crowd and turned back to the grave. His gaze pierced the soil for any disturbance and found none. The dirt remained hard and packed, the tombstone worn with time. Sighing, he took out a small scroll and wrote down the words he knew his Queen needed to hear:

It remains untouched.

He twisted back into his crow form, accepting the pain of shifting as he spread his wings and flew, the scroll tucked firmly into his talons. The air rushed under him, pushing him into the sky. Myrenna would be in her tower waiting for him and, for the first time in a while, he would be bringing her good news.

A torrent of tiny brown fingers scratched Snow's skin as she was hauled through the brush. It was like needles prodding into her milky skin and draining her blood. She kicked and struggled, yelling when she couldn't break free. There were too many of them, their beady eyes black and depthless, drinking her in with greed.

Her breath came out in sharp bursts, fear dragging at her limbs like tar. She could no longer hear her friends, could no longer see the forest path they'd followed. She could only smell wood and leaves and … ash. If she was to die, she hoped it would be swift.

A voice hissed inside her mind at the thought, but she pushed it away. If she did die, she hoped the rebellion wouldn't falter. Hoped they still somehow rallied her kingdom, still saved her people. Still gave Hansel his dream.

With her eyes squeezed shut, all Snow could see was him.

Hansel.

Golden hair kissed by sunlight, a smile that melted the coldest nights, the scent of pine and wood lingering in his embrace. She sobbed as his image faded, dissolving into darkness. Tiny hands clawed at her, yanking her ears, pulling her hair, twisting her lips.

Then it stopped.

Snow curled into a ball where she sucked in her breath, the shuddering quiet and foreboding. She didn't know how long she stayed like that, but when she felt the shivers in her body recede, the final blow to her life never come, she finally blinked.

She was in a clearing within the forest, trees lining the edge in a semi-circle. No eyes or hands were to be seen, but there was a stillness to the air that reminded her predators were still nearby.

To her left lay a creek, the trickling water the only sound breaking through the trees. 'Malak?' she croaked. She expected her voice to be stronger and cringed when it was barely a whisper.

She scanned the woods, finding nothing but shadows. Her skin itched as if she was being watched. 'Florian?'

When nothing responded, despair crowded her mind, sinking into her bones. Where were her friends?

Where was she?

'Pip?' she whispered, jolting at the sound of the rustling leaves. She hugged herself. 'Anyone?'

Her chest hurt and her eyes burned with tears. She was totally and utterly alone.

Lost, the taunting voice murmured. *Powerless.*

There was a truth to the words. Snow had been alone before, had been isolated, ignored, even locked away. But she had never been *lost* and alone before. This time there was no familiarity. No castle guards. No friends. No bedroom or hidden library rooms. Here there was only secrets and strange beasts.

Her horse was gone. She had trusted the beautiful animal, and look where it had landed her. It had spooked at the first sign of danger and fled with *everything.* Her pack. The food. Hansel's axe.

The reminder of losing Hansel's axe loosed a sob from her chest. She hated the horse. Hated the man who had given it to her.

Her memory was a blur. She didn't know which way led where. The trees were too close together to show a pathway out, leaving her little light. She trembled and ran her hands up her arms. There was a chill, but she wasn't sure if it was from the cool trees. She bit her bottom lip as she tried to contain her rising fear, choking it down. She would not cave. Not here when she only had herself.

'Don't be rash,' she whispered to herself. 'Be calm. Be clear.'

Being impulsive was a fault of hers. She was prone to being reckless, lashing out when she was hurt or found an enemy. When she'd woken and seen the Seeker with all her weapons and those tight leathers, she'd attacked without thinking. Not that she'd regretted doing it at the time. Even now, thinking of the Seeker left a sour taste in her mouth.

Were the Seeker and Hansel alone again? Were they wrapped in each other's arms? Were they laughing as she was abandoned in the forest? Her thoughts warped, spiralling into images of them laughing together. Would they even look for her if they knew she was gone?

The flutter of a leaf caught her attention, and she whirled around to see large dark eyes. They glinted back at her, then disappeared.

'Hello?' she called, her voice sounding clearer. To her left there was another scuttle, and she whipped her head in that direction, eyes and heart alert. 'I won't hurt you if you won't hurt me.'

The brush behind her moved.

She was surrounded.

Alone.

Lost.

Helpless.

Tears pricked her eyes as she tried to swallow. She had just pushed a loose strand of hair behind her ear when one of the creatures finally emerged. She stepped back at its advance, only halting when it seemed to study her. The wood nymph was smaller than expected – roughly the size of her calf – and thin and spindly. It walked on two pointed legs, its arms twigs and its fingers leaves. The nymph's head was round with huge dark eyes, and atop its skull was a cluster of grass and moss.

'Are you a wood nymph?' Snow asked.

The creature shuffled forward, and she flinched, but it merely tilted its head.

'Where am I?' Snow asked. 'Why did you take me?' She moved slowly, unsure whether it was for her sake or the creature's. Not that it mattered, she was the one surrounded. She was the one in danger.

Hansel would be calm. Myrenna would be indifferent. And Malak would be … growling.

Do not be rash.

'Pretty,' the wood nymph clicked. The creature assessed her, the clicking of its tongue unnerving. It walked with quick, jolted movements as if its head were slightly too large for its thin body.

Snow lifted her arms, reaching out her palms to show she held no weapons. Though she wished she did. 'I need to go back to my friends. Could you show me the way? Leave me be?'

'Pretty,' the nymph echoed. Another two crept out from between the trees.

I don't like this.

The ground rumbled as the roots of the trees shuffled, allowing more nymphs to pop free. Some seemed to grow from the bark itself, others melding into the tree as only faces or limbs.

'I cannot stay here. I must return to my friends,' she said firmly, hoping the sharper tone would somehow convince them.

'Drink, drink,' one of the nymphs said, skittering to the creek. This one's hair differed from the others, leaves piled so high that it almost doubled the creatures height. It blinked at her, moving between the Princess and the creek.

'Cut and bloody,' another with moss covered skin murmured.

'Drink, drink.'

'Stop that,' she snapped.

The closer they came, the more her panic took over. Everywhere she looked, another nymph was appearing, slowly filling the clearing with hungry eyes and too much curiosity. Spindly fingers reached for her, and she squealed, shoving them back.

The sharp cuts from the journey had begun to sting. She was coated in dirt and blood, the wounds making her skin blotchy and pink. She touched the back of her head and found a lump from where her head had hit the soil before she'd gone unconscious. She must have looked like a carved piece of meat.

'Drink, drink,' the nymphs clicked in their strange tongues. 'Cut and bloody.'

She spun around, ready to flee but was her path was blocked by three more of them. 'Hey!' she said. 'I need to find my friends!' She veered to the right, only to be stopped by more. She pivoted, shoving the nymphs away as she tried to flee, to gain some sort of ground. The clearing filled with the creatures, their voices crashing together. Snow blocked her ears, a tear slipping free.

Drink

Drink

Drink

Drink

'What if I don't want to drink?' she screamed, the trees closing in. Her breaths became shallow.

They boxed her in like prey.

'Cut and bloody,' they repeated.

Snow stumbled as she tried to get away, but the nymphs cornered her by the edge of the creek. 'I don't want to drink,' she sobbed. 'I want to find my friends.'

Cut and bloody

Drink

Drink

Drink

The echoing clicks of their voices drove her mad, ringing through her skull like a nail hammering into metal. Hands reached out. Her skirt was pulled. A touch lingered down her arm. Their wide eyes swallowed her vision.

'I AM A *PRINCESS! DO NOT TOUCH ME!*'

She fought against the nymphs as they crowded her, pushing her into the creek. Water pooled around her ankles, then her knees. When one jumped onto her chest, grinning with moss covered teeth, she screamed. Her foot stumbled, throwing her off balance, and she crashed into the water. It splashed around her, soaking her clothes, and a pair of hands pressed her down into the mud. The wet earth dragged her further under, her scream muffled by the cold weight of the water. She couldn't breathe, couldn't think.

With her last remaining strength she heaved, somehow throwing the nymphs off. She clambered forward, trying to get out of their reach, but they didn't follow. She slowed as she neared the opposite side of the creek, the nymphs tilting their head in one movement so freakishly deranged that she stopped breathing for a moment.

When the nymph with the leafy tower hair stepped forward, she shivered at the thought of their hands all over her, panic rising. Snow raised her arms. 'I'll drink,' she panted. 'I'll drink.'

She cupped a handful of water, raising it to show them, and drank. The liquid poured down her throat but instead of a cooling sensation it was as if she had swallowed molten lava. Her cheeks flushed as sharp pain crossed her wounds, causing her to groan. Snow curled into herself, her body trembling, her breath coming in ragged gasps. Her voice cracked as another scream fought to break free, but the sensation of pressure suddenly vanished. Silence flooded in, suffocating and cold, leaving her gasping for air in the eerie stillness that followed.

The wood nymphs backed away and tilted their heads.

Snow's eyes darted to her arms where her bruises began to pale. The cuts on her arms closed, the skin turning pink before smoothing over. It itched, the sensation soft and strong at the same time. 'What in the Godmother is this?'

'Pretty again,' another nymph said. The warmth pooled through her once more and she fell into blackness.

XIV

The Tooth of a Dragon

Brufell had been pacing for three hours now, waiting for Bronson to wake up. He'd accepted the bargain with the trolls, whatever that meant, but had insisted they wait to finalise terms until Bronson awoke. Luckily the Irksall had agreed, giving him until morning before they would meet again. It was still early by Brufell's calculations, the sun not yet risen, so he still had time before they called.

No matter how hard he'd tried to sleep, his relentless thoughts had kept him awake, his mind churning. There

173

were too many unknowns, too many things that could go wrong, that he had no control over. They were camped at the edges of the Shadow Forest, the name apt for the darkness that loomed from the trees. He could have sworn he'd seen eyes watching the camp, heard the slow scrape of claws nearby and the howl of something vicious in the distance. At least the looming presence of the trolls seemed to be keeping the forest's beasts at bay. For now. But it still didn't stop the ache of how far he was from the Seven. He didn't like not knowing what was happening further south, whether his kin had found their cousins in the Peaks of Carfell, or whether the Seeker had awoken the Princess, or if Myrenna's wrath had obliterated them, leaving nothing but ash and death in her wake.

It was the not knowing that made Brufell uneasy and restless, like spiders scratching under his skin.

He took another look at the thick forest nearby, the mountains looming in the distance, and wondered if he'd made a mistake. The rest of the Seven expected Brufell and Bronson to arrive in the Peaks of Carfell in a week or so. He had no way to communicate what had happened with the trolls, had no way to warn them they wouldn't be arriving when expected and not to worry. But in the turbulent times of war, a favour owed could be the difference between destruction and the realm's hope. It was no small thing to hold a troll's debt, and if it meant calling them to arms, then that is what Brufell would do.

Hard choices would be made in the coming battle, ones that Brufell refused to feel remorseful about. There was no room for doubt in war; only the will to survive.

Brufell heard Bronson stir just before dawn. He opened the tent flap to find the pixie rubbing sleep from its eye beside him.

'Where are we?' Bronson asked, eyes wildly scanning the jumbled campsite surrounding them. 'What in the beige-as-porridge are those tents, why does my mouth taste like dirt, and *what* is that awful sound?'

Bronson's hair was tousled, a touch of colour returning to his cheeks. He looked a cauldron lot better than he had up on the mountain pass, and it loosened some of the tightness Brufell had been holding in his chest. 'That would be the sound of sleeping trolls and, unless you wish to wake them, I'd suggest you lower your voice.'

The pixie squeaked out a curse Brufell couldn't understand, but it was Bronson he watched. The younger dwarf's eyes widened a fraction, the last remnants of sleep disappearing. 'Of sleeping *what?*'

'You heard me,' Brufell replied curtly, wanting to get this explanation over as soon as possible. 'You're injured, Bronson, not deaf.'

'Rude,' Bronson muttered.

Brufell tossed him a plain shirt and a vest that used to be the deepest green of the forest but was now more reminiscent of old moss. 'Get dressed and I'll answer your questions.'

Bronson did as asked, leaving the front buttons of his vest undone as he huffed his way towards the tent entrance. He shoved Brufell out of the way, and made it all of three steps before he halted. 'Godmother help us.'

'Now, before you do anything reckless, I need you to remain calm.'

'Remain calm?' Bronson hissed. He spun around, eyes wild with a bottled fury that Brufell knew all too well. Bronson wasn't the first to find anger, but when he did, the dwarves and the realm knew to buckle down against his whirlwind of emotions. 'Are we in the same realm right now? Or are you up with the giants in the clouds? We. Are. Surrounded. By. Trolls.'

'If you insist on stating the obvious, then this is going to take a lot longer than I'd hoped.'

Bronson narrowed his gaze. 'Oh, I'm sorry. Am I inconveniencing you somehow now that I'm awake? What in the cauldron is going on, Brufell?'

Brufell didn't have time to coddle him. 'What do you remember?'

Bronson shook his head, no doubt about to say something scathing, when the pixie squeaked. Nearby, a troll had rolled over, a bubble of snot popping wetly over the troll's nostril as he slept.

'I need you to tell me what you remember,' Brufell said, his voice lowering with command.

Bronson crossed his arms and glowered at the older dwarf. 'I remember the mountain pass, and being robbed by trolls. I remember digging, and then nothing … until there was a bowl of brown sludge which tasted like arse. Then I woke up in a tent with my kin telling me we're surrounded by sleeping *trolls* like it's no big deal.'

Sometimes Brufell forgot how much older than Bronson he was. Whilst he was not as old as Bonyx, he was still one of elders of the Seven. Bronson was closer in age to Bryn, and only a few years older than Rabbit and Beetle. Meaning they were centuries apart, creating a gap in their experiences that was impossible to close.

Softening his voice, he proceeded to fill Bronson in on all that had happened.

'They survived the fog dragon?' Bronson gasped. 'How?'

'I don't know, but whilst some lifeblood remains in them, it's small and they need a cure.'

'And they want it from us?'

'Not exactly,' Brufell muttered, hating how loud the dwarf was speaking. 'They want information.'

Bronson tilted his head, his brows furrowed. 'What could we possibly know that they don't?'

Brufell held back a sigh. 'If you had ever bothered to look, you'd know the libraries in Parador are extensive.'

Bronson pulled a piece of invisible lint from his shirt. 'I didn't take you for a reader.'

Brufell let the jab slide. 'Reading aside, I need more information, and I need your help. You've always been better at gauging others than me. You might be inept at everyday tasks but you're good with people, with creatures. They like you.'

Bronson placed a palm to his chest and gasped. 'Is that a compliment, Brufell?'

The old dwarf huffed and crossed his arms, unimpressed with Bronson's ill-timed humour. His glare unfortunately didn't deter Bronson's enthusiastic babbling.

'I just need to revel in this for a moment. No, Bronson, stop whistling. Bronson, why do you put that stuff around your eyes? Bronson, make sure you only buy from the list I gave you – I know you like to shop.'

'I don't—'

'Bronson, you need to learn how to fight. *You might be inept at everyday tasks but you're good with people.*' Bronson's voice turned into a deep rumbling sound and Brufell narrowed his eyes at the mocking tone. He did not sound like that. 'War is coming. Silly songs won't win battles. Weapons and well-trained soldiers will.'

'Enough!' Brufell roared, loud enough to quieten the trees and make Bronson pale. The pixie clutched Bronson's vest, mouth agape at the massive shadow that loomed at Brufell's back.

Warm, rancid breath smacked Brufell's neck like rotted meat, making him turn around slowly. Tuk smiled down at him as if they shared an inside joke.

'He's so big,' Bronson whispered.

Tuk crossed his meaty arms, his mottled green skin stretched tight. 'Irksall waits for you.'

'Grab your stuff, Bronson,' Brufell ordered, not breaking his gaze with the troll. Tuk's nostrils flared, and Brufell silently dared him to sniff him.

Bronson donned his shoes in silence, but when he went to grab a knife, Brufell stopped him. 'No weapons.'

'But—' Bronson protested.

'Old dwarf already try,' Tuk said, smirking. 'No. Weapons.'

Begrudgingly, Bronson followed suit, though he kept close to Brufell's side as they navigated through the maze of sleeping trolls and mismatched tents. Brufell kept pace with Tuk, though for every one of the troll's steps he had to take three.

When they arrived, the Irksall sat higher in his cot than he had before. Shatk still remained on his rickety stool in the back, enthusiastically gnawing on a platter of grey scarat meat, practically sucking the marrow from its bones.

'Delightful,' Bronson commented upon entry, but his voice was too high-pitched for the humour to hit.

Brufell shot him a warning glance as the Irksall took a sip from his cup and nodded towards the younger dwarf. 'Yer look better than ya did.'

Bronson grimaced and moved closer to Brufell, nearly stepping on the older dwarf's foot in the process. Brufell sighed internally before motioning towards the stool he'd sat on the night before. While Bronson was healed, he still looked pale, and the walk here had made his breathing shallow.

Bronson pulled the stool closer towards the tent entrance and took the seat, placing the pixie lightly on his knee. The little blue creature took in every detail but halted on Shatk for longer than necessary, the scarring on his eye pulling at his skin.

Clever little thing, Brufell thought. Even if Bronson ever lost Brufell, at least he had the pixie by his side.

Pulling forward another seat, the two trolls waited patiently for Brufell to begin.

'I've spoken to my cousin,' Brufell said, 'and he agrees that a bargain would be beneficial for the both of us.'

Shatk's gaze snapped to Bronson as the troll dropped a half-gnawed bone on the plate. His lips puckered as if he'd eaten something sour. 'Arrogant creatures,' he muttered.

Ignoring him, Brufell said, 'A while ago, my kin and I found a treasure in the mountains. We kept it safe, but over time we noticed odd things happening in the realm. Beasts that usually kept to forests started wandering. Pieces of land stripped of colour and life. Strange stirrings in the wind.

'My kin and I decided to separate to investigate these matters, and ended up in Troll's Keep.' He paused to let the information sink in before he continued. 'It was there that an acquaintance showed us to its … nest. It was docile then, but from what we can tell, it's controlled somehow. We didn't learn much more than that, but we did meet a survivor.'

Shatk narrowed his eyes. 'Who?'

Brufell tilted his head towards the pixie. 'The little one.'

The attention of both trolls fell on the pixie and the creature carefully shuffled closer to Bronson.

'He doesn't have the same symptoms,' said the healer, noting the lack of black lines inked on the pixie's skin.

'No,' replied Brufell. 'That's because we believe he didn't come into contact with the fog dragon. His colony did, though, and the whole place was massacred.'

Even now, a shiver crossed Brufell's bones when he thought of the pile of tiny bodies littered throughout the caves: shrunken, lifeless, dead, all piled on one another in a mass grave. He had seen death many times, but never as grievous as that. He could see the children clutched to the adults in terror, the hollow eyes staring back at him. It was etched into the core of his memory just as the fields of death from war were.

Inhaling with the sharpness of his memories, Brufell continued. 'From the decay and destruction left behind, it was clear that the fogged beast had come through the mountains.'

'You are giving us nothing of value,' the healer snapped. 'Only sad, petty tales that do not help at all.'

'Hold yer temper, Shatk,' the Irksall ordered, lifting his drink towards Brufell. 'Go on.'

Brufell glared at Shatk. 'There are wicked things stirring and I'm not sure how much you know about what is happening outside of your own troubles … but a real war is brewing. Carnell and Bellatorre are on the brink of something big. They are rounding up any species and locking them away in the Queen's mines. Looking for cauldron knows what, but whatever it is, the Queen wants it badly.

'We believe the fog dragon is being controlled by her. She holds great power, but we don't fully understand how she's controlling it. We know that wherever it goes it sucks the lifeblood out of the living, including the very earth we walk on. It's destroyed colonies and chunks of forest, eating its way across the land.'

The Irksall frowned. 'Why?'

'We believe the fogged beast is looking for Princess Snow,' Bronson said. He fidgeted with a piece of cloth, the material twisting in his fingers.

Brufell gave him a small nod.

'I heard she was poisoned,' said Shatk.

Brufell nodded. 'She was. We don't know if she's awake but there's a lot of people looking for her and she's in danger. A rebellion has formed in her name, and many in the kingdom are willing to overthrow the Evil Queen.'

'So, she's already grown an army?'

'Not exactly,' Brufell replied.

The healer smacked his lips, wiping his hands on his clothes. 'She either has an army or there will be no war. Only death for her. If what you say is true, the Queen already has many followers and an army. She also has magic.' His face contorted on the last line. 'Filthy magic.'

'We believe that if we can find those who are ready to help, we may be able to win. It's a long shot, but we're willing to take it. The Queen won't stop with the Princess. Do not think you will be safe within these mountains while she lives.'

'So, the Princess is the cause of all this?' the Irksall rumbled.

'No!' Bronson chimed in. 'It's the Queen's doing – Myrenna. She controls the dragon.'

'Forgive me, Irksall,' said Shatk, 'but it doesn't matter who controls the fogged beast. We need to know how to kill it and heal our people.'

'It does matter who controls it,' Brufell interrupted, turning to the white robed troll. 'Do not think she will stop when she finds the girl. Once she has Snow, she will have full control. She will be able to move everywhere and anywhere. She will kill and slaughter whenever she likes. Even you in the north will not be safe. She will not stop at Bellatorre. She has Carnell already. She's at war with Perridorm. Her beast roams the forest and mountains. What makes you think you're any different?'

The Irksall frowned at his drink, his large eyebrows covering most of his eyes. 'Skulsheer will protect us.'

'Skulsheer has not come yet,' Brufell pushed. 'You must fight and prove yourself to Skulsheer before you are worthy, remember?'

The Irksall hissed, 'I know my own beliefs.'

'Then you know what I ask of you as payment for our help.'

Shatk jumped to his feet, and pointed a thin finger towards Brufell, his voice full of venom. 'You wish us to fight? In a war that doesn't concern us?'

The Irksall raised his hand, silencing the other troll. 'A debt will only be owed when ya do yer part of the bargain.'

The tension in the tent thickened, the silence heavy. It was as if the wind outside had stopped, the realm going quiet as if it too, waited to hear his answer.

Brufell had always been one to slash a sword first. Diplomacy was a new trick to him, but it was a challenge he would embrace. It was a battle in its own way, but with words instead of weapons. 'I hail from the Mines of Parador. We have a great library – one full of magic and many healing scrolls. There is knowledge there that has won wars, saved thousands.'

At that, the healer's sharp eyes glinted in the candlelight.

Brufell took a breath before continuing. 'I know your aversion to magic, healer. But it's neither good nor evil, it just is. It exists whether we use it to carve our own path or not.'

'We will not succumb to the use of magic,' he seethed. 'It is not right. The Skulsheer would condemn us all.'

'You forget that your Skulsheer is magic, but that's not my point. My point is that the library holds very useful information. Information you need.' By this point, Brufell's voice was pleading. 'When I entered your camp, someone mentioned a dragon in these parts. Not the fog dragon but a real dragon, one that hails from the clouds above, where giants roam. Is this true?' He was met with silence. 'Because if it is, fate has smiled kindly on you.'

'There was a sighting,' the Irksall confirmed, taking another sip of his drink. 'Some of my clan even went to kill it. Use its meat as food. We wanted to salt it, keep it cool to get us through winter.'

Bronson snorted but hushed at Brufell's glare.

'Why does a dragon matter?' the healer spat, his full attention on Brufell.

'Because, Shatk,' Brufell began. 'The tooth of a dragon can restore someone's lifeblood.'

The healer's eyes widened, his mouth curling in disgust as he turned to his leader. 'He does not know what he is saying! A dragon cannot be a cure. It is a killer and one that has taken its wrath out on us.'

The Irksall watched the older dwarf, assessing him for any sign of a lie. 'You swear on it?'

'I swear on my own kin.'

'Enough to make a promise?' the Irksall asked.

Brufell knew the ties to a promise and, though he hated it, he gave a curt nod. The Irksall smiled as he raised his cup. 'Then a promise it is. If this is true, dwarf, then it looks like we're going dragon hunting.'

The healer threw his hands in the air as Brufell gave the Irksall a smile, holding his stare. 'And then we go to war.'

Sweat coated Malak's back, fear potent in his mouth as the forest lashed out. He swung his sword desperately, only managing to keep the moving branches at bay. But no matter how many he felled, only more came. The others were spurred into action behind him, Pip and Florian shouting as the horse reared on its hind legs. Malak barely missed the animal's front hooves as he dodged another branch.

He could barely make out Florian's screams, his efforts to calm the stallion failing miserably. Malak hardly registered as the branches whipped his skin when he heard the undeniable scream of Snow and froze. It was enough for the branches to get one up on him and smack him in the stomach. He stumbled back, wheezing at the impact when another branch lashed out.

From the corner of his eye, he could make out Snow. She crawled along the ground, fighting her own battle as Pip shrieked something he couldn't decipher. Malak slashed and parried and fought. Each step brought him closer to the Princess, where he could protect her.

The ground rumbled as roots broke from the earth, overtaking every inch of the forest path. Malak barely missed another whip when Snow screamed so loud that it sliced into his heart.

Malak stumbled, catching himself as Snow's feet slid into the brush and disappeared. He roared as he swung again, his sword an extension of his arm. The woods seemed to scream as he slashed the writhing branches into splinters. As a troll, he wasn't as swift as Hansel, but he held brute strength that the huntsman did not.

A flash came from his left and Malak twisted to see Florian, screaming in a high-pitched voice as a branch latched onto his feet and swung him upside down. Malak ducked as the Prince was violently swung around. Florian sneezed mid-scream, the branch pausing for a second before he sneezed again.

Malak didn't hesitate. Sword gripped in one hand and his club whacking at the tendrils of branches reaching for him, he slashed at the tree tethering the Prince, screaming a battle cry. He managed to snap one, the next shuddering under his sharp blade and releasing the Prince with a *crack*.

'Take this!' Malak yelled to Florian, shoving his club into the prince's shaking hands.

Malak turned to Pip, who was frantically pulling at his flute, the golden instrument giving off a yellow sheen in the dark. Malak swung again as another vine lashed out. 'What are you doing, Pip?! Go after the Princess!'

The elf placed his mouth on the edge of the instrument and began to play.

Malak shouted again as the music took over. The air fizzled, the magic forming around them. Before he knew it, Malak's limbs moved of their own accord. It was so unlike the metallic tang of magic he had tasted many times before, and he licked his lips. Pink smoke oozed from the pipe as the branches froze.

Suddenly the branches began to sway to the unearthly beat.

Malak's arm twitched before curving around his stomach, trailing a line across his stomach. His foot hit the ground to the beat, his hips following soon after.

And then, he began to dance.

'Pip!' Malak shouted, panic lacing his tone.

Malak's leg came up in a kick, his body twisting into a position he wasn't familiar with. He tried to pull back, to stop, but it was useless. He was a puppet on strings. 'Pip,' he shouted again, but the elf was lost. Far away somewhere in the music.

Malak's sword clattered to the ground, making him grit his teeth with frustration. *What in the cauldron does the elf think he is doing?*

Florian stood before him, arms reaching towards the sky in a pirouette. 'What is happening?' the prince asked, his voice high pitched. 'I seem to be moving without consent.' His arms lifted higher, his toes pointing in a graceful dip.

Malak tried to fight against the hold and failed, his beefy arms swinging out in a circle. His foot slid forward, his toes pointing as his hips followed suit. He growled as his arms reached out to Florian, taking him in a graceful embrace before spinning him elegantly.

'I'll kill him,' Malak roared.

Florian's wide eyes fell on the elf. They were two dolls under the control of their master and his blasted flute. Sweat trickled down Malak's forehead as he strained against the pull. He hated being controlled. Hated being told what to do. Not to mention the fact that Snow was out there. She needed them, needed *him,* and yet he was trapped in a musical cage.

He was going to shove that flute straight down the elf's throat after this.

The troll and the young prince linked arms and began to spin, twisting around each other as if they were at a ball. The branches followed, looping and bending as the music played.

'Stop that blasted flute!' Malak yelled as he twirled Florian, gracefully lowering the Prince into a low dip.

Florian let out a crazed laugh at the absurdity of it all. 'If it wasn't for the pipe, I'd say this is rather lovely.'

'Pip, I swear on the Godmother you'll pay for this!'

'I mean,' Florian began, his breath rough, 'he is saving us, isn't he?'

Malak looked above him at the branches swaying to the beat. They may no longer be under attack, but the troll still had a sick, crawling feeling coating his skin.

Florian's face turned pink as they twirled, his cheeks puffing up. Malak stretched his back, holding his chin high. The forest was his audience and the path his stage. His rough calloused hands swallowed Florian's as they spun, their feet moving in sync. Malak glared at Pip on the forest floor, legs crossed as if he were settling in for story time.

'We don't have time for this,' Malak said turning to Florian.

The Prince's face had puffed up, his eyes watering slightly as he looked apologetically at the troll.

'Why does your face look like that?' Malak said over the music.

'I … I …' Florian gasped, shaking his head. 'I can't hold it.'

Realisation dawned on Malak. As he held Florian's waist, the Prince's face only a pixie from his. 'Don't you even think about—'

Florian's mouth opened and he released the wettest, snottiest sneeze. Mucus flew in Malak's face like rain. He took the Prince into another dip.

Malak held back the bile building in his throat.

It was disgusting.

And phlegmy.

Malak's eye twitched, his hands gripping Florian's tighter than before.

'Ow!' Florian squealed. 'You're holding too tight.'

'Am I?' Malak gritted.

'I'm sorry,' Florian whimpered. 'My allergies.'

But sorry wouldn't be enough.

Malak had always been a calm troll, one who understood things his kin did not, and he liked that about himself. He liked cleanliness. He revered knowledge. And he held his anger in check so well, using his mind instead of brute strength as a preference. But now, his choice was failing him. The anger boiled just below the surface as Florian stepped out, then back in, to the beat. Malak's eyes darkened.

Florian gulped. 'I—'

'If you ever tell anyone about this, I'll deny the whole thing,' Malak said through clenched teeth. 'I'll kill you first. You understand that, right?'

The Prince's cheeks flushed red as the music rose, the branches lashing at each other in smooth, swift motions. Florian's jaw tightened as Malak's large green hands squeezed tight, crushing his small bones. Just as the music hit its peak, Florian dipped again, and Malak smoothly twirled him towards the path.

The troll's dark eyes met Florian's. 'As soon as this stops, you have to find Snow.'

Florian's sweaty hands gripped Malak's as they glided across the dirt. 'Me?'

'You can track,' Malak said. 'You can find where the wood nymphs took her.'

'What about you?' the Prince asked as Malak wrapped him into his chest.

Malak growled from deep inside his throat. 'I'll be dealing with the Pied Piper.'

The Little Red Dragon

Brufell's weapons clinked at his side as his short legs made good time.

'Why did the dragon settle in the Mountains of Eyrie?' Bronson puffed from behind him. They made their way up the mountainside. The incline was steep, leaving the younger dwarf breathless. 'Wouldn't the floating isles be better, considering that's where the dragons once existed? I need to stop.'

Brufell paused and turned to see the young dwarf resting his hands on his knees, his breath coming out in short, sharp bursts. The pixie flew beside him, his tiny wings buzzing.

'I don't know why the dragon settled here,' Brufell replied. 'But it isn't important. There's another band of trolls in this region and we need to keep moving.'

'How are you not tired?' Bronson huffed, his face flushed. 'Are you made of steel?'

'Surely for one so young you should be able to keep up.'

'And you should be retired.'

Brufell snorted before his eyes softened at his kin. 'You have one minute.'

Whilst Bronson sat down, Brufell looked ahead. He could see the faint green outline of Tuk as the troll stopped and waved down at them. It was just the four of them. The Irksall, still recovering from his injuries, had remained with his clan, sending his second, Tuk in his stead. The grinning troll was certainly rough around the edges, but at least he'd stopped looking at Brufell like a snack.

Brufell had told Bronson it hadn't mattered why the dragon had settled here, but something about it gnawed under his skin. It was a question he'd asked himself many times since agreeing to help the trolls.

The halls of Parador were full of stories, including ones about dragons and old kings. They even had a hall of heroes, where art displayed stories in vivid carvings. He remembered being a small dwarf and sneaking there, staring at the armour and war trophies of the great dwarves before him.

There had been one story he'd sat in front of and admired for hours: the squares of art outlining the tale of a great dwarven dragon rider named Frode. He'd followed the story dozens of times, his fingers trailing over Frode's twisted limbs and the dragon's wings. But it was one scene where Frode sat on the dragon's back, the entire colony of dwarves watching from below, that he'd favoured most.

'You might not be tired, but aren't you even the slightest bit afraid?' Bronson asked, pulling Brufell out of his daze.

Brufell dusted off his pants, the dirt flying free from weeks of build-up. 'Afraid of what?'

Bronson threw his hands up. 'Oh, I don't know. Maybe you're afraid because we're on the run from an evil queen? Or because we survived Troll's Keep and somehow became friends with trolls? Oh! Or maybe because we're about *TO WALK INTO A DRAGONS DEN!*'

Brufell stared at him. 'Are you afraid?'

Bronson shook his head slightly, the kohl around his eyes bringing out the colour of gold. 'Of course I'm afraid. I've been attacked, I've been kidnapped, I've been starved, lost, beaten. I'm tired, Brufell, and not just from this mountain.'

'I know the journey has been hard, cousin. On all of us,' Brufell admitted quietly, rubbing at the ache in his chest. His bones had seen more than their fair share of battle. 'But war is coming. It's already *here* for places like Perridorm. The Queen means to conquer this realm until we're all but a footnote in the ashes of the history she rewrites. We need allies and if it means a debt owed from trolls and braving a dragon's den, then that's what we will do. For the Seven. The Princess. The realm.'

'The realm is cruel,' Bronson pouted.

Brufell nodded. 'Yes, it is. Things crawl in the dark. But remember, darkness and light both exist here. Magic breathes magic, and where there is evil, there is good. You've been sheltered, and I fear in our complicity to protect you we've also hindered you. I cannot comfort you here, I can only tell you to hone that fear. The way you have done before.'

Bronson's eyes watered, but before he could respond there was a shout from ahead. Tuk waved from a narrow path further up, before pointing towards what looked to be a cave entrance. He lumbered ahead, a buoyancy in his steps that Brufell didn't feel.

Brufell reached out his hand. 'Our minute is up. We need to keep moving.'

Bronson followed, but his shoulders sagged as if he held the weight of their conversation. The pixie flew ahead, its short wings fluttering across the rocky ground.

Brufell's eyes roamed the dusky mountains. He craned his head at how far the highest peak disappeared into the sky, hidden behind streaks of red and orange, sunset not far off. The clouds puffed around its edges, white with specks of grey, like sea foam. Peaceful, almost.

Until a throaty caw shattered the air, a wave of black cresting the sky.

Tuk yelled from above, his loud bellow ringing down the mountainside like a deep horn, and Brufell noted a shadow within the clouds. It moved differently to the clouds, sharper more succinct.

Fear raced up Brufell's spine. He lunged for Bronson, grabbing the cringing dwarf by his vest and hauling him up the rocky incline, squashing them both into the narrow gap of rock that hid them from above.

'My kohl,' Bronson gasped, crestfallen as his signature eyeliner tumbled out of his pocket. It rolled down the incline, lost to the mountain as Brufell gripped him tight enough to bruise.

'*Shh,*' Brufell hissed.

Bronson went to argue but froze as the sky turned to a shrieking swarm of black, raw cries smothering the clouds with an inky spiral of feathers and claws. The sound ricocheted inside Brufell's skull, and he hoped Tuk had also found cover.

Brufell dared a peek through a narrow crack in the rock. As the cloud of crows descended, the echoes filled the mountains, bouncing off the rocks like a thousand bells. Dozens and dozens of them flew, their beady eyes scanning the land below.

'The Queen's murders,' Bronson whispered.

The older dwarf held his breath. He dared not move, his arm braced across Bronson's chest. The pixie hid in a tight crevice. Had the Queen's crows followed them, found out their plans, or did they continue to search for the lost princess? Brufell could only hope that Snow remained hidden, that everything they'd done hadn't been for nothing.

All three of them held their breaths as the murders spun back before flying over the mountains closer to the south. When they were gone Brufell yanked Bronson's tunic, bringing them back into the light. 'We need to move faster.'

'Does that mean the Princess is still safe?' Bronson asked, gathering his belongings.

'As safe as she'll ever be while the Queen lives. Come on.'

They raced up the mountain and met Tuk on a narrow path carved into the surface of the mountainside. Tuk waved them on, the troll now eyeing the sky at intervals should the crows return.

By dusk, they had set up camp on a broad ledge near the mountain's peak. Tuk sat by Bronson, the dwarf smacking the troll away when he leaned in for a sniff.

Brufell wandered towards the edge of the camp and looked out before him. The view was magnificent. The mountains spread out below them, served like a fine dish. The cloud line hovered like a roof under the stars. He could see the valleys and the ruby sheen of the river against the dying sunlight. He felt like he stood in the sky, staring down below at the realm as if they were tiny cogs in a giant clock. It unnerved him. Mostly because he enjoyed the tunnels and the safety that came with them. He was a dwarf through and through. And it was a heritage he was proud of.

On his left, the flutter of small wings let him know the pixie was nearby. The creature's scarred little body looked savage against the serenity below as it settled on the soft grass at his feet.

Brufell smiled. 'I suppose we should give you a name if you're sticking around. What about Blue?'

The pixie twitched its nose in disgust.

'No?' Brufell asked, trying to think of a name that would suit. 'How about Pix?'

The creature gagged.

Brufell tried to think of names that were relevant. The creature had stolen their food upon their first meeting. He'd also bitten the trolls when they had attacked. He could try for something soft, but that wouldn't do. 'What about Oryx? It's a type of metal found in Parador. It's a tough blue stone, like you.'

The pixie considered it before he puffed out his chest, and nodded. Oryx it was.

'You know, Oryx, I've never seen a dragon,' Brufell began. 'But I know of a dwarf who has. His name was Frode.'

Oryx's eye shone in the darkness as the fire crackled behind them. Turning towards the dwarf, the pixie crossed his legs and waited.

Brufell chuckled. 'You want a story?'

The pixie nodded, eager.

'I usually leave those to Bonyx, but considering he's not here I suppose it's up to me.' He lifted his axe and sword from his straps and placed them carefully on the ground, then swung his feet over the ledge. He reconsidered, and shuffled back from the sharp drop.

He was brave, not stupid.

'Frode had been born on the coldest winter in the second age of the dwarves. That's a long time ago, if you don't know.' He cleared his throat, trying to shake off how wrong it felt to be telling the story instead of Bonyx. 'Frode was born so small that the birthing maiden had called him a monster. You see, Oryx, his bones had been weak, bent slightly and morphed. But, despite his condition, his mother still loved him. She ignored the cries from the others to kill him, and told him to do the same.

'As he grew, it was apparent that his limbs weren't improving, growing at odd angles. The dwarf king blamed mixed blood as the cause and, as such, deemed the deformed dwarf an abomination.

'In her love, Frode's mother hid him away amongst the furthest reaches of the caverns. She would bring him food and toys. By day, she would leave him to work in the forges, and by night she would tell stories so he did not feel so alone. Sometimes she would bring him gifts. Little trinkets and tricky machines that he loved to take apart and put back together. For a dwarf so broken, he had a great talent for creating beautiful things.

'Sometimes he would sneak out, following his mother, and watch her work. He felt as if his bones had been bent because he was trapped, the weight of stone too heavy for his body, like the bulk of the mountain itself pressed upon him.

'One night, Frode overheard a tale of a secret door at the top of the mountain. Once his mother was asleep, Frode climbed the great halls to find this magical door. Several cycles he did this, never finding it. Until the night of a great celebration: the King's birthday.

'But Frode cared little for the King. What mattered was what he had found – a door, hidden within an ancient carving of a great dwarven queen. When he placed his hand in hers, the stone wrist twisted, and a gateway yawned open. For the first time in his life, Frode stepped beyond the mountain and saw the stars.'

The pixie's eyes darted up to the night sky and silence crept in. Turning around, he noticed Tuk and Bronson had approached.

'Go on,' Bronson said.

A flush crept up his cheeks and Brufell ran his finger along the hilt of his axe. 'Bonyx does a far better job.'

Taking a seat, Bronson gave him an encouraging smile. 'Bonyx isn't here, and you have a story to tell. What did Frode do next?'

'Well,' Brufell said gruffly, his cheeks warm. 'Frode sat at the door and stared at the stars every night. They became his friends and his companions. He shared his secrets, his wants, his desires, and so on. Until, one night, something changed.'

'What happened?' Bronson asked.

'On that night,' Brufell said, 'Frode saw a dark cloud cover the stars. It moved like the wind, soaring towards the mountain with such ferocity that Frode grew wary. He felt the stars blink at him. Warning him, perhaps. All he knew was that the shadow grew larger as it came closer, turning into huge, leathery wings that spun in circles.'

Bronson leaned in, urging Brufell to continue.

'When the shape landed at the top of the mountain, Frode felt a vibration along the walls. But Frode was a curious dwarf. He couldn't resist the mystery. He followed a path leading from the door up the cliffside. When he reached the top, he found himself face to face with a red dragon.'

The pixie hiccupped as he gorged on some biscuits.

'How much has he eaten today?' Brufell asked.

'Not enough, or he wouldn't still be hungry,' Bronson replied.

'Oryx could eat a whole field.'

Bronson smirked. 'Named the pixie, have you?'

'More Frode,' Tuk insisted, watching Brufell keenly, for once not looking at him like he might be a meal.

Brufell stole a biscuit and held back a laugh at the pixie's creased brow. 'Frode had never seen a dragon before. The creature was smaller than expected. The dragon was hesitant but did not fly away as Frode approached. Instead, it spoke to him.

'"*Why do your limbs twist the way they do?*" it asked.

'"*They say I'm broken,*" Frode replied.

'"*Who are they?*" the little dragon asked.

'"*The dwarves.*"

'"*What is a dwarf?*"

'Frode had frowned at the question. So great were his mother's tales of the dwarves that he assumed everyone knew of them. Thinking carefully, Frode answered. "*Dwarves are dwarves. They live underground and carve many great halls. They mine the earth and live best in the mountains.*"

'The dragon considered him, its red tail sliding across the slope. "*Then why are you out here above the world when you live best in a mountain?*"

'"*Because I am not like the others,*" Frode replied.

'"*I'm not like the others either,*" said the dragon.

'"*And why are you here?*" Frode asked.

'"*I've lost my mother.*"

'Frode thought of losing his own mother and decided that it wouldn't do. "*You can share my mother,*" said Frode.

'"*I cannot have a dwarf for a mother. I am a dragon.*"

'"*Where did you last see your mother?*"

'"*Above the clouds. I'd just learnt to fly, and she was teaching me to hunt but I dove too low. I wait here to see if I can find her.*"

'Frode was sad for the dragon. No mother and no dinner would not do. "*Do you plan to wait here a long while?*" Frode asked.

'"*Long enough that she shall find me.*"

'"*How will you eat?*"

'"*I do not know,*" the dragon said.

'"*I shall help you,*" Frode declared.

'Climbing back down through his secret door, Frode took a leg of ham and some bread from the kitchens. Upon his return, the dragon was curled in a ball, its eyes glassy. Frode placed the food before him. "*I do not know what dragons eat, but this is what I can manage.*"

'"*Thank you, dwarf. How can I repay you?*"

'Frode thought carefully before he asked if he could hear about the dragons.

'So, for several nights, instead of talking to the stars, Frode listened. When over a week had passed, Frode brought his new friend food and found the dragon solemn, tears sliding down its red scales.

'"*Are you okay, little dragon?*" Frode asked.

'"*I fear my mother has forgotten me,*" the dragon said.

'"*Mothers do not forget their children,*" said Frode. "*Why do you not fly home to find her?*"

'"*I do not know the way. I cannot fly alone.*"

'"*Then you shall not fly alone. Where is it you live?*"

'"*In the floating isles.*"

'"*Then the floating isles is where we shall go,*" Frode declared.

'Upon the next night, Frode snuck into the library and went through many scrolls before he found a map of the realm. In his excitement, he ran towards the secret door and scrambled to the top. But Frode was not alone.

'In the shadows, his mother watched, for she had seen him leaving and did not know where he went. Crawling up the hill to the dragon, his mother followed, watching as Frode struggled to climb with the scroll in hand.

'When Frode met the little dragon, he was not met with thanks but a wild roar that shook the hills. For the red dragon had seen Frode's mother where he had not.

'When she saw her crippled son with such a ferocious beast, she grabbed Frode and cried, *"What are you doing, my son? Running away to spend time with a beast!"*

'In his plea, Frode ran towards the dragon and spread out his arms so as to protect him. *"I am also called a beast, but you have told me I am not just because others say so. Are you so quick to be like the rest?"*

'Frode's mother dropped to her knees. *"But you are still a dwarf!"*

'*"And he a dragon,"* Frode said. *"I will not let you harm him."*

'*"It is not me who shall harm, but him!"* she said, pointing to the beast. *"I'm your poor mother, and upon this night I shall be killed."*

'The little dragon's wing curled across Frode as his mother watched in terror. *"I will not let you hurt my son!"* she cried, before pulling out a sharp knife.

'The red dragon roared, his chest rumbling like a storm. The mother dwarf dived, the knife glinting in the dark as she shot forward.

'*"Get on my back!"* the dragon cried, and Frode obeyed.

'*"I do not have a saddle,"* poor Frode said, gripping to the dragon's scales.

'*"Then you must hold on tight!"*

'And with that, the dragon and the crippled dwarf shot into the skies. Wind blew at Frode's knotted hair, his fingers barely holding on as the dragon swept into the night, rising to meet the very stars that Frode had watched.

'They were in a universe of light. Twinkling white surrounded them, the air frigid and wild against Frode's skin. His bones ached from the cold, but did the dwarf let go? No, he did not.'

Bronson's eyes lit up as Brufell's hand moved like tiny flying birds.

'Did he make it?' Bronson asked, 'To the floating isles?'

Brufell smiled and understood why Bonyx did what he did. Telling the story and controlling the narrative was a piece of magic in itself, a way to share history and an adventure in terms others would understand. Leaning forward, the old dwarf grinned. 'They did.'

'What next?' Tuk asked, holding the remnants of a bone from dinner.

'They found the dragon's mother,' Brufell continued. 'She was overjoyed when her youngling had been brought home. She was, of course, far larger than her son, but Frode hadn't minded. It was the first time Frode had been welcomed. He lived with them for a time, learning to work with the dragons and flying by their side as they hunted, and the red dragon grew.

'But over time, Frode missed his mother. He wondered what had happened to her and his kin. He remembered her love and the stories she told. Just as the dwarves had misunderstood him, his mother had misunderstood the little dragon. To make things right, he and the dragon flew back to Frode's old home.

'They landed on a warm afternoon and Frode walked through the hidden door that he had come to know, but he hadn't been welcomed by his mother. He searched far and wide for her, but she was gone. The home lay untouched, the halls half-forgotten and the forges dark. In his desperation, the crippled dwarf approached the King. The crowd flinched at his appearance as he entered the royal quarter, but Frode didn't care as much as he once did. He stood tall – well, as tall as he could – and approached the throne.

'The King looked old, his beard white and withered, the lines across his face etched with scars and cracked like dry soil.

'"*I am Frode,*" the crippled dwarf declared. "*I return to find my mother.*"

'The King was disgusted at such a dwarf, scowling at the bent and broken thing before him. "*You have no mother. You are a beast!*"

'"*I am no beast, I am a dwarf, and I have come for my mother.*"

'It was then the crowd parted, and standing there, her brown curls frizzing under the candlelight, was an older woman with a cane. But Frode knew her eyes – the shade of warmest chocolate – and he shouted in glee.

'"*My Frode,*" she said. "*I thought you were dead.*"

'"*I am not dead, I am alive, and I am here for you.*"

'"*But what of the dragon?*" she asked.

'"*He's here with me. I rode him here from the floating isles to come find you.*"

'"*Lies!*" cried the King. "*No dwarf has ever ridden a dragon. Never since our creation.*"

'"*I have seen the dragon,*" Frode's mother said. "*I told as much when Frode left us.*"

'"*Stories told to children.*" The King waved. "*Kill the ugly beast!*"

Brufell grinned at the gaping mouths of his companions, playing with his voice in a way he'd never done. It seemed he, too, had fallen into his story.

'Frode ignored the King and the King's guards. Taking his mother's hands, he said, *"Come with me. You shall love to fly. Leave the forge behind you. You are too old now to work there. Come with me, and I shall care for you as you once cared for me."*

"'Oh, Frode," she replied. *"The forges are all but done. They lie cold and have done for years. Nothing can ignite them."*

"'Dragon fire could," Frode said.

The King laughed. *"You are full of lies. You have no dragon."*

"'I shall light your forges if you let us go," Frode said with more bravery than he felt. *"I shall bring back the beating heart of this kingdom. Or will you kill me without trial? Without proof?"*

"'You are no dwarf," the King said. *"There will be no trial for you."*

'At that, the walls shuddered, the caverns echoing a monstrous sound. The roar of a dragon. The King shook as Frode smiled. *"I shall light your forges, and you shall let us go."* Frode lifted two fingers and whistled. The call bounced off the walls, and in moments a great red dragon dropped from the ceiling.

'The dwarves fled in terror. The King hid under his throne as Frode turned to his friend. The dragon's stomach rumbled, and a burst of fire shot from its maw and ignited the frozen forge. Orange and red and blue blazed through the caverns in raging light. Taking his mother's hands, Frode carried her onto the dragon's back.

'*"What is your name?"* the King asked.

'*"I am Frode."*

'The crowd shouted in applause, calling out his name in a song and a cry. *"Frode the dragon rider!"* they yelled, filling his blood with glee.

'Frode spent many long years with the dragons and his mother, outliving even some of the oldest dwarves. He wrote a chronicle of his life, which I believe still sits within the libraries of Parador. It's how we know of the dragon tooth and its healing properties. It's how I know that a dragon living in a cave is not common. Dragons like to fly free just as Frode wished to fly free.

'You asked me earlier, Bronson, if I was afraid. I am afraid. But not because of a dragon. I'm afraid that we'll fail, and I will never see you or the rest of the Seven again.'

Brufell let the silence linger as he finished, his breath a little uneven.

Bronson's eyes watered, black beginning to bleed onto his cheeks from the kohl. 'I want to be more like Frode.'

Brufell couldn't help but smile as he said, 'Me too.'

XVI

The Tune of The Pied Piper

There was a tug from the recesses of Rumple's memory as he scratched at the damp stone beneath him. His mind had been spinning, pushing him under as it always did. A silent battle between himself and the memories of friends and foes. He twisted, groaning as he fought against vision after vision. One broke through like shattered glass, cutting at the walls of his fractured mind.

For so long he'd believed he couldn't be broken. He'd spent an age building his walls and empire to protect himself. And upon the full moon he'd not only bent, but snapped entirely, uttering the one secret he'd tried so hard to hide.

Nona.

Would Nona forgive him? Would she ever come for him?

No.

She didn't react that way. Didn't see things in the same ways as others.

The Seer. The Creator. The fourth Grimm.

She blazed in his mind in blinding colours, her red tent and grey eyes burning into his skull.

He hit himself, the pain a reprieve from the searing memory. He'd not meant to break. Had never meant to break. He'd sworn an age ago that he would take her secret to her grave.

There had been four Grimms, four sisters. But most histories only mentioned three.

She'd hired him to do it that way, to work through the minds of those who knew and seal it away in an unknown place that nobody could find.

He'd sworn. And he'd broken it.

The Queen's eyes had glowed in joy at the name. Faint recognition morphing her features like a mother recognising their child.

He'd been weak. And now he would pay for the betrayal.

He squeezed his eyes shut as the tug came again. It was small. A tiny pinprick on his wrinkly skin. He felt a shift in the air. One that was warm, unlike the freezing cage around him.

It was magic. Magic he was familiar with. Magic he'd not felt in an age. It echoed through his memory, breaking through the fog of wherever else he'd been. His nose twitched as he sniffed the air. Caramel and sugar filled his lungs. His fingers roved along the cold stone wall of his prison. He lifted his head, pointed ears pricked as he listened for the sound.

It was a beating heart in a world of colour. It was a symphony. Life and joy and grief wrapped into one melody. Rumple relished it.

As it reached its peak, he lifted his crooked fingers and grasped at the air like trying to catch a firefly in daylight. It had been fifty years since he'd heard this music. Fifty years since the song had burrowed into his very soul. The pied piper was playing again. And though Rumple sat beneath the dungeons of Bellatorre, covered in blood and scum, he hummed.

For music healed better than any medicine in the world.

Malak tackled Pip just as the music ceased, smacking away the pipe like a disease. The elf's bones popped as he hit the ground. He was a mere leaf to the tree that Malak was. Slight and delicate and small.

But Malak didn't care. Fire filled his core at the memory of dancing cheek to cheek with Florian. The mucus from his sneeze still took residence on his face. 'Pick that flute up again and I'll club you to death,' Malak growled.

Pip's eyes grew large as Malak hovered over him. He wasn't so smart-mouthed now. The branches receded, folding back into themselves as if they'd never awoken. Pip pushed against Malak with little success and went limp. 'I suppose a "thank you" for saving your lives isn't coming anytime soon?'

Malak gritted his teeth. 'You saved nobody. The Princess is taken, and that snivelling Prince is all we have to track her.'

'Then why are we still here?' Pip frowned. His hands smacked Malak's large green bicep. 'Get off me, you fool. If she's gone, we must find her.'

Malak sighed and released him. He stood, dusting off his elbows, and eyed where the horse had bolted. The blasted animal had ridden off, taking most of their belongings with it. 'Snow could be anywhere by now,' Malak began, glaring at Pip. 'No thanks to you.'

Pip grumbled something unintelligible as he grabbed at the flute a few pixies away.

'If you're wanting to say something, Pip, just say it.'

Placing the chain back around his neck, Pip eyed the troll. 'I said,' Pip began, 'that trolls are blockheaded fools.'

Malak growled. 'And elves are useless – free or enslaved.'

Pip pressed his mouth into a thin line before heading for the trees.

'What?' Malak asked. 'Nothing wise to share now?'

Pip shook before turning around. 'I will not be chastised by someone so young and naïve. Florian can at least track, and I can provide knowledge of the wood nymphs who took her. What do you have, Malak? A club? You have no knowledge of the creatures who dwell here, or any ability to hunt Snow down when you lose her. You have neither the skill nor the experience to help her in this instance and you punish me for my quick thinking? I saved you with that quick thinking, I'll add. You may not have liked it, but are you alive? Does your heart continue to beat? You stand here arguing with me and hating me because I played my flute. Now you know exactly why I don't like to use it. And instead of thanking me, you attack me.'

Malak stood by the tree line, his shoulders deflating. Pip's words hit him like a blow. Despite his stature, Pip somehow managed to look down his nose at the troll and it made Malak feel five years old again.

He eyed the path where Snow was taken and, without so much as a glance at the elf, began to break through the brush. He was still angry, but the little pest was right: Snow took precedence over everything.

But right now, he didn't have to admit it.

XVII
The Unexpected Visitor

Dread flew hard and fast.

He aimed for the tallest tower as night covered the land. Lights flickered below him in shades of gold and white as the city began to fall to sleep. It reminded him of the sea at night with the reflecting stars. Where the old gods watched and judged. Even now, he felt them watching. The ones who had dwelled even before the Godmother and the Grimms. Gods he knew to fear.

He held back a shudder.

He tucked his wings in tight as he dived, the city clear. At this height he could see the bright coloured paints of the houses, the dips and curves of the cobblestone streets as tiny black figures hunched towards their destinations. A drunken man cried below, the echo of a song following.

Dread veered to his right and eyed the castle's towers, the white glow piercing the night. He could make out the Queen's favourite window on one of the lower towers. When she wasn't with her mirror, she spent it there, poring over the same scrolls again and again. He'd watched her from the sky sometimes, stared as her dark hair fell over her shoulders, the silky strands shining against the candlelight.

That same candlelight flickered as he approached. The flap of his wings and a caw was all he needed to announce his arrival. She met him at the window and without a word snatched the scroll from his talons.

Her fingers yanked the ribbon, pulling apart the paper with such fervour that Dread tilted his head.

Her red lips twisted into a wicked smile as she turned towards him. 'Stay hidden and stand guard. I'll be going out for a while.'

He nodded and spread his wings, letting the night air lift him into the sky. With a loud caw, he called to his murders, each one crying back in symphony.

Snow awoke covered by a strange cloth, cocooned so tightly that when she moved, the whole thing shifted with her. She blew a strand of hair from her face, blinking against the murky light.

Frowning, she reached out and tugged at the scratchy material. It stretched open slightly, revealing a sky tangled with branches. She turned, trying to get a better sense of her surroundings when the world lurched.

She squealed as everything flipped, her body slipping free from the cloth. Instinct took over and she scrambled for purchase, latching herself onto the material that had betrayed her. It stretched and swayed with her weight, bouncing in time with her panicked movements.

That's when she realised.

It wasn't just cloth. It was a hammock.

Heart pounding, Snow swallowed hard and dared to look at the forest floor below.

Way, way below.

Snow's breath came fast and shallow as she clung to the hammock, her fingers digging into the coarse fabric. The forest floor swayed far beneath her, a tangle of roots and shifting shadows. Her pulse pounded in her ears, but it wasn't loud enough to drown out the sound slithering through the trees.

Click. Click. Click.

A shudder ripped through her. That unnatural sound crawled beneath her skin like cold fingers tracing along her spine. It was the last thing she'd heard before the darkness had swallowed her whole.

Her grip tightened, knuckles white against the rough weave of the hammock. She swallowed hard, forcing herself to stay still.

'Silly,' a voice chided.

Snow jolted at the sound, finding a wood nymph standing nearby. It held a bowl, its lipid eyes blinking at her as it watched from a makeshift wooden platform. Its grassy hair was thick and long, flowing down its body and gnarled limbs in a waterfall of green leaves.

Snow's throat went dry, the dizziness threatening to overwhelm her as she held back her nausea. She was so *high*. 'Help,' she whispered, her voice coming out raspy.

The wood nymph rolled its eyes. 'Silly, silly.' It placed down the bowl and turned its back to the Princess.

Her clammy hands started slipping. 'I said help me!'

Shaking its head, the creature moved to a small crevice where its wooden fingers disappeared. Its tongue poked out as it searched for something.

Snow squealed as the branch holding her moved, shuffling her towards the platform. With a thump, her body hit the solid wood of the platform, and she scrambled away from the ledge.

'Silly,' the wood nymph said again, collecting the bowl.

'How was I supposed to know …' Snow started. The wood nymph moved away. 'Hey!' she called. 'Where are you going?'

She tried to follow, the narrow ledge creaking under her weight. Her chest contracted as she realised how thin the platform was. She bit on her lip, choking down her fear as she tried to follow the nymph, but it didn't slow down. In fact, she could have sworn it quickened its steps.

'Hey! Stop!' she called again. Her muscles trembled, vertigo taking hold. She dug her nails into the bark of a tree for security.

The wood nymph ignored her, moving with ease towards some large, twisted vines. Beyond, she noted more platforms, some carved, others melded wood. The nymph crossed a trunk attached between two lush trees.

Bridges, she realised.

The bridge the nymph crossed linked to another platform and another tree. More hammocks littered the area. More platforms. More *everything.* As if every structure floated amongst the top of the forest.

Snow gasped. At first glance, she'd seen only treetops and the long fall should she drop from the sky. But staring at it now, watching the nymph skip across the trunks, she realised it was a city. A very neat, very clever city.

From this distance, the specifics were lost, but she noticed doorways in trunks, the flicker of a light in a window. There were staircases and balconies and roads attaching every tree to another route. A nymph carried a screaming child, another blew leaves out of a carved window. There was the pop of a nymph as it scuttled along one of the platforms in a hurry.

'How many of you are there?' she breathed in wonder.

By now, the creature had turned around a bend. Snow ran after the nymph, only to watch as it walked straight into the trunk.

And disappeared.

Snow halted and reached out her hand, trailing her fingers over the bark where it had gone but finding nothing. There was no door. No entrance. She pressed her fingers harder, feeling for a groove or latch, when she heard another clicking sound. She twisted around and caught another wood nymph coming out of another tree with a *pop.*

She held her breath, but the jerk of her fingers caught its gaze. Its huge, depthless eyes locked on Snow for a moment. Then it backed away and dashed back into the bark.

'What in the Godmother is happening?' Snow whispered, wondering if she'd hit her head and this was all just a warped dream.

Pop—!

Snow swung around at the sharp crack of noise behind her, pivoting again at the cascading sounds of *pops* and bursts that flooded the forest.

She turned so fast, her eyes racing to keep up with what she was seeing. Nymphs moved in and out of the trees in succinct and silent motions. Some had hair filled with flowers sprouting from their heads, whilst others had moss or grass. Tiny lights flickered like fairylight from bulbs throughout the trees, casting a haunting glow over the creatures.

The ladders and bridges and bark stretched and grew, each tree with a different shape and platform. Some of the nymphs were smaller than others, crying out when their parents morphed into wood.

Her legs crumpled and she fell onto the platform, eyes wide at the busy scene before her. She'd been taken, stolen away like she meant nothing, and then discarded by the nymphs like a forgotten doll. A plaything. She sucked in a deep breath, trying to remember how to stay calm. This wasn't the castle, there were no walls or spells keeping her in.

You will never be trapped again, a voice in her mind promised, *This is not the Silver City.*

She'd barely had a moment to collect herself when another *pop* sounded and the wood nymph with the bowl was back.

Snow backed away, her heart thrumming so fast she was sure it would burst. She bared her teeth, growling in threat at the creature as it neared.

The nymph only sighed, looming over her with an air of quiet exasperation. Yet they had stolen *her*.

The snap of a branch from far below made Snow flinch, her hands curled into fists, arms trembling as she tried desperately to remember what Hansel had taught her.

Feet braced, hands up to protect her face. Knee to the groin and flee to safety.

Which worked great in theory when she wasn't wearing a tattered dress and stained slippers, her body bruised and battered.

Snow tensed as the wood nymph dropped the bowl, not bothering to acknowledge her fighting stance as it peered over the edge of the narrow platform they shared. Her heart stuttered inside her chest as its mossy eyes widened, clearly unsettled by what it saw below.

The nymph started backing away as she crept closer, stupidly intrigued by what could scare a wood nymph enough to make it scuttle back. She searched the ground, fighting vertigo as she held onto a branch, and gasped at the hint of pale blonde hair she saw tucked between pockets of mahogany and green. She didn't dare hope, until she heard his telltale sneezing.

Snow lunged for the edge, desperate as she called, 'Florian!'

The wood nymph was by her side in a second, its fingers latching onto her elbow. Snow threw the nymph off, growling like some animal. She could be as wild and as unhinged as the dark hounds if it meant freedom. Meant seeing her friends.

The wood nymph glowered at her, clicking something she couldn't understand. But she didn't care, not when Florian was so close.

'Florian!'

The nymph tugged her again and she lashed out. Her fingers yanked its hair, and she threw it over the edge. The nymph's scream tore through the treetops, a raw, piercing sound that sent a shudder through Snow's bones. She watched, wide-eyed, as its body tumbled, limbs flailing in a blur of bark covered skin and tangled hair.

Leaves and twigs snapped in its wake, a violent cascade of motion, but instead of the sickening crunch of impact, there was … nothing. No thud. No final gasp.

The shrieking cut off abruptly.

A branch lashed out from nowhere, snapping the creature up and stealing it away. Breathing hard, Snow considered what she had done. She had almost killed it. But, surely, she had a right to live when she'd been trapped like a butterfly in a jar for so long?

Overwhelmed, her eyes welled up, her body shaking with shock. Florian was still below, his steps as clunky as a troll in the dark. But before she could call his name again, her scream was muffled by a hand over her mouth, a dozen nymphs clamouring to keep her contained. She pushed back, only for their grip to tighten.

A wood nymph snarled in warning as she thrashed, a group of them holding her down. She blinked back tears as Florian's voice echoed from below, the call of her name so close and yet so far away.

Snow fought back, tossing her body on the platform when the nymph with the bowl appeared again. 'Silly,' it seethed.

Several nymphs pinned her down and she kicked out, her heels smashing the wooden platform in the hopes Florian would hear her. She gnashed her teeth as one of their hands slipped, and she bit hard into its wooden arm. It yelped as a sharp jolt spread through her jaw. Most likely a tooth, and she tasted blood.

Spitting it out, she growled. 'Get your creepy little fingers away from me! Florian! FLORIAN!'

Just as she managed to kick off another one, the nymph with the bowl growled at her, and smashed her across the head.

Stars blinked across her vision, her mind racing with every possibility, every angle. She would not be trapped. Not again. Never again.

Her rage coiled inside her, bellowing and burning. Snarling, Snow dived, her nails ready to scrape, regardless of the fall below. The spindly fingers loosened as she pushed. Just as she thought she would break free, more *pops* echoed, the wood nymphs arriving in droves. Snow was tackled, fingers and arms and limbs trapping her. She cried out as they pulled her against the tree, yanking her inwards. The bark burned, piercing flesh. She shrieked at the top of her lungs—

Until the tree swallowed her whole.

Dread waited at the broken edge of the castle's aviary, watching as the Queen paced on her balcony. He'd stood at this vantage point on so many occasions, waiting for her to step into the open night and invite him into her rooms. To beckon him to her.

But she never did.

Tonight was no different. Dread hid in the shadows of a pillar, his Queen muttering something under breath. She'd morphed into an old crone before his eyes, her once-smooth skin now saggy under her sleek black cape. He noted the hunch in her back and the way her hand curved as she lifted her wrinkled wrist.

The sky thundered above him, lightning spearing down as the Queen did her work. He couldn't deny the thrill he got when he saw her change. The quickening pace of his heart every time she used her power. It beat through him, like a jolt of energy he retained and released only for her.

His change was painful and slow. But hers was pure, undiluted magic.

He loved it. Loved her.

The night lit up in a white blaze, the old crone breaking free in a flurry of black ash. By the second flash, she was gone.

Dread smiled from the shadows, his eyes searching the sky for one more glimpse and finding nothing. Content, he stood there for a while as the rain fell in sheets around him. His hair was drenched, his clothes dripping as he stared at where she'd been. Even when she was gone, her presence lingered.

He knew she'd gone to the grave to find whatever it was she was looking for. He didn't understand the disguise, but Myrenna never did anything without motive.

He twisted one of the rings on his fingers absently when a groan echoed from behind him. He turned, and saw the dark shape of a single crow twisting into human form.

Trik shook off the lingering black feathers as he completed his shift and walked towards his brother. 'Staring after her again?' Trik smirked.

'You would too, if you ever saw what I saw,' Dread said casually. 'She's magnificent.'

Trik laughed. 'That was never under question.' His eyes narrowed on the harrowing storm. 'I always liked it when she brought forth storms. You could almost feel the electricity in the air before it even came.'

Dread watched him a moment before moving away from the open doorway to enter the shelter of the aviary. 'What are you doing here, Brother?'

'There's a lull in the war effort.'

Dread gave him a small grin. 'A lull?'

Trik shrugged. 'There's no movement. It's a stalemate.'

'And you thought you'd take a vacation?'

'You know we don't get vacations.'

Dread shook his hair, water droplets falling onto the cold floor. 'Lull or not, it's good to see you.'

'You too, Brother.'

Dread clapped his hand on Trik's back, and they moved towards the centre of the room where a set of seats and a round table lay. Dread sat upon the stone chaise and wiped the water from his weary eyes. Lightning flashed, filling the damp air with warmth.

Trik pulled at the lantern on the table and set the candle inside alight, the orange glow drowning out the darkness.

Dread noted the shadows under his brother's eyes. There was a seriousness about Trik, a warning to others. But it was usually for show. Trik laughed easier than Dread, found easy pleasures in ways Dread couldn't. There was only one indulgence that Dread was willing to worship, and she smelt of lavender and blood.

Trik was a ruthless general, one made for brews and brawling. But he was a solid leader, too: he didn't take anyone's shit, and was the first to put a traitor of the crown to the noose.

The one weak spot Trik possessed was their feckless brother.

Out of the three of them, Trik was the reasonable one, the one able to find middle ground when their younger brother flittered off into his dreams and Dread obsessed over one topic. It was why the silence and tight shoulders bothered Dread. Why, even though Dread appreciated the visit, he was wary.

Dread crossed his arms, bracing himself. 'Tell me why you're here, Trik. There are always lulls and you never travel out this way.'

Trik leaned back, resting his elbow on the edge of the seat. He wore the Queen's uniform, the purple and red dusty against the dim stone beneath him. It was marked and torn, old blood coating the sleeves in shades of brown. His golden buttons held a brassy sheen, and his skull had been shaved to the skin. He looked so different to the clean, shiny uniforms the officers wore in the city.

If Dread was honest, Trik looked like fairy shit. His cheek bones were sagging into his jaw like he'd turned into one of the lifeless beings he fought.

'The dead aren't rising as quickly as they once did,' Trik said. 'Not that I'm complaining. It means the princess is growing weak, and it's giving me ample time to heal the soldiers instead of sending out my own half-dead army.'

'Do all the soldiers look like you?'

'Rugged and handsome?' Trik smirked.

'Dirty and destitute.'

Trik rolled his eyes. 'In one of your serious moods again, I see? I know I look half dead. It's why I'm here. More men arrived from Carnell, and we finally have a break in the bloodshed, but I don't know how long for. It's a never-ending cycle, Brother, and I'm afraid we might not outlast a teenage girl. Do you know how embarrassing that would be?'

Dread snorted.

Sighing, Trik stretched out his legs, his worn boots squashing some loose feathers lying on the floor. 'Lucky for me, I'm not entirely here for the Queen. I wanted to see you, actually.'

'Could it not have been done through the bond?' Dread asked, raising his brow. 'You've flown a very long way, and leaving your post seems like a risky choice.'

'Well, it's risky information,' Trik replied, and he sighed again. 'Have you heard from our brother? Have you found him?'

'You know I haven't. What's this about?'

Trik pulled at his earlobe, an old habit when he became nervous. Dread eyed the movement, noting a scar running from Trik's skull down to his temple. By the colour of it, it looked fresh.

'I'm concerned he's been compromised,' Trik said. 'Either taken or turned. Or dead. He's been quiet too long. Even the murders haven't seen or felt him, and my concern is turning to anxiety.'

'You don't have an anxious bone in your body.'

'No,' Trik challenged, '*you* don't. You were always the logical one.'

Dread frowned. 'He's not dead. He's too clever for that.'

'And if he's turned?'

'Then you were right to come in person as a precaution, but I doubt that's the case, either. He's unpredictable, but he's always put family first.'

'Myrenna isn't family in his world.'

'His world is make-believe,' Dread growled. He couldn't hold back the venom in his voice at his brother's choices. Their youngest brother had always been impulsive. He'd followed them his whole life but had seen the world in a different light, consistently arguing about what was right and wrong. Over the years, he'd been successful in dividing the three of them with his antics. Mostly pulling Trik along with him and leaving Dread to be the big, bad brother.

Dread stretched out, but his muscles were still tight. 'If you're concerned, I'll prioritise the search for him. I'm to stay in the city, anyway. If he's done something stupid again, I'll find out about it.'

'And you'll take care of it?'

'I always do.'

His brother was silent a moment, before he said, 'If you're to stay here, who will be at the mines?'

'I have keepers there who maintain order. My beasts are loyal things, after all.'

'Speaking of beasts,' Trik started. 'You don't happen to have more of those harpy-looking things, do you?'

'You mean the shaiths?' Dread asked. 'No. I don't.'

Shaiths were some of Dread's least favourite beasts that dwelled in the mines. They resembled the now-extinct harpies but only because of the mixed breeding of blood backdating over a thousand years ago. They were more a mix of a harpy and wraith. Their black wings were shaped like bats and their humanoid bodies were tight with leather skin. Their eyes were pale and white, with mouths that held no lips. Most of them were female, the males rarely born. But what Dread hated the most about them was the shrieking noise they liked to make. It was ear-splitting. So, when they urged each other on and got started, it was almost impossible to shut them up. It had interrupted too many of his nights at the mines and he'd punished them accordingly – not that torture stopped them, either.

'We've had no newborns in over a year. I can't spare the few I have. We're already low on rations and stardust, raiders hitting the few carts we do move. I need them. They're my eyes in the sky while the murders are out looking for the Princess.'

Trik nodded, his eyes hollow.

Dread prodded more. 'Why do you need them? Is the army and the other beasts I sent not enough?'

Trik shook his head. 'It's not that. I just think the princess of Perridorm is almost at her peak. I need the extra bodies to push that little bit harder. To break her.'

'To break a little girl?' Dread smirked. 'Surely even you are capable of that.'

Trik stared daggers at his brother's comment before he stood. 'Enough. I have a long flight back, and I'd rather spend the night with an ale in my hand and a woman in my bed.'

'And how will your Huntress feel about that?' Dread teased.

'Artemis will get over it,' Trik replied.

Dread waited a moment before pointing to the stairs by the east doorway. 'Get cleaned up.'

Trik watched him silently, pulling at his ear again.

Dread continued, 'But before you go, what message did you need to send Myrenna?'

Trik paused halfway across the room, his eyes glinting. 'It's about Snow. I wanted to inform her that, though we can't see her, we can smell her. The Princess is close to the war front and the beasts have got her scent. I've sent a pack of dark hounds into the forest. If the Godmother has blessed us, she'll be found soon.'

'Now, that information is useful,' Dread said, moving towards the ledge again and waving his hand. 'The ale is in the cellar.'

'And where will you be?' Trik asked as he met the candlelight outlining the door.

'I'll be getting us the best girls in town.' Dread grinned, twisting into a crow.

XVIII

The Misbegotten Prince

Florian weaved his way through the forest, his feet careful as he stepped over roots and grass. The air smelt damp, and there was a coldness in the wind he wasn't used to. Verdant moss climbed up bark and scattered itself on rocks, the leaves of a thick plant he didn't recognise rushed his shoulder, and the soil was soft enough that his boots left imprints.

Florian eventually followed the trail to a clearing, where a narrow creek broke the silence. He halted by the treeline, the telltale itching at the back of his throat threatening a sneeze. But it never came. Perhaps Pip's herbs were just the remedy he needed.

He was still surprised at the elf's kindness, even if Pip had practically tossed the herbs at Florian's face.

Florian pushed down the thought and followed the trail towards the water. Leaning down, he eyed the slipper-soft footprints but came up short when he noticed they only entered the water but didn't leave. Florian knew wood nymphs dwelt in trees, water being left to the darker realms of the south with the mermaids and sea nymphs.

Florian—

His name was a whisper on the wind, coming from somewhere nearby. Head perked, Florian followed the sound. It was distant, though close enough it echoed off the trees, seeming to come from the sky. Florian braved a look up, only to find a roof of green branches.

Slight movement caught his attention as a tiny clicking sound came from his right. He pulled his sword free and took careful steps forward. His hand squeezed the hilt, his fingers turning red.

A howling wind whipped up the leaves of the forest and he shuddered.

Please don't attack again, he thought.

A twig broke. Florian gripped the sword with both hands and at the sight of a shadow, he swung. His feet caught, tripping on a root. But before he could fall, a large hand gripped his wrist, holding him up.

Florian sighed at the sight of Malak before a brush was shoved to the side and Pip stepped through.

'If I'd known how hopeless you are with a sword, I would've been training you with Snow,' Malak berated him, propping the Prince up and securing the sword at Florian's side again.

'I've had training,' muttered Florian, rubbing the back of his hand against his nose.

Pip snorted, also unimpressed. 'With what, a tree?'

Malak's lip twitched, but he didn't push further. 'Is she here?'

'The trail ends at the creek,' Florian replied. 'They go to the water, but then they stop. I can't track her any further.'

Pip looked above them, his watchful eyes scoping the branches. 'Then she's here.'

'Up there?' Malak asked. 'I don't see anything.'

'Just because you do not see it, does not mean it doesn't exist.'

'Don't start with me,' Malak said, nearly chomping off the elf's head. 'You're already on my "bad" list.'

'Oh, your "bad" list?' Pip said, rolling his eyes. 'How positively awful. To be on your list!'

Malak growled.

'Is Eve on your list, too?' Pip continued. 'Perhaps we could make tea? Reminisce on all the ways we've offended the poor troll.'

Malak pulled out his club, ready to pommel the elf.

'Enough,' Florian said firmly, standing between them. He was so sick of them bickering. Especially when they were in unfamiliar territory. He almost felt like a parent with two squabbling children. 'Let's just do what we came to do: get the Princess and save the realm and all that.'

Malak and Pip looked at him in surprise when his cheeks heated. 'She's in the trees,' Florian sputtered, 'What now?'

'We climb,' Pip replied flatly.

'Those trees are as high as the towers in the Silver City!' Florian gawped.

'Climb anyway,' Malak said, and latched a thick hand onto the knob of the tree.

Snow gasped in the dark. Her fingers trailed the hard wood, her stomach roiling with indignation. There was usually a heat to her rage, a fire that burned deep in her core. But today it was cold, as cold as the ice-ravaged Mountains of Eyrie. It pinched her lungs, making it hard to breathe, to *think* past the cage of wood and rage that tore at her throat and threatened to swallow her whole.

She needed to get free. *Now.*

Her fists bashed against the wood, the darkness too heavy. She screamed again, her body thrashing at the wooden coffin around her. She couldn't be trapped again, she *wouldn't.*

She ignored her bleeding nails. The way her eyes burned with unshed tears. She was far too hollow for that, far too raw. Time became nothing and endless as Snow battered against her cage, digging and scraping and screaming. It wasn't until her her bloodied fingers scratched weakly that she loosed a guttural sob.

Her back scraped down the shredded bark and she curled into herself, making her body as small as possible.

Imprisoned, a voice inside her echoed.

Her mind darkened.

Trapped.

Snow sneered at the words, her breaths loud even to her own ears.

She hated wood nymphs.

Despised them.

In the bleak darkness of her prison, she imagined tearing them apart. Piece by piece. Limb from limb. There would be no mercy given when they granted none. They would not be a part of her new world. They would not be welcomed into her kingdom – or any other, for that fact.

They would *burn.*

And she would be the one to strike the match.

Malak's wrist twisted as his fingers grazed the hard bark. He wasn't built to climb trees, or scale mountains. His large hands barely fit into the slots or covered the knobs, causing him to slip and strain his ligaments. He eyed Pip above him, nimbly climbing with grace, and he held back another growl. He was being outrageous, but something about the flute taking control of him had gotten under his skin.

For so long, the only semblance of control he'd had was over himself and his emotions. It was the only thing he *could* control, considering he'd been unable to command his fate. Even after he'd left Troll's Keep, the realm held rules for creatures like him, expectations and stereotypes on who or what he should be.

Most of the time he could push the fear aside, tuck it deep inside and squash it down. The belief of a better world with Hansel and Snow was a glimmer of hope in the gloom. The belief that kept him going, helped him endure.

The flute had been a slap in the face.

Florian grunted from below and Malak peered down at the golden-haired prince, his face splotchy and alarmingly red. 'You, okay?'

'Yup,' the red-faced Prince wheezed. 'Just peachy.'

He didn't look fine at all, but Florian wasn't Malak's concern. The Princess was.

They climbed further, and Malak's nostrils flared. He could smell magic now, the hint of musk and bark, metallic waters, and fresh leaves.

'Watch out for a clicking noise or a *pop*,' Pip warned. 'It means the nymphs are close.'

'Have we thought about what happens when we reach them?' Florian puffed. 'Suppose they don't want to give her up?'

'Just let me do the talking, without interruptions for once,' Pip remarked, climbing nimbly to the first ledge.

Malak dared to eye the forest floor below and sucked in a breath.

They were high. *Very* high.

'Did you hear what I said?' asked Pip, standing lightly on the ledge.

'Yes,' Malak said through gritted teeth. 'But we're not promising anything. You know a promise is a powerful thing.'

Pip waved away his concern before eyeing the trees above him, seeing something with his elvish eyes that Malak couldn't.

The troll ground his teeth, latching on painfully to another knob in the tree to leverage himself up. He was about to lift his foot when a vibration moved along the tree, followed by a quiet *pop*.

Florian caught up, his head reaching just below the troll's left foot. 'Why have we stopped?'

Malak was frozen as he assessed the creature sticking out of the bark. The nymph tilted its head in interest, its large dark eyes assessing Malak with patient curiosity. All Malak could do was stare. His muscles burned, and his breath was short. Before he could ask what it was doing, the creature melded back into the bark and disappeared.

'Pip,' Malak said calmly. 'Florian.'

Florian wheezed, his fingers red with strain.

'Don't move,' ordered Malak.

Pip did as he said, freezing on the platform and standing ready. Florian, on the other hand, groaned, his teeth clenching. 'I can't, Malak. My fingers are slipping.'

'They know we're here,' Pip murmured.

Malak heard the scrape of a boot as Florian's foot slipped. The prince squeaked, latching onto Malak's leg. Malak dropped a few pixies and let out a grunt.

'Just keep moving,' ordered Pip. 'They know we're here, so staying still or continuing to move makes no difference.'

'Florian,' Malak warned.

'Sorry,' the Prince wheezed, thankfully finding another foothold that wasn't his leg.

Malak heaved himself upwards, his body shaking as he reorientated himself. To the left, Malak felt another vibration, the wood shaking against his palm. But there was no pop this time, only a shudder. 'Do you feel that?'

'Feel what?' Florian asked.

Malak moved closer to the spot where he'd felt the vibration and placed his ear against the bark. A barely audible shrill came from within.

'Pip?' he asked. 'Can the wood nymphs turn into trees?'

The elf laughed. 'Of course not. They can blend into the trees themselves and on occasion take someone with them.'

'Could they take someone and then leave them inside a tree?'

Pip was quiet a moment before answering. 'Only if there's a gap of some sort. During the transition into the wood, nymphs must take hold of the person, or they'll burst apart or die in that form. But if there's a room, or a space, some kind of solid place, then I suppose, yes. They could.'

Malak waited another second before the thump came again. 'I think someone's inside this tree.'

'What?' said the elf.

'Am I speaking Aurelian? I think someone's inside the tree. I hear thumping and shrieking. As if someone or something is trapped. I think it might be Snow.'

'How do you know?' Florian asked.

'I don't, exactly,' Malak replied. 'But I know Snow, and she wouldn't be locked away again without fighting back.'

Malak maneuvered to a more secure hold, his foot dragging on the bark as he hung by one arm and used the other to take out his sword.

'What are you going to do? Hack at the bark with your sword? You're just as bad as the Seeker. You won't get her that way. It's too thick.'

Malak growled at the elf, the anger still boiling from earlier. 'And what do you suggest?'

'I suggest we speak with the nymphs. They can be reasoned with.'

'They locked her up!' Malak shouted, his arm shaking.

'But they didn't kill her.'

Malak lifted his blade, ready to strike, when Florian's hand gripped his calf. His pale blue eyes stared at the troll. 'I know you're angry, but Pip is right.'

Malak took a breath, holding the Prince's stare before he reached back and smacked his blade into the tree anyway. Bark sprayed, and he turned his face as he swung again, his body barely holding on.

'What are you doing?!' Pip cried.

'Getting their attention,' Malak growled. The tree groaned as he slashed again, carving deeper with each hit. Florian watched with wide eyes as Pip groused from above. Just as Malak went to swing again, a body appeared from the bark, a nymph's hand reaching out in a plea towards Malak. Before he knew it, another jumped from the bark onto his back, grappling his arm that held the sword.

Malak growled at them in warning, and they paused. They were tiny – little sticks he could shake off.

'We're here to trade,' Pip said from above. 'Tell your masters.'

The wood nymphs waited a beat, glaring at Malak and his sword.

'Put your sword away, Malak, or they won't agree.'

Malak snarled before placing his sword back its sheath. The two wood nymphs gave a curt nod then pointed to the treetops.

'Great,' Florian groaned. 'More climbing.'

But Malak didn't hear him. His vision had honed onto the ledge above them, his thoughts only of Snow and her freedom.

When they'd all reached the platform, Florian shook out his hands. Minor cuts bit into his skin from the climb like shards of glass. His muscles trembled from the strain. He panted. His brain was fit, but his body was not.

Useless, his father's voice echoed through his mind.

He shook it off, eyeing the trees surrounding them, squashing down the terror once more. He stood on a wooden platform high in the trees, the edges melded into the thick trunk. It was circular. The edge a freefall should one step too close. It was enough for him to move closer to the trunk where Malak sat, his broad shoulders barely fitting between two protruding branches.

Pip stood comfortably just around the bend of the trunk and lit his pipe. 'Remember,' he said, 'let me control the conversation.'

Florian tried to reply but his voice only came out as a rasp.

'They pop from the trees,' Malak said, regaining his breath too. 'Listen for it and they'll soon follow.'

Pip waved them forward. 'Let's move.'

Around the trunk, moth-like hammocks drifted in the canopies of leaves like floating clouds. Florian gasped. Bridges of thick trunks lined paths to each tree linking the forest like the nerves of a brain.

'The books don't mention this,' he breathed, eyes sparkling.

'I doubt any of those philosophers you've read ever made it this far,' Pip said, taking a puff of his pipe. Smoke blew around them and Florian's nose twitched. It smelt of tobacco and apple.

'I suppose not,' Florian said. 'Perhaps I could write about it.'

'Perhaps you could,' the elf said.

A warm feeling spread through Florian at the thought: his name written across the leather of a well-bound book, his adventures and knowledge printed forever in ink. 'I don't think anybody would read anything of mine. My father would burn it before anything I wrote could even be read.' And just like that, the warm feeling evaporated.

'Perhaps it could be a chronicle, considering your capture by the giants. The adventures of the misbegotten Prince,' Pip said.

'The misbegotten Prince,' Florian mused. 'Oddly enough, I like it.'

Pip chuckled before blowing out more smoke. It came fluidly from his nose as a *pop* came and a wood nymph appeared. The creature's nose crinkled at the smell before it clicked his tongue.

'Smoking their relatives probably isn't a wise choice,' Florian pointed out.

Pip scoffed.

'The misbegotten Prince is right,' Malak said, coming up from behind. His eyes glinted in amusement at the name. 'You're smoking plants – the very things they are and what they protect. Put it out.'

Pip huffed. 'I suppose you're right.' He snuffed out his pipe, then placed it back in his pocket. He turned to the wood nymph. 'My apologies.'

The wood nymph pouted, and clicked at them, 'Come, come.'

Florian peered over the ledge as it groaned under Malak's weight. Flowers bloomed in all colours from holes pierced through the bark. Lilies of orange and pink, marigolds of brightest purple and dahlias of gold. His fingers itched to touch them, but vertigo set in, and he wobbled.

'Careful, Prince,' Malak said, gripping him. 'One step at a time. I'm already trying to save one royal, let's not add to the tally, yeah?'

Florian smiled at him gratefully. They followed silently after that, crossing many bridges and passing platforms until they reached one that was stretched between an oval of trees. An ornate platform was suspended between eight trunks, stretching across the expanse like a town square.

Malak stepped carefully onto the platform, testing the strength of the wood before finally deciding to trust it. Florian took longer, trailing his fingers along the joints of the wood, marvelling at the beauty of it. It was as if the platform had grown from the trees itself, becoming a thread and making them one whole being.

'We're getting further from the Princess,' Malak said to Pip, as they walked towards to the centre of the platform.

A deep groaning echoed through the air, strong enough that Florian felt it in his bones. He gripped Malak's arm as the eight trees surrounding them shifted. The wood morphed, pulling out like stretching seams as faces began to form on each trunk.

One had the largest nose Florian had ever seen, and another to his right had a small, pointy chin. Their eyes bulged, the wood becoming smooth with their faces. They breathed a sigh collectively, causing the leaves to rustle.

Pops shot forth as wood nymphs crawled through every crevice until the three companions were surrounded.

'It has been an age since we had others visit,' a female voice cooed.

'An age since another has walked our forest,' came a deep grumble.

'Perhaps they are here to take what is ours?' another called.

The last wooden face looked half asleep, his eyes drooping against his large lips.

The wood nymphs cried out in clicking noises.

Florian gripped Malak's bicep tighter. The troll patted the prince's arm and eyed Pip, who was so insistent on being their voice.

Pip stepped forward, raising his arms. 'We are here to trade. To reclaim what is ours.'

The tree on Florian's right groaned again. A set of mushrooms scaled his wooden lips. 'A trade? What would us wood folk have that you desire?'

Pip gave a bow of respect before he replied. 'My companions and I are searching for our friend, a woman, who was taken by your little ones.'

A chuckle came from behind them. 'Taken by the little ones? She must be beautiful.'

Pip nodded. 'That she is. We require her back.'

The one with the large nose spoke. 'And what will you trade for one so beautiful? It must be a heavy price.'

Florian felt the muscles shift under Malak's arm. 'Malak?' he whispered.

'She's not some possession for them to take,' the troll gritted.

Pip continued speaking, weaving his words with ease. 'We have many treasures. Ones of gold and magic. Name your price.'

Wind cut through the platform as the trees creaked, their eyes watchful.

'We do not hoard such items.' said the female face, her skin mottled with moss. 'We are different to others of our kind. Not all nymphs are the same, and we take offence to the comparison. If she is a living human and as beautiful as you say, then she is worth more than any of your trinkets. For she is more beautiful for being so futile. The stars will have her.'

'Mmm, yes,' said another. 'A living treasure holds far greater value than mere trinkets. The stars will value her greatly.'

The voices echoed in agreement, the platform shifting with the vibrations.

'A trade is better than you deserve,' Malak snarled.

Pip frowned at the troll. 'What are you doing?'

Malak ignored him. 'You stole her, and we could have stolen her back. Ask your little ones. I could have chopped that tree until she came free.'

A trunk with large eyebrows squinted at the troll. 'Stolen? We only take what is of value as you have stolen from us.'

The female chimed in again. 'You have stolen our leaves to smoke, our trunks for your houses.'

'It is one half of the other,' said the one with the small, pinched nose. 'Like looking into a mirror.'

'Have you not stolen our very wood to keep yourself sheltered? To keep warm? You cannot lie here. We have seen you through the eyes of our kin, cutting us away to build weapons of war.'

Malak licked his lips before he said, 'What would you have us do to survive?'

The one with the mushroom lips smiled. 'You could ask.'

'And would you say yes?' asked Malak. 'Would you have let us take it as a gift?'

Florian squeezed Malak's arm as his voice rose. He could feel the panic in the troll's movements, his urgency to save his Princess. To care so strongly for someone was something Florian didn't understand, but he tried to understand anyway, envisioning if it was someone close to him, like his mother. And though he didn't understand fully, he hoped that one day he would.

To fall in love would be one of the greatest gifts.

It's what he had held onto when he had no love anywhere else. His books had shown him the power of it. It held the ability to heal when nothing else could. Even though he knew great love was rare, he still hoped the Godmother would bless him.

One day.

'War is coming,' Pip intervened before the trees could answer. 'What you stole is the key to stopping the bloodshed.'

'*War,*' the one with the thin nose drawled, 'is already upon us. With every one of us you burn.'

'This war is different.'

'All war is different depending on who you are. You will fight yourselves, and we will remain,' another said. 'As we always remain.'

Pip looked drawn, his features in shock at the severity of the trees' tones.

Florian stepped forward. 'But you won't survive this one,' the prince said shakily, trying to be brave. 'This time *is* different. You would have felt the curse that came across your northern kin in the Dark Forest. The fog that saps the life from the very soil. The dragon of smog and mist. We might cut you down for survival, but they wipe you out without hesitation. Without remorse.'

'One evil for another,' hissed the female tree.

'I'm sorry.' Florian dropped to his knees. 'I'm sorry for what we have done. But without the Princess, we cannot hope to be better. To do better. Perhaps, once this is over, we may come to an agreement. I'm a prince of Carnell and she is a princess of Bellatorre. We go to Perridorm for aid and, perhaps, with our influence, we can spread word to the other kingdoms. To bring peace.'

The trees were silent as Florian pleaded with them. The leaves rustled as the filtered sun began to die out. Darkness crept in with every minute.

'"Perhaps" is an empty promise,' one echoed.

'It is all I can offer,' the Prince whispered.

The trees murmured before the one with mushroom lips spoke. 'We will consider.'

They groaned as they morphed back into bark, leaving the group standing in silence.

'That is the most we can hope for with the wood folk,' Pip said, gripping Florian's shoulders. 'The misbegotten Prince may not be an apt name for what you've just done.'

Heat flushed Florian's cheeks as the elf gave him a rare smile.

'What now?' Malak asked, helping Florian to his feet.

'Now we wait,' the elf said.

XIX

The Grimms' Grievance

Trik's voice came through the darkness, jolting Dread from his thoughts. *'The hounds have caught a scent. We think it's her. They're close.'*

Dread flew above the Silver City, his wings aching from the hours he'd spent scoping the city below. Half the city was shrouded in darkness, the rest lit up by the fairy lanterns Myrenna loved. He'd wandered almost every one of the streets, checked every patrol, and scoped every tavern, finding nothing but dead ends at each turn.

If he was being honest, it was driving him mad, the thread holding him together fraying.

Tell me when she's found. Alive, he replied.

'Was there any other way, Brother? You've been clear.'

Dread didn't miss the underlying threat. None of the three liked to be told what to do or how to operate, but Dread had no other option. *Alive,* he repeated.

Trik only replied with a complying grunt before cutting the connection.

Dread's frustration edged into anger as he cawed into the sky. It was imperative that Snow remained alive. The hounds were accurate, but they were also vicious. Without the right trainer or correct command, they failed to stop, tearing apart whatever flesh and blood had driven them mad for the scent. Their teeth were sharper than knives and their skulls as solid as rock.

He had plenty of them in the mines, each one a reminder to those in service that, should they try anything, they would pay for it with their blood.

Dread soared into the main square, the white pillars and carved stone darkening under the dwindling twilight when he heard the call of the murders. The sound pierced through his skull as it rained across the air. He perched on a statue, tilting his head as the murders passed the outskirts of the city's walls, one flying ahead of the others in a cloud of ash.

Myrenna.

Despite not finding his brother, the sight was a welcome relief. She was home. She was safe.

And he was whole again.

Bronson pathetically attempted to comb back his unruly hair with a small twig as they awoke the next morning. His fat fingers grasped at the delicate stick when it snapped, causing him to swear under his breath. He'd hardly slept at all, the bright flashes of Frode flying upon a dragon's back bringing him hope but also acute fear. He'd twitched throughout the night and when he'd finally given up on sleep, he'd reverted to his usual coping strategies: worrying and grooming.

In the early hours of the morning, he'd found a waterfall by the mountain's edge and washed himself. Once clean, he'd opened the small mirror he carried. He jolted at the sight of his hair. He'd always found that if he looked respectable then he would feel respectable too. Taming his hair was like claiming a piece of control amongst the turmoil but, though he was washed, his eyes sprouting golden tones behind the kohl around them, his hair remained wild.

Just like the dragon and Frode.

His fingers shook again as he tried to run them through a particularly difficult knot, staring daggers at the traitorous stick comb. He *would* tame it. He *would* find courage in this mess. And he *would* do it with panache.

Bronson pulled at a stubborn knot as Brufell yawned from across the burnt-out campfire. His eyes were puffy and red, groggy after a night of telling stories. 'I see you've bathed,' he said, sitting up. 'Are you so eager to meet a dragon after last night's tale?'

Bronson hissed as he gave up, too annoyed to answer. The cooking pans from last night's meal remained by the burned down coals, begging for a wash, and Bronson was desperate for a distraction. Ignoring Brufell, he collected them all, enjoying the way they clanged, the sound somehow helping with his shaken state of mind. 'I'm ready when you are.'

Brufell frowned at him, his long, greyed beard matted with dirt and twigs. Most of the metal accessories he'd worn had fallen out on their journey, the braids loosened into kinked hair that, frankly, Bronson found offensive.

Brufell stretched, his hunched back cracking as he stood. 'Well, you might be ready, but I'm not. I need to bathe, as well. Could you point the way?'

Bronson didn't meet his eyes as he nodded to a narrow pathway.

The old dwarf shook his head as he reached for Tuk, the troll still hiccupping in his sleep. With a swat, the bubble protruding over the troll's mouth popped and Tuk shot up, his half eyes open with sleep.

'Come on, Tuk. Let's go wash and leave the little one alone.'

Bronson pretended to be busy as he laid out the pots, his mind attempting some semblance of organisation before their voices finally faded. He sighed as silence enveloped him, and dropped onto his knees. He was exhausted, his bones weary and cracked.

Stories were supposed to make us feel better, to help us escape. But something within Bronson felt different after hearing about Frode. He wanted to be like Frode: to be brave and curious and wild. But he wasn't.

He missed home and a warm hearth. Missed haircuts and baths and playing jokes on Beetle. He had all the traits that made for homebodies and good food; all the things adventure did not approve of. Traits, that didn't change history.

It was a dreary thought, one tugging him down as he remembered he couldn't even comb his cauldron damned hair.

There was a tug on his sleeve from Oryx, the pixie staring up at him with concern. Bronson's eyes stung at the pity, but he wiped them quickly away before the others could see.

Letting go, the pixie motioned some signs – Bronson's and his way of communicating.

'*Do you need more rest?*' Oryx asked.

'No,' Bronson said, attempting a smile. 'I just need something nice to happen again. Something normal.'

'*Why is normal important?*'

Leaning back, Bronson took a breath. 'It's not important,' he started, pausing to think before he answered. 'It's that normal is the expected. It's the knowledge of food in your belly and a place to sleep. Normal is knowing your family is happy and that you will live to see a new horizon. Normal is important because it's safe.'

Oryx's eye darkened and he kicked at the dirt.

Bronson rubbed his eyes. 'I'm sorry, I didn't mean—'

'*I do not have normal,*' the pixie signed before flying off.

'By the cauldron, I stuffed that one up,' he muttered. He grasped the pans, feeling like a right twat.

Bronson had Brufell, but the pixie had nobody. Turning around, the dwarf yelled out before Oryx could disappear. 'Normal is nice. But so are friends!'

The pixie halted, buzzing above a cluster of red poppies.

'We will have normal again one day,' Bronson said. 'And you'll be there, too. With us. Your new family.' His voice quivered at the last part. An offer and a question.

Oryx's smile was sad, but he didn't fly off, which Bronson took as an acceptance of his apology. Together, they tidied the camp.

Bronson had just doused the fire when a howling wind gushed through the campsite, tossing his newly combed hair across his scalp. He blocked his eyes from the spray of dirt as a resounding crash echoed across the camp.

There was a crack in the trees, the mountain groaning under some kind of tidal wave when he saw *something* crossing the trees.

'Bronson!' Brufell shouted, the dwarf and troll rushing back to camp.

But Bronson didn't register the warning, or the panic in Brufell's voice. He could only watch in horror as the tips of the forest bent and groaned under an invisible pulse of air coming his way. The force stretched across the land, crushing everything in its path.

Bronson ran.

Oryx squeaked as Bronson hauled the creature into his shirt and dived to the ground. He became a shield, his body covering the tiny creature just as the invisible wind hit like a raging storm.

Bronson couldn't hear the others, only the ringing in his ears as he flexed his muscles and held firm. The blast hit, rolling him down the hill. The wind was a torrent on his senses, etched in magic and power. There was a shudder across his skin, filled with wind and fury and sadness. He could only let it take him, only hold on to Oryx with whatever strength he had to give.

He was stopped by a large boulder, his back cracking on impact. He braced harder, the magic roiling through him. Bronson felt the shift in the world, the warning Brufell had been rattling on about for weeks.

Change was happening, and it was happening faster than he'd anticipated.

Dread sat near a market stall that specialised in Myorcaian wine and swallowed the rest of his drink. The barrel in front of him grazed his stretched-out legs as he sat on a wonky stool. His contact had never showed up.

Eyes glazed, Dread peered at the patrons around him. Most of them were men, out and about away from their wives and enjoying the night air. Suspended fairy lanterns hung above him, lining the alley in an ambient glow. A girl ran to each table, collecting glasses, and hesitated when she saw Dread's was empty, too. She licked her lips before speaking. 'Shall I get you another, Sir?'

Dread couldn't help but snort.

He was not a sir. He was not even a real man.

He was a crow. *A murder.*

She swallowed, her eyes flitting from the glass back to him when he smirked. Some of the men watched him from the other tables as he nodded. She loosed a breath before her shaking hands took the glass. With a nervous curtsy, she rushed behind the stall.

Dread gave the men an arrogant wave, ensuring to show them his white teeth. When they promptly looked away, he chuckled. He never grew tired of smelling it.

The fear.

He leaned forward, twirling the large silver ring on his finger. He grazed over the emblem of wings and the carved eyes. Myrenna had gifted it to him when he'd joined her ranks, when she'd pulled him from the mess he'd been and given him power. His youngest brother has forgotten how poor they'd been. How luck determined whether they'd eaten or not. It was why he was so flippant with orders, why he'd never appreciated the opportunity the Queen presented.

Dread still hadn't found him. Hence why he was drunk.

He was distracted when the lights flickered above him, the fairies shivering inside their glass cages. Dread frowned at them as the girl came back, leaving the cold, hard glass on the wood. Condensation dripped down its side, and while his stool was wonky, the table was not. So why, then, was it shaking?

The girl jolted as Dread grasped her wrist, her light eyes wide. He ignored her fear this time as he asked, 'Do they do that often?'

She shook her head, unsure. 'Th-the lights?'

'No,' he growled, 'the pavement. Of course, the lights. Don't be daft.'

Her eyes watered, but she answered. 'Never. Fairy lights are powered from the fairies themselves.'

'That's what I thought.' He released his grip.

The girl pulled away, her skirt trailing behind her as she fled.

The men around Dread had gone silent, each patron eyeing the lights with wariness before they flickered again.

Dread sniffed the air.

Metallic, mixed with … incense.

Magic. Powerful old magic, to be precise.

He swore as his table shook, his wine spilling onto the pavement. A crack echoed on the horizon and Dread turned his gaze towards what resembled a storm on the outskirts of the city. The wind raged, making the buildings groan. But it was the normally familiar sky that was changed. Dust and debris rippled in a wave, an invisible force of might crashing towards them without a care of who it devoured.

The barmaid screamed, and before Dread could brace himself, the wind shot through the alley like a tornado, swallowing everything whole. Dread barely had a moment to breathe before it hit, crushing him into a pale-yellow wall. His bones crunched, stars spotting his vision. Just as he blinked, the barrel he'd been sitting at hurtled towards him.

And smashed into him like a troll's fist.

XX

The Tides of Change

Snow's nails snapped as she ran them over the wood. The smell of her blood was soothing as she saw and heard nothing else. There was an odd comfort in bleeding. As if it were a reminder that she wasn't entirely blind in her sensory deprivation. She'd screamed for hours, lashing out curses before her mind had wandered. She'd even considered praying but had given up almost instantly. The Godmother had not helped her before, so why would they now?

Snow had resigned herself years ago to the fact that the stars and the Godmother wouldn't listen. So many years she'd prayed after her mother's death. After her father had fallen ill.

Prayer had been soothing then.

But it had not helped her.

She'd been set free, only to be trapped again. Perhaps this was her fate. Her destiny. She was to always be a toy. A piece of property. Ready to be called and used at other's whims but never her own. She hated them for it. She hated the wood nymphs for shutting her away and ignoring her; hated Myrenna for isolating and using her with that hideous mirror. She hated her parents for leaving her in the first place. And sometimes she even hated Malak for dictating her every move, for telling her what to do and where to go.

Her shoulders were heavy, the air thick as she continued to scrape down her nail beds.

Scrape and sharpen.

Scrape and sharpen.

That's what she did over and over, her mind locked on this one thing she could control.

She jolted as the tree groaned around her, a crack rippling through the air. There was a scream from somewhere outside, her prison creaking. Snow scrambled back, realising she had nowhere to go. She braced herself, bark falling from the roof of her prison when the whole tree shuddered.

She ground her teeth, her limbs shaking as the force of an earthquake hit. A power so mighty that bark broke, shattering against Snow's side as she was thrown against the wood. She barely had time to cover her eyes. Barely had time to breathe as she was blinded by light before the darkness tumbled in.

When everything settled, she coughed. Her eyes watered as she opened them, her hands feeling for something familiar. Her body ached, and her wrist was tender, as if she'd sprained it. She inspected it, trying to look for bruising, when she realised she could *see*.

Watery light filtered through an opening in the wood, just big enough for her head to fit through. She scrambled towards the opening, reaching out for that small taste of freedom. The breeze on her face was cool as she sucked in fresh forest air. Her lungs ached with the smell, but each breath filled her chest with new vitality. One that promised freedom. Revenge.

She clawed her fingers into the opening, tearing back the now-weakened bark. She ignored the sting in her wrist, ignored the sharp pieces of bark biting her skin. She tore the opening, a wicked smile of her lips, a laugh bubbling up her throat as the light expanded, her freedom so very close that she could taste it.

She was not a damsel. She would not be distressed. She would not wait for someone to save her.

Not this time.

And covered in blood, dirt and wood, the Princess began to break out of her prison.

Pip's fingers lingered on his flute as he waited for the elder trees to decide. The wood folk were stubborn, so for them to consider a trade was a blessing.

He shuffled on the platform, his bottom going numb from sitting for so long. To distract himself, he eyed the golden prince on his left, his feet swinging off the platform as he rubbed his nose.

Pip hoped the herbs would help him, perhaps allow people to take him a bit more seriously. Pip had fallen for it, too, seen Florian whimpering in that cage with the giants and thought how pathetic he'd been. Especially considering the amount of vomit that had left his mouth. The stench alone had been inconceivable.

But the Prince had surprised him.

Florian had somehow become the unsung hero, the one to convince the council to consider Snow's release.

'How do you think Malak is going?' Florian asked.

Pip tucked the flute back into his shirt. 'How should I know?'

Florian peered at him curiously. 'Malak has been Snow's protector for years and she's currently trapped by wood nymphs. He's awfully calm about it all. I half expected him to continue hacking at every tree, but he's just … moping.'

Pip peered over his shoulder to where Malak lay, on one of the makeshift bridges connecting two trees. The troll had mentioned something about an oath he'd made in the past, which Pip put down to annoying chatter in their conversations. He'd listen more, but frankly he didn't want to.

'You should check on him,' Florian said, tugging at his shirt.

'How about *you* check on him.'

'I'm not the one who keeps fighting with him.'

Pip narrowed his eyes. 'What's that supposed to mean?'

'It means,' Florian replied softly, 'that we only have each other. You were with the giants, too. We both know what it's like to be trapped and helpless. We know what it's like to feel alone and not have anyone who can help us.'

'I'm failing to see your point,' Pip sniped.

'What would you have given for someone to ask how you were when you were a prisoner? To check up on you, to free you.'

Pip wanted to slap him with a retort but found the words halting his tongue. When had he gone soft?

With a huff, Pip stood. 'Fine.'

Stomping over the wood, Pip made his way towards Malak. He halted on the thicker platform before the bridge started. The troll was lying down, an arm slung over his face as if to block the sun out.

'How are you faring?' Pip asked.

'You know how I'm faring,' Malak grumbled, not looking up. 'We're waiting on some wood to tell us if we can have the Princess back. Do you know how ridiculous that is?' The troll sat up, his eyes meeting Pip's, though the elf was standing. 'It's insulting.'

Pip was about the respond when he sensed a shift in the wind. There was a scent of incense on the air, a metallic tang coating his tongue that he tried to place but couldn't. The hairs on the back of his neck stood on end as he assessed the trees. 'Something's coming,' Pip said urgently.

'Let them come,' Malak said, lying back down and ignoring him.

Pip hobbled across the bridge and whacked him with his flute. 'This tree will not hold. Find a platform. NOW!' The elf rushed along the trunk as the stench of strong, *familiar* magic filled the air, the wind rising with a warning as the branches rustled violently. The land shuddered, quiet before the ripple came, the crack and tear of wood, shrieking.

Pip and Malak barely made it to the platform when the force hit, an invisible wind throwing them backwards. Pip's head cracked against the trunk and the platform shook violently. Florian squealed, dropping to the floor.

The branch Malak had laid on no longer existed, the remnants of cracked and splintered wood the only sign it ever existed.

The three of them held tight to any branch they could find as a roaring torrent on wind attacked them, bracing themselves against the onslaught until there was only unnerving silence. Pip panted, his fingers bone-white. Blood pooled from his temple, his eyes wild.

The platform groaned the same time Malak did – then snapped.

Florian screamed as the platform disappeared, Malak crying out before he fell, dropping towards the forest floor.

It was a fall he wouldn't survive.

The stone in the dungeons shifted. It was only a ripple; a tiny hum, but Rumple felt it under his fingertips as he sat hunched in his corner, tracing the aged lines with care. His cellmate had been quiet these past few days.

It was odd. His neighbour was a creature of connection. An old soul full of stories and histories. Rumple would have loved to have bathed in his cellmate's dreams, to float amongst the memories and devour them.

But without the spindle he couldn't.

Their last conversation still sat with him: the most they had ever spoken, and it had cleaved through the voices he so desperately tried to silence.

'He tries to take her apart. To break her. To see how she ticks,' Rumple had chuckled to his neighbour. 'But she won't without *me*. She won't work without me.'

Rumple remembered the colours of that moment, flashing before him as he swum through dreams, and how it had felt to be with *her* – to weave the spindle's magic as he had once done, to touch and soothe her.

But it had been the stranger's words that affected him. Embedding themselves deeper the more he thought about them. 'She will not be corrupted, for she has you. You are hers as she is yours.'

'She is mine as I am hers,' Rumple repeated.

It was a mantra. One that had seen him survive for months at the hands of the Tinker. Still, it had not been enough.

The monotony of the dark and the cold was another form of torture. His friend now lay silent – either asleep or meditating, Rumple guessed. He sensed the trickle of magic from the creature occasionally, the kind used when a thread is pulled in the world. A thread usually plucked when one's life wound to another. Or to send a message. He didn't know who his neighbour tried to contact, nor did he ask. Speaking was too hard now, his voice rusty from little use.

He curled closer to the stone, the small bumps across the wall a reminder that not everything was perfect, never completely smooth. If you looked close enough, you could always see the spoiled exterior.

The vibration came again, insistent and harder. Rumple frowned, his fingers halting and his mind breaking free in a rare moment of clarity. And then he heard screams.

He covered his ears, the world cracking as an explosion rattled through his cell, throwing him against the wall with such intensity he felt the crunch of his bones. He sucked his teeth, his pointed ears twitching at the ringing that shot through them. When silence fell, he gasped, his body trembling, and he suddenly knew – knew who it belonged to, and what it meant.

The fourth Grimm had died.

'No,' he wheezed. 'Impossible.'

But it was possible. The weight of his responsibility in revealing Nona's name was crushing and desolate.

What have I done?

He tried calling to his neighbour, but it only came out in a rasp.

She was dead. Nona was *dead*. And her power was releasing back to the realm it once helped create.

Rumple bit his knuckles and choked on a sob. He could never ask for forgiveness now. Could never hope to see her again. Curling into himself, Rumple rocked back and forth like a child in a crib.

And let out a hoarse cry.

Sap smeared Snow's fingers as she clung to the side of a tree, the remnant of her broken prison below. She was weak from lack of sleep, her skin more red than white as she climbed towards the wood nymphs home.

When she had emerged from her prison, the first thing she'd seen was the debris littered along the forest floor. Snapped branches and fallen wood strewn everywhere like bodies after a battle. And they were bodies, she supposed. The wood nymphs were a species of their own.

She grunted as she lifted herself up, then wiped her sleeve across her face. More sap stuck to her, and she tried to wipe it away but instead got it stuck on her mouth. It tasted sweet on her lips, like honey and the sweetcakes she used to steal from the kitchens.

Licking her lips, Snow took in her surroundings. She knew she should run, descend the tree with quick surety and bolt into the trees to search for her friends. But if she did, she wouldn't forgive herself.

She needed Hansel's axe.

The axe was her only tether to him. She'd already lost him once, and she refused to lose the last piece of him she had left. It was risky, but what kind of ruler would she be if she couldn't face some wood nymphs? She was going into a war, after all, and that required facing things head on, doing things yourself instead of relying on others.

She could not run.

Not now.

Her fingers stretched towards the ledge of the platform above. It was close enough that she could reach with a jump, but if she missed it meant death. The floor loomed below, laughing as she took a deep breath.

It's now or never, the voice inside her said.

She pushed off with a yelp, her hands stretched out, the air flying around her shoulders before she grasped the platform. Her legs swung out, dangling below her as she heaved herself up. Her breath came out in sharp bursts. Her body thrummed with adrenaline, her heart pounding in her ears.

Yelling echoed across the trees and her skin prickled as she recognised Florian's high-pitched wails.

Her friends were close.

She bolted across the makeshift bridges, smacking away the low-lying hammocks. She couldn't see the wood nymphs – didn't care to look for them – as she followed the sounds of her friends.

She crossed bridges and trees, passing platform after platform as the trees blurred into one another. Her eyes pierced through the leafy pathways but never found her friends. She could hear them, but they never got closer, the green and brown mixing into one swirling vortex with every turn she took, every branch she crossed.

She panted, slowing to rest. The wind rustled the trees and Snow turned in a slow circle. Each leaf looked the same, smelt the same, blinding her in its monotony.

'Where are they?' she whispered to herself.

If your friends are here, then why did you have to save yourself? the insidious voice inside her said.

Snow frowned at the question, the voice only a whisper in her mind. She refused to acknowledge it, putting it down to her own insecurities as she began her hunt again, this time slower. Despite the lush foliage, her skin crawled at the feeling of being watched. She was in the open, defenceless and alone. She needed time to think, to assess. She thought of Hansel's lessons, reminding her to be patient.

She hid amongst some thick brush growing from a large trunk. Her friends' calls echoed again, but she hesitated this time. What were they doing amongst the city of the wood nymphs if not saving her? How did they know she was here?

She closed her eyes, stilling the shaking that had begun in her hands. There were too many questions and not enough answers. Snow gripped her palm, rubbing it in small circles as she listened to the distant voices.

They could be trapped, too, she thought.

Or it is a trap, the voice inside her mind echoed.

The wood nymphs had tricked her before. Echoing her friends would make her hasty. Rash.

She would not be such a fool now.

Snow wavered, caught between what she knew to be true and what was illusion. She couldn't stop her tremble when she heard the telltale *pop* that burst up ahead. She flinched and scrambled backwards on instinct.

That sound. She'd never not hear it in her nightmares.

Peering through the gap of her hiding place, she noted one of the wood nymphs rushing across the pathway. A knife with a wooden handle was pinched between his gnarled fingers, his face twisted with disgust.

Snow held her breath, too afraid to move as the creature opened a hidden door in the trunk with the press of its fingers. Inside was an alcove where the sun glinted on weapons made of steel, wood, and other materials she didn't recognise.

The leaves rustled with her movement, and she froze.

The nymph's head spun at the sound. He clicked his tongue, angrily pushing aside some of the debris as he ran across one of the bridges towards the shouts of her friends.

Carefully exiting the brush, Snow quickly stepped across the platform, fumbling towards the alcove. Her eyes widened as they fell upon a hoard of weapons. Nestled amongst them she saw the familiar carving of a handle: Hansel's axe.

Florian's scream shattered the air.

They are fine. They can handle themselves.

They might not be real, the voice said again.

Hansel's axe was all that mattered.

She blocked out their pleas and bent down under the curved roof of the alcove, its smooth sides touching the tips of her dark hair. She gritted her teeth against the fear that swept within her to be inside a tree again, but this time she at least had a weapon. Several of them.

She picked up Hansel's axe and stroked its edge. She could smell the worn leather and the faint hint of smoke – a smell she recognised as home. Then she heard another scream.

'Shut up,' she whispered. 'It's a trick, Snow. Don't let them trick you.'

She sifted through the weapons, her mind pushing against the urge to run towards the screams. To help.

'This is your chance, Snow. You finally have your freedom. It's a lie.'

Her hand gripped the axe, and she snatched a knife with her other. The hilt was made of black leather, the seal of a stamp burnt into its surface. The weapon was light in her hand, the grip secure and balanced. She shoved it into her pocket when she spotted her mother's silver pen. The last she'd seen of it had been on the back of the cowardly horse. Growling, Snow snatched it up, shoving into her pocket as well.

Filthy thieves.

Run, the voice in her head said.

She bit down the fear and the hatred, the urge to slash the festering wood creatures into nothing but shavings roaring.

But she was free. She finally had an opportunity to choose her own path. She had a destination, and she'd seen enough maps to get to Perridorm by herself.

She halted in the shadows. Why shouldn't she just leave?

She could climb down with Hansel's axe and slip into the trees without a word. If her friends were here, she was sure they would find her later. They were tough, after all. And she knew Malak would always find her – just as his oath dictated.

Some time by herself may even be beneficial to the cause.

Another shout, and she stepped back into the sunlight. She could see her path clearly before her. Her quiet escape through the forest before anyone noticed she was gone.

She yearned for it.

But in the beat of a moment her heart pulled in two different directions.

Run, the voice said again.

Shaking off her doubt, Snow grabbed the axe and made her choice.

She ran.

XXI

The Dragon and Its Talon

The ground rumbled as Brufell ran towards Bronson, his feet swift and sure. The dwarf had hit his head badly on impact and blood ran down his temple, mixing with the kohl around his eyes. Oryx grasped onto Bronson's shirt as the dwarf groggily swore, Brufell reaching him in mere moments.

'What was that?' Bronson mumbled, reaching for his head. His fingers came back red.

'Get the med kit, Tuk,' Brufell yelled as he inspected the wound.

'That really hurt,' Bronson mumbled. 'Did you get hit, too, Brooofill.'

Bronson's eyes were heavy and Brufell sighed. 'You have a concussion. Lie down.'

'Concushion?' the dwarf slurred.

Tuk was back with the med kit, and Brufell pulled out some herbs. 'Could you make that brown stuff your people brewed? I'll find something for the bleeding.'

Tuk nodded before running off to get what he needed.

'Just rest, little one,' Brufell said.

The pixie trembled as the ground rumbled beneath them. A roar echoed through the air, and Brufell turned just as Oryx thrust out a finger, pointing ahead. A great dragon sprung up from the mountain, its scales gleaming like emerald and water-washed jade. Large leathery wings blocked the sunlight as the dragon called to the sky. Its head was broad and square, with teeth as long as Brufell's sword, each one glossy like polished ivory.

Wind tore at their clothes as the creature's massive wings beat the air. With a piercing cry, it vanished into the shrouded clouds above, leaving only the echo of its roar behind.

Brufell's mouth went dry, and he turned back to making his ointment. 'Looks like we found our dragon,' he grunted.

'It sounded sad,' Bronson whispered, staring at the sky.

Concussed or not, Bronson was right. The roar had not been one of triumph but of pain. As Brufell crushed the herbs into his palm, he wondered if they were doing the right thing or if they were condemning an innocent creature to death.

It was nightfall when Bronson, Brufell, and Tuk stood outside a cave's entrance. While the top was high, the entrance itself was narrow, making it resemble some kind of scar. The edges were moss-ridden, the rock dewy from the misty air.

Brufell peered inside, seeing nothing but darkness, but there was the scent of sulphur on the air which he took as a good sign. He dropped his pack, only taking what he needed, before hiding it in the brush.

From his own satchel, Tuk pulled out a jar of glowing lights and handed the jar to Brufell. 'To help.'

Bronson stepped closer to inspect, his brow furrowing, when he gasped. 'What is this?' Bronson asked, horrified. 'How long have you been keeping fire fairies? You've trapped them! Set them free.'

'No,' Tuk replied flatly. 'We don't keep long. Use for dark places.'

Brufell frowned, but he accepted the jar gingerly, his face screwed up with distaste. He held it up by the makeshift chain melted into the glass. The light flickered off the dark stone walls, illuminating the cavern a few steps ahead, giving them enough light to navigate the tunnels. It was effective, but he noted to free the critters later.

Slowly, both dwarves entered the cave. Brufell lifted the light to check out their surroundings. The roof curved upwards, filled with nothing but smooth stone until he could only see distant shadows.

'You won't fit, Tuk,' Brufell said, turning back towards the entrance.

'Tuk go to south door,' the troll said, handing Bronson a second lantern. 'Bigger.'

'Where shall we meet you?' Brufell asked.

'Inside. You will see Tuk's arrow.'

Tuk picked up a cloth bundle, gave them a nod, and veered down the rocky path to the other entrance.

Doubt crawled under Brufell's skin as the troll disappeared. Bronson frowned at the jar he held, his pinkie finger erect. Oryx wouldn't go near it, and Brufell couldn't blame him.

'Come on, Bronson,' Brufell said, entering the cave. As uncomfortable as they were, they had a bargain and Brufell couldn't allow them to lose the slightest advantage in the war to come. The walls brushed his shoulders, the cavern roof curving higher and higher until it opened, revealing the now darkening sky.

A soft dripping sound came from ahead, and the air moistened, sticking to their clothes like honey. His shirt itched from the buildup of dirt, his torn pants long past repair. Even Bronson couldn't save them now, which was saying something. His fingers brushed against his leather vest, the ties worn so thin he could hardly tie it up each morning. It was as if his clothing had begun to reflect the unravelling inside him at the prospect of facing Myrenna.

'This reminds me of that cave with the beast,' Bronson whispered. 'You know, the one we fell into after being chased by the scarats? The one where we found the colony.'

Oryx whimpered at the comment, and Brufell patted his head.

A stab pierced his heart as the bodies of the pixie's kin flashed before him. Wrinkled grey skin and blank eyes. Thousands of them piled on top of each other in a forgotten grave.

He shivered.

Whatever power had rushed through the mountains earlier, knocking them all to the ground, had been far more powerful than the fog dragon, though both were terrifying. But it had been the smell of incense that had triggered his memory. One of Nona smiling from the edge of a battlefield. Her long hair loose around her shoulders. Only someone as powerful as her could have released that kind of power.

Or something else.

A gift for giving at the aftermath—

The words from the prophesy echoed through his mind, beating to the same drum as his footsteps. But this wasn't the aftermath. Nona had given her gifts and Brufell hoped they were enough.

The tunnel eventually opened to a huge cavern, the roof curved into an opening showing the starlight sky. Stalactites hung from the ceiling in huge, crystallised rock. They shone like icicles against the light of the fairies.

Brufell paused, taking in the sight. He stood on a ledge protruding into the dark abyss. A great chasm stretched before them, the bottom delving into complete darkness. There was no other sound but their heavy breathing and the drip of water from somewhere.

Bronson came from behind, his breath close to Brufell's shoulder as he winced at the drop below. 'It couldn't be a meadow, could it? Or a nice beach. It always has to be a death drop.'

The sound of a deep rumble echoed the through the air and Brufell squeezed Bronson's shoulder, making him hush. The stench of sulphur grew, and another rumble echoed.

Slowly, Brufell lifted his lantern, and he sucked in a breath.

Because across the divide was a slumbering cerulean dragon.

XXII

The Crow and the Tinker

Dread crushed the throat of a man behind the old theatre complex. He didn't need a knife when it came to the filth that slinked through this city, especially in these parts.

Dread's head still throbbed from the blast, the barrel hitting him with such force that he'd struggled to get back up. The city had been trashed, the debris scattered throughout the streets. His men had managed to clean what they could, enough that the Queen could have her little parade, could pretend at diplomacy with her fake black carriage and pretty soldiers. But it was still a mess.

Dread tightened his grip and sneered. He hadn't bothered to learn the man's name, not when he was as valuable as a speck of lint on one of his shirts. The man's skin was already turning pale, blood seeping into his eyes. Dread could feel the tiny veins under the man's skin thrum, where it would take only one little push to dim his life.

Dread would have liked to have done nothing more, but he couldn't. Not when he needed information. He'd already asked all the basic questions, given him a description of his brother, asked about guard routes and taverns visited. But for someone who was claimed to hold secrets of this city, he was useless so far.

'Did you think when you didn't show up to our meeting I wouldn't notice?' Dread hissed.

The man muttered something, but it was lost to the air Dread was cutting off. With a sigh, Dread released him. Gasping, the man clutched his throat, and sagged against the damp cobblestones. His trembling fingers scraped against the ground, as if grounding himself after the suffocating grip had been lifted.

The sound of the crowded city streets echoed across the buildings. The Queen's black carriage was leaving, and the city had come out to see it. Dread had no interest in the carriage, but he noted the darting eyes of the man landing on the crowd of onlookers.

Dread knew one thing the man didn't know: the peace treaty with Carnell was a lie. The King rotted in the cells, half-dead, with the rats. Exactly where he belonged.

Dread leaned over the man and gave him a menacing smirk. 'Rumour has it that you know all the comings and goings of this city. That you worked for the Dream Weaver himself.'

The man flinched as Dread grabbed him by the shirt, hauling him back against the wall.

'You also know the guards who patrol the streets. Tell me where my brother is.'

'I t-told you,' the man stammered, 'I know of no shifters in the city guard.'

Dread slammed him against the wall again and the man whimpered as his shoulder cracked.

'But I have seen one with a similar description,' he said. 'One of sleek black hair and green piercing eyes.'

Dread didn't hold back the sneer crossing his face as the man's backside bit into the wall.

The man looked up at Dread with terror. 'He frequents the Tinder Box. You can find him there most nights. He prefers to drink alone.'

Dread stepped back and wiped his hands on his pants as if he'd touched a dead animal.

'He is only low on the rankings,' the man said. 'Not much in the way of authority. If he is a shifter, then he wants to keep it a secret.'

Dread turned and walked away, leaving the man huddled in a puddle of dank water.

If his brother was purposely hiding, then Dread needed to know why. No mission was so secret that the three brothers did not know about it. It was high time his brother answered his calls.

Dread was furious.

The sky burned a deep orange as dawn rose above the silhouetted buildings of the Silver City. The sun had only just breached the horizon as Dread swooped into Myrenna's tower.

The harsh scent of mixed herbs and potions tingled his nose as he shifted. Papers were strewn across the surfaces, stained and torn. A crack ran through Dread's back from the transformation.

Myrenna was gone. Just as his sources had confirmed.

After he'd left the alley, he'd received a message from one of the guards requesting his immediate return to the mines. When he'd enquired about the Queen, the guard had simply repeated the lie that she'd left for Carnell in the carriage.

But something was off.

He had shifted immediately, flocking here with urgency. She'd only just returned from the grave he had reported to her about, had only just returned with the murders mere days ago. But she wasn't here.

All that was left was a pestle and the crushed petal of a flower.

His broad fingers stroked the edge of the bowl before he growled. Black stained the inside of the mortar, the scent similar to a decaying root.

It was nightkiss flower.

His stomach fell, a stone weighing heavily in his gut before it solidified to rage. She was not meant to leave without telling anybody. Not when she was surrounded by so many enemies. Myrenna was powerful, yes, but so were others in this realm. And there were three in particular who would love the taste of her blood.

Dread threw open the doors and took the tower steps two at a time. His boots slapped against the cold stone and the staff scattered at the sight of him. But this time he took no pleasure in it.

His focus was on one thing: his Queen.

He powered down the halls, a tornado amongst the grand portraits hanging gracefully against the walls. The gold linings from the windows shone against the newly rising sun, the glass littering rainbows across the lush carpet. Dread marched around the next corner, the floor turning from carpet to marble, and shoved the huge doors of the throne room open. The chequered tiles and stained carpet led to Myrenna's grand throne, and behind it, Dread's target hung on the wall. The centrepiece of it all.

The gilded mirror.

Dread homed in on it – on the ghastly piece of magic that gave Myrenna her gift but also trapped her, squeezing its invisible chains around her neck like a pretty animal.

But she wasn't an animal.

She was a goddess.

He hated the mirror – had always hated it – just as he hated anything that threatened her. His rage coiled in his gut, coals spitting out black fire with each step. The Queen had taken nightkiss. The one plant that could mute her magic and make her human, *vulnerable.* Myrenna wasn't naïve; she would have known precisely what the nightkiss would do to her. She never did anything without reason.

But even the mighty could fall to the manipulations of their desires.

The mirror glistened as the dawn melted through the windows, the new day burning through Dread as the fire grew. He would have to release it soon, would have to find a way to let it go.

But he held onto the rage, the anger, letting it fill his veins. He would burn for her. Would turn to ashes if it meant her happiness. If asked, he would become dragon fire.

As he reached the dais, the mirror awoke, its smoke and glistening eyes smiling down at him with mild amusement.

'Where is she?' Dread demanded.

The mirror remained silent, as if waiting for a *please* or a greeting. But he wouldn't stoop to pleasantries with such an atrocity, wouldn't bend for anything so *unnatural.*

'Where is she?' he repeated through gritted teeth. 'Why did she take the nightkiss flower?'

The mirror's eyes glittered like leashed smoke, seeing and unseeing all at once. Its shadowed smoke drifted forward, wrapping around Dread's clenched fists, tickling his skin. There was something cold and empty about the touch, something *lifeless.*

Dread tried to breathe calmly, his veins filling with more fire. The glass shivered, morphing into liquid. He saw his reflection past the dark eyes of the mirror, warped and melted like a watercolour painting. It reminded him of an old quote, a tale told by his parents about reflection and perception.

To look through a glass darkly.

Power soaked through the smoke, twisting along his skin and taunting the threads of his rage. A smooth, velvet voice filled the room and crept under skin, along his bones, piercing into his mind.

'*Hello, Murder,*' the mirror said. '*What a pleasant surprise. A long time with no visit makes a mirror that cries.*'

Dread flicked away the curling mist and growled. 'I'm not here for your riddles.'

The glass reflected back at him, shapes slithering under its gleaming surface. '*The Queen has a spirit that cannot be tamed. Though years will pass, she remains unclaimed. She cannot answer to all who follow, for she has a need to fill what remains hollow.*'

Dread growled again, his muscles going taut as he stepped forward. 'Enough games, mirror. I saw the remnants of the nightkiss petal in her tower, ground up to drink.'

The mirror chuckled. '*The nightkiss flower is poisoned but sweet, and to some it's a gift to make them complete.*'

'She cannot be mortal,' Dread said darkly. 'And if she is, she cannot do it alone. There are too many enemies, too many variables. Tell me what I need to know: where is she?'

The mirror clicked its tongue, like chastising a child at their stupidity. '*If the Queen wanted company, she would have said so. But if it's directions you'd like, I'll tell you where to go.*'

Dread hissed but the mirror only laughed. The sound a hollow, faded thing. '*So much anger for a bird so small. The higher you fly, the further you'll fall.*'

Dread was at the end of his tether. He could taste the ash on his tongue. Feel the lava in his blood. His fists clenched at his sides, his nails digging in so hard he wouldn't be surprised if he'd drawn blood.

'You won't get anything from it,' a husky voice said from behind him.

Dread whirled around to find the Tinker standing in the middle of the room, slinking as he always did, with his creepy little hands and soulless eyes. The Tinker slithered closer, his purple robes dragging along the ground behind him like a brush on a canvas and Dread defied the urge to step back.

Dread noted the wooden spindle held in The Tinker's hands and sneered. 'How would you know?'

'I know because I've tried,' he replied calmly. 'The mirror bows only to her.' Dread rolled his eyes. 'And even sometimes I question that.'

The mirror smiled again, its smoke now reaching for the Tinker's robes. Dread ignored the mirror's prodding, and closed the distance between him and the Tinker, stopping a pixie away. He loomed above the Tinker, easily a head taller, and narrowed his eyes. 'What do you know?'

Surprisingly, the Tinker didn't step away or back down. 'I gave Her Majesty the nightkiss flower. Collected it myself, just as she ordered.' The Tinker smirked.

It was that smirk that unleashed the last of his patience. Dread had the Tinker by the throat in an instant, his feet barely touching the carpet, and Dread roared. Spittle loosed from his mouth, landing on the Tinker's cheek. And there, beneath the bravado, was the Tinker's tremble.

Dread grinned, letting the fire inside him twist into a storm. 'That sounds like grounds to kill you on.'

The Tinker smoothed his features and his spindly hand grazed Dread's wrist. 'I am the keeper of her secrets,' he croaked slowly, 'not you.'

The fire in Dread's stomach flared and he gritted his teeth. The Tinker barely touched his skin, but it felt like a wolf was tearing up his insides, waiting to slash its way out and sink its teeth into the Tinker.

'How does it feel to be a forgotten toy?' the Tinker cooed.

Dread stared into the Tinker's eyes. Neither blinked, some kind of unspoken war between them. Dread squeezed a little tighter, enjoying the way the Tinker gasped. But violence wouldn't get through to him; no, it was the Tinker's treasures he valued the most.

Dread's gaze flicked to the wooden spindle, and in a blink, he seized it. He dropped the Tinker on the floor with a satisfying crack, his nostrils flaring in triumph.

'Speaking of toys,' Dread began, 'how about I break this one? You've had enough time to play with it, haven't you? Or is it another obsession? One that awakens that thirst in you. One I could take. Perhaps I should have a play. What do you say to that, *Tinker?*'

The Tinker's eyes widened. 'Put it down. *Please.*' He rushed forward, his long fingers grasping for the spindle, desperation etched into his face. For a moment, he looked no different from the beggars in the streets.

Dread held the spindle above his head and smirked. The Tinker was so slight next to him, like a fragile piece of glass that Dread would enjoy shattering.

'That is not a toy!' the Tinker cried.

Dread threw the spindle in the air and caught it easily, this little game dousing some of the anger burning inside of him.

'It is the spindle of dreams, you feathery birdbrain! Give it back!'

'This old thing?' Dread sneered. 'It's pathetic. Just like you.' The Tinker's eyes filled with cold fury as Dread held the spindle, dangling it like a carrot to a horse. 'Are you going to jump, Tinker?'

'Enough!' the Tinker yelled. 'I'll tell you everything if you just give it back. She'll go mad with rage if we destroy it.'

Dread lowered his arm, stunned for a moment. 'Is that not your speciality? Destroying things? Why would the Queen rage?'

'If all I did was destroy,' he hissed, 'I would be called the destroyer and not the Tinker. I can break things, but I can also put them back together. I like knowing how things work, what their insides look like.'

'Including living things,' Dread said flatly, reluctantly handing it back.

'Especially those,' the Tinker replied, cradling the spindle. 'You think you know things, but you do not. The fourth Grimm has died. You would have felt the power surge when it happened. Even with your black feathers and rotted brain you would have felt something *change*.'

Dread paused. He had felt the tearing rift. The clap of power that surged through whatever force had been released. It had felt like the end of something. But there had also been a beginning in it. He crossed his arms and waited.

Sighing, the Tinker stroked the spindle and stared at Dread with determined eyes. 'The Queen wants the fourth Grimm's grimoire. She desires it greatly. But to get it, she must go unseen to a place. And to be unseen, she cannot wield power. So, the nightkiss was a necessary evil.' The Tinker lowered his voice, though there was nobody else in the room but the mirror. 'I assume you already know why she needs the grimoire.'

'Because the scrolls are insufficient.'

The Tinker nodded. 'Mirror,' he said, calling to the back wall. 'Why does the Queen need the grimoire?'

A shadowed face appeared in the mirror, and it smirked, its sharp teeth bright. *'The hearts of many only feed a little. The well is dry, and the Queen is brittle. She seeks a heart that will fill her years, for without it she faces her darkest fears. The Queen seeks leverage on a bargain she sought, and she seeks a Grimm's knowledge to kill what she wrought.'*

The Tinker waved the mirror off and faced Dread with stern eyes. 'The Queen needs the grimoire to kill the Grimms. Or better yet, she needs the heart of the Princess – the purest of hearts. Without either, she will fail.'

'Why do you tell me this if she hasn't?' Dread asked.

'Because we have the same goal,' the Tinker said. 'To see her in power, at her fullest, in her glory, releasing the darkness we have both come to crave.'

Dread took a step back and dropped his arms. The Tinker was uncomfortably observant.

'The Princess has almost been found,' Dread said, uncertain. 'She knows this – I reported it only yesterday.'

'It is not our job to question her but to serve her. You and I both know the Queen has many moving pieces. Her mines being another one of them as you well know. She has reasons, and we must trust those reasons as we have always done.'

The Tinker was right. Myrenna had more than her beauty and yet he still raged. He closed his eyes and took a breath. It wasn't just the mirror, or Myrenna. The hunt for his brother infuriated him; the hunt for the Princess, too, and though he wished to stay, it was time to return to the mines. His time was up. The sandglass had run dry.

With the Tinker and the murders on watch, the city would be secure. Dread didn't know how long the mines would last without his presence. The beasts, after all, were restless.

He lifted the corner of his mouth as the Tinker's face turned to confusion. With a quick step forward, Dread punched the Tinker square in the nose.

The Tinker sputtered, clutching his bleeding face.

Dread flexed his fist, the anger under his skin receding, if only a little. 'I'd like to say it was a pleasure, but we both know I find you disgusting.'

With a satisfied snort, he left the Tinker bleeding, stormed out of the throne room, and shifted at the nearest window. He had to find his brother before he could leave the city, but then he would fly home.

If Myrenna insisted on leaving alone for one of her schemes, then he would do the same. And after that, he would find what Myrenna craved, lying deep within the earth behind a door of bones.

XXIII
The Lost Brother

Bronson's breath stuttered in his lungs, his eyes wide as he took in what felt like the edge of the world crumbling beneath his boots. Nothing but black existed in the void that stretched before him, a chasm in the earth so deep he wondered if he kicked a pebble into its gaping mouth, would he hear the echo?

The slash of night at his feet wasn't even the scariest thing in this cave. No, that would be the slumbering dragon, stretched idly along the ledge on the other side of the divide. Shadows floated over the dragon's scales, glimmering with emerald and specks of blue, oddly pretty for how its barbed tail twitched while sleeping, as though dreaming.

Or pondering what was for dinner, which Bronson sincerely hoped wasn't them. Why did he ever follow Brufell on this insane quest – who chose to search out a *dragon?*

They were in so much fairy shit.

Bronson didn't realise he was tilting forward until he felt the sturdy weight of Brufell's arm wrapping around his chest, pulling him to safety. 'Make no sudden movements.'

'Well, I wasn't planning to dance about with a tambourine,' he muttered, tugging at his vest and smoothing his hair. Things he could control.

He knew the others teased him sometimes about his fussiness, but it settled him. Being able to touch the clothes he wore, feeling the fabric of the vest he'd created, ground him.

They were almost on the other side. From this distance, Bronson could hear the dragon's soft snores. See the ripple on its shimmering scales from the open roof that revealed a starlit sky. A breeze came from the entryway behind them, and Bronson's hair tickled his forehead.

Brufell stayed close his side, the pixie tucked away inside his front pocket and nudged his chin towards the sleeping dragon. 'Dragons don't have sensitive smell. If we're quiet, we should be able to approach it.'

'It doesn't look very big,' Bronson said. 'Only a baby, if the green dragon we saw flying earlier is anything to go by.'

'Precisely,' Brufell replied. 'But if we move quickly, we should be able to catch it and grab its tooth before the bigger one returns.'

'You're not going to kill it, are you, Brufell?'

His voice was quieter than expected, guilt lingering in each syllable. While he didn't want to die being eaten, he also didn't want to harm the creature, especially when it had done nothing to them yet. Plus, if it was only a child, then that made them villains.

The sword in Brufell's hand glinted against the moonlight. 'Not if I don't have to, little one.'

Bronson wasn't sure if that made him feel better, but he nodded anyway and followed Brufell's lead. He counted his steps, avoiding looking at the darkness below. It took everything in him not to fall, his heart beating so loud it drowned out everything else. The rocks made his footing uneven, and when he was almost across, his foot slipped, and he cried out as gravity pulled him down.

Brufell's hand grasped his, and he hung against the jagged wall. He dangled above the chasm, his legs kicking out into the empty void below, finding nothing but air. There was a roaring in his ears and his breath came in ragged gasps, heart hammering against his ribs as the sheer drop yawned beneath him. This wasn't how he was supposed to die, not in an abyss with only Brufell. He was supposed to host parties where the Princess would bring her court. He was supposed to create beautiful clothes and sing ballads. His grip slipped by a notch, and Brufell hissed. Oryx shot forward, his tiny fingers grasping at Bronson's clothes to help, but failing miserably.

All Bronson could do was whimper.

The snores of the dragon ceased. Everything went still.

The hair on the back of Bronson's neck rose as Brufell grunted, using his bodyweight to lean back. There was nothing elegant about the way Bronson clambered for a grip, nothing subtle about the way he groped onto the ledge, or graceful when he was finally pulled to safety.

Quickly, Bronson scrambled back from the edge, his limbs shaking uncontrollably. He opened his mouth to ask a question when he noticed Brufell already moving the last few paces to the other side.

Of course, I almost die and the old fart forgets about it immediately.

Bronson scrambled after him, only to realise the cave had gone quiet. There was an empty space where the dragon had been, setting off the hairs on his skin. Bronson shuffled after Brufell, every shadow in the cavern now a threat. Huge stalactites dripped from the ceiling, its twin forms on the ground like jagged teeth. He forced each step to be silent, swallowing down the urge to bolt as they approached a towering stalagmite, its rough surface slick beneath his trembling fingers. He pressed his back against it, its surface cool and damp. His breath came in short, uneven pants, and Brufell's sharp gaze swept over him, checking for injuries. Oryx climbed the rock, sneaking a peek over the top, before Brufell braved a look too.

The old dwarf pursed his lips. 'I can't see it.'

'Maybe Oryx can help,' Bronson replied, deciding he'd rather eat a live scarat before exposing himself to a fire-breathing animal.

Oryx frowned down at him.

'All you have to do is see where he is and report back,' Bronson muttered, irritated that they were even here in the first place.

With a sigh, the pixie left, blending into the same foreboding shadows Bronson did not trust.

'Let's hope we can get in and get out,' Brufell murmured, keeping his voice low. 'I don't want to be around when mother dragon comes back.'

Bronson gulped. He hated it here.

Thankfully, Oryx was back in moments, pointing towards the back wall and signing something to Bronson.

'The dragon is hiding in the far shadows,' Bronson translated.

Brufell nodded. 'If we're quick, we can move from both sides and corner him.'

Oil slid through Bronson's veins at the thought. He didn't want to corner the dragon – didn't want to go near one, in fact. He had friends. He had family. He wasn't Frode.

Brufell nudged Bronson, edging him forward.

With a hiss, Bronson bounced on his feet before he finally moved. His steps echoed louder than he liked. He kept to the shadows, shifting in and out of the dark until they finally reached the back wall where the dragon hid.

Bronson swallowed. He could hear the deep breaths of the creature. He braved a glance and regretted it immediately as sharp golden eyes stared back at him.

By the cauldron, the beast was only twenty pixies away.

With the realisation, Bronson winced before running for the nearest stalagmite and hiding behind it.

Sulphur filled the air, the heat in the cavern stifling. Sweat pooled down his neck as he prayed to whatever Gods would listen that the animal wouldn't eat him. He waited for the growl that would come, the inevitable stench of burning flesh or the tip of a sharp tooth.

But all that came was a whimper.

Bronson dared a peek from behind his hiding spot, finding the dragon nearby. Its wide, golden eyes, molten like the gold beneath Parador, were filled not with fury but with fear. The dragon balanced on three legs, its head swivelling between Brufell stepping closer and where Bronson stood.

As the pixie appeared, the dragon whimpered again, tucking itself against the wall at its back.

That sinking feeling coated Bronson's skin again.

The dragon was trapped. And from the look of golden blood on its raised foot, the animal was hurt, too.

This isn't right.

Bronson hesitated, his own memory of the arena reminding him of the shaking terror at being alone and afraid, about to die. With bravery he didn't feel, Bronson stepped out of the shadows and raised his arms. He didn't exactly have a plan, not when the most he knew about dragons came from a story Brufell had told the night before, but if the creature was anything like him, he'd need to know he wasn't in danger. That it was okay.

The dragon snarled as Bronson stepped forward, but there was a pain to it that made Bronson shudder. Despite his fear, or the sight of those extremely sharp teeth, Bronson approached. Oryx appeared from the shadows and pushed on his chest in a feeble attempt to stop him, but he couldn't stop. Not when he'd already made his choice.

'Bronson,' Brufell hissed from the darkness, sharp and commanding.

But Bronson ignored the warning tone.

Blood dropped from the dragon's foot, where a claw was torn and raw. The dragon held it elevated from the ground, hindering its manoeuvrability as it shuffled back.

'Let me help you,' Bronson whispered, hoping for a tone that suggested he could help but quiet enough that he didn't sound like food. 'I have medicine. I can help you,'

The dragon eyed him suspiciously.

Bronson took another step, and the dragon flinched.

From the shadows, Brufell spoke through gritted teeth. 'Have you gone insane? Get back here now!'

The dragon snarled as it eyed Oryx by Bronsons shoulder, backing closer to the wall. But there was nowhere for it go unless it decided to trample him. Bronson supposed the creature could fly through the ceiling, but maybe the wound hindered that, too?

When he was close enough, Bronson lowered his hand to grasp at the pouch that hung by his belt. He froze at the snapping teeth that neared his face, spittle flying onto his cheeks. He whimpered as some of it rained down his cheek.

'Please,' he whispered again. 'It will help.'

Golden eyes assessed him, the dragon twitching as it sized Bronson up. If he wasn't already about his piss his pants he would have laughed. Dwarves were already small creatures; next to the dragon, child or not, he was a fairy flying beside a troll.

Bronson tried for his pouch again, the dragon letting him this time. He peeled it open slowly, before holding it out for the dragon to sniff.

'I have some medicine,' Bronson said shakily. 'It's not much, just a tincture Brufell and I made on the road, but it might help the wound.'

Bronson took it as a good sign that the dragon didn't growl this time. With another few steps, the dragon's nostrils flared, his snout only a pixie's length from Bronson's nose. The stench of sulphur was stronger now, as if the dragon was made of it. The creature's breath was hot and wet, coating Bronson in a muck that made his insides squirm.

Bronson held back the urge to wipe his face and instead forced a smile, twisting his face into something ugly instead of comforting.

The dragon side-eyed Bronson before smelling his pouch again. Bronson used the opportunity to inspect the colours of the dragons scales. Each scale was the size of a conch shell, coloured with different sheens and patterns. Bronson yearned to touch them, to see whether they were soft, or as razor sharp as the tales told.

A grumble echoed from behind Brufell's rock, and the dragon reared back with a growl.

'He won't harm you,' Bronson said, his tone taking on a hint of desperation. 'Not while I'm here.'

The dragon shuffled, the movement causing rocks to skitter across the floor. The ground rumbled, the taut air suffocating until the dragon lowered its head. Bronson could only blink as the dragon sat, its eyes never blinking, and offered its wounded foot.

Bronson swallowed his fear down, the emotion tasting like razorblades down his throat. By some miracle, he managed to keep his hands from shaking as he assessed the wound. From the looks of it, the dragon had three claws on each foot, and the one that was injured only held two: the middle claw had been torn completely off. The wound was open, dirt-encrusted, and a little green.

Bronson's nose twitched in disgust. 'We need to wash this, okay? I'm going to pour something on it to help it. It's going to sting.'

The dragon held still as Bronson pulled out his whisky flask and yanked out the cork with a small *pop*. He hovered it over the wound before he spoke again. 'Remember, this will hurt.'

As he poured the liquor, the dragon reared back, his injured leg hitting Bronson in the chest and knocking him backwards across the cave floor. There was a moment where the world blackened and the ring of Brufell's screams could be heard over the roaring in his ears.

Brufell stood firm, sword gleaming in the dim light, its tip unwavering as it pointed towards the dragon.

Bronson winced, blinking past the sharp ache in his back as he propped himself up on his elbows. His voice was quiet, almost lost beneath the dragon's heavy breaths. 'I said it would hurt. I'm sorry.'

The dragon let out another guttural snarl, but this time, it wasn't fury that sharpened its teeth, it was pain.

Brufell stood with his legs apart, his sword raised. 'Hurt him and I'll slice you to bits.'

There was a tone to Brufell's voice Bronson had never heard before and it made him shiver. But, for once, he didn't want Brufell to protect him, to stand between him and death. This had been his choice to make, his act of bravery for the quest or whatever it was they were doing.

Bronson stood and ignored the throbbing pain in his lower back from his fall. 'Let me do this, Brufell.'

'Let you do what?' Brufell snapped. 'Get yourself killed?'

'This isn't the arena.'

'No, it's worse,' Brufell said. 'This is a *dragon.*'

The dragon released a huff, before it reached out its talon towards Oryx nearby. The pixie squeaked, dodging the claw, but it only enticed the dragon. The creature's tail twitched in excitement as it followed Oryx's every move, reminding Bronson of a cat and a mouse.

Bronson touched the old dwarf's shoulder, 'Look at it, Brufell. Truly look at it. He's a baby. He's wounded. Let me help him – let *us* help him – and in turn he might help us. Remember Frode's mother? Her judgement?'

Brufell was silent, but the hardness behind his eyes had softened a little. 'We will try it your way this time,' he conceded.

With a smile, Bronson walked back to the dragon, who huffed another breath towards Oryx. The pixie, by this point, was squealing, spinning through the air as they dodged and chased one another. Ignoring them both, Bronson put on his best soothing voice. 'The hard part is over. Let me place some salve on it and then we can wrap it.'

He was about to open his pouch again when a rush of hot, foul air blew over him. The baby dragon froze, his wide eyes staring at something behind Bronson.

Though he suspected what had arrived, Bronson still turned around.

And met the teeth of the largest dragon he had ever seen.

Dread heard the bell of the Tinder Box as he waited in the shadows of a cobbler. He stood just out of reach from the square, hidden from prying eyes as the drunks came and went. He could still hear the markets down the way, the patrons packing up their stalls as the sky turned to dusk. It would be twilight soon.

This area of town was known for robberies and selling skin, the people starving and searching for scraps. It didn't surprise him the soldiers' most attended tavern lay in the dregs of the city so close to the Caged Robin and its debauchery. It also didn't surprise him his brother would be found here. His younger sibling had a knack for bad decisions.

Dread wrinkled his nose at the smell of urine and stale alcohol. It burned through his nostrils the way the metallic scent of blood did.

Across the square, three shadows emerged from one of the cobblestone streets. They howled with laughter, the sound echoing off the canal lining the square. Dread tucked himself further into the shadows as they approached.

'She was definitely my kind of girl.' one of them laughed. 'Sweet and small and innocent.'

'Innocent?' another said. 'Oh, no! I'll bet she's just begging to be swept away by a man in uniform. A ripe little thing like that? Even the Queen wouldn't deny me.'

Dread sneered, the rage still boiling in him long after his visit to the throne room.

'Hush,' the other said. 'Don't speak about Her Majesty that way. She'll do as she pleases.'

'Cauldron help us, Flynn,' one said, throwing up his arms. 'Do you ever just have a laugh?'

Flynn.

As the three of them got closer, Dread noted the shiny fresh uniforms and the neat hair, but it was only one soldier that caught his attention: the one with slicked, black hair and piercing green eyes.

'I see you, Brother,' Dread hissed quietly.

He watched the guards bicker, the argument ending as one of them commented, 'You're as dreary as a corpse.'

They chuckled as they entered the Tinder Box, music pouring out of it like spilled wine.

Flynn froze in the doorway. His green eyes swept the square, landing only for a moment on the dark space from which Dread watched him.

With a cruel smile, Dread stepped into the light, the sky finally turning a murky grey.

Flynn held his gaze, not even a twitch on his smooth, pale face.

Dread held the stare in challenge before he shot his brother a wink—

I've found you.

Flynn entered the tavern, leaving his hulking brother in the shadows.

XXIV
The Blood of Royalty

Malak was flying.

Or falling.

He didn't quite know.

After the explosion, the platform had splintered beneath him, dropping him into a chaos that felt achingly familiar – like the collapse on the mountain before they found the mines of Parador. White light seared through a blur of green, flickering past in flashes that stung his eyes, twisting dream into nightmare.

Wind whipped around Malak as the world careened by. His chest seized, then tightened further as something coiled around his torso: thick wood and twisting vines, a sudden lifeline that snapped taut, yanking him upward. Air whooshed past his ears, and then solid ground slammed beneath his boots.

Malak crumpled, limbs trembling too fiercely to hold him upright. His breath came ragged, each inhale scraping his lungs raw. He forced himself to focus, slow it down. Inhale. Exhale. Gradually, his hammering heart eased. 'Thank you,' he rasped to the empty air.

No answer. Only the rustling of leaves. The magical branches were gone. Just as well – he still wanted to carve them into kindling for taking Snow.

A howl pierced the stillness. Pip. Malak's gaze snapped up to see the elf bounding across one of the makeshift bridges, Florian close behind, panic etched into both of their faces. Pip's brown jacket was torn, though the old elf moved with a stubborn vigour. The prince's pale hair was wild, catching on branches as he sprinted.

Before Malak could rise, the bark of the tree beside him rippled and twisted. The carved face of mushroom lips emerged, eyes fathomless green pools. 'It's been an age since someone of your kind said thank you,' the tree mused, its tone solemn.

Malak straightened, muscles stiff but steady. 'You saved my life. Thanking you was the least I could do.' He rubbed his palms over his knees. 'You could have let me fall.'

'I could have,' the tree agreed, its gaze unreadable. 'But it is not our way to kill so easily – unlike others in this realm.'

Florian's frantic voice cut through the air, closer now.

'They're alive, if that's what worries you,' the tree said.

'I can hear that.' Malak smiled faintly.

The bark creature's lips curled into a knowing smirk. 'The ties of fate do not wither so easily.'

The platform shuddered as Pip and Florian finally reached him. Florian didn't hesitate – he threw his arms around Malak in a fierce embrace. Malak stiffened, unsure how to react, but gradually he melted into the prince's grip and patted his back. The prince's wild hair poked at his chin, and a twig was stuck awkwardly near his ear.

'By the cauldron, Malak,' Florian wheezed. 'We thought you were dead!'

Malak smiled down at him, warmth flickering through his chest. His gaze shifted to Pip. The old elf stumbled onto the platform, dark eyes crinkling with relief before his expression returned to its usual sardonic calm. Thankfully, he refrained from a hug, offering only a curt nod.

'The wood folk have been kind,' Pip said, his voice gruff.

'Maybe they'll save Snow, too.' Malak turned to the bark face – but it was gone, leaving behind the rough pattern of ordinary wood.

'He was just there,' Malak muttered.

'Who?' Florian asked.

'It doesn't matter now.' Pip knocked ash from his pipe. 'Come along. We'll go to the elders. Saving you means they respect you – a rare thing among wood folk.'

Before Malak could respond, Pip was already marching ahead, Florian following.

Malak hesitated, fists clenching and unclenching as he fought to ground himself. The rush of survival faded, leaving a gnawing dread in its place. His heart had found its rhythm again, but his mind raced – sharp, relentless, wide-eyed. A heavy knot twisted in his gut as restless winds rustled the leaves around him. Hope clawed at him, raw and fragile. Snow had to be freed – it was the only outcome that made sense.

But dread clung to his bones, cold and unyielding. He knew this feeling. He'd felt it just before Hansel had left to chase the Seeker. Before Troll's Keep. Before the grotto had been attacked.

This time, though, it was worse.

This time, he couldn't ignore it.

Snow crashed through the underbrush of the forest and leapt over a moss-covered log, staining her dress. She'd already managed to tear her sleeve, her porcelain skin exposed like the moon on a starless night. Mud lined the hem, her slippers long gone somewhere near where she had escaped.

Good riddance.

Her heart pounded in her chest, the thrum of her blood loud in her ears. She could taste the sweet honey nectar of the sap on her lips, a euphoria coating her senses every time she tasted it.

Twigs snapped in her wake as she ran with fervour, her soul singing at the freedom and her heart dreading being caught by the spindly hands of the wood folk. She held onto that desperation of freedom until the feeling of being inside that tree seemed far away, until the sounds of restless clicking and creaking bark was replaced with birdsong and silence.

When she thought she'd crossed enough distance, she slowed to a walk, her breaths shallow. The forest glistened before her. Bell flowers bloomed by her right, their bulbs opening with a tentative blue. She watched as a bee landed, seeking pollen, the fur on it looking particularly soft. Ferns grew in large, green bursts, dotting the trees with lush greenery and pale veins that glowed.

Exhausted, Snow dropped onto the grass with a soft thump and groaned in pleasure at the sudden stillness. It seemed so serene here, the plant-life content in what the world had to offer, so full of lifeblood and light. Her muscles let go and the tightness in her back receded as she relaxed into the grass. And though she should have wanted to sleep, her eyes lit up like a fire. Each detail, each living thing, pulsed like her own heart. Her dress was suddenly the colour cerulean, reflecting like the ocean in one of the portraits back at Bellatorre's castle. The lace had turned bronze, but in this light it seemed almost gold. Her skin was luminescent, almost silver as she soaked it all in. Maybe she wasn't just a princess or a queen. Maybe she was one of the star-kissed gods in the night sky.

She was distracted again, by the bees moving across the multicoloured flowers with a peaceful buzz, and she felt their fluttering wings. She experienced the breath of the grass as it released a sigh under her. The way the wind danced along her skin, and how the trees rustled in song.

For years she had lived in agony, everybody watching her every step with ferocity, as if she stood on the ledge of a great chasm, her sanity only a mere breeze from falling over the edge.

For the first time in her life, she was free.

Alone in a forest.

Tasting sweet nectar on her lips.

The blades of grass tickled her fingertips, soft like one of the plush rugs back in the castle, and she giggled.

She felt glorious. And wild.

Alive.

Her skin buzzed, like a happy melody was being played just for her. She lifted her fingers – were they always this pale? The dirt under her fingernails glinted and she peered closer, catching flecks of gold. It was a wonder. Her head was dizzy but the glitter amongst the dirt was as clear as the grotto's water, shining as it lit up her eyes. She noted the sap on her palms and licked her hand clean. Her body warmed at the taste, the way it tingled her tongue, and at the burst of colour behind her eyelids.

Lost to herself, Snow barely heard the arrival of a stranger. A twig snapped, a subtle sound, yet enough to make her peer between the shadows of the trees. The ground seemed to shift like the sea beneath the figure's strong strides. Snow rubbed her eyes, the urge to run feeling distant, almost out of reach.

A shadow blocked the sunlight, and she blinked, her vision becoming clearer. And she made of the shape of a man standing over her, with golden brown eyes.

'Hansel!' she squealed, attempting to get up and failing. She fell back down. He rippled like a mirage, and she squinted, barely making out his arms, the strong set of his shoulders, his sharp jawline.

So pretty.

He was smiling, his white teeth a warm welcome as he reached out towards her. Snow had never wanted to take his hand more than she did now, to share this wondrous place with him. But her body was sluggish, heavier than it had been before. She whimpered as her limbs refused to answer, the colours becoming too bright. Too loud.

The grass tickled her skin, grazing her face like a caress as she breathed it in. The groggy smile permanent on her lips. What would it be like to be this still? To enjoy nature at its best? To live in the wild like a hunter?

She didn't want to leave, didn't want to endure the war that loomed before her. But Hansel was here. And everything else seemed so far away, so unimportant.

His hand remained outstretched, calling to her against the lull of the forest. 'Lay with me, Hansel,' she murmured. 'Just for a moment.'

But he didn't reply; he merely stood there with his arm extended. The hand she still couldn't reach.

Why is he so far away?

His voice came out like chocolate, rich and smooth and sweet. 'I cannot stay with you,' he said. 'You must take my hand. You cannot remain here a moment longer.'

Oh, that voice, she thought. *That warm, beautiful voice.*

Suddenly, Hansel stopped smiling, his lips pursing as something tugged at Snow: the *wrongness* of it all.

Snow frowned at the grass as it turned a sickly brown and withered. Decay and rot slithered up her nose, the ground turned cold and hard.

Snow screeched as vines shot out, wrapping around her arms and ankles.

They are back. The wood nymphs are back.

Her back arched as the vines gripped her, growing from the soil, and piercing her flesh. They moved under her skin, and she screamed and screamed. She clawed them as they crawled further and further under her skin. Into her bones. Into her soul.

'Hansel!' she shrieked.

He stood like a statue, watching her struggle as more vines snaked from the ground. Her world tilted again, its once-vibrant life turning the world to grey—

Except for her blood.

Red fell to the ground in pools, moving through the dirt like worms. Scattering around her as it came alive.

The taste of honey in her mouth turned to ash.

'Take my hand, Princess,' Hansel insisted. 'You must run.'

But how could she?

The vines snaked across her bones, sharp pain shooting through her very core. They were in her. Within her very soul. Piercing each and every part of her. Her vision blackened, the vines now crawling up her throat. She choked.

Hansel was the only light, his warm eyes pulling her back.

With painful effort, Snow gritted her teeth and lifted her dead arm. It was as if she carried a thousand chains, the metal grinding against her skin and pulling her down. Yet, some of the vines snapped, tearing her skin and peeling her apart like a skinned animal.

With the pain came clarity.

Hansel came into focus, his hair shining like the sun. She thrashed again, pulling at the chains, screaming as it tore her skin. With a last thrash, she reached out her hand, stretching it towards Hansel as stars blinked across her vision.

She was barely inches from him when the vines snapped, and she broke free. Her hand shot forth, her body dripping with blood.

But it never met Hansel's.

He flickered in the light, fading in and out.

Snow stumbled forward. 'Hansel?' she panted.

She turned back to where the vines had been, but only untouched grass lay there. She ran her hands up her arms, noting only small cuts and bruises. Yet, somehow, the pain and terror lingered.

Her temples throbbed, each pulse sharp and relentless. She squeezed her head between trembling hands, fingers digging into her scalp as if to contain the chaos within. The ache clawed its way through her senses, making the world tilt and blur. A warm breeze rustled the leaves, brushing against her clammy skin. Her tongue scraped against the roof of her mouth – parched and cracked, as though the desert winds had carved themselves into the hollows of her body.

The sap, she thought. *It must have poisoned me.*

Except Hansel remained.

'Are you really here?' she wheezed.

Silence enveloped them as he flickered in and out of the light again.

She frowned.

It's a dream, she thought. *It's just a dream.*

But a good dream, the voices inside her mind echoed.

Hansel's eyes whipped behind her as the silence broke, the sound of howls piercing though the distance. 'You must run. *Run now.*'

'Wait,' she said, desperation in her voice. She reached out, only for her hand to meet nothing. He was gone.

Another howl broke through the trees and Snow whirled around. The cries were violent and savage, like starving dogs. She recognised that sound.

Dark hounds.

She shivered at the thought. She'd seen these beasts. Had dreamt about them many times when they called from the castle's keep, and she finally panicked. Only one animal cried for blood with a howl like that. One that had been trained to kill. That had been honed to hurt and tear the flesh of its victims. And Myrenna had loved them because of it.

Snow stumbled, breaking into a sprint. Her arms smacked away the brush as she flew over the forest floor, rocks cutting into the soles of her bare feet.

The hounds had smelt her.

And they wanted her blood.

The trees melted into one another, their twisted forms swaying like ink bleeding across wet paper. She staggered, the world tilting beneath her feet, and a cold knot of panic cinched tight around her chest. The once-thrilling freedom of solitude now clung to her like a suffocating shroud. Distant echoes rippled through the trees – screams; her friends' voices, frayed and fading. Her stomach twisted.

Stupid. Naïve. Too young. Every bitter warning she'd ignored crashed down on her. Who was she without them? Just a shattered, bleeding, drugged-up princess with no map to reality. A coward hiding behind her dreams. Selfish. Weak. Everything they'd said she was – maybe worse.

Her heart slammed against her ribs, each beat a desperate drum urging her forward. Branches lashed at her hands, stinging like wild screams, but she tore through the trees without slowing. The howls snapped closer, gnashing and ravenous, and the eerie whistle of their master sliced through the air behind her. Sweat clung to her spine, her legs churning despite the fire in her thighs. The raw soles of her feet scraped against the unforgiving earth, every step a fresh spark of agony, every blister a testament to her flight. She wasn't a princess now – just flesh, breath, and fear. A meal for the dark hounds on her trail.

Malak growled. 'Something's wrong.'

The three of them stood in front of the elders. Each carved face seemed to mock them.

The female elder spoke first, her voice scattering through the still wind. '"Wrong" is correct. We save one of you, only for another to slice at our skin,' she hissed. 'Again we have been fooled into trusting others not of our own.'

The elder with the mushroomed lips groaned as his face appeared in a trunk nearby. 'The beautiful one has tarnished you. What say you now?'

Malak had already apologised for his misgivings with his sword, and after his rescue he'd assumed they'd forgiven him for that. But nobody had called him the beautiful one, *ever.* And he certainly knew today hadn't changed that fact. They could only mean one person: Snow.

'What do you mean, "tarnished?" What happened? What did she do?' Malak asked.

Pointy nose seethed at them. 'The one you bargained for has left. She has broken through our skin and stolen from us!'

'Where is she?' Malak demanded, stepping forward. His heart pounded in his chest, rising fear biting at his core at the thought of her alone.

'Gone,' said the female. 'Running as we speak, no doubt causing more pain to our brothers and sisters.'

Malak's stomach flipped. 'We didn't help her break free. Our goal remains the same: tell us where she is, and we'll leave you be.'

'*Liars,*' big nose hissed. 'You demand information when you have broken what you promised us.'

'If I may intervene,' Pip said, stepping forward. 'None of us made any specific promises. A promise is a powerful thing, after all. But we certainly did not go back on our word. The terms were to return the Princess to us and then we would negotiate a treaty with the other kingdoms about the use of your kind should we win the war.'

The female scoffed, bark shooting forth from her mouth. 'You lie. You could not wait for us to decide, and like all those with short lives, you moved hastily. She's damaged one of our own, hacked at our skin and made us bleed. She even took the blood!'

Bushy eyebrows intervened, his voice bellowing across the trees. 'The little thief gulped it down as she fled!'

Pip's face paled.

Malak turned to him. 'What do they mean took the blood?'

'You're all liars!' the Elder's screamed.

'It means she's digested the sap,' Pip said.

'Traitors!' the trees bellowed.

'What does that mean?' Malak asked as the trees began to warp.

'Killers!'

'It means she's drugged,' Florian piped in. 'It's mind-altering. Causes visions of all sorts – not always good.'

The wooden platform groaned under them as the elders shifted their mouths, opening them wide. *'Murderers!'*

The bark split with a chorus of sharp, cracking *pops*, spraying splinters into the thick air. From the ruptured wood, nymphs burst forth in a frenzy, their eyes gleaming with raw, feral hunger. Their twisted limbs shimmered with bark and moss, vines coiling like serpents around their bodies. They moved with unnatural speed, circling Malak, Florian, and Pip in a tightening, twitching ring, their breath thick with the scent of sap and decay. The forest trembled under their wild energy, as though the trees themselves had unleashed something ancient and merciless.

'Less spouting facts, Prince, more running,' Pip suggested, backing up until he stood back-to-back with Malak and Florian, forming a defensive circle. The nymphs moved in sync, the elders morphing as the branches of the trees cracked under the newfound movement.

'We need weapons,' Malak shot back.

'We need a miracle,' Florian whispered.

'What we really need is a distraction,' Pip replied.

And then the howls came.

The trees seemed to freeze in place, their limbs stiffening as the chilling, guttural cries of the hunting party echoed through the woods. Shadowy forms emerged from the depths of the forest, moving with a swift, terrifying unity. The unmistakable rhythm of their paws pounding against the earth, like a drumbeat of doom, reverberated through the air.

'No,' Malak whispered.

They were surrounded. The wood nymphs shuddered as shadows surged through the trees in a blur of snarling fury. Dark hounds erupted from the undergrowth, their black hides rippling with taut muscle. Foam glistened at their snapping jaws, their eyes burning with savage intent. The air thickened with the sharp, metallic taste of fear, the forest seeming to hold its breath as the predators closed in.

'Revenge will be enacted,' the female tree swore. 'Your princess is doomed.'

Malak's eyes flicked to an opening – a narrow, fleeting gap in the chaos. He didn't hesitate. With a swift motion, he hoisted Florian over his shoulder and yanked Pip by the waist. His feet hit the ground hard, muscles coiling as he lunged forward and weaved through the shifting maze of creaking wood.

Florian's elbows jabbed into his back, sharp grunts breaking through the prince's protests. Pip let out a strangled yelp – one Malak hoped never to hear again. The branches blurred beneath his flying steps, splintering with sharp cracks under his weight. Behind them, the forest erupted in a shrill cacophony, wood nymphs screeching as they swarmed like furious wasps.

'Umm ...' Florian said.

'What is it?' Malak puffed as he jumped from one platform to another. The wood dropped, sliding a few pixies down the tree as the roots holding it up creaked.

'Nothing,' the Prince whimpered. 'Just maybe try to go a little faster. Not that I know you aren't already, it's just that we have, umm …'

'WHAT?' Malak yelled as he flew across another bridge.

'Nothing.'

'What the Prince means to say,' Pip said, 'is that there is an angry horde of wood nymphs directly behind us carrying sticks and what looks to be knives. They are getting closer and, in all honesty, they look terrifying.'

Malak shot forward, his growl coming out thick. 'I'd move faster if you didn't weigh so much. Florian is lighter than you. What do you eat?' His hands gripped his two friends as he slid on one of the platforms' moss-covered surfaces and chanced a look behind him.

Angry horde was an understatement; it was an army, roiling toward him at an impossible speed. From here, the tiny bodies resembled a swarm of locusts instead of wood nymphs, each one blending into a terrifying monster that would crash into them at any moment.

Malak kept running, dodging trees, platforms, bridges, and nymphs.

The forest was alive, writhing with fury. Nymphs exploded from the bark, launching through the air in a storm of tangled limbs and snapping branches. Their wild eyes glinted, fingers clawing through the space around him, some diving in front, others cutting from the sides like arrows. Pip swung his arms out as another latched onto Malak's back, attempting to throw it off. Florian only whimpered.

Malak twisted Pip around as he dodged a low-hanging branch, the wood missing the elf's head by a pixie when his feet hit more moss. He felt the slip too late, the bark too far to grasp.

Another wood nymph latched on, gnashing its teeth, when the floor fell out from under them.

The wood nymph squealed as the platform snapped, casting them into a freefall.

Florian and Pip screamed as Malak held tight.

The wind roared in their ears as they fell.

And fell.

And fell.

XXV

The Mother Dragon

Bronson's pulse slammed in his ears, drowning out everything but the thunder of fear. The dragon loomed above him, scales glossy like molten stone, eyes gleaming with a predator's cold focus.

Tuk moved like a blur, barely a flicker against the cavern's glow. Another arrow flew, cutting through the air like a streak of moonlight. It hit the dragon, straight into its eye, sinking deep into its soft flesh.

Bronson felt the air thicken, his heart slamming in his chest as the beast's roar echoed through the cavern. He couldn't breathe, couldn't think. The sound was deafening, a primal fury that rattled the very walls.

The dragon twisted, its massive body undulating in the darkness, and for a split second, Bronson saw the flash of sharp teeth. He flinched, the urge to run, to escape, overwhelming every rational thought. But his body didn't listen.

Brufell's grip tightened on him, pulling him behind the rock just as the cavern shook again.

Stay calm, stay calm, he told himself. *Don't lose it now.*

The dragon's tail whipped out, smashing against the ledge where Tuk had been only moments before. Stone broke apart like brittle bones, tumbling into the abyss below. Bronson's breath caught in his throat. How close had they all just come to dying?

Brufell was saying something, but it was drowned out by the dragon's shriek as it flung itself toward Tuk again, its wings beating the air like thunder. The cavern felt smaller now, suffocating.

The beast's claws raked the air, and for a terrifying second, Bronson thought it would tear the shelf clean off the wall. He swallowed hard, trying to push down the bile rising in his throat.

'We need a plan,' Bronson whispered, the words barely escaping his throat. His hands were shaking, but he forced himself to stay focused. He had to think. They all had to think.

Brufell's eyes were sharp, flicking from the dragon to Tuk, calculating the next move. Bronson could feel the tension in his shoulders, his stance like stone, yet his jaw was clenched with something darker. Something that said he, too, was wondering how the hell they were going to get out of this alive.

The air vibrated with the dragon's fury, and Bronson squeezed his eyes shut for just a moment. He couldn't let fear take over. He had to do something.

When he opened them again, the dragon was already preparing to strike again, its wings like a storm cloud descending. Bronson's breath hitched, but this time, he didn't look away. Not as the ground shook, and the chasm widened, opening the pit further as rock fell into its depths. The stone behind Bronson cracked, and he scuttled backwards.

'This whole place is going to come down,' Bronson yelled.

'We can't leave without the tooth,' Brufell replied.

Another stalactite fell, crashing near the baby dragon.

'I don't think the mother realises she's bringing the cavern down around us,' Bronson breathed.

The mountain shifted as the dragon drove her talons into the wall with a roar. Tuk skidded down the rocky surface, grasping his bow tightly.

'We have to save it,' Bronson said.

Brufell shook his head. 'We can't.'

'But if we save the little dragon, we can take its tooth.'

'And where will we get it out, hmm?' Brufell replied, 'He's wounded, he can't fly, and though he might be small, he's too big to take the same entrance we did. The only way he can go is up.'

Brufell pointed towards the giant opening of the ceiling where the stars poked through.

'How do you know he can't fly?' Bronson asked.

'Because he would have by now.'

'What if he's too young?' Bronson said, 'Maybe he's younger than we thought. We can't leave him here, Brufell. We *can't*. Too many have died already.'

Brufell looked to the baby dragon; his golden eyes filled with terror as the pixie attempted to pull away the rocks to no avail.

The dragon's head followed his mother. His cries came out in nothing more than squeaks.

'For once we can save instead of kill. *Please,* Brufell.'

The old dwarf's eyes softened, 'Do you have a plan?'

'I do,' Bronson said. 'But you're going to hate it.'

Dread had to return to the mines. He'd been gone too long as it was, but something gnawed at him.

Since Myrenna had left, it was as if the world had become misplaced.

He paced back and forth in the high towers of the aviary, his gaze roving the horizon. From this height, the city sprawled before him, a patchwork of life beneath the golden light of the late afternoon. The rooftops shimmered in shades of deep amber and rich red as the sun began its descent. Here and there, copper tiles reflected the light, their surfaces gleaming like freshly minted coins. Smoke curled up from chimneys, adding muted greys and soft blues to the air, blending with the warmth of the setting sun.

The city was beautiful, just like its mistress. And yet wholly undeserving of her.

He hadn't yet contacted Trik. He wasn't ready. How would he explain that their brother was playing lowly soldier, getting drunk with the flies caught in the city's web? What he should have been doing was collecting traitors infiltrating the city. But he'd also said his mission was secret. Was Flynn lying?

Dread clenched his fists. The Queen remained absent, but the Tinker had made sure to make his presence known throughout the castle. He trailed around in those purple robes of his, slinking across the marble floors like a rat wearing a fake crown.

Dread resented him for it.

After Dread had found his brother, he'd only felt cold rage. He was torn between leaving the city to follow the Queen's duty, and the duty for his family. The look Flynn had given him didn't bode well: behind that calm mask, Dread saw the burning anger.

It was why Dread hadn't approached him in the first place. Dread didn't know his brother's mission, but he highly doubted it included getting drunk in a sleazy bar.

Flynn could have been a general just like Trik, but instead he chose to linger in the shadows like a worm. He'd never had purpose and he refused one even when it was offered to him on a plate.

But Dread had bigger issues to worry about. The mines were close to finding the object, dusting off the brittle bones of the door. There was the pull of something happening, as if the death of a Grimm had started some kind of ripple effect. Gears were now in motion.

The Tinker entered the aviary, eyeing the high ceiling with disdain.

Dread halted. 'What?' he asked, not hiding the growl rising in his throat.

The Tinker smiled at him, still holding the tiny spindle. 'The mirror has requested you.'

The hairs on the back of Dread's neck stood on end. 'Why?'

The Tinker shrugged. 'I'm not its master; I fear no one is. But I'm wise enough to tell you when you're needed and to send for you.'

With a slinky bow, the Tinker swept a hand toward the doorway, his grin unsettling beneath the grimy shadows of his hood. The acrid tang of decay clung to his robes, curling into Dread's nose like a toxic whisper. Holding his breath, Dread strode past without a glance. His heavy steps echoed through the corridor, brushing past scurrying maids who ducked their heads at his approach.

He reached the throne room doors and threw them wide. The air inside was thick, crackling with an energy that prickled his skin. Dread's jaw tightened. Was it the lingering presence of the Queen, or a new disturbance – the mirror flexing its will? The Queen had hoarded its secrets, guarding them like a jealous warden. Dread had kept his distance. That *thing* was hers, her oracle, her key. He preferred not to know the truth it whispered, despite seeking it out earlier.

As the doors groaned shut behind him, black smoke poured into the chamber. It hissed and writhed, snaking across the crimson carpet like living tendrils, beckoning him forward.

Dread's boots faltered, but he clenched his fists and shook off the creeping unease. Just a mirror, he told himself, pushing forward. Just glass and shadows. But even he couldn't fully believe that lie.

'*Come here, shifter of skin,*' the mirror said with its silky voice. '*Let me show you your kin. So many battles I feel inside of you; come closer, crow, so I can see too.*'

Dread's steps were slower, careful as he reached the dais. 'What do you want?' he asked, holding his voice steady. He had dealt with nastier things than the mirror.

'*Let me show you,*' the mirror cooed. '*Come to the glass and look through.*'

Dread's breath caught as his gaze met the mirror's murky surface. The glass rippled like water disturbed by a distant tremor. His reflection stared back – but it wasn't the man he was now.

It was a boy, wide-eyed and fragile, with messy black hair sticking to a dirt-smeared face. A threadbare tunic clung to his bony shoulders. His small hands were curled into fists, knuckles white with defiant tension.

The boy's eyes gleamed with something raw – fear, anger; perhaps both – but there was no mistaking it.

It was him. And yet, it wasn't.

His head quirked to the side as two shadows stood behind him: one of a smaller build with dark hair and green eyes, the other blonde with a sharp jaw.

Trik and Flynn.

'What is this?' Dread asked. 'I don't have time for your mockery. There are things in motion. Things Myrenna needs fixed.'

'*Yes, yes, things indeed. But you cannot serve until you kill the weed.*'

'There are many weeds in the Queen's garden,' Dread replied steadily. 'I'm here to pull them out as I always have.'

The mirror chuckled, its smoke curling around Dread's feet. '*Then why does this weed remain alive? Why does it grow and thrive?*'

Dread frowned. He'd always hated the mirror's riddles, its knack for turning a simple solution into a poem or rhyme. He didn't know what the Queen saw, nor had he ever understood how it provided a purpose for her. She always had a purpose.

'Just tell me about the weed and I'll kill it,' Dread ground out. Goosebumps coated his skin where the smoke lingered.

The surface of the mirror rippled. Cold eyes stared back at Dread as the three children in the mirror blended into one, forming a slinky man with pale skin and hard green eyes.

Flynn.

'*I know you found him, Shifter. He plays a game. But he's the weed which must be slain. He lingers with heroes. His weapon is words. His influence grows and the rebellion stirs.*'

Dread tensed his jaw, hating the games the mirror played. More gears, more clocks, more moving parts.

'Can you prove it?' Dread ordered. 'Killing one's brother is no small task, and you're questionable already, whispering wild thoughts into the Queen's head.'

'*She is not so easily manipulated, your Queen. She forges her own path, but you? It remains to be seen. Proof you need?*'

What a quaint request. But wait, dear crow, I'll do as you behest.'

The voice laughed as the mirror's surface shifted again.

Flynn stood on a balcony beside a silver-skinned changeling. His eyes soft as the changeling rested her hand on his shoulder. Somehow, he seemed vulnerable, misshapen in a way that Dread barely recognised.

It made his skin crawl.

The mirror's glass followed Flynn, his uniform immaculate against the lamplight of the city. He veered around a corner, watching for followers before he entered the creaky door of a tavern. It was packed, soldiers drunk with girls, the room a whirl of noise. But it wasn't the radical behaviour that Dread growled at.

It was the lean, broad figure of a light-haired man sitting at the bar.

Hansel.

Pain shot through Dread's palm as his nails dug in.

The scene shifted. A fight broke out, bar stools and fists and blood.

Then Flynn was dragged out — flung onto the street like a lowlife beggar.

The mirror faded, maintaining Flynn's crystallised green eyes.

'How recent is this?' Dread's voice cut through the thick air, taut with demand.

The mirror shimmered, smoke curling back into its surface like a living thing retreating to its den. A slow, sly grin formed on the glass, mocking, infuriating.

'When was this?' Dread growled, his fists clenching at his sides.

'Time is a concept I'm not accustomed to,' the mirror mused, its voice languid and amused. *'But I'd say a handful of hours ago, if the image is true.'*

Dread's eyes narrowed. 'Is the image true?' His voice grew harsher, rising with anger. 'Is that filthy Huntsman in my city? Does Flynn know him? Are they still there?'

The mirror offered no answer, only a faint ripple across its surface, as if enjoying the chaos it sowed. *'So many questions, crow. Perhaps you should go — kill the weed before it can grow.'*

Dread backed away, his hands shaking.

Betrayal.

Enemies.

So close and yet so far.

'How can you see Flynn and the Huntsman, but you can't see Snow? What game is it you are playing?'

'I play one game, and it is my own. Snow was protected by something unknown.'

Before Dread could ask more questions the mirror blackened until it was silent again.

Dread couldn't go back to the mines now — not with what was happening inside the city. Not with Myrenna gone.

Clearly the people had forgotten their place.

And it was Dread's duty to remind them.

Brufell didn't run – he charged, teeth gritted, cursing Bronson with every step. The cavern yawned wide, jagged floor slick with cracks. The mother dragon's tail whipped across the ground with a deafening *crack* and Brufell dove, boots skidding on loose stone as the impact rattled his bones. The edge of the platform crumbled, revealing the endless abyss below.

Claws the size of swords slammed into the stone beside him, splintering it. He rolled, lungs burning, and saw his chance. One desperate leap and he landed hard on the dragon's foot. Her scales grazed against his palms, sharp and slick like polished obsidian. Brufell grunted, clawing his way upward as the beast's muscles rippled beneath his hands.

A sudden lurch. The dragon reared, and Brufell's hand slipped, a scale cutting deep into his palm. His sword clattered to the ground below, lost in the chaos. Pain shot through his shoulder as he clung to a single jagged scale.

Below, Bronson sprinted with the pixie trailing behind, the baby dragon wailing in panic. The mother's roar shattered the cavern walls, vibrating through Brufell's bones. Heat surged under his grip as the dragon's belly glowed with molten fire.

Tuk's voice rang out from above and another arrow sliced the air but missed its mark. The dragon barely flinched. Her rage was focused on Brufell now.

Sweat slicked his skin as he pulled himself higher, muscles screaming in protest. The dragon bellowed and unleashed a torrent of flames, scorching the rocks below. Brufell's vision blurred from the heat, but he held fast, yanking a knife free from his belt. With a guttural cry, he drove the blade between two scales, the metal grinding against her hide.

The dragon reared, thrashing wildly as the blade sank in. It wasn't deep, but it was enough. Enough to distract her.

Brufell clung desperately, blood pouring from his torn palms. His shoulders quaked, every muscle screaming as the beast twisted and stretched her neck. Her molten eyes burned into him, bright as fury itself.

'I will burn you,' she growled, her voice a searing promise of death.

Despite his fear, Brufell was defiant when he looked into the dragon's eyes. 'You'll crush us all first, if you don't stop thrashing around!'

The dragon blew hot smoke from her nose, coating Brufell with a potent sulphuric smell. His clothes stuck to him like a second skin as sweat coated his body.

'Why?!' the dragon growled. Her tail sliced into the wall as she gnashed her teeth.

He let go and slid down the dragon's body, then gripped another scale.

'Shall I stay still so you can kill me? Shoot me with your pathetic arrows?' she seethed and lashed out with her tail. 'Should I lay down as you take me apart and kill my child? Leaving nothing left of our kind!'

Brufell saw the glimmer of the baby's hide through the rock. 'We don't want to hurt you!' he ground out as he heaved himself up again. His shoulder throbbed, most likely pulled from the socket.

'You're all the same, the giants too, marching to our mountains as if we're dinner. We are *ancient* and we will not die so easily.'

Another arrow flew, this time piercing the green dragon's eye. She lurched backwards and fell. Brufell's beard whipped over his shoulder as they fell and fell and fell—

Until they crashed into the ground.

Brufell tumbled on impact and rolled off the dragons hide. The dragon's breath hissed, tendrils of smoke curling from her flared nostrils. Each of her movements was wild and violent, shaking the cavern as though the earth itself threatened to shatter beneath them.

Brufell grimaced, the tang of copper thick in his mouth as sweat and blood mingled on his skin.

The beast's remaining molten eye locked on him, burning with raw fury. Her lips curled back, sharp teeth glinting like daggers. Smoke billowed around her maw, and she let out a growl that vibrated through Brufell's bones.

Tuk yelled something from above, but it was lost as the cavern collapsed around them.

In the distance, Bronson tied a rope around the baby dragon's belly and called out to Brufell. The old dwarf twisted at the signal and waved to Tuk.

The troll stood on the precipice, his face covered in dirt and blood. He nocked another arrow.

Brufell shouted. 'Stop, Tuk! Stop shooting!'

The mother dragon's belly rumbled again. Another stalactite fell, crushing onto her side. Flame ripped free, shooting towards the starlit sky.

Brufell only had one chance. And it was dying quickly. He ran forward, pivoting across the landscape and jumped back onto the dragon's hide. He flew across the scales, his shoes barely gripping as he stopped near the dragon's maw.

'Let us help you,' Brufell yelled. 'Everything is falling. The ground will collapse if you do not get up, if you do not fly!'

'My baby,' the dragon whimpered. Blood seeped from her eye. Her wing was slashed.

Bronson ran towards Brufell, the remaining rope clutched in his hand, and he threw it to Brufell.

He caught it.

Oryx held onto the baby dragon's head, his wings fluttering behind him.

'I'm tying a rope to you, okay?' Brufell yelled to the mother dragon. 'Your baby is attached. If you wish to save him then you must fly!'

The dragon gnashed her teeth again. Her voice was a low, guttural snarl that rippled through the cavern. 'Do not hurt him.'

'He will not be harmed by me, but he won't live long if you don't move! You won't be shot again – just fly. FLY!'

With that, Brufell slid down the scales, the sharp edges tearing at his skin. He ran around the dragon's leg, tying the rope in what he hoped was a safe knot.

The floor cracked sharply, the sound ricocheting off the cavern walls like a whip. Stone groaned beneath the pressure as fractures spread in jagged lines. The dragon shifted, standing tall on its haunches, her molten eyes flicking between the dwarves, the taut rope, and her wailing child.

What was left of the floor crumbled beneath their feet, more chasm than solid ground now. Smoke billowed from the dragon's maw, rising in thick, swirling plumes. Her wings unfurled with a heavy snap, muscles taut with raw power. The hole in the cavern ceiling widened with each beat, jagged rock tumbling down in a deadly cascade. One massive chunk hurtled straight toward Bronson—

A flash of talons sliced through it, shattering the boulder into dust and shards.

The ground beneath Brufell gave way. With a desperate shout, he leaped, landing hard on the dragon's foot. His fingers trembled as he knotted the rope around his waist, murmuring a frantic prayer to the Godmother. The dragon roared, wings pumping as she lifted off.

Wind tore at Brufell's face as they ascended, higher and higher, the rope slithering like a living thing across the splintering floor. It snapped taut, yanking Bronson and the baby dragon upward. Bronson clung to the shimmering blue hide of the young dragon, his knuckles white, muscles straining against the pull.

Below, the cavern succumbed to chaos. The floor collapsed entirely, the chasm yawning wide – a gaping maw of darkness ready to swallow everything. Dust and debris spiralled upward, blinding Brufell. He gasped, the acrid air thick in his throat.

The dragon roared, wings slicing through the turbulence as they rose above the ruin. The rush of wind drowned out the shuddering crash of rock below. Brufell's heart raced, terror seizing his chest as the final wall crumbled, the cave obliterated in a cloud of dust and stone.

Then – silence.

He squinted into the swirling dust, searching desperately for any trace of Tuk. But there was nothing. His throat tightened, his mouth dry as the thought struck him like a hammer. He swallowed hard, choking back a sob. Had the troll been swallowed by the ruin?

Cold, biting wind kissed Brufell's skin as the dust cleared. His vision blurred, but through the haze, starlight glittered above them. They were too far now to go back, to look for the troll. Brufell could only swallow as they soared beyond the mountain peak, the world stretching endlessly below. Lakes glimmering like fragments of glass, rivers snaking through valleys, jagged peaks reaching for the skies.

The dragon's belly rumbled in triumph, a victorious thunder that echoed through the night. But Brufell's fear clamped down, fierce and unrelenting. His breath faltered, the ground too distant, the sky too vast. The wind roared louder, and darkness curled around the edges of his vision.

As the stars spun above, Brufell's body sagged, fear dragging him down into utter blackness.

XXVI

The Chained Princess

Branches clawed at Snow's face, slicing her skin with stinging pricks. The coppery tang of blood mingled with the sharp scent of pine, and for a brief, disorienting moment, it felt as if the forest itself were attacking her. Her lungs burned, each breath a ragged gasp as her legs faltered. The world around her blurred into a chaotic mess of twisted trunks and snapping twigs. The ground seemed to rise and fall, and her feet pounded the earth in a frantic rhythm as her heart raced.

The howls closed in, slicing through the trees like serrated knives. Each guttural sound gnawed at her resolve, sinking into her chest like icy fingers. Terror twisted in her gut, but still, she pushed on, driven by the need to escape, to survive. But with every step, the surge of adrenaline that had propelled her forward was fading fast, replaced by the weight of exhaustion.

A root caught her foot, sending her sprawling forward. Her arms flailed, struggling to catch herself and her heart slammed against her ribs. The forest seemed to tighten around her, branches arching like skeletal fingers eager to claim her. Behind her, the sounds of pursuit grew louder, a chorus of teeth and fury ready to tear through flesh and bone.

She swore she'd seen glimpses of Hansel in the trees, his voice echoing around her.

Run.

Her throat was raw. Her breath came in sharp bursts. There was no end to the trees. No way to know where she was going. She could have been running north, for all she knew, towards the peaks of the mountains and the dark things that crawled there. Or she could be running south, towards the battle where the dead pierced the cold soil and fought for a cursed royal. But what did it matter? Every direction she turned only brought her closer to the fear that clutched her soul. Whether she ran west or east, there was no escape. The trees were closing in, the howls behind her were growing louder.

The weight of her fear pressed down on her chest, suffocating her, making it harder to breathe, harder to think. She was outnumbered, hunted, and the cold truth settled into her bones. She was utterly, terrifyingly alone.

Her muscles burned, screaming as she crashed through the brush. Her panicked thoughts splintered as her body betrayed her. She knew she'd slowed. She felt it within the tingle of her fingertips, in the ache of her muscles and her blurry eyes. Her limbs felt leaden, her movements clumsy and jagged. Every step was a battle against the growing weight in her body. The trees blurred, shifting in and out of focus as her vision flickered.

Then – Hansel.

He appeared on her left, a familiar figure cutting through the chaos. Her heart, so heavy with dread just moments ago, surged with the flicker of hope. Without thinking, she lunged toward him, ignoring the fiery protests of her legs and the sting of fresh cuts on her skin. Another howl ripped through the forest, sharp and merciless.

Her breath caught, panic shredding through her thoughts. The world felt like it was slipping away, unravelling at the edges, but she clung to the image of Hansel that appeared before her. He wasn't real. Deep down, she knew that. The forest had splintered her senses, warping reality into something fractured and wild.

But even an imaginary Hansel was better than nothing.

In any world, real or imagined, he would fight for her, protect her. She couldn't bear to think otherwise. Desperation drowned reason, and she ran toward the illusion, grasping it like a lifeline.

Snow vaulted over a thick root, her breath ragged as her eyes darted through the tangled maze of trees for any opening, any hollow to hide. Her hand flew to the axe strapped to her back, fingers fumbling against the slick leather. It wouldn't budge. The strap dug into her shoulder, fighting her desperate grip.

No no no no no no—

Distracted, she stumbled, catching herself on a tree trunk as splinters bit into her palm. The howls slithered across the forest floor, slick and predatory, wrapping around her legs like chains. Her skirts tore as she pivoted off another tree, the fabric snagging on gnarled branches.

Instinct screamed at her to keep moving, but she braved a glance over her shoulder.

One glance was all it took.

Through the twisting trees, a hulking shadow shot toward her. Its muscled body blurred with speed, each stride devouring the distance between them. Saliva glistened on its gaping jaws, thick threads dripping from rows of jagged teeth. The forest warped around the beast, bending to its weight. Its skull gleamed dark and solid – a battering ram of bone and fury.

Snow's stomach turned to ice.

With a jolt, her leg seized under her. Her foot caught on a lone branch, and she fell headfirst into the dirt. A root pierced the ground and dug into her shoulder. The world stilled for a moment, black spots cutting across her vision.

Above her, Hansel stood, his figure blurred, but somehow still there. Pain was everywhere. It was in her shoulder, her ribs, her legs. She couldn't tell where it began and where it ended. All she could do was choke down air, her lungs burning as each breath felt more desperate than the last.

And then she smelt it – decay and wet fur.

The stench clawed into her lungs, sharp and rancid.

The hounds.

Ash clung to her nostrils as she tried to push herself up. She had to move, to somehow keep going. She refused to die as a snack. Refused to have her first taste of freedom tainted by the beasts who chased her. Steeling herself, she pressed her palms against the earth, only for them to come back smeared with grey. Her breath hitched at the sight before her: the once-vibrant tree in front of her stood blackened and rotting, bark flaking off like dead skin. The grass surrounding it was shrivelled, brittle as bones underfoot.

A howl ripped through the air, rattling her ribs. Snow's head snapped back, slamming into the dirt. The ground beneath her pulsed with cold dread. Hot, rancid breath coated her face, the stench of rotting meat making her gag.

She'd been too slow.

A weight bore down on her chest, crushing the air from her lungs. Gnarled teeth dripped strings of saliva, gleaming inches from her face. The sharp canines were stained with blood, fragments of bone lodged between pale gums.

Snow's breath shattered into sobs. Her scream tore from her throat, raw and endless.

The beast growled, a guttural sound that reverberated through the forest. Shadow and smog closed in, the air thick and choking. More growls surrounded her, circling, prowling. She caught flashes of movement – three pairs of gleaming eyes locked onto her, ravenous.

This was it.

This was where she would die.

Or worse.

Her pulse thundered as panic clawed at her chest. Would it be quick? Or would they tear her apart slowly, savouring her screams? Would they drag her away, leave her alive just long enough for her heart to be eaten?

The hound's claws dug into her shoulders, sharp points breaking skin. Pain shot through her, and she gasped.

Snarls swelled around her. Fog thickened, pressing in until there was nothing left but blood, shadows, and teeth.

Then a sharp whistle sliced through the air, clean and pure.

The beast stiffened, its ears flicking toward the sound. Snow coughed violently, curling into herself as the crushing weight lifted. The hound backed away, low whines rumbling from its throat.

The fog shifted, parting like a veil.

Through the smog and darkness, a figure emerged. She was slender and poised, her presence commanding the air around her. Shadow clung to her cloak, curling at the edges like living smoke.

'Hello, Princess,' she cooed, her voice smooth as silk and twice as deadly.

Snow's breath faltered. Her body trembled against the dusty ground.

The Huntress had found her.

Wind whipped past Malak's face as the ground surged toward them, faster and faster. His lungs seized, breath ripped from his throat. The insistent clicking of wood nymphs echoed like a relentless drumbeat, mocking their descent.

This was it.

Death would come swiftly now. No one survived a fall like this. He knew that all too well. He'd cheated death before – once, twice, too many times to count.

A cat with nine lives. Saved and saved and saved again.

Until he wasn't.

Flashes of memory seared through Malak's mind as he plummeted.

The Princess giggling in the library, golden light catching in her hair. Her chin lifted high, regal and defiant, each time she strode from the throne room flanked by guards.

Hansel, grinning wide as he offered Malak a job – offered friendship, as though a troll was worth the time. Swords drawn in the training yard, Hansel's voice sharp with command as he taught him and Snow to parry.

The warm scent of horses in the stables, their hooves restless against the straw. The gardens where he wandered, listening as the Queen's laughter rang out amongst her court.

And then – Troll's Keep. His father's shadow looming over him, fists clenched. The sting of blows. The guttural accusation: weak, insolent.

Villagers with twisted mouths spitting on him as he begged for work. The crumbling posters advertising the mines, which had seemed like a salvation when he was starving and alone.

The ground roared closer, the rush of wind deafening. Malak braced for it. He knew he wouldn't survive this time.

But then—

A piercing melody sliced through the air, sharp and commanding. The song wove into the air like living magic.

Leaves exploded from the earth, twisting upward in a frenzy. Vines lashed toward Malak, snapping taut beneath him. They struck like a living net, smashing into his body and breaking his fall branch by branch, plant by plant.

Pain radiated through him as he thudded against the last thick stem, breath knocked from his lungs. His vision blurred. Cold ground met his back with a jarring finality.

Malak gasped, coughing violently. The sharp tang of dirt filled his mouth. His chest heaved as the realization settled in.

He was still breathing.

Maybe he was a cat after all – one with too few lives left.

Snow's wrists burned where the iron chains bit into her skin. The links clinked with every stumble, her feet dragging through the dirt. Sharp stones cut into her soles, but she barely felt the pain anymore. A numbness had crept in, slow and merciless.

The Huntress strode ahead, her red hair spilling down her shoulders in wild waves that gleamed like embers against black leather and coarse grey wool. She moved with unnerving grace, each step silent as if the forest itself bent to her will.

Only Snow's scuffling feet broke the stillness, along with the guttural snarls of the hounds flanking them. Their hot breath puffed in the cold air, claws scraping against roots and leaves.

The forest loomed, ancient and watchful. Shadows clung to twisted branches, shifting with every flicker of movement. Snow's breath caught as she glanced at the dark silhouettes weaving through the trees – more hounds, their eyes glinting with hunger.

Her legs wavered, chains pulling taut as she nearly collapsed. The Huntress didn't stop, didn't even glance back.

They'd walked for hours, the beasts sniffing and growling with every step. Snow had fallen a few times, the hounds nipping at her ankles whenever she faltered.

Exhaustion coated her limbs and pain reverberated with every step she took. Her dress was torn, her slippers long lost, leaving her feet raw and bloody. Just as Snow thought she couldn't take another step, the Huntress stopped.

She blew her whistle, her pets diving off in different directions. Snow shivered as the Huntress's gaze flicked toward her – dark, bottomless, and unyielding.

In three fluid strides, the Huntress closed the distance between them. Snow's breath hitched. The metallic bite of the chains pressed against her raw wrists, but it was the weight of the Huntress's presence that truly held her captive.

The Huntress's scarred hands closed around Snow's chains, fingers rough and stiff. With a savage yank, she pulled Snow forward, momentum slamming her against the coarse bark of a tree. Pain jolted through Snow's shoulder, but she bit back a cry.

Before Snow could recover, the Huntress shoved her into a sitting position, looping the chains around the trunk and her torso in tight, unforgiving coils. The metal dug into Snow's skin, biting through cloth. Each pull ratcheted the bonds tighter, constricting until Snow's breaths came shallow and sharp.

Snow clenched her teeth, willing herself not to flinch as the final loop cinched into place. The Huntress tested the bindings with a sharp tug, nodding in grim satisfaction.

The woman left her side and crouched, striking flint against steel. Sparks flared in the gloom, briefly illuminating the dark around them. A flicker of flame caught dry kindling, its warmth spreading as shadows danced wildly across the trees.

The low growl of the returning hounds stole Snow's attention. They'd returned with a bloodied carcass, matted fur clinging to torn flesh.

A wolf.

The scent of iron and decay filled the clearing, making Snow's stomach churn. The Huntress didn't even flinch at the grisly offering, her attention focused on feeding the flames.

Snow sagged against the tree, ignoring the bite of the bark. Her eyes drooped. She was so tired she could feel the pain ebbing away, sapping what little energy she had left, and she closed her eyes. She heard crickets and the shuffling of the hounds' paws, but it was the steady sound of a knife carving the wolf carcass that finally lulled her to sleep.

She stands in her blue dress in front of the gilded mirror, its hungry eyes assessing her as Myrenna waits off to the side. The Queen's foot taps the cool stone as the mirror reaches forward with its shadows.

Snow whimpers as the darkness touches her skin, caressing her with careful, tentative strokes. It takes everything in her not to recoil.

To recoil would mean the wrath of Myrenna. To be locked away again.

To be trapped.

With a slight shiver the shadows retreat and Snow looses the breath she'd been holding.

'Not yet,' the mirror says. 'She is still no threat.'

Myrenna growls, like a quiet warning before a storm. The firelight from the candelabra flickers across her midnight dress, each movement casting shimmering sparks like distant starlight. The fabric clings to her frame, dark and endless – a moonless night given form. 'When?' Her teeth grind.

'She remains too young, barely just a girl. Her heart must ripen, like a clam with its pearl.'

Myrenna's manicured nails grasp Snow's arm, pinching her skin.

All Snow can do is hold the ragged sob that climbs in her throat.

'Each week we will do this,' the Queen says, pulling Snow forward. 'Each week, you will come when I call. You will not dawdle. You will not hide.'

Snow's heart hammers at the underlying threat, and she gives the Queen a tiny nod.

The Queen's amethyst eyes are hard and unforgiving.

With a knock at the door, the Queen turns. The Tinker enters, with Hansel following suit. The Huntsman stands at attention, his golden-brown eyes trailing over the Princess with concern.

'Is it time?' the Queen asks.

The Tinker nods, his purple robes hanging limp on his frail body. 'Yes, Your Majesty. The pieces are in play.'

'Good,' she sneers, pushing Snow away. 'Let's see how the Dream Weaver fares when his web is broken.'

Snow rubs at the spot on her arm that prickles with the lingering imprints of Myrenna's nails. Where she knows she'll find vicious bruises should she lift up her sleeve.

Myrenna strolls along the weathered carpet, the Tinker and Hansel in tow. She turns back to the Princess. 'Do not fret, Snowfall. Your time will come. And it will beat in my palm when it does.'

The guards' hands clamp around Snow's arms, tugging her towards the door. Her feet skid across the cold stone floor as they haul her through the dim corridor towards her room.

She waits until the lock clicks before she lets herself break.

Snow jolted awake as something heavy and hot landed in her lap. Pain still gnawed at her limbs, muscles stiff and aching from the cold and the chains. Her body protested with every movement, but instinct forced her to glance down.

A slab of meat, charred and glistening with fat, rested in her numb hands. Smoke curled from its seared surface, the scent sharp and greasy.

Snow's gaze snapped upward.

The Huntress stood over her, eyes gleaming in the flickering firelight. 'Eat.'

Snow stared at the meat in her dirty palms. 'I'm not hungry,' she said quietly.

The Huntress slapped her, the shock hitting her jaw like cracked ice. 'You will eat, and you will not be asked again.'

Snow gritted her teeth. 'I'm not hungry!' she yelled, throwing it onto the dirt.

Her stomach growled.

Traitor, she thought.

The Huntress sneered. 'We have a long journey. I know you don't want to be with me, and I certainly don't want to be with you. Eat so the journey is easier, not because someone is telling you to.' Shaking her head, the Huntress picked up the meat from the forest floor and smacked it back into Snow's hands. 'You won't be getting a new one.'

Snow's hands shook as she tried to manoeuvre the chains. Her eyes trailed the woman's back as she walked away, throwing a large piece of meat to one of the hounds who dived and tore at it.

Snow stared down at the meat, now smeared with dirt and ash. Her stomach churned with hunger, a gnawing ache that refused to be silenced.

She hesitated, then lifted her bound hands, the chains biting into her skin as she strained to bring the meat to her lips. The cold metal pressed against her ribs, but she forced herself to take a bite.

The tough flesh caught between her teeth, gritty with dirt. She gagged, choking on the grainy texture. The bitter, unsalted taste clung to her tongue, making her grimace. But she swallowed anyway.

Her body screamed for nourishment, even if it came like this – ugly and undeserved.

She sagged against the tree, the chains pressing harder with each shallow breath. Every wound throbbed, sharp and insistent. Her head spun with exhaustion, muscles quivering from strain. What she needed was medicine, sleep, and proper food. But instead, she had dirt-streaked scraps and the firelight flickering like a cruel taunt.

How unfair this realm is, she thought bitterly, *to throw my own stubbornness back at me.*

She'd fought to defy its rules, and now it punished her with survival on its terms, not hers.

And there was no escape from it. Not yet.

As she took her second bite, her eyes veered back to the Huntress, her back to Snow. The Huntress turned, meeting Snow's eyes with victory as Snow chewed the gritty meat.

Snow looked away hastily, hating that the Huntress had won somehow.

The Huntress snorted.

When Snow had eaten her fill, the dirt lingering on her tongue, she watched as the woman set up her bed roll and patted one of the hounds, who nudged his head forward in a caress.

'Where are we going?' Snow braved asking, but the woman ignored her. 'Are we going to the palace?'

If she knew the destination, perhaps she could determine an escape route. Though, that seemed highly unlikely. Her weapons had been confiscated, and the woman was larger than her; probably stronger, too. Not to mention the fact there were at least seven hounds in this camp that could outrun her. But she held onto the small hope that she could gain some semblance of control if only she knew the direction in which they travelled, the destination where she was to take her final stand.

The sap had worn off now, her vision and mind becoming clearer the further they'd walked, and though

Snow wanted to rid herself of it, she still found her heart ached a bit at the absence of it.

The absence of *him*.

She couldn't see Hansel anymore. He'd stopped appearing amongst the gaps in the trees, stopped warning her, stopped giving her comfort.

She eyed the axe by the woman's side, its hilt worn against her thick clothes. 'Are we going to the mines? Is that where the Queen is?'

One of the hounds growled at Snow and the woman clucked at it, bringing the beast closer to her as she laid down.

'Just tell me where we're going, and I'll shut up,' Snow said. 'Otherwise, I'll just keep going and you'll never get any sleep. Neither of us will.'

The woman turned around, and shot her sharp look. 'You are just as annoying as I remember,' she said.

Snow had only ever met the Huntress once. She wasn't the Queen's favourite hunter — that was reserved for Hansel. But, by the cauldron, the woman had tried. Snow remembered winter-covered gardens and a woman with hair of fire walking across the grounds, yelling at Hansel. Her lips had been coated in dark lipstick, her sharp eyes watchful.

Snow remembered the cold stab of jealousy as the snow fell like tiny droplets onto the woman's hair; the freedom of being in the open with Hansel, of having the audacity to yell at him.

Snow remembered touching her own hair in envy before skittering behind her curtains as the woman looked up to her window and glared.

Snow met those same eyes now, but her envy had been replaced by anger.

'I didn't meet many people, so it's easy to remember them all,' Snow said, her voice braver than expected. 'We were never officially introduced, so how could you possibly know how annoying I am?'

Her cheek still stung from the slap she'd received earlier; if Snow didn't choose her words carefully, the woman could easily do far worse than that.

'I can read tracks just as well as I can read people. Like you, I watched – though, I didn't have the luxury of hiding behind the palace walls.' The Huntress smirked. 'We didn't need a formal introduction. I already know everything about you.'

'You know nothing about me,' Snow bit back. 'Nobody does. Not really.'

'*Woe is me,*' the huntress drawled. 'A poor princess with nobody to talk to.' Snow frowned at the mocking tone. 'I told you. I watch.'

Snow heard the threat, the underlying message of what she knew and could do, if she pleased.

'Where are we going?' Snow asked again.

'We are going to someone who has been looking for you.'

Snow gulped. 'Myrenna? Is that who we're seeing?'

The woman stood, walking silently over to Snow, her red hair falling in waves over her shoulder. She smelt like blueberries; Snow had expected her to smell like blood. It was how Myrenna smelt before she dabbed on her lavender perfume.

'You will address Her Majesty by her *proper* title,' she warned, pulling free a knife from a holster on her thigh. The blade glittered as she brought it to Snow's chin. 'Now, shut up, or I'll have to cut out your tongue.'

The Huntress waited a beat before she backed away. 'Go to sleep.'

As the fire dimmed, the snores of the hounds echoing around them, Snow found she couldn't. Not when the Huntress had looked at her like a feast. Not when Hansel was lost somewhere in the realm. And not when the Queen was so close to taking her heart.

Her broken, beaten, thrumming heart.

Malak groaned, and Florian coughed beside him. The melody had gone but Malak knew it had been Pip. They'd be dead if it weren't for the elf. Suddenly, Malak was grateful for his company.

With a struggle, he pushed himself up, first checking on Florian before standing to search for Pip. A soft cough came from the ferns nearby, and after a few long strides, he reached out to help the dishevelled elf off the ground.

'Remind me why I chose to follow you lot again?' Pip asked, checking all his pockets.

'Something about boredom,' Malak replied, his voice hoarse from screaming. 'What are you looking for?'

'My flute. It's fallen from my throat.'

'Well, at least there's no giants,' Florian joked, though even he had a wheeze to his voice.

Pip eyed Florian with distaste and the prince went a shade of tomato.

'I'm sure it's here somewhere,' Malak interjected.

A sharp clicking sound cut through the clearing. The group froze, spinning toward the source.

Among the trees stood one last wood nymph, its slender frame barely visible against the dense foliage. Huge dark eyes gleamed under the shifting light, fixed on something golden in its grasp—

Pip's flute.

Malak's chest tightened as the nymph tilted its head, shaking the instrument as if coaxing it to play again. Pip let out a strangled yelp and lunged forward.

The nymph hissed and clutched the flute close to its chest. 'Mine,' it declared in a high, lilting voice.

'No,' Pip snapped, his voice strained. 'Mine.'

The nymph's brow furrowed, stubbornness etched in every flick of its wooden limbs. 'Mine,' it insisted, shifting on its haunches, eyes darting toward the tree line.

Gravel crunched under Malak's boots as he stepped forward, his gaze locked on the creature. Florian followed suit, inching forward with a grace Malak didn't know he had.

The nymph flinched.

'Don't scare it,' Pip warned, raising a hand to stop them. 'What are you doing, Malak?'

Malak's voice was low, measured. 'We just escaped the wood folk. I don't think being dragged back in chains is our best option.'

'That's why I said don't scare it!' Pip hissed through clenched teeth.

Florian, who had ignored the warning, lost his footing and stumbled.

Chaos erupted.

The nymph screeched, sending nearby trees trembling. The creature bolted toward the shadows, flute clutched in its hands.

'GRAB IT!' Pip screamed.

The wood nymph darted through the forest, leaping over rocks and skimming past boulders. Brush snapped and thrashed in its wake as it vanished and reappeared between trees, moving like a pixie hopped up on caffeine.

Malak bit back a curse, surging forward with long, determined strides. His companions lagged behind, their footfalls drowned by the pounding of his heart. He pushed harder, lungs burning. His boot caught the edge of a slope. Malak tumbled, the world flipping into a blur of green and brown. Branches lashed at his arms and face, the ground slamming into him with brutal force at every bounce. Air exploded from his lungs as he hit the base of the hill, momentum carrying him straight into the unyielding trunk of a tree.

Stars danced in his vision. Pain lanced through his side. A high-pitched giggle sliced through the ringing in his ears.

He blinked upward. The nymph was perched halfway out of the bark, its bulbous eyes gleaming with mischief. It swung the flute back and forth, the golden surface glinting in the dappled light. Mocking him.

Malak's fingers dug into the dirt as fury surged through him. His breath came ragged, but he didn't take his eyes off the tiny menace.

Not this time.

'You little piece of—'

A piercing howl shattered the forest, raw and primal, sending birds scattering into the sky.

The wood nymph froze, its bulging eyes widening in alarm.

Without warning, it leapt from the tree, vaulting clean over Malak's dazed form. Leaves fluttered in its wake as it hit the earth running, its legs pumping frantically. With each passing moment, it shrank into the distance, fading into the shadowy depths of the forest.

It didn't look back.

Malak shook himself as the others approached. 'I'm sorry, Pip. We've lost it.'

Pip panted. 'Fifty years I was trapped. It's my fault for not learning from my previous mistakes.'

'But it wasn't your fault,' Florian said. 'The flute's cord snapped off your neck.'

'Fault of mine or not, it's happened, and we must deal with it. One problem at a time. We have the issue of the forest being angry at us but can't leave until we find my flute and the Princess. Those were the howls of the dark hounds. Right now, Florian's tracking skills are our most valuable asset. But if we're caught, I don't have my flute to assist.'

Malak asked, 'What do we do first?'

'We find the Princess. She's always been the priority. If she's been caught, she'll be taken to the Queen's nearest outpost and, out this far, I'd say it's the camp down south near Wolf's Den.'

'What about your flute?' Florian asked.

'I'll just have to hope the little critter never understands what it does, and once we save the Princess I'll have to go back to the elders and seek their help.'

'They tried to kill us!'

'Yes, but is slavery better than death?' Pip replied, steeling his shoulders.

Florian swallowed. 'I don't know. Neither sounds appealing.'

'No, they don't,' Pip agreed. He drew a line in the dirt with a large stick, carved ridges and hills, and marked where they stood with an X. 'Let's say we're here. If the Princess has been captured, they'll try to take her here'— he illustrated a path to the borders of Perridorm—'Few people control the hounds in the army. They're foul and hungry creatures and, once they smell their prey, they become obsessed.'

'I thought they were a myth,' Florian said. 'I've studied similar creatures in books but there was never much information.'

'That's because those who encounter them usually die.'

Florian's face drained of blood, turning a pale shade of white. 'Why is everything out to kill us?'

'Because the realm is harsh.'

'And if we can save Snow, we can maybe change it. Make the realm safe,' Malak replied.

'Do you think we can?' the Prince asked.

'We don't know unless we try,' Pip said, wiping his foot across the dirt to erase the map. He peered up at the Prince, who scratched himself, and Pip whacked him with the stick. 'For Godmother's sake, stop scratching!'

'I can't help it,' the Prince said. 'My skin reacts when I'm terrified.'

'You mean it reacts when you breathe.'

'That too.'

Pip rolled his eyes.

Malak cracked his knuckles, ignoring them both. 'I've dealt with the dark hounds before, I can do it again.'

'Let's hope that's true,' Pip replied.

XXVII
The Bells of Warning

Warning bells shrieked through the thick, humid night, slicing the darkness like blades. The Silver City roared with chaos – screams ricocheting off cobbled streets, torches flickering against stone walls. Shadows flickered like spectres across the buildings as soldiers scrambled into formation.

Dread stood at the city's heart, sweat slick on his brow despite the cool sheen of his black armour. Summer crept closer, and the air clung heavy, suffocating with heat and unrest.

Above, his murders circled, their sharp eyes scanning the skies. Wings beat against the night as they waited, ready to descend at the first sign of defiance.

He'd seen the golden dwarf strung up by a fountain, her defiant stand a symbol too strong to let linger. She had become a martyr for killing the General. An expression of the people. And Dread feared what an uprising would bring. He had to show the rebels' efforts were futile, that the power of his Queen was to be reckoned with.

And he'd start with the Silver City.

The rebellion had been left to grow for too long, infecting the capital like a plague, winding its way through the alleys and veins of each heart. Dread would be the cure.

Orders rang out as soldiers broke free from the group, checking each and every house for stowaways. To go against the Queen was treason, and with treason came the punishment of death. High-level soldiers had been killed in the incident at the tavern and Dread knew it was Hansel's doing.

He only had to find him.

Flynn had last been seen on the doorstep of the Tinder Box, thrown out like a rag doll for the fight he'd started. Dread stared at the broken door, at the blood splattered across the square. The shimmering body of the dwarf still hung on the fountain, her torn dress and bloodied face as still as the statue that held her.

Someone was going to die tonight.

The city glowed orange. People were hurled from their homes, hideaways pulled free and placed into chains. For those who did not abide, Dread had given the army strict orders to burn down their homes.

Glass shattered as soldiers broke into shop fronts, one pulling forward a dark-skinned girl and locking her in chains. Dread clapped the back of the soldier, rumbling a 'well done' when she spat at Dread's feet. He barely gave her a glance.

Humans, elves, changelings, dwarves; each kind coming out of the woodwork like a termite infestation.

He grinned in the flickering firelight, his teeth gleaming against the warm glow. The sounds of terror were the Silver City's new anthem. It was a witch-hunt for traitors and thieves, for those who believed in hope.

A knife slashed across a man's throat. His eyes went dead as he dropped to the floor.

Hope was a fool's dream.

Fear was the true power.

Dread held the thought close as he roamed the streets. The city was alive, people and creatures and monsters running throughout the night. But that wasn't what caught his attention. It was the shadow watching him – the one slinking behind the crumbling walls of the ramshackle buildings.

Dread slowed his pace, instincts sharp as a blade. He twisted past a flickering lamppost and veered toward a stone-clad alley. The stench of rot clung to the narrow passage, mingling with the scuffle of rats and the faint shuffling of the homeless pressed into dark corners.

A flicker of movement.

Dread lunged, seizing a throat in one swift motion. The woman gasped, clawing at his gauntleted hand. Her wide, desperate eyes gleamed in the dim light.

'Get out of here,' he growled.

He released her with a shove, and she hit the ground. She scrambled to her feet and, clutching her skirts, fled, her footsteps fading into the night.

Silence.

Then came the sound – the deliberate tread of boots on stone. A figure emerged from the shadows, fluid and unearthly. Not a man. A shifter.

Dread's jaw tensed. He cracked his knuckles, the sound echoing against the narrow alley walls. 'What do you think you're achieving?' he asked, his voice cold as steel. He advanced, each step deliberate. 'Trying to provoke me, Brother?'

The figure's lips curled into a faint, humourless smile.

'Not everything is about you, Dread,' Flynn said, stepping into the firelight. The flickering glow played across his pale skin, igniting the green in his eyes.

Dread's breath came slow and measured, but the simmering heat beneath his ribs was impossible to ignore. 'Whatever mission you're on is over.'

'It's over when Her Majesty orders it to be.'

Dread growled. 'If she knew Hansel was in the city, I can guarantee she'd be ordering his head, not a drink.'

Flynn picked at his jacket. His uniform was bunched from his brawl at the Tinder Box, and his lip protruded slightly, blood trickling from whatever wound the Huntsman had given him. 'Your jealousy clouds you, Dread,' he said.

'This city has a disease under it.'

'And I suppose you're the one who thinks setting it alight is the best course?' Flynn said, stepping forward. 'You won't cut out the sickness out by hunting them down. You're only fuelling the larger fire. This will make the people angry. It gives them a reason to join the cause, not hide from it. You're destroying their homes, their livelihoods, taking what little they have. And when they have nothing left, Brother, they will seek out those who can provide vengeance, those who can hone their anger and give them something to do with it.'

Dread's fingers latched onto Flynn's throat with such veracity that Flynn's head cracked against the wall.

Dread was only a pixie from his face. 'I show them fear. I show them what happens when they choose the wrong path. Fear is strong. It will rule them as it rules all of us.' He dropped Flynn on the stone.

Flynn coughed and spat blood onto the ground. 'There are things stronger than fear, Brother.'

Dread sneered. 'And what might that be?'

'Hope.'

Dread growled. 'Hope is an illusion. Hope is for dreamers and weaklings. It's a filthy habit you were never able to let go.' Dread crouched down, curious as he looked over his brother's hunched form. 'What is your mission? Your *real* one. And don't give me some fairy shit about stealthing around the city and finding out who's in the rebellion. You've been silent too long. Trik is concerned.'

Dread noted the flinch at Trik's name.

Flynn's eyes came to rest on Dread's with stern determination. 'I'm to find the Commander's replacement in the rebellion, see what the succession line is, and crush it before they can rally.'

Dread stood and pulled free his knife. It glowed with the burning backdrop of the city. 'And have you found the new Commander?'

'No,' Flynn replied. His voice was calm. *Too* calm.

The tip of the knife glinted at Flynn's throat. Dread gave him a deadly smile. 'You've always been good at that.'

'Good at what?'

'Lying.' Dread pressed the blade deeper, piercing the pale flesh underneath. Dread watched with satisfaction as blood trickled down Flynn's throat, bright red against the brown crusted blood from the brawl. 'But you forget I'm family. I know you. Lie to me again and I'll push this knife so far into your throat that you'll choke on your own blood.'

'Trik wouldn't—'

'Trik is currently preoccupied with a war, and spinning a tale of your death wouldn't be difficult. I don't lie as well as you, but I do it well enough.'

Flynn's eyes were wide, Dread's threat cracking through his calm exterior.

Dread relished it. 'However,' he said, hovering on the word. 'That will not be today.'

He drew back the knife and placed it back in his sheath. He picked up his brother's arm and lifted him to his feet. 'You will report daily. You will inform me of your movements and your progress. You will no longer get drunk with vagabonds, and if you see the Huntsman again you will inform me of where he is and what he is doing.'

'What if I'm unable to? What if I have eyes on me?'

'You always have eyes on you, Brother. But you've always had a knack for escaping them.'

'And you'll kill me if I don't? That's a little savage, even for you.'

'I'll be whatever my Queen needs me to be, and you should do the same. The Commander has already been imprisoned. The rebellion is weak. Find me the silver assassin and the rest of the snake.'

'What will you do when I find them?'

The bells blared as Dread smirked one last time at his brother and ignored his question. 'I look forward to the report.'

Flynn gave him a small nod.

Dread walked away, his shoulders lighter than they had been before. He wasn't sure how much of what Flynn told him was true but at least his brother now had a leash. After all, Flynn's biggest motivation was self-preservation.

Dread marched through the streets, watching as the city turned to ash. He passed smouldering carts and overturned barrels, the remnants of a life now lost to the flames. A few bodies lay sprawled where they had fallen, their forms indistinct in the smoke. He snatched a flaming torch from a nearby stand, its light flickering like a dying star in the chaos around him. He held it with purpose, as if it were a signal to the destruction yet to come.

The markets were ahead his next target. The building was a vast wooden structure, open to the air, covered with an array of trinkets and mould. Dread knew messages had been sent here, secret meetings and under-the-table dealings. With a sneer, he brought forth the torch and lit up a faded cloth covering a stall. The flames licked at the material and jumped from one cart to the next. The fire crackled, eating away at the wood like a starving wolf.

Dread smiled.

Let them all burn.

The mother dragon stretched her leathery wings, gliding effortlessly across the jagged peaks of the Eyrie Mountains. Moonlight kissed the icy ridges and danced along her shimmering scales.

The taut rope dug mercilessly into Bronson's side, but he barely registered the pain. Below, Brufell dangled limp in the dragon's talons, unconscious and swaying with each powerful beat of her wings. The rope was the only thing keeping him from plummeting into the abyss.

The world unfurled beneath them. Tiny dots of trees scattered across the valley floor. Lakes gleamed like shards of silver. The stark contrast of white snow clinging to rocky terrain gave way to lush green hills and cascading waterfalls crashing down gleaming cliffs.

It was breathtaking.

The wind roared around him, fierce and wild, filling his lungs with exhilaration. Bronson stretched his arms wide, mimicking the dragon's wings, a wild laugh escaping his throat. The dragon's belly rumbled in response, vibrating with shared glee.

He was weightless, untamed – free.

For a fleeting moment, he wondered if Frode had felt this way. Was that why Frode had chosen to stay with the dragons? Had the pull of the sky, vast and boundless, proven irresistible?

Behind them, the mountain crumbled inward, a thunderous collapse sending clouds of dust spiralling toward the heavens like the smoke of a dying fire. Bronson's heart clenched. Tuk. Had he made it out?

He had to believe it. There was still a debt to settle, a tooth to claim to heal the sick trolls.

The stars blazed above, ancient and unwavering. Ahead, the mountains thinned, giving way to an endless expanse. To the east, the forest stretched in a dark blur, fading into the shadowy swamps beyond.

They were flying in the opposite direction their cousins' home.

Bronson's stomach twisted at the realization. Dread coiled in his chest as he imagined having to cross the mountains again – the endless climb, the biting winds, the jagged paths that cut into his boots and wore down his resolve. The memory of that journey to Troll's Keep clung to him like a weight. He wasn't sure he could endure it a second time.

He forced the thoughts away and closed his eyes, surrendering to the rush of cold air slicing through his clothes. It stung his face and numbed his fingers, but he welcomed it. The wind carried with it the clean, untamed scent of high altitudes – sharp, crisp, and unburdened by the grime of cities or smoke from forges.

A sudden squeak pierced the air.

Bronson's eyes snapped open just as the dragon banked hard to the left. The movement was graceful and vast, like a ship carving through open seas – but it wasn't smooth for everyone.

Oryx clung desperately to the dragon's scales, his tiny fingers red with strain. His wings, normally iridescent and proud, trembled as if unsure they could bear even the weight of his terror.

Bronson's breath hitched. For all the pixie's defiant chatter, he looked utterly petrified.

'Hold on!' Bronson shouted over the howl of the wind.

The dragon rumbled in response, her powerful body steadying. But Bronson kept his gaze fixed on the pixie, ready to act if the creature's grip faltered.

This wasn't just survival anymore – it was keeping each other alive.

With some slight manoeuvring, Bronson was able to stretch out his arm, managing to grab the creature and pull him close. Oryx shivered as he clutched Bronson's clothes, his unscarred eye shut tight.

Bronson's ears popped as the dragon began its descent. The rush of air dulled, replaced by the creak of strained wings and the distant roar of a river. Through a break in the dense canopy, a shimmering ribbon of water danced across the forest floor.

The mother dragon circled, her wings beating gracefully in the air. With careful precision, she lowered Brufell to the ground. Her talons released the older dwarf, leaving him still unconscious.

With a heavy thump, the mother dragon landed, sending a tremor through the earth. Mist curled around her feet, mingling with the rich scent of damp moss and river stone.

Bronson exhaled, his breath fogging in the cool air. For a moment, the chaos of flight faded, replaced by the eerie calm of the forest clearing.

The baby dragon landed soon after but with less grace. It heaved a great sigh before tumbling into the dirt, taking Bronson and Oryx with it. The mothers wing wrapped around them as they rolled, its membrane smooth and fine.

When the world finally stopped spinning, Bronson checked his pocket, finding the pixie perfectly alive and wide awake.

The mother dragon shivered, arching her wing so the open air coated the dwarf's face. He crawled out and unhitched his rope with ease before doing the same for the others.

Bronson checked on the baby dragon first. The creature was tired but uninjured from the flight, with only the bloody talon left to tend.

A rumbling voice behind Bronson said, 'Leave him be. He's alive but needs rest.'

Bronson turned to the green dragon.

The mother dragon sniffed at dwarf's motionless body. The arrow still protruded from her eye, and she winced with each movement.

'Let me help you,' Bronson said. 'Let me fix your eye.'

Her snout was in front of his face. 'The eye *you* shot.'

Bronson swallowed the guilt for what Tuk had done. 'Please,' he said. 'Tuk didn't know. Let me at least heal it.'

After some contemplation, she gave in. She rested her head on the ground and let out an unimpressed huff.

'May I?' Bronson asked, gesturing to the dragon's head. To reach her eye he'd have to climb her scales and situate himself on her snout.

She grumbled a 'yes' and, with shaking hands, Bronson began to climb. The scales edges threatened to tear his skin as he placed one foot after the other.

When he finally reached the top, he squatted near the dragon's wounded eye.

Blood spilled from her iris, its dry red flakes peeling from her scales as he assessed the wound. From the looks of it, the arrow had been snapped during the turmoil.

Bronson's stomach fluttered as he pulled some ingredients from his bag. He began to hum to calm his nerves as he cleaned and tended to the dragon's wound.

She winced and groaned as he twisted what was left of the sunken shaft. He braced himself against the dragon's forehead, counted to three, and gave the arrow a mighty pull. The forest floor trembled as the dragon's claws pierced the dirt. She held back her roar, and Bronson began to sing a dwarven lullaby he'd heard from Bonyx.

He cleaned the dragon's eye using the makeshift ingredients in his pouch. She flinched from the pain but overall remained calm, trusting Bronson to do his work. When his pudgy fingers finally placed on the bandages, he had to get up and lean over the dragon's forehead to reach the top part of her wound. When he was done, he crawled back to the ground, landing with a soft thump.

The dragon turned her head and looked down at Bronson with her one golden eye.

Bronson said, 'Just try not to rub it, and if we're still together in a few days, I'll check it again. We don't want it to get infected.'

The pixie assessed Bronson's handiwork, giggling as it pointed to its own damaged eye.

Bronson chuckled. 'He says you're both the same now. Says you'll both have a matching eye.'

The dragon snarled at that, biting towards the pixie, barely missing. 'I'm a dragon. I have nothing in common with an insect.'

'It's a pixie, actually,' Bronson said.

'We are not the same.'

Bronson found it easier not to respond and walked over to Brufell. He went to work on the dwarf's cuts and bruises. Considering what Brufell had achieved, the wounds were minimal.

Bronson smiled at the warrior before him. The mother dragon moved closer to watch as he applied the paste to Brufell's nicks and cuts, the dwarf still asleep.

'I've never carried anything that wasn't food before,' the dragon commented. Its golden eye glittered and Bronson had to remember how to swallow.

He didn't think he'd ever get used to such a creature.

Bronson took off his jacket and placed it over the older dwarf's body. 'We are mountain folk, dwarves; we aren't accustomed to being carried, either.'

With a heavy thump, the dragon sat, her tail whipping across the grass. 'Why did you save us?' she asked.

'I'd say you saved us,' Bronson said, taking a seat on a nearby log. 'Flying out of there wasn't easy, but you managed – carrying all of us, as well.'

'He still flew,' the dragon said, motioning to her youngling. 'I'm just sad it was his first real flight.'

'He'd never flown before?'

'Not for that long or that much. I'm afraid I've pushed him too far.'

The little dragon's breaths had evened out in his sleepy haze. His scales glimmered against the moonlight, reflecting hues of blue and silver and gold. Paired with the rushing water, the scene painted a very peaceful picture.

Bronson smiled. He thought about the Seven and wondered if Bryn could ever carve it accurately. The dragons across the walls of Parador, adding it to Frode's adventures. It would be something of beauty, just like the crystal coffin.

'When was his first flight?' Bronson asked.

'He flew to the chasm where you found us, and injured his talon when he landed. That's why we remained there.'

'He was alone when we found him.'

'I was searching for food and a safe place to go,' the dragon said. 'I smelt the troll and rushed back, instead finding the both of you threatening my youngling.'

'I was trying to help him. To fix the wound.'

The dragon clawed the ground, stretching her neck forward. 'I only saw a threat. It's a mother's prerogative to protect her little one. I saw him in pain, and I smelt blood and something foreign.'

Bronson gave her an understanding nod.

Brufell hiccupped in his sleep.

'I'll help your youngling when he wakes. I didn't finish tending to his wound, but I'll fix the talon.'

The ground shifted slightly as the dragon backed away, curling its large, spiked tail behind it. 'Why were you there?' she asked. 'I smelt nothing of any creature in that chasm and all of a sudden you showed up. What were you looking for?'

We were looking for you. To kill you.

He opened his mouth, but the words lodged in his throat. He could lie, of course, but somehow, he knew the dragon would know. He wasn't particularly keen on being turned to ash.

Bronson began, 'We made a bargain with the trolls. War is coming and our kingdom needs allies. They said they would help us if we helped them. We found the chasm because we were looking for it. For you. For a dragon tooth, actually. It has healing properties and can help them.'

'Wars will always rage. Illness will always exist. Why should I care, when I'll outlive you all?'

'Because the illness was caused by dark magic. From a dragon made of fog and shadow. It sucks the lifeblood from everything. The war is to stop the one who controls it.'

'A dragon made of fog?' she asked. 'Start from the beginning.'

Bronson didn't know where to begin. His mind clutched at every detail, every trail they'd followed before all of this began. He started his tale at the road to his cousins in the Peaks of Carfell, how they found a lost princess amongst the rubble and took her in. He spoke of the crystal coffin, the broken and dying places of the forest; he spoke of the Seeker and the Queen and how they'd trailed across mountains to find the dragon of smoke and darkness.

The dragon remained silent as Bronson's words fell like wine poured over the edge of a glass.

When he'd summed it up as best he could, his shoulders drooped. A weight he'd long been holding released.

The dragon pondered his story for a moment, considering her words. 'Magic like that has not been seen for a long time. Few in the realm have the ability to survive such a force and most of the time they aren't your friends. This Queen was once mortal?'

'We believe so, yes,' Bronson replied.

'Then she has either been gifted this magic, or stolen it. That also means her magic is not natural. Something like that would drain her immensely. She would require finding it elsewhere if she cannot control it on her own.'

Bronson nodded. 'She eats hearts. That's why she wants the Princess. Snow has a pure heart and can grant her immortality. If she gets her hands on it, she will be unstoppable.'

'Hence your war?'

'It isn't my war,' Bronson replied. 'It's for the realm. If the Evil Queen isn't stopped, she'll take over everything. She'll continue to divide everyone and control us. She'll kill Snow.'

'I'm curious, dwarf,' the dragon said. 'I understand why you wish to help the Princess and stop the Queen, but why do you help the trolls after what you've told me about them? They kidnapped you, tried to kill you, and yet you help them. They could pull out of your bargain easily even if you do heal their kin. So, why?'

Bronson fiddled with his hands, not quite knowing where to look. His eyes landed on Brufell, still peacefully unaware.

'Because not everybody is inherently evil,' Bronson replied. 'The trolls have their issues but not all of them are the same. Just like dwarves, we have good ones and bad ones, but we shouldn't be judged as a race. Just because one troll tried to kill me doesn't mean another will. They have trolls dying and, if it was me in that position, I'd want help, too. Even if they don't follow through on their bargain.'

'You are different from others,' she replied. 'You are a rare breed.'

'I've been called worse things,' Bronson joked.

The dragon leaned in close. "Different' is a compliment. Many can play the same game and follow the others, but they will not be the ones who find truth or peace. You are different because you choose to do right though you have no reason to.'

'Does that mean you'll help us?' he asked.

'I will consider it,' she mused. 'For now, we must rest. In the morning, we can decide what to do next.'

'I'll take watch, then.'

She walked over to the little dragon and spread out her wing, covering his small body in warmth as he curled into her. Bronson tried to get comfortable but found without his pack he'd have to make do with a rock as a pillow. He shuffled around, staring at the stars before the dragon lifted her head. 'Will you sing?' she asked. 'Like you did before?'

He'd been so accustomed to his kin blocking out his tunes that having someone ask for a song made him nervous. He was thankful for the cover of night when a blush crept up his cheeks.

He cleared his throat. 'It would be my pleasure.'

XXVIII
The Fires of War

Snow was jerked awake by the stench of rotten food and hot breath. When her eyes finally fluttered open, she jolted back at the sight of a drooling maw looming over her. She instinctively recoiled, pressing herself into the rough bark at her back. Her pulse thudded in her ears, quick and erratic. Chains tightened against her chest as she struggled to steady her breathing.

The creature huffed, its milky eyes gleaming with primal curiosity – or hunger.

The Huntress whistled as she approached and the hound backed away, allowing Snow to loose her breath. Her gaze trailed over the already packed-up camp, the Huntress close enough for Snow to smell her damp skin and hair. Everything about it was so mundane, so calm despite the fact there was a death threat hanging over her head.

The Huntress unravelled her chains, the rattle of the metal jarring amongst the quiet forest.

With a kick from the Huntress, Snow was up, the chains weighing heavily on her creaking body.

'We're not far,' said the Huntress.

Dew lingered on the rocks, and dirt caked her feet from the moist morning. Snow wrinkled her nose, shivering from the cold. She'd hoped it had all been a bad dream, one where, after, she would wake in the grotto, Hansel's body curved next to hers. But she supposed that was the real dream.

The walk was harder today. Snow's limbs were stiff from the broken sleep she'd had. Her mind had taken hours to quieten, visions of hearts and blood and torture streaming one after another, flooding her mind. Hansel hadn't returned — not even after she had closed her eyes. Tears threatened to spill as the Huntress carried Hansel's axe on her back. The Huntress was lithe, her form strong.

Like Eveline, a little voice cooed.

Snow pushed the thought away, zeroing in on that wild, fiery hair. The Huntress thought she knew Snow, but Snow knew of the Huntress, too.

Long before chains and her trip through the forest, Snow had loved watching the lives that moved through the castle halls. When her eyes had grown weary of words and intricate illustrations in her books, she'd let the living stories unfold around her. Servants had scurried with trays, courtiers had glided with hushed whispers, and amidst them all was the Huntress – sharp, fierce, and always shadowed by one of the Queen's crows.

Snow had seen her stride through the grand arches, boots striking stone with purpose, summoned at the Queen's whim. The Huntress never lingered, always vanishing like a flame snuffed out. A character ripe for invention, Snow had imagined a hundred tales about her before she had ever heard the woman speak.

She'd caught the Huntress once, half-naked and wild in the castle maze, tangled among the narrow, twisting paths. The air had smelt of crushed roses and damp earth. Snow had frozen, wide-eyed, as the woman arched against a man, her moans threading through the hedges like forbidden music. The man's eyes met Snow's, dark with amusement as a knowing smile curled his lips.

Snow had gasped, heat flooding her face, and fled.

Her breath had come in sharp bursts by the time she reached her chambers. Her cheeks burned as images seared into her mind: the gleam of sweat on exposed skin, the raw intimacy of lips brushing lips, bodies moving in rhythm.

She'd wondered then, what it would be like. To be that entwined with someone. To feel hands mapping her skin, breaths mingling in shared heat.

And then she had almost died as she thought of what it would be like with Hansel.

Her blood had roared, leaving her frazzled. Overwhelmed.

The thought of it brought heat to her cheeks now. Of how she had run from such a simple thing. Of how she shied away from such thoughts, envisioning a dream that could never be.

But maybe it could be.

Hansel had always been with her, and if she managed to escape, get to Perridorm and find the rebellion, she was sure to win back her crown.

She would claim power first, and then she would claim the Huntsman.

Hansel would be a great king: a man of the people, a commoner become royalty. A united king and queen ruling Bellatorre: living proof that 'happily ever after' could exist.

Her thoughts were pulled from her when teeth gnashed at her ankles. She was swaying again.

But Snow's dreams were futile if she didn't take back her crown. And right now, the odds were against her.

She needed a way to win, a way to defeat Myrenna.

Power, the voice inside her head said. *You need power.*

Snow shook off the thought as the trees began to thin and the hounds rushed forward. The woman smiled at them warmly, like a mother with her children. Snow shivered at the chilling comparison. The day the Huntress became a maternal figure would be the day the realm fell to ruin.

Dusk had begun to fall, the sky shifting from a soft lavender to deeper shades of indigo. Pockets of orange lights flickered in the distance, floating like watchful eyes in the darkening horizon. They glowed faintly through the thickening trees, the distant reflection of lanterns or fires, their warmth unable to reach her where she stood in the cold embrace of the forest. She was careful with her steps as the ground steepened. She slipped a few times, much to her chagrin, but she blamed her bare feet. At this point, she couldn't feel the poor things. The Huntress's cruel hands caught her and pulled her forward, her grip tight enough to bruise.

At the crest where the trees broke stood a city of tents, each one unlike the last. Some spanned the width of three trolls, others the size of a single bed. But it was all of them clustered together that made Snow hollow inside. Horror dawned inside her as she took in the camp, how each tent stretched down the hill into the valley below, so far that they blended into the horizon.

As the Huntress pushed her forward, Snow's mouth grew dry. The camp was the size of Roserock, perhaps bigger. Smoke billowed around the tents where soldiers moved amongst one another, reminding Snow of just how alone she was.

Snow faltered and the Huntress tightened her vicelike grip. 'No dawdling,' she whispered into Snow's ear. 'The woods aren't the only dangerous place for a woman.'

Watchful eyes tracked them as they strode through the camp. Men and women alike lifted their heads from fires, conversations halting mid-sentence as they regarded the newcomer, shadows dancing across weathered faces. Some whispered in hushed tones, their voices sharp and secretive. A few lay sprawled in makeshift bedding, while restless figures wandered aimlessly, boots kicking up dust.

The air was thick with the mingled scents of smoke, roasting meat, and sweat, sharp and cloying. Snow's nostrils twitched in distaste.

A sudden movement made her tense. A man leaned toward her, his hand hovering just out of reach, eyes gleaming with raw hunger as they roved over her body.

Snow's stomach twisted. Even with the Huntress's firm grip on her arm, she felt naked under their scrutiny – an object on display, shiny and new, tempting hands eager to claim and play with her.

The Huntress pulled free her knife with a growl. 'Back off.'

With a snarl, he retreated, but his eyes still followed Snow, etched into her back like a promise. She could feel all their stares, like a finger trailing across her skin.

Powerless, her mind whispered.

'Shut up,' she whispered to herself.

The Huntress eyed her curiously, but Snow just stuck out her tongue.

As Snow's gaze swept over the camp, she took in the grim details etched into every face. Shadowed eyes spoke of sleepless nights, while bruises bloomed in violent hues across skin already marred by battle. Some wounds were ghastly – jagged scars puckering flesh, stumps where limbs had once been. Each face was stark with pain, painted in the harsh palette of blood and darkness.

What horrors had they seen?

The weight of it pressed against her chest, thick and suffocating. Snow's legs wobbled, her balance slipping. The Huntress hissed in frustration, tightening her grip as Snow faltered.

'Stop stumbling. You're like a newborn fawn trying to walk. At least show you can step straight, or they'll eat you alive.'

Snow tried to follow the instructions, but something niggled at her. Fear, perhaps, or anxiety.

Always alone, the little voice in her head whispered.

She agreed with it.

After what felt like an eternity, Snow and the Huntress arrived at a large tent near the centre of the camp. It was grey like the others; the only different detail was the large crest stitched into its side. One with a red apple.

A sharp whistle pierced the air, and the hounds vanished, weaving through the maze of tents with uncanny swiftness. Snow barely tracked their departure before two guards came into focus, flanking the entrance to a large tent. Their expressions were blank, backs rigid as though carved from stone.

Without a word, the guards pulled back the heavy flaps, the canvas rustling like dry leaves. The sudden shift in warmth and scent was jarring – woodsmoke fading into something richer, musky with leather and stale incense.

Snow had no time to process it as her chains were removed, her wrists raw and angry. A firm shove sent her stumbling forward. Her knees struck the thick carpet with a thud, pain shooting through bone. She winced, the rich fibres cushioning her fall doing little to dull the sting.

The soft touch of the Huntress's cloak snaked over Snow's hand as she stepped beside Snow and waited. Snow yanked back her hand, grasping it to her chest and, as she raised her eyes, met the eyes of a bald, scarred man.

A memory cut through Snow. Of him half naked in the maze. His knowing smile and wink branded into her skull.

The Huntress's lover.

The crow.

Snow looked away.

Sheer curtains hung from the ceiling, fluttering from the open doorway. Neat, wooden furniture was scattered:

a chair by a small table, a bed by the back on a platform, and, in the middle of the room, a large table littered with a map of the realm and figurines.

A war map.

The Huntress had brought her to the border of Perridorm and Bellatorre, then.

'Dread was sceptical,' the man said, grinning at the Huntress. 'When he sees we finally caught her, even he can't be a grump about it.' He seized the Huntress, his lips crushing against hers with raw intensity. Her body softened under his touch, yielding as a low, breathy moan escaped her lips.

Snow's scowl deepened, the ache in her body flaring anew, sharp and insistent.

The man was the first to pull away, though the ghost of a smile lingered on the Huntress's lips – soft, intimate, and utterly out of place. It was a smile that didn't belong in this world, in this place of blood and captivity.

A knot of frustration and something darker twisted deep inside Snow. That smile, that stolen, private moment, felt like a betrayal of fate. It wasn't just a smile; it was a fragment of another world, a world Snow had been forced to leave behind when she stepped into the shadows of this one. When her father had married Myrenna then died.

Her throat tightened as the bitterness welled up, like bile rising, tainting everything.

'Pick her up,' the bald man ordered. 'Let's get a good look at the Queen's prize.'

The Huntress pulled Snow's hair, tearing her head back.

Snow whimpered.

The man clicked his tongue. 'Easy, Artemis. She might be our prisoner but she's not to be harmed.'

'The Queen said we couldn't kill her. Harming her was never specified.'

The man gave Artemis a knowing smile. 'That is true, but she's our guest. At least, until the convoy arrives.'

'I say we skip the pleasantries and peel her skin off. The Queen only needs her heart. The other organs are ours.'

The man shook his head and frowned at the Huntress. 'Normally I love your savagery, but for now could you contain it?'

She rolled her eyes but didn't argue his point, instead looking at Snow like she was an insect. A particularly annoying insect that Artemis would love to crush beneath her boot if the Huntress's sneer was anything to go by.

'Get up,' the Huntress – Artemis – said, pulling at Snow's torn sleeve.

With unsteady feet, Snow stood, the muscles in her legs crying out in pain.

Slowly, the man circled her, his eyes assessing. 'You've been difficult to find,' he said. 'Nothing has worked – magic, the murders, even the hounds. Not until that strange explosion, anyway. Whatever magic it was, it hid you from all eyes. Including the Queen's. That's not an easy feat and, if I'm completely honest, it's impressive.'

Snow lifted her chin, eyes defiant.

He gave her a slow smile, disarming the insult she held at the tip of her tongue. His hair might have been shaved down to the scalp, but he wasn't unattractive. His teeth were straight, his jaw defined, and when he smiled, there was a hint of playfulness behind his eyes that made her pause. 'You're a pretty little thing, aren't you?'

Artemis scowled and yanked at Snow's hair, tugging her back. She winced at the pain in her skull as the General waved the Huntress away. 'Get a grip, Artemis. I haven't found a new favourite toy.'

Artemis growled. 'I'm not a plaything, Trik.'

Trik tilted his head, his eyes drifting from Snow, locking on Artemis's glare. 'No, you're not. But your jealousy makes you immature and no better than a rabid animal. Pull it together.' Trik infused his voice with lethal command, making Artemis straighten, though her sneer remained. 'The Princess is to remain unharmed – for as long as I say so, anyway. I would never replace you. You're my favourite menace.'

Artemis remained silent, but Snow could feel the anger radiating off her.

'You both look starved,' he said, 'We'll get you some food, and perhaps the little Princess here can answer some questions before she leaves with the convoy.'

'What could you possibly want to know?' Artemis asked, a biting tone to her voice.

The chains rattled as Snow righted herself, shaking with the urge to lash out. But Artemis wasn't looking at her now, she was stepping towards the General, her eyes burning bright. 'She's a spoilt princess hiding from her fate. The Queen doesn't want her questioned, otherwise she would have said so. She's a runaway and a brat,' Artemis said through gritted teeth. 'She's had nothing but pure luck to save her. I say lock her up and send her away.'

The General just stared at the Huntress, bored. 'We've had this discussion before, Artemis. She's my prisoner, I'll do with her what I like.'

Artemis growled. 'She might be your prisoner, Trik, but I'm the one who found her. I'm the one who got her here – and in one piece, I might add.'

'And as always, your skills are not underestimated. You've never needed coddling, so I won't give it to you now. Either you eat with us and deal with my questioning, or you can go eat with the soldiers where they'll appreciate your glum demeanour.'

'I'm not putting up with this fairy shit,' Artemis bit back. 'You can find someone else to warm your bed tonight.'

'You'll probably just cut their throat if I do,' he remarked.

'Probably.' She smirked, then spat on the ground next to Snow. 'You touch him, and I'll cut out your heart myself.'

The tent flap quivered in her wake as Artemis left, the air still heavy with the scent of sweat and anger. Snow's scowl lingered as silence crept back in, broken only by the faint rustle of canvas and distant murmurs outside.

Trik sighed. 'I know she seems … unrefined. Believe it or not, she can be charming when she wants to be.'

Snow suspected it was more than just loyalty. Artemis may have been wild and ruthless, but there was no denying her striking beauty – and likely her prowess in bed. Heat prickled at Snow's neck, and she bit down hard on her tongue, desperate to banish the unwelcome thought.

Trik motioned to the wall. 'There's a basin over there filled with fresh water to wash your face and hands. After that, we'll eat.'

Snow didn't want to comply, but she felt the dirt crusted over her face like a second skin. She didn't even want to consider her smell.

Slowly, Snow obliged. The basin was made of wood and marble. Above it stood a plain round mirror. As she cupped the water, Snow braved a look, horrified when she gazed at the half-dead stranger before her. Dark circles lay under her eyes and small nicks coated her skin. She was bruised, dirty and savage. The one thing that hadn't dulled were her eyes. Her eyes blazed an untamed blue, fierce and defiant, burning back at her reflection as though daring it to look away.

The water stung her torn nails and open cuts, but it was relief to wash off some of the damage the forest had wrought. Long gone were the days of her being pristine in the castle, draped in fine clothes and tucked away among cushions. Though, if Myrenna had her way, Snow wouldn't have many days left. And this beautiful, beating heart of hers would be gone.

After she was done, a guard handed her a towel and led her to the dining table towards the back of the tent. Trik sat ready, his napkin placed carefully across his lap as though he were dining with Myrenna and not a prisoner.

As Snow reached the table, the smell of food almost overwhelmed her. The last meal she had eaten had been the rank cut of meat that Artemis and thrown at her. In the centre of the table was a platter of roast beef, covered with rich gravy. Potatoes and fresh vegetables sat on the side, steam wafting from them as she picked up her knife and fork.

Trik chuckled. 'Surely a princess doesn't need to be shown how to cut her meat?'

At that, Snow dropped the cutlery. 'I'm not hungry.'

She was being ridiculous, but eating remained the only thing in her control. And she would cling onto her stubbornness while she could.

'Yes, you are,' Trik said calmly, not looking up at her. His knife carved into the tender meat and her mouth watered. 'You're practically drooling on my nice linen, Princess. Surely you realise that to survive, you must eat. Being in the world hasn't amplified your beauty, it's only harshened it.'

'Beauty isn't everything,' Snow snapped, choosing to ignore the dirt she couldn't completely clean from her hands.

'No,' he replied with a mouthful of food. 'But it's a useful tool in getting what you want. Beauty is power. If it's used right.'

Power. Why did everyone seem to have it except her? Myrenna and her blasted mirror had power over Snow. The realm held power over her choices as a future queen. Even the rebellion she'd yet to find controlled what her next move should be. The Huntress had overpowered her with a whistle and her hounds.

Perhaps Trik had a point about there being power in her beauty, in what she could control.

He nodded towards his food. 'It's not poisoned. There's no apple pie here.'

She flinched.

The sharp clatter of cutlery against a plate made her stomach twist with hunger. She reached for the knife, her fingers curling around its cool handle. In its polished surface, her reflection flickered back – a gaunt, wild version of herself. Could the blade sever his artery cleanly? Hansel had shown her where to cut, how fast the blood would spill.

Trik chuckled. 'Try it and you'll be locked away before you can blink. I know you think you can fight, but I assure you I'll win.'

Heat flushed her cheeks as she dropped her eyes. To fight, she would need her strength, her wit. Finally picking up the fork, Snow sliced into the meat. The tender cut of beef melted on her tongue, and she felt the wild beast of hunger claw at her stomach. Her hands shook as she tried to hold back the urge to rip into the food with her bare hands.

'Good,' Trik said, taking another bite. 'Food can be scarce and wasting it would make Vlad mad.'

When she didn't reply, Trik said, 'Vlad is the cook. He's very good, but also passionate about food wastage. Especially when there's a war.'

'Who is Dread?' she interjected, bringing up the name he had mentioned when she'd entered.

'And she speaks!' he laughed. 'Now, now, don't pout. I don't get royal company often.'

She wanted to say something smug but held her tongue.

'You might not have met me before – not formally, anyway,' Trik said, shooting her a wink, 'but you've certainly met Dread. Big guy? Long hair? Very stern expression?' Despite the scar cutting past his ear, his smile was genuine.

She didn't trust it.

'I've seen him,' she conceded.

'I don't doubt that at all,' said Trik. 'He has a way of being at the castle just when something is about to happen.'

'How do you know him?' she asked, taking another bite.

'He's my brother.'

Snow's food turned to ash in her mouth. She hadn't expected that. But when she looked up, Trik was calm, the warm smile still on his face

Snow had met Dread, of course – several times. She had just never known his name until now. She could feel his rough hands on her as he hauled her from the throne room to her quarters. See how his eyes would sparkle when Myrenna was being particularly cruel.

Yes, she had met Dread.

Brother.

The word pulsed through her as she sat before the general of the army. Trik was slimmer than Dread but, now that she truly looked at him, she saw the similarities. He held the same harshness, the defined jawline, the piercing green eyes. Perhaps it was written in their genetics, to be as sharp as a blade. To cut through the world as if it were soft flesh.

Trik watched her put the pieces together before he spoke. 'You know what we are.'

She gave him a small nod. 'I know what you are.'

'Say it,' he urged.

She hesitated.

'Go on – say it.'

'You're the three brothers.'

'And what are we?'

'Birds,' she replied.

Trik snorted as he took a sip from his cup. 'Crows, Princess,' he corrected. 'If Dread heard you call us just birds, he'd cut you through the middle and he'd do it slowly. We are *crows.*'

'You're murderers,' she whispered.

His eyes sparkled at the comment. 'We can be. But we are also more. We are magic. We are linked. We are the executioners of her army. We are shapeshifters. Skinwalkers and mimics. We are a lot of things.'

'You are only one thing to me,' she said.

'And what is that exactly?'

'Monsters.'

'We've been called worse,' he said, shrugging.

'Why am I here?'

'You're here to satisfy my curiosity. Now that you've had your turn, it's mine.' He placed down his cutlery, resting his elbows on the table. His eyes grew dark, but he held the smile on his face; solely focusing on Snow. 'What was protecting you? And why is it now gone?'

'I don't know,' she replied. It was new information to her.

Trik twitched, but the smile remained. 'Who are you travelling with?'

'I was travelling alone,' she lied.

He raised an eyebrow. 'I'll try again. Who were you travelling with?'

'Nobody.'

His smile faltered. 'I know you were found alone. But with your background and inexperience of the realm, you would have been quick work for the wolves if you were alone. So, I'll ask one last time, who were you travelling with?'

She remained silent and his eyes glittered with malice.

He shook his head when she didn't reply and sat back in his chair. 'You're lucky Artemis chose other company tonight. She'd have a knife to your throat already.'

Snow slammed down her cutlery. 'Then why don't you?'

At that, his voice darkened. 'I usually prefer politeness rather than pain but I'm not above it, *Princess*. I'm an executioner, after all. Do not push me.'

Goosebumps spread across Snow's skin.

Trik pulled a jagged knife from under the table and placed it next to his goblet. 'Artemis wasn't lying when she said the Queen mentioned nothing about harming you. I will protect you from others but I'm not willing to save you when you're already on the Ever After's door. I require information and you will give it to me, *willingly*. Otherwise, we will take the difficult path.'

She eyed the knife carefully. Its handle was carved from bone, rough and weathered by use. The jagged steel edge resembled a crude saw rather than a proper blade. A pang of longing struck her – Hansel's axe was sleek, balanced, and true, deadly in its precision. This thing was primitive, but it would have to do if it came to that.

She should have felt fear. But she didn't. There was only rage. She was no longer the girl locked away behind castle walls. She had been poisoned, poked, kidnapped, bossed around, and now she was being threatened.

She was powerless.

Yet, once upon a time, so was Myrenna.

She was not just a princess. She was a survivor. She was tired of being demure, of being scared.

She let the rage fester beneath her skin, coaxing it to boil in her blood and turn molten in her core. Her glare was a weapon, sharp with loathing and brimming with dark promises. Poison pulsed in her gaze, a silent vow of retribution that clung to the air between them.

Don't be rash, her mind whispered.

Kill him, came another voice.

Snow slowly picked up her cutlery and cut into the meat, lifting it to her mouth casually. Trik eyed her suspiciously, but she gave him nothing of what lingered under her skin, of what threatened to be unleashed.

The longer she was away from the palace, the more she understood the realm and how people worked. Books had once been her window to the realm, but now she was living her own story, one that revealed the realm's true face in ways no tale ever had.

She held onto the rage, letting the food melt on her tongue though she tasted nothing. The longer she travelled, the longer her list became. The list of those she would cull as soon as she had the chance.

When she became Queen, she would rule equally and firmly. But she would not forgive with ease, nor would she forget.

The wood nymphs would pay for locking her inside a tree. Myrenna would pay for crushing her people. The entire war front would be dismantled and every single one of them would have their heads chopped off and mounted along her walls like a prized collection. She would bathe in their blood, drink in her revenge, and salute to those left standing.

Trik saw the glint in her eyes. The promise. But he didn't act.

Snow didn't know if she was impressed or infuriated.

Her fingers gripped tightly around her knife. In a blink, she spun it in her palm and dived across the table. She was quick, but not quick enough to stop Trik as he twisted from his seat and grabbed her by the back of the neck. Her face collided into the table with a hard blow.

Her ears rang, something cracking in her jaw as Snow slid to the floor, gravy on her chin. She blinked back surprise, gasping to breathe.

Trik's boots were covered in muck and grime as he leaned down and growled into her ear. 'Try that again and I'll show you just how powerless you are in my camp. When my men are done with you, not even your beauty will save you. You see, that's the trick, *Princess*. Beauty is only powerful when you wield it. Otherwise, it's nothing but a curse.'

'I'll kill you!' Snow screeched, thrashing violently as guards stormed into the tent and seized her by the arms and shoulders. Their grip was iron-clad, dragging her outside as soldiers paused their duties to gawk at the commotion. Her body writhed with fury, teeth bared and snapping in Trik's direction. He followed behind, his face disturbingly neutral, unfazed by her wild struggle.

He straightened his jacket, the knife gleaming in his hands. 'I was really hoping we could have a civil conversation.'

Snow's ankle hit the mud with a squelch. 'And here I thought you liked to roll around with savages,' she spat.

Trik's eyes grew dark, but he didn't respond as he stepped past her and led his men through the tents.

Firelight flickered as they reached a decrepit building surrounded by tents, with two guards at each entrance.

With a creak of the door, Snow was pushed inside, then shoved into a tall, narrow cage that sat on the dirt, a rope tied to its top. Her eyes roved the ceiling, meeting wooden beams where the rope was attached to a pulley.

It was an old barn.

She staggered forward and was met with the steel clang of the cage doors. A heavy padlock was attached before the guards stepped back. The cage shifted as she balanced, and Snow clutched the bars, feeling like a bird with her wings clipped. A guard pulled a heavy chain from the doorway and the cage swung, lifting higher and higher until it hung from a suspended wooden beam. Dizziness fell over her, her skull throbbing. Her fingers trailed her forehead where she was met with a warm trickle of blood.

The cage was so narrow she was forced to stand, her shoulders brushing against the cold, unforgiving bars. Trik stared up at her, his eyes sparkling as the guard tied the rope tight. 'Let's see how you play after a day or two without food, water, or company.'

With a feral growl, Snow spat, the gesture futile as it fell with a silent splat on the ground.

Trik merely gave her a disgusted look and pulled at his jacket sleeves like a gentleman about to go to dinner. 'Check on her regularly,' he said to a guard. 'I'll come back later.'

One day, you'll kill them all, the dark voice inside her echoed.

Tears pricked at her eyes and the rage she'd desperately clung to at dinner ebbed away, replaced by icy fear. Snow pressed her face against the cold, unyielding bars of her cage and let out a scream that clawed its way from the depths of her soul.

She screamed for her losses, each one a scar etched across her heart.

She screamed for the broken, jagged parts of herself that she barely recognized anymore.

She screamed out her rage, raw and searing, and for the fear that gnawed relentlessly at her resolve.

Her voice fractured, splintering into a cracked, pitiful whimper until it abandoned her entirely.

Yet even in silence, she kept screaming – inside her mind, where no one could silence her fury.

XXIX

The Unlikely Rescue Attempt

The absence of Pip's flute was like missing a limb. He'd only felt this way a few times in his life. The first had been with Rumple and the second time with the giants. This third time was worse somehow, his confidence cracking with its loss. The other two times he'd learned from his mistakes, applying logic to everything he did. It's why it had been tied to him in the first place.

But he had nobody to blame but himself. He had been stupid. Careless.

His family had once locked the pipe inside a puzzle box and hidden it within the fields that surrounded their family home. This was before it was stolen; before his family died under the control of their new masters.

That had been a long time ago.

Since then, Pip had found fortune and fame with the Dream Weaver – before falling out of regard and turning to his own games. Then he lost big time when he met Bogart.

He shook his head at the thought. The idiocy of not protecting the flute as he should after all this time was ludicrous, yet he'd still managed to lose it. To one of those horrible wooden creatures, too.

The Princess was in danger, but he couldn't help but feel the pull towards leaving the quest and searching for his flute. He was only supposed to be here temporarily, anyway. He was here to help courier Snow before leaving for Rumple.

The spindle in the wrong hands could turn this whole war, princess or not. It would mean disaster. And though he still resented the Dream Weaver, that sense of loyalty lingered. The urge to prove himself. He wondered if it would ever go away. Or if the urge would remain, whispering to him in the dark confines of his mind.

A whistle from ahead jostled him from his thoughts.

Florian waved them forward, flapping his arm energetically like they couldn't see him perfectly already.

'He needs to work on his subtlety,' Pip murmured to Malak who strode just in front of him.

'I think that's why he did the bird whistle.'

'You know I didn't mean the whistle. I meant the flapping of his arms like he's about to take flight, as if we can't see him. Every creature in the forest can see him.'

'He's useful,' Malak said. 'Be nice. I'll check the perimeter to ensure there's no one else. Perhaps you can enlighten him as to how he can be more *stealthy.*'

'Do I look like a tutor?'

'Well, you're bossy enough to be one.' Malak smirked.

Pip waved him away. 'I wouldn't have to if you two didn't act like idiots.'

'Coming from an elf who lost the one item that controls his freedom.'

Pip swung his stick, but Malak dodged it. Laughing deeply, the troll veered off, checking for intruders.

As Pip got closer, he noted the red hues of Florian's face had returned. His nose was pink, his shirt sleeve riddled with snot from wiping it. 'Put your arms down, you ninny,' Pip chided.

The Prince lowered his arms, wiping his nose on his already-crusted sleeve. 'Sorry. I just got excited. Look.'

They entered a small camp. The fire's embers were still warm, tracks freshly pressed into the dirt.

'It's recent. Several hours, maybe,' Florian said. 'I found indents in the dirt over by the tree there with grazing on the bark.'

'We're alone,' Malak said, coming through the trees. 'And I think we're further behind than we thought. Perhaps half a day. They'd be closer to the border than expected by now.'

Pip frowned.

'We won't make it in time,' Florian said. 'Not with our scent and the speed they're going. They'd see us before we got there.'

'We've got no other option, then,' Pip said, poking the fire. 'We'll have to meet them at the camp. Try another way.'

'You're doing that thing where you hatch a plan, aren't you?' Malak asked. 'Your eyes get darker, and you stare at something for a long time.'

Pip ignored him, thinking in a way he hadn't been required to do in a long time.

What would Rumple do?

The others waited as the wisp of an idea came to him. It was improbable – almost impossible – but Rumple had always loved a distraction.

Pip turned to the others. 'We need to sneak in somehow, and when everyone is distracted, we'll take her when nobody's around.'

Malak snorted. 'How do you distract an army of thousands?'

'By doing it when the army of the dead crawl from the earth.'

Florian gulped. 'That's suicide.'

'It might be, but it's also a chance,' Pip replied.

XXX

The Tinker's Toys

Dread stood on the balcony of the throne room, smoke billowing amongst the debris. He rested his forearms against the parapet watching the Crystal Lake shine against the sun. It was a giant jewel amongst the rock, the ash and dirt of the city bruising its peaceful surface.

He hadn't slept. He'd spent the whole night rounding up prisoners, most of whom would face beheading or hanging over the coming days. He'd found Flynn, but there had been no sign of Hansel, or whoever it was he stole from the fighting pits under the tavern. They'd escaped somehow, slinking back into the shadows and vanishing.

Dread twitched at the thought.

Was his control slipping? Or was he only on edge because Trik was at the border and Flynn was on the loose? With Myrenna gone, he was a bubble drifting along the wind, afraid that the slightest thing would pop his outer shell.

He'd not had an update on the bone door, either. Did he stay? Or did he go and resume his duties as his Queen had ordered?

It tore at him.

He heard the quiet breath of the Tinker behind him as his robes glided across the tiles. 'Do you suppose she'll thank you for burning down her city?' the Tinker said. 'Or do you think she'll just burn you instead?'

Dread remained staring at the horizon, holding back his urge to crush the Tinker's bones with his fists. 'The only way to stop infection is to cut its core. The city was just an artery on the way.'

'An artery that now continues to bleed,' the Tinker replied. 'Is that what you thought when you began burning down the market?'

Dread didn't want to know how the Tinker knew that, so he remained steady, watching as the light refracted off the water's surface in hues of peach and violet. So vastly different to the darkness of the mines.

'The market was their trading hub. A place for messages and sabotage. It couldn't stay.'

The Tinker paused. 'Did you also know it was the most useful place for the Queen's spies? Without it, she'll be blind. The rebellion will find another way to communicate, and she won't be able to control it now. You know how she gets when she doesn't have control.'

Dread ignored the sinking feeling in his gut, the shard of fear that sliced just under the surface. Had he been too hasty, acting on impulse without thinking through the implications? Even he didn't believe the lie as he said, 'When she sees how many we've caught, she'll see the benefits outweigh the risk.'

The Tinker stepped beside him, resting the small wooden spindle on the railing, and raised his dark eyes to Dread. 'I hope for your sake that's true.'

Dread turned to him and immediately regretted it. The Tinker wasn't smiling but he didn't need to. His eyes shone in triumph as if he'd already won whatever rivalry this was for Myrenna's favour. He didn't care if Dread lived or died. He didn't care what the Queen wanted, either. He just liked power, the ability to play with his toys and break and build them without repercussions.

Dread eyed the spindle, the only thing the Tinker seemed to care for in this whole realm. 'Let's not lie to each other, Tinker. Are you here to gloat or to be helpful for once?'

The Tinker's eyes glittered and a thin smile played on his lips. 'I'm always here to help. The gloating is just a benefit I rarely get to enjoy.'

Dread leaned back. He could smell the ash on the air, the remnants of the fires now diminished. Suddenly it didn't smell so sweet anymore and left a stale taste in his mouth.

'Have you figured it out yet?' Dread said, pointing to the spindle.

'Almost,' the Tinker mused, cupping the spindle with both hands. 'It's a tricky little thing. I haven't broken it because I'm not entirely sure I can put this one back together. It seems to operate in conjunction with its master – a tie of sorts between the two souls. It's alive almost, but can only be partly controlled because Rumple is yet to fully comply.'

'I thought you'd broken him.'

'He's mostly broken. His mind now tricks him, and I use that to my advantage. Want me to show you?'

Dread almost snarled. 'I don't want your tricks today.'

'Not on you,' the Tinker laughed.

Heat crept up Dread's cheeks and he turned before the Tinker could see.

'Meet me tomorrow, in the throne room,' the Tinker replied, enjoying Dread's discomfort. 'I'll show you on one of the prisoners. Bring no one else.' Dread didn't reply, but the Tinker didn't mind. Instead, he grinned at the view before giving Dread a mocking bow. 'Tomorrow,' he repeated.

Dread leaned forward, his forearms pressing hard into the stone barrier. He didn't want to know about the Tinker's experiments, but he also knew he was screwed without the Tinker's help.

And though he denied it, his curiosity had been piqued.

XXXI

The Warnings of Dreams

The icy wind bit into Brufell's skin.

He stood on a grassy knoll overlooking a battlefield, the clouds casting grey shadows over the ruined land as bodies lay splayed across the once-verdant surface. The heavy steel of the axe he carried pulled on his hip, the hilt encrusted in gold and lined with gems only mined in Parador.

It was dwarven-made, strong and thick. A gift from his father.

Brufell scanned the horizon. He'd been here before, had stood on this very hill, watched this same graveyard with deep sorrow. He lifted his gloved hand to his face, feeling the fresh stubble of a young dwarf. He touched the breastplate, the indents worn and scarred from battle.

He was in a memory, coated in the illusion of a dream. His bones were still stiff from age, his mind not as free to wander as it once did. He remembered this battlefield, but he had been a different dwarf then, prone to ideals of glory and heroism instead of safety and cynicism. Though, he had been a survivor. That remained unchanged.

And he'd felt guilt for years.

A shadow moved and he turned to see a hooded figure standing amongst the smoke. A long cape billowed behind her, and her grey eyes shone beneath long lashes. Dainty hands clasped each other, pale against the black she wore.

'This is a dream,' he said to her. 'This battle has long been forgotten.'

'Ahh,' said the woman from behind her cloak. 'But should it have been?' She lowered her hood.

The lines in her face were fine compared to his previous dreams. He'd seen her over the years, in dreams or whispers and rumours. She was a Seer, a watcher, a witch.

Lady Nona.

Her skin was smoother than the last time they'd met, her hair thicker, with loose curls half tied back in braids that whirled on top of her head.

'I didn't forget,' Brufell said. 'Memories are one of the wounds that never heals after war.'

'Do you know why I chose you? Why I also chose Bonyx and Eveline?'

Brufell took a breath, fresh pain searing in his heart at the corpses of dwarves among the dead. 'I don't usually assume why anybody does anything. Especially not those with powers like yours.'

She cupped his chin, pulling his face towards hers. 'I chose you all because you each have something in common.'

'You mean death?'

'No, not death. You have faced dark paths and yet each of you retain hope. You look at the world in all of its poisonous ways and still hope it could be better.'

Brufell snorted, pulling away from her. He squeezed his axe, connecting him to what he had felt that day in battle. It was a comfort but also a haunted memory; a tool from the day his youth and ignorance had been torn from him.

'You've died,' he bit out. 'How are you here? Why are you here?'

'Magic as powerful as mine can never be fully erased. It lingers in parts of the realm I impacted most. The cauldron. My grimoire. Even in the Seeker herself.'

'I suppose I shouldn't be surprised,' he said.

'No, you shouldn't.' She smiled. 'But we're not here for that. War is coming. Eveline fights to gather the tools she needs to defeat the Queen. But I fear she doesn't understand what that power means. She has a target already from those who choose to harm her, and that will place her in more peril. She must do it alone, but that does not mean we can't protect her from here. She has saved the Princess, but she must now find dark and dangerous things. You and Bronson must get to the rebellion: the Six are not whole without you. Together you are stronger.'

'I think you mean Seven,' Brufell corrected.

Her greys eyes fixed on his before she placed her palm on his chest. 'I mean Six. Beetle's heart no longer beats to the sound of this realm.'

Brufell stepped back, something sticky curling in his gut. His mouth went dry. 'No,' he said. 'Impossible.'

Nona gave him a sad smile. 'Death comes for us all. I'm sorry I had to be the one to share this news with you, and that you must grieve alone. It's why it's crucial that you find your kin. Lift your blade and protect the realm once more.'

Brufell was shaking, but it was as if he stood far away, staring down not at the corpses but at himself as he died inside. It was as if smoke was being sucked out of a room, the air leaving him as he went utterly numb, breathless.

He had felt grief. He had seen death. Each time it had taken something from him. He had always been able to stand up, always found reason to continue going, but now he was hollow, scraped from the inside out like the gutting of an animal.

Little, quiet Beetle.

Beetle who played in the grass, who longed for adventure and glory. Beetle who delved into Bonyx's stories with such vigour he'd ignore the Seven until he wanted another adventure.

'The grotto …'

'Is gone. The Princess has awoken, and she runs. The others, including your cousins, have found refuge with the rebellion. Bonyx lies locked under the castle. There is nothing left for you here. Not anymore.'

'What of the fairies?' Brufell asked, his voice husky and hollow.

'Gone, too. They put up a brave fight.'

'A brave fight means nothing when all that's left is death.'

'A brave fight means their spirit lingers. Where they stood and fell, they shall linger forever. Just as I linger now.'

Brufell stepped back, suddenly angry. 'Since the day you invaded my dreams, I have seen nothing but ruin following me. You twist words. You speak of prophecies and yet there is only sacrifice. You may infect Bonyx's mind, but you are no longer welcome to infect mine.'

Her lips shaped into a thin line as he continued.

'I cannot do this with you anymore. I cannot protect my heart and my kin and the realm at the same time. I must tell Bronson, and you must leave.'

'The Seeker—' Nona started.

'Can protect herself.'

Nona's eyes darkened, the muscles in her jaw tensed. 'That is not for you to decide. This is far from being finished. You must go to Carfell—'

'What is finished is this conversation – just like this battle,' Brufell said.

Nona gasped as he lifted the axe with strong, firm hands.

And he shoved it deep into his gut.

Malak, Florian, and Pip hid within the tree line as smoke curled around the campfires of the army. Malak could see the line where the camp ended and the road stretched out towards Wolf's Den, the nearest village. Burning lanterns dotted the tents, each one a reminder of how many soldiers lay between him and his princess.

Shame twisted his insides for not protecting her. For letting her go. He'd made an oath and failed.

After they'd figured out their next move, the three of them had stopped to sleep, only lighting a fire long enough to cook something and prepare the allergy tea for Florian. The fire was a risk, but Florian's sneezing and sniffles were a bigger one.

Malak shuffled as sharp, dried sticks bit into his skin.

'How long do we wait?' Florian asked from the dark. 'Are they expected to attack soon?'

'We wait as long as it takes,' Pip replied. 'Could be an hour or it could be a day.'

'We could be here a week, and the Princess would be dead by then,' Malak grumbled.

Pip sighed. 'So dramatic. It won't be a week.'

'You don't know that,' Malak said, 'so stop pretending you do.'

'What's that?' Florian asked, pointing to a group of men walking through the camp.

'It's just the officials. Probably going to the General to report,' Pip replied. 'Or to drink.'

'Surely even the Queen's men aren't dumb enough to drink when an attack is imminent?' Malak said.

'When there is war and you're ready to die, troll, you'll take what you can of life's pleasures,' Pip whispered.

'I didn't mean the men,' Florian said. 'I meant the shadow next to them. The one following.'

Malak's interest was piqued. His eyes roved past the officials, focusing on each tent and burning light until finally resting on a slim figure donned in black. The figure moved in and out of shadows, zigzagging across the camp.

Whoever it was, was definitely following the men.

'Who is that?' Malak asked. 'Someone alone in a camp that size and they think they can just sneak around? That's a death wish.'

'They seem to be doing well, though,' Florian remarked. 'Look at them move.'

'We can see them too, Florian,' Malak replied. 'But I want to know *who* they are, not *what* they are doing.'

'I'd like to know the same thing,' came a voice from behind them, the low echoing growls of dark hounds following.

The three of them turned slowly, Malak ensuring to keep his hands up as they came face to face with the pack.

A red-headed female stood amongst them, her face warped with anger. Her coat was made of fine fur, the hues of grey and white stark against her hair. She lifted a long knife and pointed it at them as the hounds surrounded their prey.

Malak's stomach dropped.

The Huntress.

'I'd also like to know who you are and why you're watching my camp,' Artemis said, raising her other hand. 'But tonight, I'm not feeling very patient.'

'We can explain,' Florian stammered.

'I don't care,' she replied.

Then she blew the whistle.

XXXII

The Breaking of Beasts

Malak flung out his arms as a hound hurtled toward him, its jaws snapping inches from his face. He barely caught hold of its thick, matted fur, muscles straining as he fought to keep it at bay. Hot breath blasted against his skin, reeking of blood and decay.

He gritted his teeth, shoving the beast away – only for another to crash into him from the side. Fangs tore into his flesh, a searing pain exploding through his arm. He screamed, but the sound was lost to the snarl of the beasts, the clash of steel, and the terrified cries of his friends.

The Huntress laughed, her crimson hair matching the blood on her blade. Blood poured from Malak's arm as he struggled against the crushing weight of the hound. Drool dripped onto his skin, hot and foul, as raw panic clawed at his chest. He thrashed, driving a desperate fist into its jaw, the impact jolting up his arm. The beast yelped and staggered back, its hungry eyes locked onto him. Malak sucked in a sharp breath, fists clenched. Despite how his body screamed in pain, tonight would not be the night he was defeated, not when Snow was in danger and so close.

As the hound charged, Malak readied himself, his swing wide as the beast dove for him. He struck the hound's side with a fierce blow, sending the creature tumbling across the grass. But before he could catch his breath, another leapt at him, fangs bared, eyes wild.

This time, he was ready.

Malak's fist met the beast's jaw with a force that sent a sharp crack echoing through the trees. The hound yelped, its head snapping sideways as it staggered back.

Malak had no time to catch his breath when another lunged, teeth bared, eyes wild. Malak twisted, muscles coiling as he ducked beneath its snapping jaws. His hands found purchase around its torso, rough fur bristling against his grip. With a guttural roar, he heaved the creature over his shoulder and threw it into the underbrush with a sickening thud.

The growls didn't cease. More shadows circled, hungry and unrelenting. Malak rolled his shoulders, blood dripping from his knuckles, his breath misting in the cold air.

Two more sprinted towards him.

They lunged, a blur of snapping jaws and matted fur. Malak swung without care, his blade meeting flesh with a sickening crunch. A yelp cut through the chaos, but there was no time to register it. Another hound was already upon him.

He kicked out, boot colliding with ribs, sending the beast sprawling. Claws raked across his arm, burning hot, but he didn't slow. He fought like a storm given form, striking, shoving, twisting through the relentless onslaught. Blood – his and theirs – spattered the dirt as he barrelled forward, every movement fuelled by raw survival.

On his right, Pip's cane flew, smacking away the hounds as they approached. Florian held his sword to Malak's left, swinging the weapon around without direction as hound after hound dove forward.

Artemis' cackle rang through the trees, mixing with the growling barks of her pets. To her, it was music; to Malak, it was murder.

He'd always hated the woman, from every flounce in her step to the way she eyed the staff with contempt at the castle. She used to spit on the ground when he saddled a horse for her, and he'd avoided the kennels whenever she was in town, hoping to never meet her hounds.

Fate truly was deranged sometimes. Much like her pets.

The hounds lunged, and the group fought back, parrying with whatever skill they could muster. Snarls and steel clashed amongst the trees. Malak groped for his sword and found his sheath empty. His heart slammed against his ribs as he whirled, scanning the darkness. Then he spotted it – his club, lying by his pack. He sprinted, diving for the weapon just as a hound snapped at his heels. His fingers closed around the familiar wood, and without hesitation, he swung.

Wood met bone. The hound's teeth shattered, flying from its maw as it recoiled, shaking its head. But if the blow had dazed it, the fresh blood dripping from its mouth only made it more terrifying. Its sleek black body gleamed in the dim light, muscles coiled beneath its hide, ready to strike. Its nostrils flared, drinking in the scent of fear.

I won't survive this.

Malak's could only brace himself, readying for a kill or to be killed. Then Florian screamed.

Malak turned.

The prince was covered in blood, his sword thrown into the dirt several pixies away. His leg was twisted, the hound's locked jaw yanking him through the dirt. Another howl echoed as the snap of Pip's stick rang in his ears. The elf raised both fists and screamed out profanities. 'Come and get me!'

Malak's mouth went dry. They were outnumbered and out skilled. But he wasn't ready to give up. He'd endured too much hardship, too much sorrow.

Somewhere out there was hope. Love. Family.

Snow.

He'd faced worse in Parador with the wraiths, worse in the grotto; this time, he would not fail his friends.

A deep growl rumbled through the night as two hounds sprinted toward him.

With a raw battle cry, he surged forward, raising his weapon high. He swung low. The first hound lunged, and Malak's club met bone with a brutal crack, the impact reverberating up his arm.

Fuelled by adrenaline, Malak turned, eyes locking onto the Prince. Snarling hounds surrounded him. Malak didn't hesitate. With another savage roar, he tore through them.

He slammed one in the ribs, feeling the crunch beneath his strike, then swept the legs out from another, sending it sprawling.

Florian screamed as another hound lunged, plunging sharp teeth into the prince's skin. Malak dropped his club and ran for him.

Malak latched his green hands around the hound's jaw and wrenched it open. Teeth tore free from Florian's leg, and the prince staggered back with a sharp gasp. But Malak didn't let go. His grip tightened as he pried the beast's maw wider, bone cracking beneath the pressure. A sick snap rang out, and the hound went limp in his grasp.

With a fierce shout, he hurled the lifeless body toward its master. Where it landed with a heavy thud at her feet.

Artemis wasn't laughing anymore.

With a whistle, she recalled her last few hounds, and stepped back, her skin pale. Malak noted a sheen of sweat on her forehead, her pupils wide with fear.

How does it feel to be the victim? he thought.

Malak tasted blood as he picked up the club and twisted it in his grip. There was something empowering about releasing the strength his body housed. About being able to release the frustration and anger he'd been keeping deep inside.

A rumble reverberated through his chest. 'We're here for the Princess, and you're going to give her to us.' He didn't recognise the voice that came out, or the anger that echoed underneath his skin. But he only had one purpose, one path, one promise: to protect Snow.

His confidence dissipated when the woman cackled. 'You won't find her,' she said. 'Her heart has already been claimed.'

Malak lunged.

His swing sliced through empty air as the woman blew her whistle and bolted, abandoning her beasts to finish the job.

A searing pain erupted through Malak's body as three hounds sank their teeth into him, each maw tearing into his flesh. He lurched forward, chasing after Artemis, but the weight of the hounds dragged him down. Blood filled his mouth, the metallic tang thick on his tongue, and darkness crept at the edges of his vision. His steps faltered.

With a furious roar, he ripped one hound free and flung it aside. Another he struck with a brutal punch, feeling bone shatter beneath his knuckles. But the third held fast. His knee buckled, a sharp wince escaping his lips as, ahead of him, a flash of red hair vanished into the trees.

Malak thrashed against the last hound, his energy ebbing. He wasn't sure if he could fight off the last one, wasn't sure if he had it in him. His vision wavered, black creeping in at the edges, his skull pounding like a war drum.

Then a figure burst through the trees. A shout. A blur of movement. Pip.

The elf swung wildly, his stick cracking against the hound's side. Another strike. Another shout. Then sweet, sweet relief.

Malak staggered back, his shoulder slamming into the rough bark of a tree as he fought to stay upright. He sucked in a desperate breath, the world spinning, and then – there was Pip, standing between him and the beast.

The hound snarled, its muscles bunching, ready to lunge. Pip held his pitiful weapon aloft, but he was nothing more than a snack in the beast's eyes.

Blinking back the pain, Malak pushed off the tree, closing the distance in two strides. With one swift, brutal twist, he snapped the hound's neck and watched as the life drained from its eyes.

Malak dropped to his knees and gasped in air. He didn't know where the pain ended and where it began, but from the feel of his ribs, he'd broken a bone.

Pip panted beside him. Malak couldn't see any blood, but the elf's clothes were torn, his skin covered in mud and leaves.

'We need to move,' Pip said. 'She'll be back with reinforcements.'

But Malak couldn't hear past the roaring in his ears, the way the world narrowed onto the hound's lifeless form. His breaths came out in short sharp bursts and his heart ached. Blood was everywhere, black bodies splayed at odd angles.

A weak whimper broke through the night, snapping Malak's gaze toward it.

Florian lay nearby, clutching his wounded leg. Blood seeped through his fingers, and beneath the torn flesh, bone gleamed stark and pale where the hound's teeth had torn deep.

But it wasn't the wound that pierced through Malak's chest.

It was the fear in the prince's eyes.

Snow woke to the slow creak of her cage descending. The chains groaned, metal scraping against metal, until the floor met the earth with a dull thud.

Her body protested as she stirred. Her stiff limbs refused to obey, joints cracking like brittle twigs. She felt like a skeleton unearthed from a forgotten grave, broken and pieced back together all wrong.

She groaned as she hit the ground, the stillness rattling through her.

The clattering of keys rang in her ears before the door swung open and firm hands picked her up.

'One night and you look as if you'd been fighting the war for weeks. It seems living outside the castle doesn't suit you, Princess.'

She peered at Trik through her lashes. The Huntress loomed just behind him, her expression dark with fury, lips pressed into a tight, unforgiving line.

'Let me break her,' Artemis demanded. 'Let me see her *bleed.*'

Trik ignored the comment as he lifted Snow up by the elbow, his fingers digging into her skin. 'Artemis is in a mood this morning. It seems your friends killed her pets.'

Snow's eyes darted up and met the cold fury of Artemis. She caught the hard clench in her jaw, the ripple of control barely holding. A slow, defiant smirk tugged at Snow's lips.

Her friends had come.

'She'll be easy to break,' Artemis said, holding her hunting knife. She glided forward and gave Snow a cruel smile. 'Let me do it, *please.*'

Trik held out his arm to stop her, the gesture firm and commanding. Artemis obeyed, but from the flared nostrils,

Snow knew it was a short leash – one that could be broken if pushed hard enough.

'Let's hope she is,' Trik said to the Huntress. 'But you won't be the one to do it. The convoy arrives tomorrow, and she needs to be alive. Then the Queen will have her.'

Snow went rigid.

She is coming for you.

She couldn't run now. Trik's grip was iron and, if the look in Artemis's eyes was any warning, she'd be dead very soon.

She envisioned it now: rewinding the clock and spinning back to the afternoon where everything had changed. She would have taken Hansel's hand and run, left through the passages that reached out to the maze and let Hansel carry her when they'd passed the castle walls.

Her thought was forgotten when Trik pulled Snow towards him. 'She's bloodthirsty today,' he whispered, smelling of ale and blood. 'Your friends *really* pissed her off.'

Snow's mortality hit her like tsunami. Her heart thrummed in her chest.

Twanging.

Singing.

Roaring.

She would be fine once her friends came. They would save her. Malak would always save her.

Trik pushed her forward.

Artemis put away her knife and grabbed her other arm.

'She's going to my tent,' Trik said. 'Don't give me that look, Artemis.'

The woman gripped Snow's arm tighter as they exited the building and took the path to the general's tent. Artemis's breath was hot on her ear as she whispered, 'I may not be able to touch you now, but when the Queen is done with you, I'll skin your corpse like a freshly caught fawn. I'll adorn you on my wall as a prize, and then I'll bed Trik underneath it.'

Snow shivered in disgust. 'That says more about you than it does about me.'

She was shoved forward through the entrance of Trik's tent. The plush carpets had been pulled away, replaced by the skin of some kind of bear. In the centre, a wooden cross had been erected, chains and iron linked to it for hands and feet.

Snow knew a torture device when she saw one. She'd seen enough of them when she'd been sneaking through the castle. She backed away, hitting the hard muscle of Trik's chest.

He pushed her against the rough wood, the grain biting into her spine. 'I offered you an easy way, and this is the road you chose. Don't forget that.'

Snow thrashed, limbs flailing, body twisting, She would not go. She couldn't. But the guards were faster. They surged forward, hands clamping down like iron shackles, wrenching her into their grasp.

A sickening weight settled in her gut as she watched Trik turn his back to her, his steps casual as he approached a table laden with bottles of amber liquid. He poured himself a drink, swirling the goblet in his hand before offering another to Artemis, as if this were nothing more than an evening's entertainment.

The first strap cinched around her wrist, the leather biting into her skin. Then the next. Her breath came in ragged gasps as they fastened another around her ankles, locking her into place. She struggled, pulling against her restraints, but they only dug in deeper, unyielding.

Her body was splayed open, her arms stretched wide like a set of obscene wings.

She tilted her head back, blinking against the harsh glow of the fairy lanterns swaying above. The tiny creatures inside flailed, their frantic movements casting restless shadows across the tent, mirroring her own struggle. She saw herself in them. In their panic, in their silent pleas for escape.

A single tear slipped down her cheek. She wasn't sure if it was from rage or fear. Maybe both. But she refused to sob, refused to give them that satisfaction.

Artemis laughed, but the sound felt distant, warped, as if drifting from another world.

Snow shrank into herself, retreating to a corner of her mind that felt sealed off. Safe. The voices she had come to recognize whispered from the shadows, their cold, low tones rising like a bitter wind.

Trapped.

Weak.

Alone.

She was a lone star in an endless galaxy. An animal hunted as prey. She was a princess with no kingdom.

Deep within her mind, she found a dark space. A small, locked box where nothing could touch her. She reached for the lid, pried it open, and crawled inside just as Trik's voice cut through the haze.

She curled into herself, lowering the lid, shutting out the world. Darkness embraced her. A single sob slipped past her lips.

Then the knife cut into her skin.

XXXIII

The Princess and The Assassin

Brufell woke to the sharp, panicked screech of Bronson. He jolted upright, heart racing, only to find his companion flailing wildly, swatting at a bug that had dared to land on him.

He turned over and groaned. His skin was sticky, leaves and dirt clinging to the concoction Bronson had spread on his wounds. His head pounded and the image of Nona still floated just underneath the surface. 'Where are we?' he asked.

The golden eye of the dragon hovered above him, warily watching. 'We're north. Far from those who harm us.'

Brufell sat up and rubbed his skull. It was as if a hammer had hit him a hundred times.

Bronson came over and knelt beside him, offering him a bowl of stew and the remainders of stale bread. 'Can you eat?' he asked.

Brufell took the bowl gratefully. His stomach churned at having eaten so little for the last few days. Bronson smiled down at him as he took his first mouthful, letting the meat soak on his tongue.

The young dwarf had come a long way from his early days of cooking back at the grotto. The meat was tender, juices seeping with each bite, perfectly seasoned with just the right touch of salt.

Brufell noted the smudged kohl around Bronson's eyes and his neatly combed hair. For a moment, he almost looked like the old Bronson.

'You look put together,' Brufell remarked.

Bronson grinned back. 'Are you saying I look nice? Is that a compliment, Brufell?'

Brufell grunted.

Bronson clapped in glee. 'He must have really hit his head!' he said to the mother dragon.

Her belly rumbled with a laugh, smoke unfurling from her nostrils. There was something less terrifying about her now. Maybe it was the fact she wasn't growling at them, or maybe it was because Bronson sat near her scales without flinching.

Nearby, the baby dragon played with Oryx, the pixie zooming in and out of greenery in a game of hide and seek.

'It seems I've missed something,' Brufell said to Bronson. 'What happened?'

Bronson was beaming. 'We're friends now.'

'Oh?' Brufell asked. 'How did that happen?'

'You saved us,' the dragon said in her deep voice, 'and you accomplished what I could not. He healed my baby.'

Brufell looked back to the trees and noted the bandage on the dragon's foot.

'The dragons are looking for a safe place to call home, and I think I know where to send them,' Bronson said quietly. 'In Frode's story you mentioned the floating isles. Not many creatures can reach the points of the islands and it's so far north nobody will think to look there. Not after the dragons were sent to the land of giants. And I thought that, maybe …'

Brufell raised his eyebrow.

'I thought maybe Frode's dragon might have kin that remain there. So, they aren't alone. What do you think?'

Warmth spread through Brufell's chest, filling him with something he hadn't felt in a long time. Maybe Lady Nona hadn't been so wrong after all. Maybe, just maybe, a spark of hope still lingered within him.

'I think that's a great idea,' the old dwarf said, gripping Bronson's arm.

'But,' Bronson whispered, 'we won't be able to go back to the trolls. Not without a tooth.'

Bronson was right. Options had become more limited the further they travelled. The deeper they went, the more problems came up, and not the other way around.

'I know,' Brufell replied, biting into the bread. The sharp edges scraped against his cheek, rough and stale, but he welcomed the discomfort. He'd eaten worse. 'But we'll figure out a way – we always do. You are kind little one. Do not let the realm take that away from you.'

The mother dragon lowered her head beside them. Her chin was almost on the ground as she tried to match the dwarf's height. 'If it is a tooth you require, then I can provide such a thing. It would be a small price for finding us a home.'

'Really?' Bronson asked.

The dragon chuckled. 'My youngling is due to lose one of his baby teeth. Some are already loose. With a little wiggle, a tooth should be easy.'

At his mother's call, the baby dragon scampered over, tiny claws skittering against the ground. It tilted its head up and opened its mouth wide.

'Go on,' the mother urged.

Brufell chuckled as Bronson froze, his body rigid with hesitation. Carefully, he reached inside the dragon's mouth, his fingers brushing against sharp, tiny teeth. With a twist and a wiggle, one came loose. Bronson yanked his hand back, eyes wide.

The youngling released a smoky little laugh. 'I won't bite you.'

Bronson's face broke into a smile as he held up the tooth. It was small, fitting neatly in his palm, its pearly surface gleaming in the light. 'We can help the trolls,' Bronson said. 'Thank you.'

The mother dragon rubbed its snout along her child's neck and purred, then turned back to them. 'Could you show us the way? To this place called the floating isles?'

Brufell finished off the dregs of his stew and stood, his body cracking as he moved. 'I'll draw a map. Do you mind dropping us off at the troll's camp on the way?'

The dragon grumbled something about trolls that Brufell missed before replying, 'I'll drop you close but I won't bring my youngling near the trolls, so you'll need to walk the rest of the way.'

Brufell couldn't see the fault in that, so he agreed. They'd planned to spend one more night where they were and, in the morning, fly out. He only hoped the sick trolls could last that long.

With the tooth now safely in Bronson's pocket, and a possible army of trolls, their luck was turning around.

Snow was numb.

She burrowed deeper into the locked box in her mind, clinging to the shredded embers of herself, the more the knife cut into her body, over and over.

She forgot when her voice finally broke. It could have been with the knife. Or the hot poker that had branded into her skin. At one point, an open flame had burned into the pads of her bare feet. But with each stab of pain, she only lost herself further, clutching at the dark corners of her mind, where only she and the safety of her voices remained.

She knew her body was splayed on the cross, her limbs fodder for torture, her skin a sickening canvas. Numb and broken and tortured, Snow barely felt it when they hacked off her hair, tearing chunks from her skull. She had a dim memory of the Huntress bragging she'd add Snow's hair to her fur cloak.

All she knew was the beat of her heart, the way it remained steady in her chest. She timed her breaths, using it to focus and forget.

One, two, three—

If her heart lived, so did she.

Her friends would come.

But what if they don't? the voice inside her echoed.

She remembered Trik's face twisted in rage as his fist slammed into her. Pain exploded through her skull, but she hung there, silent and unmoving, absorbing every blow. She let the agony carve itself into her bones, storing it away deep inside. She would keep it. Use it. Harness it.

She added their names to her list, envisioning their heads spiked to the gated walls of the Silver City.

She would cut them all.

Behead them all.

She held onto those names, clinging to them like talismans. Reminders of what happened when she was hurt.

Pain pulsed through her in slow, uneven waves. Light danced behind her eyelids, a hazy smear that made her head throb. She couldn't remember how long it had been since anyone had touched her. Her body hung limp from the wooden cross, broken and battered.

Voices drifted in from beyond the tent – urgent, panicked shouts about an intruder, followed by the scuffle of hurried footsteps. One swollen eye cracked open, her vision swimming as her mind crawled out from the darkness.

The tent flaps rustled. She struggled to blink, to focus, trying to peer from behind the box she'd hidden in within her mind. A shadow moved before her. Her heart seized, and she flinched, bracing herself for Trik's harsh voice.

Instead, she met the eyes of a perfect stranger. Perhaps Trik had sent a new torturer.

He wore black, the smooth folds of the tight outfit hugging his figure. He was tall and lean, his figure sharp against the dim light. There was stubble on his jaw, and a pulsing vein in his neck she couldn't look away from. His skin was bronzed, richer and darker than any she'd seen before, smooth and flawless. A strange urge flickered within her to reach out and touch it, to feel its warmth beneath her fingertips. But her body refused to obey.

Her wrists screamed in aching pain from the chains.

The stranger placed a finger to his lips. But the voice inside her awoke.

Be quiet, it whispered.

The stranger's hands moved swiftly, fingers expertly untying the bindings. The straps fell away, and she collapsed to the ground, her body crumpling like a discarded rag.

Her limbs trembled as she tried to push herself up, but her strength was gone. Even the smallest movement felt impossible.

The stranger knelt beside her, producing a vial of shimmering silver liquid. Without a word, he lifted her chin, his touch surprisingly gentle. Though panic speared through her, she had no energy to fight off his touch, to stop whatever the liquid was. Cool glass pressed to her lips, and the concoction slid down her throat, icy and bitter.

'Quickly,' he said, his voice husky and dark. 'It'll give you strength.'

Whatever the tonic was, it burned.

The stranger hushed her again as she choked. He propped her up, his short black hair curling at his scalp.

She couldn't stop staring at his eyes and she felt herself melting into them as the pain receded. Her vision cleared as energy returned to her limbs. She clenched her fists, testing out movement. She looked at him with wide eyes, but he frowned, lifting her up.

'Quickly,' he said again. 'It won't come all at once, but you'll find you can move more now. I'll explain later, but we must run.'

Where could they run? They were outnumbered in the middle of an army camp run by the Evil Queen, where everyone wanted to kill her.

The horns sounded.

The stranger swore as he gripped her arm. 'I thought we had more time.'

She wanted to ask what he meant but her breath came out raspy, barely shaping words. 'Who are you?'

He didn't answer, pulling her along before he opened the tent flaps. He jolted back as the general walked towards his tent, his men readying their weapons.

'Stars help us,' the man whispered. He whirled on Snow. 'Is there another way out of here?'

She didn't know – she hadn't been conscious – so she just stared at him. She had two options before her now: Trik, who's echoing voice from outside speared through her core with fear; or this man, who seemed to be helping her. Snow took a breath, leaning into the energy that was building under her skin.

The stranger narrowed his eyes before shaking his head. 'The rumours said you had a fire in you but all I see is a mute. You had better be worth this.'

She would have normally been insulted, would have swung back at the jibe. But she was inside her box, clinging to the safe dark place where numbness consumed her.

The stranger yanked her arm, pulling her behind the partition placed near the back. She shivered. The heavy march of Trik was like a snap to her bones for every step he took. She still felt his *touch* all over her and quaked.

At least she could stand on her own now. Her fingers tingled, her body slowly waking from a very long sleep.

The stranger pulled free a knife as Trik's voice echoed through the entryway.

Snow's heart thrummed, her breath halting as he tore at the cloth wall, creating a jagged opening.

Trik entered and Snow's fingers pressed into the same bruises he'd created. She shrivelled into herself, her breath shallow in case he heard, in case he found her again.

The general spat out orders in force. 'Time's up. Leave a group to secure the camp. Get the rest of the men. The lull is over. I want the fifth regiment placed ...' his voice trailed off.

Shit, Snow thought. *He knows. He sees.*

She peered through the gap of the partition. Trik stood in full uniform, his shorn head and pale scar stark against the clean cuts of his men. Trik swore as he stared at the now empty cross. The empty tent. His eyes darkened.

Snow could feel his rage from here, rippling off him like the heat from dragon fire. She closed her eyes, focusing on hiding, on breathing. But when she opened them again, she didn't see Trik. She only saw blood.

Blood that stained the floor, pooled like a slaughterhouse.

Her blood.

Trik roared as his men stepped back. He unsheathed his sword in one clean motion and swung at the cross before shouting more orders. 'Get Artemis! I want the Princess found. *NOW!*'

The stranger gripped her elbow and pulled her through the tear he'd created in the wall. The cold air bit her skin as the camp flared to life, and she faltered. Lost in the sight of her own blood, the stranger led her along the edge of the tent, sticking to the shadows as they waited for soldiers hastily gathering weapons and shouting as they ran past.

A horn blared, shouts and screams ringing out from the west. The stranger pulled her along, trailing in and out of hidden places and shoving her back when more soldiers came.

She heard the howls of the hounds and cowered.

They will find me. I am going to die.

Not today, the voices in her mind said.

But the stranger remained calm. Strong.

The two of them zigzagged until Snow realised they were heading west: towards the battle. She halted her steps, pulled her arm out of her rescuer's grip and hugged herself again, frantically looking for another path, another way out.

'What are you doing?' the man hissed.

'It's the wrong way,' Snow said, her voice a croaked whisper.

He shook his head, frustration flickering in his eyes. 'It's the right way, there's just obstacles which I'd hoped to avoid. You're not making this easy.'

Her throat was raw, freezing the inside of her mouth like frost. 'The dead have come. We won't survive. There is nothing that way. I have friends. In the forest.'

'Your friends won't last long here. The dead won't hurt us. Not with me.'

She didn't say more, didn't have to when a loud crack ricocheted through the camp. The ground shook, the very soil echoing the fear inside Snow as it announced what was coming.

'They've started,' he whispered. 'We have to move.'

'How do I know I can trust you?' she choked.

'Because you have no choice.'

'We always have a choice,' she said. 'Don't we?'

'Only the privileged have choice, and right now you're not in your castle.'

'I—' she began, but stopped as another set of soldiers ran past.

'Stay here and die if you want. I won't stop you. But I'm going west, with or without you.'

He hadn't lied. With a quick scope of the path, he skirted along the tent and broke for the edge of the camp.

Freedom, the voices inside her mind battled. *Revenge.*

He moved like wind.

Alone, the voices whispered.

Her friends hadn't saved her, but the stranger had.

One heartbeat was all it took. Snow charged, holding back the urge to call out. She darted across the gap between tents, swift and silent, her heart thundering in her chest. He caught her in the shadows and smirked at her as she caught her breath, frantic energy surging into her veins.

Whatever he'd given her, it had worked.

Snow smiled back, the taste of freedom on her tongue. Until she froze at the sight before her.

Beyond the line of tents lay trenches and men, wood and thorns twisting into a barrier. Beyond that, soldiers stood at attention, their weapons ready as they braved for attack. Further out, in the shadows and darkness where the land stretched and lived in fog, corpses pierced the earth, breaking free of the soil. Their eyes were blank, some with loose skin and torn limbs, each one in a state of different decay, screeching the most horrific sound Snow had ever heard.

She gasped as the stranger pulled her back, his eyes warning her to be silent.

But it was too late. She'd already seen them.

The dead.

'You need to breathe,' the stranger said. 'We can't die today. I promised Adanna I'd return home.'

'Adanna?'

The name rang through Snow's memories, but she couldn't grasp it, couldn't fight through the sludge of her memories as fear consumed her.

He shoved a sword into her hand and wrapped her palm around the hilt. He grabbed a bow from nearby, donned the arrows, and urged her forward.

The sword was heavy in Snow's hand, built for someone bigger and stronger than her. But the weapon calmed her;

at least she wasn't completely defenceless now. She lifted the sword, feeling it like an extension of herself.

'I guess I don't need to ask if you can use it,' the stranger said. 'Don't lose it. I can't replace it.'

She nodded.

'The halopod liquid won't last long,' he continued, readjusting his weapons. 'I have a horse just on the outskirts to get us to Felldryn. We need to move fast.'

She felt the beating of her own heart. She listened to the whispering voices of her mind and cleared her thoughts. The sword was her anchor to the world, the man a key to her prison. She stepped outside the box in her mind and closed the lid.

Her fear still lingered but part of it ebbed away, replaced by the fire inside of her she always stoked. She embraced the adrenaline swimming through her veins.

'Adanna is the princess,' Snow said, claiming the memory. 'Her brother is Odion.'

The stranger's eyes glittered. 'Yes,' he replied. 'Now, let's go.'

They crept along the edge of the camp, the air crackling with tension as the Queen's soldiers braced to charge. Fear rippled through the ranks, visible in the nervous shuffling and hushed, uncertain whispers.

Just as the army tensed to spring, the man leaned close, his breath hot against her ear. 'Run.'

She didn't hesitate. They bolted as the army erupted in a deafening roar, the formation surging forward. Snow's legs pumped beneath her, leaping over holes, bones, and discarded weapons. She ran with the soldiers, her feet pounding the earth, heart racing.

But as she reached the front line, she didn't stop. She kept running.

Right towards the charging army of the dead.

Brufell frowned at the space between the mountain range and the sea as the two dragons carried the dwarves through the Mountains of Eyrie. The air was bitter the higher they rose, the dips and curves roiling his belly with each deep thrust of their wings. He wasn't sure he'd ever get used to flying. It was almost like falling without an end.

They'd agreed the dragons would have to fly high for a time, and only under the cover of night. It was too risky otherwise; the old towers of the dragon hunters who claimed their hides might not all be forgotten. Despite the dragons moving realms, he'd seen firsthand dragon skin moulded to chairs, old skulls placed in taverns as if it were a picture and not remnants of great beasts that once littered the land.

Brufell clung to the dragon's back, Bronson close behind. His eyes watered but he could make out the youngling struggling with the winds. With the little dragon's lack of long-distance flying, he was wobbly at best.

Bronson had done his best to heal the creatures, but even then, their wounds remained fresh, and the mother's balance was askew thanks to the damage to her eye. Another reason he felt like spewing into the clouds.

Brufell had explained the story of Frode, of how the dragons had settled in the floating isles, and it had been enough to convince the mother to at least try. That was all he could ask.

Brufell's ears popped as the dragon glided to a small clearing, southwest of Troll's Keep, landing with a thump on the soft grass. Sliding off with shaky fingers, Brufell stumbled onto the ground, resembling a drunken sailor more than a battle-weary old dwarf. His cheeks were flushed from the bite of the wind and Bronson was no different. The younger dwarf's hair stood at odd ends, unkempt and tousled. Yet, from the grin plastered on his face, Brufell guessed he didn't seem to mind.

Bronson opened his pack, quickly pulling free a smaller bag with a strap. With swift, smooth motions he wrapped it to the mother's leg for future needs. Bronson had packed with care the night before, filling the bag with ointment and bandages for the two dragons' wounds.

'May the stars grant your wishes,' the mother dragon said to them both. 'Thank you.'

'And may the Godmother bless you,' Bronson replied.

Brufell wasn't much of a believer, nor was he fond of goodbyes, but he repeated the words anyway. Bronson smiled at him with approval before he secured his things.

Oryx hugged the baby dragon and Brufell bowed low to the mother, his beard touching his knees. 'I hope you find peace.'

The dragon's golden eye glittered as she twisted her neck. 'You too, warrior. You have seen too much death.'

He nodded and she heaved a hot breath. 'Before you go, take this.' She reached forward and plucked a scale from her leg with a claw. It glittered in the light and changed colours depending on the angle you held it. It was sharp at the edges but soft across the smooth surface.

'It won't bring you peace, but it will help. Dragon scale is sturdy – almost impenetrable.'

He turned it over in his hand. The green reminded him of the grotto, of the leaves and lush plant life. 'Impenetrable, hey?' He smiled.

'Some used to place it over their heart,' she replied. 'As a gesture of what the dragons meant to them, but also to protect themselves from steel should an arrow try to pierce their heart.'

He bowed again. 'Then that's where I'll keep it.'

Her eye sparkled as she gave him a small nod.

Bronson grunted as the pixie whined, sobbing into the young dwarf's shoulder.

'Is he okay?' Brufell asked.

'I don't know anymore,' Bronson sighed with resignation. 'You ready to go? We need to use what we have left of the light to reach the camp.'

Brufell smiled and clasped Bronson's shoulder.

Bronson rolled his eyes. 'Don't look at me like that.'

'Like what?'

Bronson shrugged out of his grip. 'Like you're proud or something.'

'I am proud.'

Bronson groaned. 'Let's just go. I'll whistle a tune and you can chastise me along the way.'

Brufell chuckled as the dwarves set out, taking a steep path down the mountain. He glanced back just as they descended the hill and took one last look at the two legendary creatures stretching their wings. With one powerful thrust, they took flight.

And their light shimmered into shadow.

XXXIV

The Murder's Kin

Florian had always known Malak was a troll. It was hard to miss. The sheer size of him, the greenish hue of his skin, the pointed ears, and those formidable teeth. He'd known from the start, yet he'd never been afraid.

Not like he'd been back home, anyway.

With Malak, he'd always felt safe. Troll or not.

Tonight, that had changed.

Malak carried him now as they sped through the trees, the troll gritting his teeth at his own injuries as they ran as far as possible from where the hounds had found them. Florian would mumble out tips every now and then about minimising their trail but found his voice coming out in a higher squeak than usual. Though, that could have been from the nauseating pain shooting through his body, or the way every jolt sent him into a cold shudder.

He knew logically he shouldn't fear Malak. He'd also never seen what a troll could do. Had never experienced terror seize him the way it did when Malak charged those beasts. He'd snapped the necks with ease, and the sounds still echoed throughout the Prince's mind.

But what had really terrified him had been the blackness to his eyes and the pure animalistic roar that had escaped his lips as blood coated his very pores.

Even the scary woman had been terrified.

Malak had apologised profusely since, had slowly tried to engage Florian after the attack. But Florian had been in shock, staring at the friend who had now become an utter stranger.

Pip had merely grumbled that they needed to move on, needed to find safer ground. That was Pip – ever the practical one. He always had a plan, even if it didn't exactly work out how it should.

As the three of them slowed down, Malak's breath came out in sharp bursts, his heart hammering against Florian's body. Florian hadn't meant for Malak to carry him so far, not when he was already exhausted. Guilt slid through the Prince as Malak placed him gently on the ground. His eyes were soft now, back to the warm brown Florian knew.

Malak took a careful step away, as if to prove he meant no harm. Which only made Florian feel worse.

Florian leaned into the soft earth, avoiding Malak's gaze. The grass cushioned him, and for once, the air wasn't setting off his allergies. The herbs had worked wonders, yet the ghost of a sneeze still lingered, the phantom itch of a rash threatening to surface. It was a cruel reminder that his body was never meant for the wild, never built for open skies and endless horizons.

Florian's wounds throbbed, each pulse of pain like a hammer against his skull. The gash in his leg was worse than he'd thought. Blood spilled freely, soaking into the torn fabric of his trousers. He pressed his fingers against it, and they came away slick, the red spreading over his palms in warm, sticky rivers. His breath hitched as a fresh wave of dizziness hit, the world tilting slightly at the edges.

'I'm so sorry,' Malak said again, his voice cracking at the end. Pip eyed Florian's wound carefully, his jaw tightening at the sight. 'There's nothing I can do without more supplies or a proper healer.'

It was all the concern Florian would get, and despite his pallor, a smile tugged on his lips.

At least Pip was consistent.

The night was quiet after the attack, the forest holding its breath. No creature dared stay this close to the beasts that roamed the army. If Florian had his choice, he'd simply leave, too. Warnings of the dead army marching in this region rang through him, slicing him with fear.

Pip murmured something to Malak. The troll nodded, and knelt before the Prince, towering over him still. 'We'll be back,' he said. 'Just try to relax and keep pressure on the wound.'

Florian may have been inept at most things, but even he wanted to give the troll an eye roll. He knew how basic injuries worked. What bleeding out meant. But mostly, he now *felt* what bleeding out was like. The books never prepared you for that. Sweat beaded on his forehead, his body trembled, and he felt like he was drowning in a frozen lake. He looked pale – paler than usual, anyway, his moon-kissed skin usually falling into a shade of red or white.

After a moment, Malak stood, deciding to follow the elf. Florian blinked as they disappeared through the trees into shadow.

The prince released a breath, and fell backwards, letting his body sink into the dirt. His head spun and he focused on the cool wind, the way the grass tickled his skin.

He closed his eyes for a moment, his injuries pulling him under. He blinked, trying to stay awake. But he also wondered if there was a point.

Nobody wanted him here, not really. He'd never been wanted. Not at home. Not with the giants. And even when he was told he had a purpose, it had been Malak who had saved Snow.

Snow, who was now in that camp, alone.

He thought back to his escape from Carnell, his shaking hands as he told the stableman to prepare his horse. The way he'd sobbed in fear when the animal pounded his hooves across the dirt as he rode it north.

Fear wasn't new to him. It was a part of him.

Leaving his home had been his first step to working with his fear. Embracing it instead of letting it take control. Since then, he'd seen the mountains, experienced magic, played at diplomacy, and barely survived an attack from the dark hounds.

Still, he was afraid.

Though, he didn't want to hide from it. Not anymore.

His wound burned. He could hear the rustling of the leaves, the light trickle of a hidden creek, the quiet whisper of the grass. And he smiled. In the short time since mounting that horse, he'd lived. *Actually lived.*

Florian exhaled slowly, sinking into the weight of his exhaustion. The fight was over. The fire in his veins had burned low, leaving only embers, flickering and fading.

Maybe it was alright to stop now. Maybe, just maybe, his ending lay here.

A clicking sound snaked across the forest.

Florian's eyes fluttered open, his vision blurred and hazy. Florian forced his sluggish limbs to move, his fingers digging into the damp earth. His wound burned, sharp and insistent, but he ignored it and squinted into the darkness.

The shadows beneath the trees shifted. Wooden limbs creaked as a nymph crept closer, blending with the shifting shadows. It moved with a cautious grace, inching towards the injured prince.

A glimmer caught the sheen of Pip's flute as the wood nymph clutched it in its tiny hands.

'Hurt,' it said.

Florian gave a tired nod as the creature peered at the prince's injury.

The nymph leaned in, nostrils flaring as it sniffed the blood. Its eyes widened, a hungry glint flashing within them. Green, mossy hair twisted wildly around its head, crackling with energy.

The flute dangled from a short rope tied around its neck, swaying with each jerky movement as the creature grabbed

Florian's sleeve. Its wooden fingers were rough, splintered at the edges.

Florian hissed in pain as the nymph tugged, forcing him into a sitting position.

'Water,' it said in its strange clicking tongue. It pointed into the shadows of the trees, its body buzzing with urgency.

'I don't understand,' Florian replied through a pained sigh. 'I need medicine.'

The wood nymph nodded, pushing on Florian. 'Water. Water.'

'I can't—'

'Come,' it said, interrupting him. 'Come. Come.'

Florian eyed the forest; the others were long gone.

'I can't,' Florian said, his body shivering. 'I'll die. I'll bleed out.'

The wood nymph shook its head. 'Close.' The nymph's eyes watered as its hands came back covered in blood.

Florian touched the fleshy wound, the fragile rips of skin and the warmth of his blood.

I'm going to die anyway, Might as well embrace this fear, too.

With a push, Florian heaved himself up. His legs were weak, and he tipped forward. The wood nymph pushed him, its arms shaking against the Prince's weight.

'Water,' it clicked, clutching Florian.

The ground shifted beneath Florian's feet, the world tilting and swaying like the deck of a ship in a storm. Every step felt uncertain, as if the earth itself had turned to liquid, pulling him sideways, threatening to drag him under. The two of them stumbled through the trees, branches clawing at Florian's arms as he pushed forward. Dark spots fluttered at the edge of Florian's vision, growing larger with every shaky step. Sweat trickled down his back, dampening his tattered clothes. His eyes, heavy with exhaustion, barely held open as a new sound cut through the haze. 'Is that water?' he mumbled.

The wood nymph darted ahead, splashing into the shallows with frantic energy. It cupped its hands, lifting the cool liquid and letting it spill through its fingers. 'Drink.'

'I don't know if I can,' he said. Death called to him. It whispered in the dark, singing a new but familiar song in the night as his knees hit the shallow water. Pain reverberated through his hips, but it was somehow far away, as if it were simply part of his being.

The wood nymph squealed and caught his head before it cracked on the ground.

'Drink,' it said, its shaking body pulling at Florian's sleeve. 'Drink.'

Florian couldn't move. Blood pooled from his leg and left streaks of red in the stream. His energy waned, his eyes fluttered.

A vision of his mother appeared before him, her arms open, smile warm and inviting. He tried to reach for her, his heart aching, when something cold touched his lips.

Water.

He gasped as it slid into his mouth, but the relief was fleeting. It burned like molten fire, searing and sharp.

The wood nymph scurried back and forth, bringing the water in tiny handfuls, each drop igniting him from the inside. The liquid trickled down his throat like sweet poison, setting his veins ablaze.

Florian's body convulsed. He screamed, the sound tearing from his lungs and echoing through the trees. Agony crashed over him in waves, each flame licking at his bones, searing through every muscle.

His body felt like it was on a pyre, consumed by fire. And just when he thought he would shatter into ashes, the world went black.

XXXV

The Uncertainty of Friends

Florian wasn't sure how long he slept.

When he woke, energy surged like lightning through his muscles. His limbs moved with too much strength. Too much life.

His legs lurched as he stood, and his fingers roved along his wound. But he was clumsy, like he'd drunk too much brew.

And then he cried.

His wound was healed, the skin sewn together in fleshy pink.

The forest around him remained the same, the creek trickling its soothing sounds as the wood nymph clicked in joy.

Florian laughed as he picked up the creature and embraced it. It squirmed in his grasp, squealing in a sound Florian was familiar with. Still, he didn't let go.

'You saved me,' Florian said through a sob. His cheeks were wet with hot tears, his eyes blurry with relief.

As Florian placed it back on the ground, the wood nymph smiled, placing its hands on its hips in triumph.

Florian paused. 'Why would you help me?' The wood folk had banished them. Chased them through the forest and threatened his friends. 'I thought you hated us,' he said.

The wood nymph considered Florian, dropping his arms, and kicking the dirt. He pointed to the break in the trees where Florian had lain and said, 'Bad.'

Turning his finger to Florian, he poked the prince's chest. 'Good.'

So, not all the wood folk believed them traitors.

'They aren't all bad,' Florian replied with a smile. 'I don't know how to thank you.' He had nothing to offer – except for his promise. 'I'll make sure I talk to the kingdoms. I'll petition for the wood folk.'

The nymph gave him a smile and jumped. 'Good.'

Warmth flushed through Florian, creeping up his neck. But this time it wasn't allergies. It felt good. 'I do have to ask, though …' he said, pointing to the creature's neck. 'The flute. May I trade for it?'

The nymph considered him, touching the flute gently with its wooden fingers.

'I know you don't like him, but it's the elf's and it's a family heirloom. Very important to him. Just as the forest is important to you.'

Florian slowly leaned down, pulling free his hat. The wilted feather attached to it danced in the wind, and he gave it a small, sad smile. 'A trade that important needs another important trade. This hat was given to me by my mother. She's gone, but I think maybe you might like it.' His hands trembled as he handed it over, letting the wood nymph assess it with its wide eyes. Its wooden fingers roamed the material, and it sniffed it before placing it on its head.

The wood nymph twirled, and Florian chuckled. 'Very dashing.'

'Dashing,' the nymph repeated, giving the prince a stern nod.

With quick movements, the nymph shoved the flute into Florian's hands. It was cool beneath his touch.

The slow smile spread on his lips. For once, he'd *achieved* something. Even Pip couldn't be mad at him now.

Another twig snapped and the call of Malak's deep voice cut through the dark. 'Florian?'

'Over here,' Florian cried out.

The wood nymph skittered away, pausing at a tree. Its eyes flicked between the tree line and the Prince.

'I'm okay,' Florian said, wrapping his fingers around the flute. 'Thank you. Again.'

With one last nod, the nymph ran into the bark, the feather flying above its head as it disappeared.

Malak's heavy steps approached, the sound of a *pop* followed closely behind. The troll sighed with relief as he saw the prince. 'Florian!' he yelled. 'By the Godmother, we thought you were dead.'

'Or taken,' Pip gruffed from behind him. 'How did you get here?'

Florian stood, his body getting used to the new energy that flowed through him. 'The wood folk saved me – but that's a story for another time. I got you something.'

He tossed the flute to Pip.

The elf caught it one-handed, and his eyes widened. 'How did you get this?'

'That doesn't matter,' Malak said, 'How did you heal yourself? How are you alive?'

Florian shrugged. 'The water has some kind of healing property, which is fascinating. But it also puts you in a blacked-out state. How long was I gone?'

'Gone long enough that there's movement at the camp,' Malak said. 'They're preparing for something.'

Pip pulled the flute over his head and patted it against his chest. 'What did the wood folk ask for in return?'

'I promised to petition the kingdoms for them.'

'Interesting,' the elf said. 'But you're right: a story for another time.'

Florian was glowing. He'd done something right for once. Done something *meaningful.*

Malak helped Florian up and led the way back to the edge of the forest. They squatted near the treeline, taking in the camp below. Malak was right, the camp was busy.

Pip frowned, his lips pursing as he took in the campsite below. The flickering torchlight cast long, jittery shadows over the churned earth, illuminating rows of soldiers tightening armour straps and sharpening blades. Smoke curled from dying fires, mingling with the distant clang of metal and the restless murmur of men. Beyond them, the battleground stretched wide and open, a bleak expanse beneath the heavy sky, where banners flapped in the rising wind.

'The army is going to battle,' Pip murmured.

Malak snarled. 'Snow is down there.'

Then he was gone, a blur of motion as he navigated down the slope. With a squeak, Pip and Florian followed. The damp grass hissed beneath his boots as he tore through the underbrush, his form blending with the shifting shadows of the forest's edge.

Florian's breath hitched, and he forced his aching legs to move, nearly stumbling as he followed. The descent was treacherous. Roots jutted from the soil, rocks were slick with moss that threatened to throw him off balance. But he pushed forward, his focus locked on the distant glow of firelight.

Pip moved with more fervour than Florian had ever seen before, the elf managing to skitter past him and meet Malak who stood at the edge of a rocky outcrop. As Florian reached the crest of the hill, a roar shattered the air, rumbling across the valley. Florian's stomach twisted as his gaze fell upon the battlefield below.

Lines of soldiers marched toward the front, their armour gleaming beneath the pale light. They moved in rigid formation, shields locked, spears poised. But the earth beneath them cracked and split, shadows clawing their way up from the soil, dark and twisted.

And at the head of it all, breaking through the chaos, were two figures: a princess with blue fire in her eyes, and a black-clad stranger at her side. Together, they charged straight at the army of the dead.

Florian's heart lurched. Snow.

'Prepare yourself, Prince,' Pip huffed beside him. 'It looks like we're going to war.'

'We don't even have a plan!' Florian squeaked.

But there was no turning back now. War was here, whether he liked it or not.

He wasn't a soldier, or even a very good prince, but this: running headlong into death, heart hammering, body breaking, for the sake of the people who still had something to live for, seemed right. Even if they didn't have a plan. He might not have been able to break her curse, but he'd be cauldron damned if he let her die now.

Florian barely had time to brace before Malak moved again, a blur of fury and vengeance as he tore down the hill. Pip followed, swift and sure-footed.

And then Florian ran.

XXXVI

The Tinker's Prize

Dread watched as another body swung on a rope, the crack of their neck still ringing across the cobblestone streets. It had only been a day, but it felt like a lifetime. Dread's eyes veered from the bodies to the castle, the flame in the tower igniting with warning that the Queen resided inside.

But he knew she didn't.

His bones were tired, and he checked his timepiece. The Tinker would be waiting for him. Dread nodded towards the guard and left the square as another line of prisoners dragged their chained feet up the wooden platform. The drop and crack of their bodies echoed behind him as he cut through the alleys towards the castle.

His body was heavy, like the eyes of the city judged him as he strode past. The marketplace was a husk. People crowded around a broken shopfront where tears and cries of years of hard work filled the air with newfound misery.

He'd never failed Myrenna before, had never needed to apologise. But failure was slowly sinking into his bones like an anchor dropping further and further into the bottom of the sea. He only hoped he could recover from this, that Myrenna might just forgive him. But his doubt was a seed already planted.

He cracked his knuckles, then shook them out as he approached the castle's large gates. The lieutenant at the front shuffled as Dread passed, wary with the shifter's presence.

His misery hung from him, profound and potent.

The sun blazed a bright, unforgiving white. The clouds had receded, leaving the sky wide open, the heat sharp enough to sting his skin. It was a stark contrast to the cool shadows within the castle. Dread wiped the sweat on his brow as the relentless warmth pressed against his dark uniform.

He couldn't help but feel the sky was laughing at him, purposefully shining in protest against the violence happening below. He could still hear the cracks of their necks, even now.

He'd only taken a few steps when the guard coughed. Dread slowed, halting before turning slowly.

The guard swallowed, his face bright and blotchy. 'Sir?'

'Yes?' Dread asked, drawing out the word with clear disdain.

'It may be nothing, but I feel as if I should share that two guards came through earlier holding a prisoner.'

Dread bit back his irritation and frowned. 'All the prisoners are in the square. Why weren't they directed there?'

The guard swallowed again, standing at attention as Dread's shadow blocked out the sun.

'They said it was the silver ghost with twin blades. She was hurt, in chains, and they were taking her to the Queen.'

Dread's heart stuttered as he peered towards the castle. 'How long ago?'

'Umm …' The guard faltered. 'I'm not sure.'

Dread's arm shot out, his fingers wrapping around the guard's throat. A growl escaped his lips. 'How long ago?'

'Half an hour, maybe?' the guard choked. 'They were escorted by the Tinker's new guard.'

Dread dropped him to the ground and shot toward the castle. His bones cracked with the transformation, reshaping him into a lone crow.

The shift was swift and painful, but it felt like instinct, a seamless change that freed him from the weight of his human form. He soared through the air, wings cutting through the wind with the sharp precision of a predator. The landscape blurred beneath him, the castle's towering spires pulling closer as he banked left, gliding smoothly over the curated garden.

Each beat of his wings brought him nearer, and soon the Queen's tower loomed ahead. He circled once, his sharp gaze scanning the windows and shadows, before diving toward it. His claws gripped the stone with a fierce precision as he landed on the window's edge, his chest rising and falling with the intensity of the chase.

Dread's failures amplified all over again. Flynn's smell was all over this. And he wasn't going to let the weasel ruin what little Dread could salvage. Papers fluttered through the air like falling leaves as he shifted back into his human form, his boots hitting stone.

The room was empty.

Good.

They'd not found Myrenna's scrolls.

Dread charged towards the door, pulled it open with fervour, and ran down the stairs. The alarm hadn't been called yet, but it was only a matter of time. He took two steps at a time, shoving the servants into the walls as he flew towards the Tinker's dungeons.

Down the hallway, the cool whisper of the Tinker echoed through the air, green smoke filling the corridor like a poisonous gas. Dread pulled back, waiting for it to fade before he approached.

The Tinker cackled at the three bodies lying in his stairwell, unaware of Dread's presence and he kicked the silver one, his eyes glittering in triumph. Dread approached slowly, his muscles taut.

When the Tinker lifted the spindle, eyeing it hungrily, even Dread flinched. 'I'm so close. She'll be so pleased.'

Dread gritted his teeth and stared at the intruders. Silver skin lay crumpled against a set of broad shoulders and light brown hair. Dread flipped the body over with his boot, a smug smile curling his lip.

The Huntsman.

Dread loosed a growl, his fist tightening with rage. His first strike landed square on the Huntsman's jaw, the satisfying crack of bone sending a shiver of triumph through him. He relished the feeling, the long-awaited release of all his frustration.

His fist pulled back, ready to strike again, when something halted him. A familiar figure came into view, and Dread's heart skipped a beat at the sight of his brother's slick black hair.

Flynn.

Dread's nostrils flared. He stepped back and called to a guard nearby. 'Get me some men to carry two prisoners.' His large hand grabbed the collar of Flynn's uniform and lifted his unconscious brother up.

'There's three intruders,' the Tinker corrected.

'The changeling and the Huntsman can go to the dungeons,' Dread said, coldly. 'The third one is *mine.*'

The Tinker didn't say anything, opting to step back with a curious look in his eyes.

'The meeting is postponed,' Dread ground out as he dragged his brother's limp body towards the aviary.

XXXVII

The Brothers that Broke

Dread sat at the edge of the aviary, his legs dangling from the ledge when a groan echoed from behind him.

He's awake.

Flynn hadn't been knocked out for long, but it had been enough for the rage to cool inside of Dread's gut. Only last night his brother had conceded, had promised, to report to him. Only last night Dread had reminded him of his place.

And already he'd been betrayed again.

Most people trembled before Dread, but not his brother. No, Flynn was the worst kind of incompetent. He was stubborn, too.

Dread turned as Flynn sat up and rubbed his eyes, adjusting from whatever fog the Tinker had used. In that moment, Dread didn't care what the spindle did, didn't care what the Tinker wanted to show him. All he cared about was the need to pound his brother into dust.

'I suppose you think you're clever?' Dread said, stepping towards the stone bench Flynn sat on. 'Lying to me with your slick tongue and then completely blinding me. What is it you're hoping to achieve? The city is in ruins. The traitors have been pulled from the rubble. The Queen is soon to return, and yet you choose to, what? Break into a castle you have access to?'

He stormed forward and smashed his fist into Flynn's face, the crunch satisfying.

Flynn dropped onto the marble, blood seeping from his mouth.

'You were supposed to report,' Dread seethed. 'You were supposed to be loyal. When were you going to tell us your mission was complete? You knew the silver assassin was the Commander, and yet you remained with them? *Why?*'

'Does it matter?' Flynn said, spitting blood onto the floor. 'You'll beat me up either way.'

Dread growled. 'I beat you because I hope one day you'll see reason.'

'Reason?' Flynn asked, sitting up. 'You see this as reason?'

Dread loomed over him, the anger burning inside of him. 'I can't protect you from this, brother. I don't want to protect you from this. You've crossed too many lines. Told too many lies. Betrayed me too many times.'

'Then we're at an impasse,' Flynn said, wiping his mouth.

Dread watched his brother carefully. He was calm – too calm for the situation he was in. But Dread knew his trickery wasn't over.

Dread cracked his knuckles. 'Why did you do it?' he asked, his voice dropping an octave. 'What did the *filthy changeling* do to you?'

Flynn flinched at the tone.

Dread's mouth curved up at the side. 'What was that?' He continued stepping forward, 'Don't like the term "filthy changeling?"'

Flynn glared at him, his lips thinning into a line.

'No smart comment now? That's odd for you.'

Flynn stayed silent and licked his lips, his fingers placed calmly on his knees. It irked Dread, but he was too curious. But then pieces fell into place, whirling through Dread's mind with such sudden clarity that he wondered why he hadn't seen it sooner.

Flynn's silence. His absence. His change of mind.

Dread smiled. 'She didn't *do* anything to you, did she? It's what your heart did to you. You're *in love* with her.' He couldn't help the rough laugh that broke free.

Flynn glowered at him.

'She's already dead, Brother,' Dread said. 'And if it isn't at the hands of the Queen or the Tinker, it'll be done by me. When did you become so *weak?*'

Suddenly, the ground rumbled, an alarm echoing through the stone walls. Flynn's knee twitched and he turned to Dread, a smile playing at his lips. 'You do what you want, Brother, and I'll do what I want.'

Dread's smile disappeared as the sound blared from below, ringing louder with each passing second. 'What have you done?' he whispered.

'I'm righting my wrongs.'

It happened before Dread could blink. Flynn dived, his hands transforming to talons that shot towards Dread's face. Dread barely had time to turn as they slashed across his skin and Flynn shifted, black wings erupting from his arms as he leapt towards the open air.

The rage in Dread exploded as hot blood coated his neck. His body cracked, pain shooting through his bones as he transformed. His crow was triple the size of Flynn's. More brawn. More muscle. More *everything*. It would tear his brother's form into tiny little pieces.

He flattened his wings and let loose a raging scream.

With a flawless dive, he smashed into Flynn mid-air, his claws clasping onto Flynn's back with vicious accuracy. They pierced through flesh and Flynn cried out.

Dread threw Flynn into the tower wall and his brother toppled, skittering down the stone's side before he stretched out his wings and righted himself.

Flynn coughed as the bond clicked.

'*Trik!*' Flynn cried out. '*Trik, can you hear me?*'

You cannot win, Dread said. *Trik is busy.*

Flynn flew towards the lower levels and Dread followed, his large wings and talons spreading wide. Flynn dodged his next attack.

Dread cawed in anger.

His little brother was fast, but he wouldn't escape, not from Dread. The two crows veered around a tower, the wind carrying them across the skies. Flynn's wings scraped against stone as he took a sharp turn. But Dread knew this castle, knew its walls as if it was his own skin, and cut through a window. The staff cried out as he shot through the room and flew out the other side, crashing into Flynn.

Dread's talons tore into his brother's skin, ripping free his black feathers. His beak was covered in blood, the metallic tang coating his tongue.

Suddenly, the sky filled with wings, murders cawing at the fight as a great black cloud descended on the castle. But Dread could taste his vengeance, too, and it was sweet.

Flynn hit another wall, a bone cracking.

I've got you now, Dread seethed.

But something was happening below.

A rumble reverberated through the castle. Stone broke below and Dread pulled back, his eyes scanning for the cause.

With a shriek of fury, Flynn launched himself from the shadows, his talons slashing through Dread's feathers and into his flesh. Before he could react, Flynn's beak sank deep into his neck, blood welling up from the wound in a hot, searing rush.

Dread's entire body shuddered, his chest heaving as the sting of the attack consumed him. He let out a guttural caw, the sound ragged and filled with fury, echoing off the stone walls like a battle cry. His claws flexed, desperate to retaliate, but Flynn was relentless.

They spiralled through the air, bodies locked in a twisted dance of violence, blood and feathers flying in every direction. The howls of the surrounding murders grew louder, a chorus of feral cries as they swooped in to witness the chaos. The wind whipped past Dread's ears, tearing at his senses as the ground loomed closer, like a hungry beast eager to claim its prize.

Dread sank his claws deeper into Flynn's side in an unspoken promise. *If I fall, you'll fall with me,* Dread ground out, tearing into Flynn's side.

He dug his talons in, ripping through flesh, his brother's roar of agony ringing in his ears.

In the final moments, as the earth rushed up to meet them, Flynn wrenched free, squirming out of Dread's hold like a snake shedding its skin. The ground reared from below, but it was too late. Before he could right himself, Dread smashed into the earth. Where he felt every bone inside of him snap.

XXXVIII
The Bones that Break

Snow couldn't breathe. She was terrified.

She swung her sword, screaming at the oncoming army with a ferocity she didn't know she possessed, when a decaying, mutilated corpse ran past her.

Her limbs shook as she forced deep, shuddering breaths into her lungs. Any moment now, one of the dead would turn, its empty eyes locking onto her, its withered fingers reaching, and then pull her into the soil and bury her.

Perridorm had an army of these things, each one more decayed than the last.

More ran forward, meeting the enemy with a soundless cry. While she shuddered at their nearness, just close enough for the air to brush her skin, they never made contact. She slowed, turning around just as the Queen's men collided with the army in a bone-shattering crunch.

Snow stumbled in the mud as men and weapons clashed, blood spraying like rain. A horse broke through the crowd, a soldier charging towards her.

Snow raised her sword, her arms shaking, when an arrow pierced his skull. His eyes glazed over, and he slid from the horse, collapsing lifeless on the ground.

Snow shook as the battlefield churned around her. The clash of metal against metal rang in her skull, a relentless din that drowned out her thoughts. Screams and roars wove together in a terrible symphony, punctuated by the sickening crunch of bodies breaking and the heavy thumps of the fallen. The noise rattled through her bones, so overwhelming that she bit down hard on her tongue, the sharp taste of blood grounding her for a fleeting moment.

If she wanted to live, she had to keep moving.

She had to make it to the other side.

Arrows whizzed past, barely missing her as she ran. She dodged a strike, raising her sword to deflect, but an arrow pierced her opponent's neck. Someone shouted, but it was lost in the mayhem until her arm was tugged. She stumbled as the man in black pulled her along, keeping by her side as she picked up her pace. They dodged bodies, the sharp edges of swords, the call of an arrow as it was sucked into the mud. Without the arm pulling her along, Snow would have been lost. The battlefield was a writhing mass of bodies, the scent of sweat and blood thick in the air, clogging her lungs. Every breath carried the stench of iron and decay, the desperation of men fighting to stay on their feet as corpses clawed their way from the earth.

Bile climbed up her throat as she shouted at the man in black, but her voice was lost to the sound of battle. Her bare feet were slicked with mud. She dodged bodies and lost weapons, barely sidestepping a blade on the ground before she could cut open her foot.

She'd chosen to enter a battlefield with no shoes and no armour, relying on a magic potion. She could hear Malak now, chastising her for her recklessness.

Her *foolishness.*

She raised her sword and swung to the left as a soldier attacked, and urged her body towards another steed when more enemies broke through. One roared as he charged her, his armour clinking. She screamed, her muscles burning and swung. Blood splattered across her torso as the blade cut through his face.

Another cry, and an arrow pierced the horse's hide.

All she could do was stumble back. Her sword felt like lead, dripping crimson onto the soiled ground, but she didn't feel fear, or regret, or grief.

She was oddly … Exhilarated.

Glorious.

Free.

She'd killed her first man – slain someone in battle like the queen she was meant to be.

And she *liked* it.

With new fervour, she ran, her feet gliding over the upturned soil like a dancer. She laughed, her voice flying free over the screams.

Freedom, the voices echoed. *Power.*

The man in black shot his last arrow, barely missing a rider that careened through the crowd. The rider wore a helmet of gold, a red braid flying behind them as they charged towards Snow.

Helmet or not, Snow knew that rider from the set of her shoulders alone.

Artemis.

The Huntress smiled with hunger behind the golden plates of her helmet.

Snow should have felt fear, or the touch of despair, but she didn't. There was only rage. It blinded her as the man in black dropped his bow and ran towards Snow.

She dodged another body, her legs aching but never ceasing to stop.

The woman was quick, precise.

Snow's breath was raw as she stole a look behind her.

Just in time to see the glint of the Huntress's arrow pointed towards her.

XXXIX
The Hound's Huntress

Snow's vision honed onto the arrow as the Huntress drew back her elbow. Her smile was one of triumph as the horse carried her forward.

She was a queen of the forest. A hunter. A shadow.

Snow veered to her left, dodging the arrow, but shrieked when her ankle snapped under her. Mud coated her skin as she rolled over, her sword a few pixies away.

The Huntress was off her horse in one smooth glide, when a shadow cut in front of her. Snow's mouth went dry at the sight of Malak's sword clashing against Artemis's, a scream escaping the Huntress's lips.

Florian and Pip broke through the darkness, screaming her name. But they were too far off.

The black-clad stranger reached her first, grabbing her under the elbow and pulling her forward. 'Get the sword and keep moving.'

She shoved him away. 'What are you doing?'

'Get off her!' screeched Florian, as he ran towards them.

The battle raged, more soldiers breaking the ranks as decayed bodies crawled from the earth.

The Huntress swung her sword and Malak met it with his own. The clash of metal drowned out the death around her. She clenched her teeth.

She'd run once, but she wouldn't run again.

She grabbed the sword discarded nearby, the squelch from the mud oddly satisfying as she stumbled over another limb protruding from the earth.

'The halopod won't last! You have to run!' the man in black screamed.

And she did run – not away from the battle, but towards it.

Malak fought fiercely, each blow he landed met by another from the Huntress. His face remained stoic, unshaken in the face of the onslaught. But Snow felt it. The fear, laced with a relentless tide of fury propelling her forward.

The battle came in flashes. Malak striking against Artemis. The man in black cutting down a soldier. A corpse rising from the ground. And Snow, running, and slashing, and screaming.

The Huntress, a figure of cold precision, disarmed Malak with a swift motion, her eyes gleaming with the promise of victory. Artemis raised her weapon high, poised like an executioner preparing for the final strike.

Horror wound its way through Snow, the blade aimed for his chest. She screamed.

Then Snow collided with the Huntress.

XXXX

The Irksall and The Lost Clan

The camp was empty when Bronson and Brufell arrived. Smoke from the fires drifted softly into the sky as they weaved their way through the huts towards the Irksall's tent.

'Where is everyone?' Bronson whispered.

Oryx zoomed around the camp, but when he came back, he shrugged and signed to Bronson.

'He says every tent is empty except for the sick.'

'Well, that's where we need to go, anyway,' Brufell replied. 'Let's start there.'

The camp wasn't dishevelled; it was still relatively neat, considering trolls weren't known for cleanliness, but it was *quiet*.

Bronson groped for the tooth in his pack, clutching it.

They lifted back the flap and met the healer. Shatk's robes were soil-stained and his eyes were wild. He strode around the tent shouting orders, the other trolls fumbling with the directions. Bronson coughed, hoping to gain his attention but immediately regretted it when the troll noticed them.

'YOU!' he screeched, stomping forward. 'How *DARE* you return here after what you did! I told him not to trust you, not to bargain.'

Brufell took a step forward, blocking Bronson from harm's way before growling at the troll. 'We have the tooth. I don't know what you think you're accusing us of, but we've held our end of the bargain.'

The healer's nostril's flared but he paused. 'You have the tooth?' He held out his palm. 'Give it to me.'

'I'd rather give it to the Irksall,' Brufell replied sternly.

'The Irksall has left with the others,' Shatk seethed. 'Give me the tooth.'

Bronson peered over Brufell's shoulder, eyeing the sick trolls and the black veins that ran under their skin. 'Where is everyone?'

Shatk narrowed his eyes and snarled. 'They've gone to avenge Tuk. To defeat the dragon and kill our enemies that betrayed us.'

'Tuk is dead?' Bronson whispered.

The healer gave a savage laugh. 'Tuk is alive but he told us of your lies. Of how you stopped his arrows and saved the dragons. Of how you left him to die in the cavern.'

'We have to stop them,' Bronson said. 'They don't know we have the tooth. That we didn't betray them.'

Shatk stretched over them; his yellow teeth gritted as he held out his palm. 'They left this morning. You'll have to run to catch up with them. Give me the tooth.'

'You won't know how to use it without us,' Brufell replied. 'Bronson will stay here with Oryx, I'll go find Tuk and the Irksall.'

'But ...' Bronson said.

'Make the cure.' Brufell ordered, 'Save them, and I'll save us. You can do this.'

Worry curled in Bronson's gut, but he nodded anyway. He had to help. War hadn't been his calling, but this had.

'You touch him, and you'll have me and your Irksall to deal with,' Brufell warned before leaving.

Bronson looked up to find Shatk staring at him darkly. 'I'll not have your magic kill them.'

'It won't kill them, it'll cure them,' Bronson huffed.

'It has to,' he sneered. 'Otherwise, I'll be sucking on your bones next.'

With a gulp, Bronson turned to the pixie. 'I'll need something to write with so the healer can help.'

Oryx's scarred face sneered back at the healer, but he got to work quickly.

Bronson turned to Shatk. 'I'll need you to follow the directions closely whether you like them or not. Otherwise, they'll never survive.'

Shatk's lips thinned but he gave a sharp nod. 'What do you need?'

Brufell's weapons clanged against his hips as he ran. His muscles burned, his chest heaving, but he didn't slow. The icy wind bit at his face, but he was numb to it, his focus fixed on the hill's crest.

He reached the top and his breath caught in his throat.

The clash of metal and roars of battle echoed up the mountain, the air thick with dust and blood. Brufell swore under his breath, his fists tightening around his weapons as he took in the mayhem below. The valley was a churning sea of chaos. Trolls attacked one another in brutal combat, swords slamming against spears, clubs swinging with bone-crushing force.

Picking up his pace, Brufell ran. He looked for Tuk or the Irksall, failing to see through the turmoil of bodies and blades. He was jostled as a troll knocked into him, and a thick arm swung as Brufell ducked. Ahead, through the disorder, he could see the edge of a fur cape, the shimmer of a silver bow shining through the gaps of flailing limbs and battle cries. Of course the Irksall would be in the thick of it all, injury or not. Brufell could only grit his teeth as he charged forward, meeting the onslaught as a troll ran at him, slamming down his weapon in the dirt. Brufell slid past him and released his axe. He slashed it across their calves, freeing blood. In a mere moment, he was back up, arching the blade and slashing downwards into a troll's neck with a wet crunch.

Brufell yanked the blade free and ran.

The trolls trampled the ground. Blood sprayed. Fists swung. Brufell dived under limbs, cut through bodies, and tried not to fall. The benefit of being small, at least, was remaining unseen but if he collapsed, he was one giant foot away from being crushed.

Brufell made it to the middle quickly, where the Irksall was bringing down foes with his arrows. Brufell ran forward, and the Irksall spun, his mouth twisting into a snarl as he raised his bow.

'We have the tooth!' Brufell screamed, still running forward despite the arrow pointed towards his skull. 'We have the tooth!'

The Irksall frowned, distracted momentarily, when a troll escaped the crowd, roaring. Brufell barely had time to react. A massive, spiked club swung for the Irksall, and he lunged, his sword raised. Metal met wood with a shuddering impact, the force rattling down his arms. Brufell's grip faltered, and he rolled, breath ragged.

Steel flashed as he unsheathed a smaller blade, driving it deep into the troll's lower spine. A bellow of pain. A heavy body collapsing.

Another roar and Brufell twisted. Another troll ran for him, another club, already swinging. But his blade was too small. There was no time. No escape.

His breath caught.

An arrow buried itself deep in the troll's skull.

'By the Godm—' Brufell's feet went flying under him as he was launched into the air. His shirt caught under his chin as he met the stench of the Irksall's breath.

His eyes were hard, a cold rage behind them as he snarled at Brufell. 'The tooth?'

Brufell gripped the Irksall's wrist. 'It's with Shatk and Bronson at the camp.'

The anger in his eyes receded.

Hope, Brufell thought.

'Tuk?' Brufell choked out, hating how his feet dangled below him. He felt undignified, like a pet being cuddled against its will.

The Irksall smiled, pointing to his left flank. 'He is fighting, over there.'

With a thud, Brufell was dropped on the ground, his legs groaning on impact. He looked up as trolls dropped to the ground, blood pooling into the dirt. The clang of metal still rang as the battle raged on, and between the bloodshed and the destruction, Brufell made out a familiar figure.

Tuk was grinning, his fist crunching into the jaw of another troll. He held a bow in one hand, using it to catch a wild swing. Wood met bone with a dull thud. With a twist and a step, Tuk drove the bow's end into another's gut, forcing out a wheezing grunt.

'Who are we fighting?' Brufell panted.

The Irksall shot another arrow at an approaching troll. 'The other clan.'

Brufell's beard tickled his knuckles as the wind blew. The battle was shifting. The crowd parted as another troll stepped forward, draped in spiked metal armour. His face was partly fleshy, a burn mark marring his once-green skin.

'Is that the other Irksall?' Brufell asked, allowing himself to gaze at the warrior beside him. But the Irksall failed to reply. The crowd paused. The valley fell silent. Brufell's ears rang in the quiet as the two Irksalls faced one another, one marred, and one pristine.

Brufell wasn't sure he was breathing as they stepped towards one another, grim expressions and taut shoulders the only warning of the blood about to be spilt.

Silence broke as the one in the armour blew a great horn. It reverberated through the field, rippling through Brufell's bones. The clans separated. The burnt troll grinned, his eyes alight with hunger as he looked down at Brufell.

'You mixing with dwarves now?' the troll said to the Irksall. 'How *weak.*'

The Irksall growled in response, his knuckles white on his bow.

The burnt troll only sneered. 'I've been waiting for this.'

The Irksall dropped his bow and stepped forward. 'Not as much as I have.'

The burnt troll dropped his weapons, too, and cracked his knuckles. There was a moment of utter stillness, as if the world waited on bated breath. Brufell's heart hammered in his chest, blocking out everything before the hammer fell.

The crowd roared, drowning out everything as the two Irksalls charged. The impact of their bodies rippled through the mayhem, like giants clamouring together. Brufell stumbled back as the crowd roiled forward, vying for a view the battle.

Blood sprayed as they collided, fists and teeth and screams blending into something brutal.

Violent.

Chaotic.

The surge of bodies pulled him back. Brufell fought, scratching and pushing against limbs as the blurry shapes of the leaders attacked again and again. Roars and growls filled the air. Flesh tearing, bones cracking. Through the chaos, he spotted the Irksall with the fur. With a primal roar, the Irksall knocked a troll to the ground and drove a brutal kick into its face, the crunch of bone audible even over the noise of battle.

The crowd roared – some in anger and others in triumph – as the silver bow was passed through the crowd and given to the victor.

The Irksall raised his arrow, claiming his triumph. Brufell could only hold his breath, wedged between two giant bodies as the burnt Irksall was pinned to the ground. He thrashed, but there wasn't much behind it as the victor pulled the bow taut, then released.

The other Irksall went still.

XXXXI

The Hunted Huntress

Snow braced her arms as Artemis's fingernails slashed into her cheeks. They scrambled through the filth, mud sliding across her skin. Snow's eyes burned with wild desperation, every inch of her flesh screaming in pain and rage. Blood and dirt matted in her hair, dripping into her eyes, but she didn't flinch. With a snarl, Artemis grabbed her arms, yanking them to the ground and pinning them down with terrifying strength. Snow writhed beneath her, but the weight of Artemis's hands was unyielding, her grip a vice as she forced Snow into the muck.

She was dead. This was it. The moment she died.

Artemis's eyes were savage, her hair caked in blood and dirt. She grinned cruelly, and bit deep into Snow's shoulder.

Snow screamed as skin tore, pain shooting through her side. Artemis yanked her head back and spat onto the ground. With a shriek, Snow bucked, kicking out just as the huntress released her grip. Snow's nails raked the air as she tumbled away, and Artemis cackled, raising goosebumps on her skin. Snow heaved in a breath, but it was raw. Pain pierced her shoulder as she scrambled to stand. Artemis remained on her knees, teeth coated in gore as she snarled at the princess.

She reminded Snow of the hounds, the way they growled, gnashing at skin and bone as if they'd never been fed. Forever starved for blood.

Snow peeked behind her, finding Malak unconscious. Florian and Pip were close, running towards them. 'Take him away,' Snow gasped, her voice raw with desperation as she locked eyes with Florian. 'Now!'

Florian stumbled, an argument on his lips, but she turned back to Artemis, giving her a grin of her own.

Artemis's smile slipped at the challenge. Then she stood and unsheathed her sword.

All Snow could smell was smoke and blood and sweat. It invigorated something within her, as if she'd never awoken from the crystal coffin, not truly. For years she'd been under a spell, dampened into someone naïve, someone lost. But there was something freeing about facing your enemies, standing tall when it felt like the realm was against you. When all you'd ever been was a nightingale trapped in a cage.

Snow raised her chin, a challenge in her eyes as she met Artemis's stare.

Artemis swung the sword with ease as she assessed Snow. Her eyes narrowed at the look Snow gave her, as if even she didn't recognise the woman before her. 'I'll enjoy hanging you on my wall.'

Snow's gaze skirted the mud, landing on her sword strewn a few pixies away. An arm protruded from the dirt, digging around. A shoulder appeared, then a head. Dead eyes watched her as it groaned, reaching towards the weapon.

Snow saw the flicker of movement, and her heart stopped a beat. But before she could act, she narrowly dodged the shining metal of Artemis's sword as the huntress swung.

Snow ducked, her fist rising to meet the Huntress's jaw in an uppercut.

Artemis grunted, stumbling back. It was only a moment, but it was enough for Snow to run. Taking her chance, Snow pelted over the mud, her feet flying across the battlefield. Artemis followed, cackling. Snow's foot collided with something sharp, sending her into the mud. She squealed as a hand grabbed her ankle, pulling her down. Her shoulder collided with bone with a sick crunch and her chest constricted as she stared down at a mutilated hand. The corpse gripping her made a horrific sound, its limbs cracking as it broke free from the battlefield's soil.

Snow snarled and kicked its face, then tackled the half-dismembered body, choking on the smell of decay as she threw her fists into the soldier.

The corpse screamed, dust flying from its mouth as she snatched the blade and stood on wobbly legs. Wind blew strands of hair across her face as Artemis spat out a tooth.

Blood on her lips, the Huntress swung her weapon. Snow raised her blade in response, the clang of steel reverberating through her arm.

'I'll skin you after this,' Artemis seethed as she swung again, Snow barely managing to dodge. She parried, each thrust harder than she remembered, more powerful than Malak and Hansel had ever dared to do.

But fighting was a dance, too.

Snow feigned to the left, her steps tricky on the uneven ground. But Artemis took the bait. The Huntress swung wildly, just as untethered as Snow's attacks. The princess ducked, and brought her sword upwards in an arc, narrowly missing Artemis's gut.

The Huntress growled and attacked again, this time with more fervour. But Snow had learnt her steps. She let the rage simmer under the surface. She couldn't hold back her smile as she swung again, their blades clashing together like lightning one strike after another. Snow feigned again, but Artemis didn't fall for it this time, instead moving against her blow and smashing Snow's chest with the hilt.

The breath ran out of her. She felt the tingle receding, the halopod ebbing away. Her legs shook, a headache forming on the edge of her skull as she righted herself and lifted her weapon.

Voices rang from afar, like walking through a dream. Snow heard her name, the shout of a warning, a scream.

But she didn't care.

She had one goal.

The Huntress.

Artemis strode forward, blood in her eyes, as a corpse broke free from the dirt behind her. Snow waited for the Huntress to notice, for the woman who was adept at hunting and killing and skinning to notice.

But she didn't.

Eyes on the corpse, Snow ran forward. She feigned left, and dropped and spun on her knees. She came up behind Artemis, surprised it had worked, and unleashed the remainder of her strength. She tore Artemis's side.

The Huntress released a howl as blood dripped down her torso. She spun, meeting Snow's blade with a roar, disarming her.

Snow stumbled back and fell into the mud.

From the depths of the mire, the hand of a corpse reached out, its fingers curling around the back of her neck with a grip like iron. Snow froze, her heart pounding in her chest as she looked into the lifeless face of the dead, its eyes blackened, hollow, and still. The corpse blinked. A moment of silent, eerie acknowledgment before the world around her spun into chaos once again.

Artemis charged forward, her scream cutting through the air like a blade, fury in every step. She raised her sword high, the tip gleaming in the dim light, a queen preparing to deliver judgment on her kingdom. Snow's pulse thrummed in her ears as the sword hung in the air, poised to strike.

The world slowed down, the beat of Snow's heart steady as the sword glinted, then fell.

She wanted to close her eyes, wanted to shut it all away, but found she couldn't.

Freedom, the voice echoed inside of her. *Death.*

Then she saw Hansel, his face pushed through the fog. He smiled at her.

He was dazzling.

With everything she had left, she smiled back as Artemis's sword lunged forward. There was only one viable path for the direction it travelled.

And then everything went still.

Artemis's eyes grew wide. She coughed up blood. Snow blinked through bloody eyes and the huntress staggered forward, the sword dropping from her grip. And then Snow saw the blade protruding from her chest.

The corpse let Snow go.

Artemis released a groan, the sound ricocheting through Snow like a song.

It was *beautiful.*

Awful.

Artemis collapsed, her red hair trailing behind her like fire as she crashed into the dirt with a heavy thud. Standing behind her, his sword coated in blood, was the man in black.

Snow could barely breathe.

'Are you alright?' he asked. He grabbed her hand and helped her stand. The sound of battle rang in her ears, the world speeding up as she stood.

The man in black turned towards the corpse that had grabbed Snow, and shouted, 'Hold them back!'

The corpse turned, running towards the Queen's army.

Florian shouted something from nearby as Snow wobbled. Before she knew it, the stranger had her in his arms, carrying her across the fields as the others joined.

She remembered blood and bodies. Her body being strapped to a horse. The warmth of the stranger holding her close as they galloped into fresh fields. The stars flickering above her. But what she remembered above all was the absolute glee in seeing the life leave Artemis's eyes.

A scream tore through the pits as whips cracked, shedding skin across a dwarf's back.

Dread frowned, watching it all from his tower's window. He sat in a chair, his bones grinding like a pounding drum as they slowly healed themselves back together.

His murders had carried him home, back towards the mines. He was lucky he wasn't a corpse. The thought brought bile to his throat every time he felt the bones cracking from his fall.

His guards had been loyal, bringing him food when needed, outlining reports, but it still didn't soothe the ache within him – the one where he needed to move, to *fly*.

He'd been out for days, and despite his shifter ability to heal quickly, it didn't ease the pain. Since then, he'd been reduced to this chair, unable to walk or move or shift.

Flashes of Flynn burned through his memory. The smaller bird twisting, shifting just enough to slip from his grasp before Dread plummeted. Flynn had looked at him, just for a second, emerald eyes gleaming with something that wasn't regret. It wasn't fear, either.

It was satisfaction.

Dread had always known his brother was a coward, slithering in the shadows, hiding behind others when things got too heated. But this? This was different. This was betrayal in its purest form. Flynn hadn't just let him fall, he had ensured it.

He was a traitorous, spineless bastard.

Dread ground his teeth, rage swelling inside him, drowning out the pain. If he survived this, he would rip the satisfaction from Flynn's face and replace it with something far more fitting. Terror.

In the meantime, he was reduced to this. A man broken.

Dread didn't know if Myrenna was back, but he'd had word about the Tinker's death and the prison break. His only hope now remained with uncovering the prize beneath the bone doorway. That, at least, he could do from his chair.

The whip cracked again but the prisoner had long passed out from pain.

The punishment for an uprising within Her Majesty's mines was a public whipping and, if they were lucky, a swift death.

Dread usually preferred to squash out any kind of rebellion quickly and silently, but the Queen had other views. She believed that death made them martyrs, and if done quietly, it did not send the right message.

'Public is best,' she would say. 'Show them what will happen if they choose unwisely.' He wondered how much of that opinion was hers, and how much stemmed from the mirror. Either way, he would obey, but that didn't mean he had to watch.

Dread was cruel, but watching the torture sometimes made his skin crawl. Not that he felt much of anything after the numbing potion he'd been given.

He now had to find his way back to Myrenna's graces before her return. Because when she came back to her burned city, the freed prisoners, and the dead Tinker, she would rage. And Dread would be here, finding what semblance of dignity he had left.

The crowd of recruits below surrounded the podium, some hanging from the cliffs and crevices lining the pit. Chains swung amongst the orange glow and the decayed podium stood tall amongst the rock and dirt.

His beasts cried out as the third whip echoed across the rock. He watched with a smirk as blood trickled in rivulets down the dwarf's back.

It was nice for someone else to feel pain, at least.

When the whip ceased and they pulled the recruit free, Dread's eyes roved the crowd. The shivering, dirty recruits watched in horror as the next prisoner was hauled onto the podium. Some didn't look at all, choosing to close their eyes. Some watched without blinking, their pride shining through despite the horrors. And some flinched with each whip, the sound a harsh lullaby for their dreams that night.

He noted a changeling below, gritting his teeth with each whip as it fell on the new traitor's back. With his hooked talons and dark skin, he was in far better condition than the others. Stronger. Meaner. Dread wondered how long he'd been here, whether he was broken in.

That's when Dread noticed the dwarf beside him. He was young, fresh-faced and rosy, just like all recruits were before they understood the mines. But it wasn't that which drew Dread's attention. The dwarf didn't stare at the podium at all.

Instead, his brown eyes stared up at Dread, unblinking and unforgiving.

Dread couldn't move his feet, but he could certainly move his hands. With a wicked grin, he flicked his hand forward, replicating the motion of the whip as the crack echoed below.

With a shiver, the dwarf looked away.

Dread didn't.

He could see the dwarf's spirit even from here.

And he looked forward to breaking it.

Epilogue

Princess Adanna sat on the cushions of her bay window, eyeing the grey clouds that loomed above the castle. They were thick with water, their bellies about to release an onslaught of rain.

She hugged herself, her trembling arms layered with bandages from the last battle. Memories rattled her, each death bright and blinding. Some were too hard to grasp, others a painful reminder of the cruelties of life. But there were some that gave her peace. A voice on the other side, a hand held at a bedside with whispers from loved ones.

Adanna looked over her shoulder at the ancient wooden sword. It lay by the door as her maid tidied the room, unknowing of the pain that came every time she used it.

She turned back towards the window. Adanna hated the rain now, hated the downpour and the chill it brought to her bones. She hated the constant visions that crept across her memory of walking down the slick steps as everyone was murdered by the woman in black.

She was pulled free from her thoughts at the shuffle of her maid. 'Will you be okay, Miss?'

Adanna turned and noted the bloodied bandages, the bowl of red water as the maid attempted a curtsy.

'Go home, Laurie,' Adanna replied. 'Before the rain hits.'

Laurie nodded. 'He'll be home soon, Princess. Odion always survives. You couldn't wait any longer. He will understand.'

Adanna was too exhausted to argue with her, to bite back at the surety of her tone. Laurie was right, Odion was strong. But he was only human.

And she had unleashed death upon him.

He hadn't hesitated when she'd told him of her dream. Of her vision about the Princess locked away in the enemy's camp.

They had held the Queen at bay, but for how much longer?

Adanna was running out of skin to cut, of blood to bleed. She was covered in the scars of it. Her skin that was once rich umber now had a grey pallor to it. Her hair that had once been thickly curled lay limp around her shoulders. She looked like the dead she raised from the ground. The shadows under her eyes were a permanent fixture since the day the evil Queen had attacked.

Princess Snow was a shot at alliance, at righting the wrongs done to them. Adanna only hoped the Princess was as they said: ready to start a new, peaceful rule. Adanna was tired of death. Tired of worrying. Tired of everything.

The door quietly clicked shut behind her.

She shivered as the first few drops of rain cascaded down the glass. She ran her fingers along the window, the grounds turning a shade of grey when she glimpsed them outside – a group of five, with her horse. A body hung from the saddle, with dark hair, and Odion sat with a straight back, clad in black. Beside him trailed a troll, a human, and an elf.

Joy flooded through Adanna as she stood, but dizziness overwhelmed her. Laurie burst through the doors, rushing to her side and urging her to sit.

'I thought I'd told you to go home,' the princess murmured.

'I was, but then I saw him – the prince. He's returned!' Laurie helped Adanna into the wooden wheelchair by the door and straightened out her dress. 'They'll be up any moment.'

Adanna gave her a small smile, her body weak, and let Laurie push the chair.

They veered down the corridors, taking the lower floors to the entrance way. After the attack, some of the castle had been amended to suit her condition. Ramps lined the stairwells, and most of the business in the kingdom was held on the lower floors, including her personal rooms.

It was impractical for her to climb the towers now.

Not that she was ready to face those rooms yet.

Laurie floated over the smooth floors as the group entered the keep. Odion was helping one of the healers to carry the Princess. The others were escorted off to the infirmary rooms, but Odion stayed behind, casually climbing the front steps. His mismatched eyes looked over his sister before he broke into a grin. 'You look radiant.'

She knew she didn't, but it was so good to see him that she didn't correct him. She only asked, 'No hug for your sister?'

He was covered in mud, sweat, and who knows what else, but she didn't care. In a few quick strides, Odion stepped forward and lifted her from her chair, much to Laurie's indignation.

Adanna laughed, the sound light and free as Odion spun her around, her skirts flying out behind her. She giggled into his neck and breathed him in, holding onto his strong, sure form.

Over the scent of battle filth, he smelt of orange and metal. Of safety and home. And with his return came the changing of tides. The moving of winds.

It meant something Adanna hadn't felt in a long time.

Hope.

End of Book Three

The Little Lord

A SHORT STORY

There once lived a little lord, with buttons of brass and tassels of gold.

His small estate lay by the cliffs of the sea, where the waves crashed against the rock like a violent lullaby.

Others in his realm lived the same way, though not all were as little as he. And not all held the same gentleness of heart.

Lords littered the land, with no king to rule them, each with their own laws and governing rules. And though they traded and met once a year, it was a land divided, ruled by greed and lust.

Sometimes when the little lord couldn't sleep, he would leave his grand home and walk down the sandstone path that reached right up to its very edge. It was on these uneasy nights that he would pray to the stars, counting them one by one as they glittered back at him.

On one night, after his seventh birthday, when the little lord could not sleep, he walked down that familiar path and met a stranger. Their cape billowed behind them as the wind rushed up the stone and crashed over rock. The waves were ravenous on this particular night, and the lord could feel the spray, even from this height, sprinkling over him.

'You are in my spot,' the little lord said to the stranger.

The moon waned above them, casting pale light across the black furs that lined the stranger's hooded cape. 'Can it be your spot if everything is owned by the stars?'

The little lord frowned, about to correct the stranger on who exactly owned the land, but froze when the stranger turned.

Delicate, pale fingers drew down the hood, and there stood a beautiful maiden, her eyes like the grey of the crashing sea below. The little lord was immediately enamoured, and the stranger smiled.

'The stars have gifted me with this land,' the little lord said, if a bit uncertain.

The maiden smiled, bringing forth dimples that almost stopped the lord's heart. 'They have gifted us all.'

Stepping forward, the little lord gave a bow. 'What is your name?' he asked.

But she did not answer. She instead looked towards the stars, her grey eyes shining in the pale light. 'If you could make a wish to the stars, My Lord, what would you wish for?'

He was shaken by this response. He did not know what to wish for, so instead said the first thing to come to his mind. 'I wish for a strong, white steed so that I may have a friend.'

Tilting her head, she gave him a smile. 'Then perhaps we will meet again. Go back to your bed.'

The little lord nodded, not wishing to see her go. His eyes went heavy all of a sudden, and when he awoke the next morning, he was perfectly tucked into his silk sheets.

That same morning, he found a small wooden horse by his bed. With glee he picked it up and played with it for the whole day. The little lord would stroke its mane, and when he did, the horse came alive.

When the little lord's advisor found the toy, he took it from the boy and shook his finger. 'You must not get distracted, My Lord. Toys are for children, and you are no child. I shall take this toy, and you will return to your schooling and duties.'

The little lord was devastated but he let the advisor take it away.

From then on, the little lord would trail the sandstone path each night in the hopes he would see the maiden of the stars. But she did not appear again until his twelfth birthday.

With the land's growth, the little lord grew too. His shoulders filled out his suit with the yellow trim, and his brass buttons were fashioned into silver.

On the night when the maiden finally appeared again, the little lord bowed, his eyes sparkling with anticipation.

He had longed to see the maiden again, and now that he had grown, he was sure she would be amazed.

At his approach, the maiden pulled down her hood. Her hair fell down her back in rich waves. The wind kissed her cheeks, bringing forth a rosy glow. The little lord swallowed. He had forgotten the extent of her beauty and vowed to himself that he should never forget again.

'My Lady,' he greeted.

She nodded before giving him the smile he longed to see. The dimples crinkled on her cheeks.

'You are in my spot,' the little lord said.

'Can it be your spot if everything is owned by the stars?' she replied.

He grinned, his many nights of waiting finally coming true.

'Why do you come here?' the little lord asked.

'Why do you?'

He blinked. His nightmares had brought him here. But after years of visiting the stars and sea, he instead replied, 'I come to hear the sea and talk to the stars.'

'And what do they say?' she asked.

'They say nothing,' the little lord replied. 'I talk to them.'

She smiled again and raised her eyes to the sky. 'And what do you tell them?'

'I tell them about my land and my reputation. I tell them what I long for and I tell them of a little wooden horse that once came alive when I stroked its mane.'

The woman turned. 'Tell me, little lord. If you could make a wish to the stars, what would you wish for?'

The little lord had not anticipated that she would ask the same question. He had only hoped to see her beauty once more. But under the cover of moon, he forgot what he was about to say and gave her an answer. 'I wish for a magic quill, so that I may finish all my homework and have time to play.'

Her eyes glittered again before she turned back to the sea. 'Then perhaps we will meet again. Go back to your bed.'

Before he could speak, he awoke as daylight broke, tucked under the covers of his silk sheets.

This time, there lay a wooden quill on the end of his bed.

Again, the lord had a fruitful year, his estate becoming one of the wealthiest in the realm. The boy would use the quill to write down his demand and he would receive a letter in return. Sometimes he obtained a letter from the far reaches of the north, and sometimes from the sea. The boy never questioned who responded, only that he always had an answer, and could spend his afternoons in the woods by the estate.

The other lords now asked him for favours, taking on his advice with fervour as he grew. But as each cycle passed, he found their eyes dimmed and their questions menacing.

His advisor found him one afternoon with the quill floating mid-air and grabbed it. 'You must not get distracted, My Lord. You must learn by doing it yourself. I shall take this toy, and you will complete your learning.'

But without his quill, the little lord lost his time in the woods and lost the instant responses. Eventually, his borders were breached by the lords who resented him.

And as the seed of war grew, each night when the little lord couldn't sleep, he would walk the familiar sandstone path.

When his sixteenth birthday came, the little lord walked up the sandstone path and met with the beautiful maiden. Her hair was braided across her skull, the lines perfectly entwined with a small headpiece that shone silver in the white light.

'You're in my spot,' he said, bowing.

'Can it be your spot if the stars own everything?' she replied.

The little lord smiled. He was older now, but still enamoured by her beauty.

'Each night I walk this path in the hopes of seeing you,' he said. 'Perhaps one day you may come see my estate?'

Her stormy eyes glittered at him under full pale moon. 'Do you still talk to the stars?' she asked.

He nodded. 'Only when I cannot sleep.'

'And what do you tell them?'

'I tell them of my home. Of my schooling and duties. I tell them of the lords who bring war to my borders and the woods that grow darker with each year.'

This time, the little lord dropped to his knees. 'My Lady,' he said, 'I will own nothing if the other lords take what is mine.'

'Then tell me, little lord. If you could make a wish to the stars, what would you wish for?'

He had thought about this and prepared for it. The little lord no longer needed a companion or a tool for his studies, for he desired something else. 'I would wish for a sword, so that I could defeat my enemies and live in peace.'

The woman did not smile this time. Instead, she turned to the stars and raised her hood. 'Perhaps we shall no longer see each other again. Now go to your bed.'

And with that, he found himself tucked within his silken sheets as the sun came over the horizon.

Upon the next morning, the little lord found a wooden sword at the edge of his bed. In his joy, he took it to training with him and found it unbreakable. But it did not come alive as the others.

When it could not slice the skin of his enemies, the little lord was resigned to leave it in his rooms. The advisor did not take it this time, as a wooden sword was no distraction. So, as the armies of the lords descended upon the estate, the little lord forgot his gift and instead took up steel.

For years, the little lord battled the other lords, managing to push them back. But after one heavy battle where he lost a lot of good men, the little lord took to his bed.

Another year passed, where the little lord became of age, so it was time to marry. He was without an heir, and as such, remained vulnerable amongst the greedy and spiteful lords. His advisors brought forth many beautiful maidens, each more talented than the last. But no matter how many maidens he saw, he only thought of one.

The Lady of the Stars.

On the night of his twentieth birthday, instead of fighting with his men, the little lord took the sandstone path, leaving his people to bleed. His shoes had been shined, his hair had been combed, and his buttons had now been replaced with gold.

Straightening his new coat, the little lord looked up and saw the maiden waiting along the edge of the water. His hand shook slightly as he gave her a bow, greeting her with their familiar saying.

'You are in my spot,' he said with a smile.

'Can it be your spot if everything is owned by the stars?' she replied, turning towards him.

The little lord had prepared for this meeting, but he was still breathless when she removed her hood.

'Could it be, that you become more beautiful with each passing year?' he asked.

He expected a smile, but she merely stared at him, her lips pursed in a fine line.

'Tell me, lady,' the little lord said. 'Are you a lady of the stars? Despite my searching for you, you only appear here one night every few years under the moon.'

Her hair had been pinned this time. Each curl twirled into fine twists with specks of silver. She matched the sky above her, shining even amongst the dark. 'I'm a creation of the stars. Just as you are.'

He stepped forward. 'Where do you go when you leave this place? So that I may find you again.'

She clasped her hands together, a curl falling loose across her brow.

His heart sped.

'If you could make a wish to the stars, what would you wish for?'

He knew the question was coming, but it had been too soon, with too few questions answered. But he knew his answer.

'I would wish for your hand, so that you may marry me and have my heirs.'

But she did not repeat her farewell this time.

'How has your last wish fared?' she asked instead.

He thought of the wooden sword gathering dust in his estate. 'It lies unused,' he replied honestly. 'I could not make it come alive like the others, and it did not wound my enemies.'

'You have not used your gift properly,' she said. 'So, you will not have more wishes.'

The maiden stared at the stars and, with a soft voice, echoed, 'Go back to your bed.'

When the little lord awoke, he was seething with anger. His estate was the finest in the realm, he was called handsome and rich, he held power and influence, and he was *good*.

He could not understand why she would disappear and reject him so.

In spite of himself, he could not forget her and instead forged forward, growing his estate more and more.

Within the next twelve cycles, the little lord married, and though she was not the woman of the stars – plain by those standards – she was kind and lovely.

An heir she did bear, but it happened on the night of a large attack.

As the coffers shrunk, his medallions running low, his estate turned to disrepair. And each time he returned to his rooms, he stared at the wooden sword.

One night when he couldn't sleep, he donned his dressing gown and headed toward the familiar sandstone path.

But the woman was not there.

'Tell me, husband,' said his wife one night. 'Why do you leave so late to walk to the cliffs?'

The little lord felt silly sharing his story, but he had grown to love his wife and so he told her about the wooden horse and the magic quill and the wooden sword.

'If this is true,' his wife replied when he finished, 'then perhaps you should try the sword again. You have a son now, and he will have nothing if the battles do not end.'

The little lord knew she was right, and so he picked up the sword.

Again, the sword never broke no matter how hard he pushed it, it also did not slice the skin of his opponent.

On one afternoon, after heavy training, the little lord tripped on his feet, his advisor having bested him, when the sword slipped and sliced his skin.

The advisor rushed forward and took the sword. 'You must not get distracted, my lord,' he said. 'A wooden sword cutting a lord is no ordinary thing. I shall take this, and you will use steel as a real warrior does.'

But this time something had changed. In a flurry, the little lord's other advisors rushed in and told him to come to the woods immediately.

The little lord ran in haste, taking his sword with him, and when they reached the edge of the woods, they found their enemies slain.

'How could this be?' his advisor asked.

'I do not know,' the little lord replied.

When he returned to his silken sheets that night, he turned to his wife and told her about his day.

'You say these items are magic, and the sword was to slay your enemies?' she asked. 'I say that, when you have cut yourself, something else comes alive to slay those who wish to harm us. Just as the other gifts came alive.'

The little lord pondered this.

So, when another battle came to his lands, the lord cut his skin, testing his wife's theory.

She had been right.

Upon the first drop of blood, a great army emerged from the soil. One of death and decay. Some were dressed as civilians and others were soldiers that had been slain from previous battles. The little lord's horse skittered at the sight, but he stroked its mane as he once did with his toy and watched as the dead saved his land.

From then on, word spread, and each lord placed down their weapons and surrendered to the little lord, crowning him king.

He reigned for a long time, having many children with his wife, and named the land Perridorm.

And as time passed, the lord continued to visit the familiar sandstone path.

On his sixtieth birthday, he donned his robe and followed the path to the cliffs.

And there the maiden stood.

She had not aged a day, her supple skin smooth against the harsh lines of the King's face.

'You are in my spot,' he greeted her.

'Can you call it your spot if the stars own everything?' she replied.

He laughed and looked to the stars. 'The stars have blessed me, indeed. Tell me, Lady, if the stars could wish for anything, what would it be?'

The woman smiled and bowed to the king. 'They would wish that you kept this peace and honoured them with a celebration each year.'

'Then they shall have it,' he declared.

The woman turned, her eyes becoming sad as the seas crashed below. 'We will not see each other again. But I shall watch from above and each year, when they celebrate the stars. I will be there from afar. Now, go to bed.'

The King smiled, waking up in his silken sheets as the dawn pierced through his glass windows.

The following day, the King announced that, each year, for his birthday, they would hold a grand celebration. Not for his birth, but to give thanks to the stars.

And each year, the people rejoiced with food and dance and the unity of their people.

Whilst the kingdom danced, the King would take the hand of his wife and kiss it.

'Your kingdom thanks you for bringing it peace,' she would say.

'My kingdom should thank the stars,' he would answer.

The End

Acknowledgements

When I started this journey in 2018, I did not expect to write one book, let alone three. It's a surreal feeling, one laced with anticipation, anxiety and a whole lot of excitement. So many people are involved in the publishing process from artists, to editors, marketing and so on. As an indie, there aren't enough words to express my gratitude to those who have supported me or the work that's been put into this.

Originally, this book was a challenge to write. Not because I didn't have a clue of what I was doing (though most of the time I don't) it's because it was written when I experienced true grief for the first time. My brother passed away on February 1, 2021. It's been four years and I still feel it sharply.

When this book was mid draft, I distinctly remember sitting in ICU with him and reading snippets of The Gilded Mirror. I remember discussing plot lines and asking what he thought. I remember his excitement was palpable despite his condition — so I owe a lot of this series and my desire to finish them to him.

After his death, I struggled to continue this story when I returned home. I remember writer's block took my hands and locked them in chains. No matter how much I stared at the last scene, I could not find the right words. It took four months to get out of that and start again but I'm grateful for that break. The time to reflect really let me see this story in a broader light and helped me bring rich colour to it. So, thank you Trent, I hope the Ever After is holding you close.

Dante is a tribute to him.

As most of you know, this series has been republished after I split with my previous publisher. I had three books released and three under contract, meaning once this book is out in the world, I'm finally free. It also means that when the next book lands in your hands, it will be the first new book I've released in over three years. To say I'm beyond excited is an understatement.

But none of this would be possible without the help I mentioned above.

Thank you to my partner, Jared, who wants me to kill off everybody but pushes through when I ignore him for months on end in another world.

Thank you to my parents, who are both avid readers and didn't crush my heart when they read the books. Your honest opinion means the world. To hear you love these characters as much as I do makes this worth it.

To my colleagues and friends, who support me and purchase my books.

Thank you to my BETA Readers.

Candi — You not only read these books once, but multiple times to make sure they're the best they can be. Your feedback and support is invaluable and none of this would exist without you.

Bri — You have been with me since the concept of TGM was one sentence. I love talking books with you and taking dinner dates by the waterfront.

Ingrid — We might have met under wildly traumatic circumstances but having you in my life not only as a writer but as a friend had been an absolute honour.

Thank you to Paris and the Loire Valley in France, who made editing this book decidedly less dreary with the perfect views, perfect cheese and perfect wine.

Thank you to Daniel, for sticking with me as my editor and believing in this series as much as I do. We too met under strange circumstances but I'm grateful for every edit, word change, suggestion and reshuffle.

Thank you to my readers, who go on this magical journey with me and continue to buy my books. I love seeing your theories and favourite characters. I love engaging with you on socials. I love this community. I see every social media post, every recommendation and every review. You make this worth it every day. I owe everything to you.

This book is my most important to date, one with a huge chunk of my heart written into its pages. I hope you loved it and I can't wait to give you more magic in Book Four.

I hope all your wishes come true!

Kim xx

For updates and bonus scenes, you can
join K E Barden's Newsletter by
scanning the QR Code below.

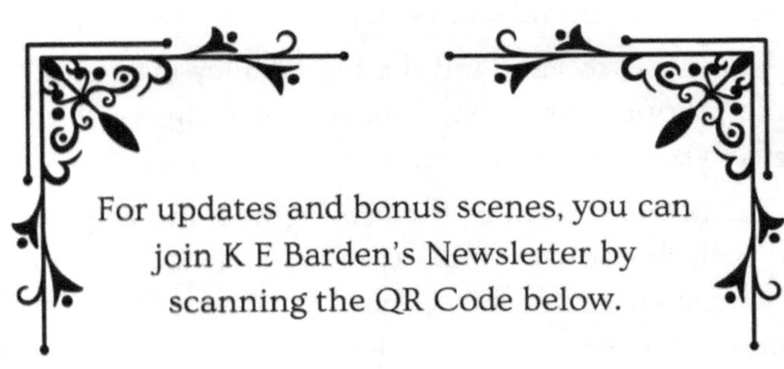

About the Author

K E Barden is an independent author based in Brisbane.

Her first book, The Gilded Mirror was written entirely on a mobile phone and the dent in her pinkie finger proves it.

When she isn't writing, you can usually find her spoiling her high maintenance cat, building fairy castles, or comparing her real boyfriend with her book boyfriends.

Her books are a combination of fiction, romance and fantasy with the express intent of stealing you away from reality and creating characters that will become your entire personality.

You can find Kim on social media @ KEBardenAuthor

Authors Note

Thank you for making it this far. I hope you enjoyed A Glass Darkly.

Reviews are the lifeblood of indie authors. Without them, there's a very high chance our books fade into obscurity. If you are enjoying the Finding Ever After series please take the time to leave a review on GoodReads, Amazon, Social Media, or anywhere you want to share.

Thank you, *Kim xx*

www.ingramcontent.com/pod-product-compliance
Lightning Source LLC
Chambersburg PA
CBHW031730180726
48283CB00005B/1444